THE PRICE OF LIFE

THE PRICE OF LIFE

by

VLADIMIR LIDIN

Translated by
Helen Chrouschoff Matheson

HYPERION PRESS, INC.
WESTPORT, CONNECTICUT

Library of Congress Cataloging in Publication Data

Lidin, Vladimir Germanovich, 1894–
    The price of life.

    I. Title.
PZ3.L6199Pr5 ₍PG3476.L56₎   891.7'3'42   72-90300
ISBN 0-88355-011-3

Originally published in 1932
by Harper & Brothers, New York.
Copyright 1932 by Harper & Brothers.

First Hyperion reprint edition 1973

Library of Congress Catalogue Number 72-90300

ISBN 0-88355-011-3

Printed in the United States of America

And just before I leave this life
A sound familiar I shall hear;
Dreaming that friend or brother dear
With gentle hand wipes from my brow
The cold drops, which suffused but now
My face in its last agony,
And, in a whispered melody,
Sings of my own beloved land.'

Lermontov.

THE PRICE OF LIFE

CHAPTER I

It was nearly five o'clock on a day that Kiril Bessonov would always remember. The professor was just finishing his lecture on applied mechanics. With sweeping movements, he was sketching parabolas and circles on the blackboard, every now and then giving a tap with the chalk as he elaborated his diagrams. Somewhere between a hundred and a hundred and fifty men and women students crouched over their notebooks, taking down formulas, sketches and calculations. It was one of those warmish days that often come at the end of October before the winter sets in; when the pallid dawn is shrouded in a clinging mist, and, in the depressing, hazy dimness, the big town with its dripping roofs seems to be drowning, while shivering, lonely, tense men and women hurry hither and thither, as though they were shuttles weaving the threads of their whirling urban life. It is one of those days on which the whirl, nay, even life itself, seems to be utterly futile, as though planned solely for unpleasantness and mutual exasperation.

Professor Chelishev lectured on applied mechanics, and his course was one of the most difficult and abstruse. While figures and formulas flew from his hand like light-winged swallows, it was difficult to realise in their airy flight that they represented the measured progress of gigantic mechanisms. A well groomed man, with a slight touch of grey at the temples which did not detract from his air of youthfulness, Professor Chelishev had been a military engineer and a successful inventor. He liked the semi-circle of cropped or tousled heads straining to assimilate the complicated puzzle on the blackboard which was the product of his brilliancy and knowledge. And he liked, too, the flexible modulations of his own baritone voice softly penetrating to the farthest corners of the lecture theatre. The students, especially the women, always had a sense of slight but not unpleasant shyness when they talked to him. At this moment, a good many of his audience were not so much taking in his formulas as listening to the sound of his voice and watching the rapid movements of his small white hands.

Kiril Bessonov was one of these. He had begun by conscientiously taking down sketches and figures, but had fallen into a daydream, merely hearing the professor's voice while he stared over the sea of heads at the blackboard covered with curves and intersecting lines. The classroom seemed to him like a big ship drifting, through the humid dusk which showed against the windows, towards the harbour of the five o'clock recess. The soft baritone voice, the rustle of paper, all his surroundings, had become for the moment unsubstantial, unreal, and he found it pleasant to abandon himself to the fleeting oblivion, relinquishing all effort to listen or to understand. He leaned his heavy golden head on his hands, peasant fashion, and became absorbed in his own fancies. The professor rose, moved from his chair to the blackboard, drew a line, and returned to his place. Behind Kiril, in an upper row, a note was passed from hand to hand till the paper hit his nose and fell on his notebook. He looked round and saw the faces behind him in smiles. It was from Sverbeev:

'Don't sleep, my friend,' it read. 'Life is beautiful, and if you have a rouble it can be even more beautiful. Don't disappear after the lecture, let's go out together. I have something important to say to you.'

Bessonov turned round again. Sverbeev, sitting on the bench above, gave the impression of a face that was all long nose and smile. Professor Chelishev raised his voice, going on speaking while he gathered up his notes, and there was a rustle of paper and movement all round. The lecture was over.

Most of the students lived in a huge hostel which had formerly been a workhouse. Its dismal corridors seemed interminable in their length, and a dreary panorama showed through the grey light of the solitary window at the end of each of them. The rooms formerly occupied by paupers now held students' beds and large drawing-boards on which plans and blueprints were pinned. Married students lived separately, but the younger, unmarried ones shared rooms – several of them together. In the evening the corridors were dimly lit by solitary lamps, there was a blue blackness behind the windows, and there the hard student life went on, study, weak tea in mugs, and the occasional twanging of a mandoline. Here, as in every government institution where years are spent in the acquisition of knowledge, every spring saw a migration back to the country, to the provinces, to a summer job, and every autumn the corridors hummed with the homing flock, whose sunburn faded day by day to the pallor of town and study and student life.

Sverbeev was waiting at the entrance and they went out together into the grey dusk. A Scotch mist beaded nostrils and eyebrows with tiny drops of moisture, and the street lamps, like smears of rust in the fog, cast little light on the damp, murky darkness.

'I meant what I wrote in that note, Kiril,' said Sverbeev, bending nearer with his long, pimply nose. 'Life, my boy, is a very jolly thing if you know how to tackle it. Learning is one thing, and living is another. Let's go to a pub, and I'll tell you what I mean.' It took the students some time to reach the end of the long wet street. 'Here we are,' said Sverbeev at last. 'This is a topping place; they have a Tzigan chorus here that will move you to tears. Let's go in and warm the cockles of our hearts.'

Kiril followed him into the tavern. It was still early, and many tables were empty. They sat near the platform, and Sverbeev ordered two beers. 'I don't drink beer,' said Kiril as he took off his cap and gave his head a characteristic toss to shake his golden hair.

'Do you suppose I do? It's only to pass the time away and listen to the Tzigans.' Still wearing his grey cap, Sverbeev cupped his head on his two hands, and glanced gaily at Bessonov with protruding eyes which were usually about as expressionless as those of a duck. Though Bessonov was not intimate with Sverbeev and had no particular liking for him, Sverbeev had made advances from the first, as though he had taken a fancy to the golden-haired boy about whom there still hung something of the fragrance of the peaceful countryside. And so it happened that Sverbeev had become his guide in the great city which was so apt to bewilder a newcomer. Sverbeev did not live in the hostel but in Bronni Street,and Bessonov was glad to have at least one place to which he could go for human intercourse on holidays, when the hostel was empty, and loneliness, like the cobwebs, filled every corner. Sverbeev always had visitors, often women students, but the main thing was that he managed to organise his life in accordance with his desires: forcefully, and always with success. At the bottom of his heart, Bessonov had been glad to get his note, although he had meant to devote his evening to work.

The waiter brought two bottles of beer and a little dish of pickled peas. 'I don't advise anyone to drink Corneiv beer, it makes your head ache, but the Three Hill ale is first rate,' said Sverbeev. 'What do you say, shall we have some biscuits?' He clinked his glass against Bessonov's, took a drink, and said 'Women are queer creatures. . . everyone of

14

them cherishes some fantastic notion of her own. . . Wonderful! You sit here drinking beer not thinking of anything in particular, while extraordinary things are happening. Ah, my boy, life . . . life is a cunning mechanism, and the only way to win out is to drive it. Well, I suppose you've guessed what I've got to say?'

Almost frightened, Bessonov replied with the utmost sincerity, 'No, Theodore, I don't know.'

'I'm talking about Tania, Tatiana Agourov. What eyes! But I don't believe in the innocence of anyone nowadays. I know you're gone on Tania. . .'

Bessonov passed his hand over his forehead with a gesture of pain. 'You're talking nonsense Theodore.' But the image of Tania as he had seen her a month ago in Sverbeev's room rose in his mind – Tania, the little student in a flame-coloured jumper, with chestnut brown hair cut like a boy's, and deep blue, almost black, eyes between which was the hard line of a tiny furrow, and with a slight irregularity of teeth which gave a singular charm to her smile. They had met several times, and though they had never exchanged a word she had made a deep impression; so perhaps Sverbeev was right in surmising that Tania had inspired the first poignant dream of Bessonov's city life.

'You drink your beer and listen,' went on Sverbeev, 'and drop all that purity tosh. Nobody wants it. Times are holey now, not holy. To tell you the truth, I was very glad when I thought that you and Tania might click. You suit each other so well – she's dark, you're fair – "the golden boy," that's what they've nicknamed you. But things don't seem to have turned out quite that way.' Sverbeev broke off a bit of his biscuit, munched it, and went on 'We're students, we have professors to teach us, and while we are trying to nibble at the edge of science the professors are taking the women students. I have it from a reliable source that things are

15

not all that they should be between Chelishev and Tania.'

Bessonov suddenly felt hot, and his blood tingled as it rushed up to the very roots of his hair. After a pause, he asked 'How do you mean. . . Chelishev!' burying his burning face in his tankard to hide it.

Sverbeev put a few pickled peas in his mouth: 'Tania has an affair with Professor Chelishev. It's quite simple and quite human. But, I ask you, Kiril, can we sit calmly by and let the professors walk off with the women students for their own amusement?'

'No, of course not,' said Bessonov, speaking quickly and without thinking, for he did not know why not, or how they could stop it. Then he put his tankard down with a thud.

'Let me tell you, my boy; speaking in general, if you have come to Moscow to live a clean life, Moscow will swallow you up in three months. Everybody here has to show his mettle or else go under.'

Whether from the beer, from what Sverbeev had just told him about Tania, or from the atmosphere of the room, Bessonov suddenly felt light-headed, as though the hard bone of his skull had crumpled up like cardboard; and the thought of Tania, which had been torturing him a moment ago with feelings of frustrated tenderness, wavered away into a shadow as though there were no longer any such person. 'Well, what about it?' he said after a second of silence. His voice was hard and rough. 'Why are you telling me about her? She's nothing to me.'

'Now that's just feebleness on your part; it's not strength. If you take that sort of line, anyone will do you that wants to. No, Kiril, you must remember the main thing: nowadays *everything* is permissible; war and revolution have ploughed us up pretty thoroughly. As a matter of fact, life is not worth living if you can't allow yourself everything. The granite of knowledge! That's all very well, but suppose you crush the granite, what then? You become an engineer and are caught up in overproduction. There are openings for a hundred engineers, and there are three thousand of us. A hundred can just exist on bread and water, and two thousand nine hundred are candidates for the cemetery. At the best, they may get a job as draughtsman in an office or become a railway clerk – at some little wayside station like Licobor. There will be marriage, of course, from sheer boredom, a canary, children – and, at Licobor, grey monotony, wind and wretchedness, with the passing trains as the only link with life. No, my boy, I mean to build up a different sort of life. I want a life in which to live no worse off than anybody else, to have devilishly beautiful women round me, and beautiful women are plentiful enough to lift by the spadeful"

Sverbeev poked his long nose towards his companion and winked. 'Let's join forces, Kiril; I really mean it. I sized you up the moment I saw you. A lad like you ought not to be wasted. Only listen to me. I fought in the civil war from Siberia to Warsaw and saw every side, from the Partisans to the Poles, and I know the values of things, I know the value of life.'

He was quite merry now, and ordered more beer. Bessonov also felt elated. He lost sight of the main point – Tania – his head at the moment being filled with thoughts of the extraordinary life that Sverbeev promised. How it was to be obtained did not worry him. Sverbeev knew how to find the right way. Bessonov was not used to beer and was easily fuddled by it, so that he kept on wanting, and then forgetting, to ask Sverbeev what he meant by suggesting that they should join forces. Weren't they leading the same life together now? But Sverbeev explained of his own accord.

17

'Always concentrate on your own interests; that's the most important thing. Push on with your shoulder, without any compunction. If you show pity for anyone, you will be trodden underfoot. Don't pity anyone; go on, and, if anyone gets in your way, give him a push with your shoulder. If he does not give way, give him a good shove, and don't look back. That's philosophy. And believe me, people are always making up harrowing stories. But now about the most important. . .'

At that moment there was a confused noise on the platform, and the Tzigans appeared on it, bringing with them an atmosphere of restless animation.

The sallow, slender women with their thick eyebrows, wrapped in scarlet or yellow shawls, jingled their bracelets as though they were chains. Among them was Nastia Vorobiev herself, a dark will-o'-the-wisp. Without hurrying, the women took their seats in a row. The men, with waxed moustaches and loose jowls like pointers, stood up behind them. A ribbon-bedecked guitar vibrated, and a few notes flowed from it and rolled away like pearls. A tall dark woman led the singers. With glowing eyes, staring almost indifferently over the audience, she began to sing in a harsh, high voice that seemed to chill the room. The penetrating, monotonous voice went on until she brought the song to a climax on a high note, and the thunder of the whole choir took it up. There, in the tavern, the Tzigan song rose high and guttural, accompanied by the heavy bass of the men, which seemed to give a solemn emphasis to its overwhelming yearning. Suddenly, in a pause, Nastia herself began to sing. In a deep contralto, as though she were singing a litany at matins, she stirred up that inexpressible yearning, and other voices echoed her, while the be-ribboned guitar swayed to and fro, until its music ceased in a crashing chord.

18

In the intoxicating atmosphere of melancholy longing produced by the guttural Tzigan music, Kiril laid his heavy head on his arms. Sverbeev listened, nodding his head in time to the song as though he were conducting it with his long nose. At last, turning his head he said: 'How well the devils sing! And now, Kiril, listen to me; this is what matters most. You can get Tania in two ticks if you'll really take the trouble. She's not a bit happy with Chelishev, of course; it's only a game, a sort of playing at turtledoves, see? If you handle the thing properly, you can make Chelishev look a perfect fool. And, you ought to know that Chelishev is damned rich. He was paid for two of his inventions, and he's on five committees, to say nothing of his lecturing. He lives in great style, so you certainly needn't feel any compunction about him.'

But at that moment Nastia began to sing again. Once more the guitars sounded, and the thin leader, moving her shoulders, and nothing but her shoulders, danced with tiny steps toward a Tzigan who was fingering his guitar with intense passion, plucking the strings as though he wanted to break them. And again the air became full of that same delicious yearning. Bessonov listened to the song with bowed head, and Tania seemed to him to be infinitely desirable, perhaps because she seemed now to be more real, and something definitely within reach.

They stayed on in the tavern for another two hours till the room was drowned in smoke and human exhalations. When they went out into the wretched wet street, it did not seem wretched to them. Walking away from the tavern, they paused under a street lamp. In the light which it diffused, they could see the tiny drops of rain like gnats circling round it.

'Well, come to-morrow about five,' said Sverbeev. 'We'll discuss it all then, and perhaps Tania will show up.'

'I'll come without fail,' replied Bessonov quickly and warmly.

There under the lamp, they said good-bye. Sverbeev was at once swallowed up in the fog. Kiril, still filled with an undefined but joyous yearning, wandered back through the misty rain as though carried forward to his fate in an invisible net.

CHAPTER II

WHEN a snowstorm raged for a week, the whole town became white and silent and meek. Then the thaw with its miserable drizzle made the streets like soft, muddy jelly, and the town looked itself again – sinful, soaked in human meanness and the menace of evil days to come. On days like that, the trams, with their headlights resembling yellow, bloodshot eyes, made the rounds of their ordained orbits like monstrous, drenched dragons. There were surging crowds at the stopping places, men with their necks muffled in scarves rushed across the dirty snow heaps, and out of the wineshops burst steam, the smell of alcohol, and snatches of song with a tinkling tambourine accompaniment, or a tune madly played on a concertina.

On Sunday evening, Bessonov left the hostel. He had spent the day over the plans of a suspension bridge for a term examination, and all through the day, from the midst of his calculations of girders and stays, the figure of a girl with deep blue eyes and chestnut hair cut like a boy's, kept rising up to evoke a vague bitterness, and to scatter his mathematics like a flock of sparrows. What Sverbeev had said about her the day before had not added to the distance between them or soured his feelings for her; on the contrary, she seemed nearer, perhaps because, from being a fleshless dream she had become comprehensible, frail, and of the earth, human. All that day his thoughts had been utterly disjointed, thoughts of her dimmed by figures and drawings, which, in their turn, had been obscured by her; so that by the evening his head was in a whirl, and he was glad to go out and plunge into the fog. He walked slowly through the streets for a long time, breathing in the cold, damp air, and gradually ridding himself of his spiritual confusion. He glowed inwardly with a bitter-sweet tenderness at the thought of meeting Tania before long. And he thought, too, that it was good to have one's own individual dreams amid the bondage of city life. He wandered through many streets until at last he reached the Tverskoi. It was crowded at that hour in spite of the mist and mud. Speeding taxis dashed past with shiny black hoods – young couples were driving out to the Petrov Park, green and dank with the wet. The dense holiday crowd pushed its way to the yellow light of shop windows which were displaying photographs from cinema films. Near the lamps and lighted windows one could distinguish the falling drizzle, but beyond them all was a misty blue darkness, and distant street lamps looked like pale and ineffective moons. Illuminated boards loomed up at intervals bearing a red police baton or a notice 'Look in both directions before crossing the street.' But there was such incessant hooting in the fog that it was useless to stop and look, one had to rush across the street as best one could at full speed, jumping over the puddles.

In Strastnoi Street, near the tram shelter, men were hurrying down a stairway, while others, still fumbling with their buttons, emerged with much dignity. A whole crowd of women were strolling about by the shelter, some in hats, some in kerchiefs, singing as they walked with voices which suggested that they all had colds. On an advertisement kiosk a crowd of crocodiles were tearing to pieces an elderly gentleman who was mournfully diving among them. Crossing the square, Kiril passed the austere statue of Pushkin, with its head of stone curls, and went down the boulevard where red lamps flared at the edge of the pavement as tram signals. Sverbeev lived in one of the blind alleys just off Bronni Street which had provided dwelling places for the poorest students from time immemorial. Times changed, landladies died, the lodgings became more and more crowded, but the students' dens remained unaltered, with the same paraffin lamps on the windowsills, and the same dreams for the hungry, visionary inmates. In the alley, dark as an Arctic winter, Kiril suddenly realised what it was that had been so violently agitating him since yesterday. It was, of course, not Tania and their few meetings, at which they had not exchanged a single word – it was the passionate longing for a kindred spirit roused by his isolation in the great city. From the very beginning, he had suffered from loneliness, and it had been inevitable that he should sooner or later create some image to satisfy his craving. That was what had happened in regard to Tania. He had warmed to her as unlike the girl students he knew and avoided because of their carelessness in manners, in dress, and often, in their loves. There was about Tania something essentially feminine, modestly chaste and fragile, and yet there was an enchanting strength in the almost childlike face with its deep blue eyes and serious little mouth. And now he had learned something about her that was not in the least in keeping with her appearance, something that should have repelled him and turned him from her; but, to his surprise, it did not in the least repel him but awakened a burning flame of illicit passion that seemed to draw her nearer to him. At the thought that he might see her in a few moments, he felt excited and quickened his steps. He finally reached the house and climbed the stairs, which smelt of cats. On the third floor, he found a door covered with endless instructions as to how often to ring for each inmate. He discovered that he had to ring eight times for Sverbeev. Pressing the corroded button eight times, he heard the unpleasant yapping of a toy dog behind the door. Sverbeev let him in a moment later.

23

'Ah, Kiril, we were just talking about you,' and he led the way past the kitchen and through the dark passage.

The sputtering of a dozen primus stoves in the students' rooms made the place sound like a factory. They went on to the end of the passage, that was blocked by cupboards on the top of which all kinds of hampers and bundles were piled. Sverbeev's tiny room was no wider than a skittle alley. A woman sat on the bed smoking, with her legs crossed like a man. She glanced quickly at Kiril. Her pale grey eyes conveyed a sense of shamelessness. She was broadly built, and not bad looking in a coarse way. 'Vera Nikolsky' she said in a peculiarly deep voice that was almost a baritone. 'And you are Bessonov? We were just talking about you.' Abashed, Kiril hurried to a corner between the sofa and the cupboard.

'Don't be afraid of Vera,' said Sverbeev seriously. 'She's a good sort, and a student, too; but in another trade, she's an artist.'

Kiril noticed that the pale grey eyes went on staring at him enigmatically and with an air of appraisal. 'Look here, what have you got into that corner for? Get out of it, lad,' and Sverbeev seized his leg. 'This is our golden boy that I told you about,' he went on. 'I wish you would make a man of him. You might take him to see the poets, he does a bit of scribbling himself.'

'Do you write poetry?' asked Vera, and her deep unnatural voice so embarrassed Kiril that he could not speak. But he got used to her in a few minutes. Her speech was frank, and a bit coarse, indeed everything about her was a little coarse, her build, her cropped hair of a neutral colour, neither fair nor dark; her masculine poses; her smoking. . . But there was something handsome about her, and for all her coarseness and masculinity, one felt that if a strong man handled her in the right way, he would find that she had a passionate woman's nature.

24

'First and foremost you must get to know the town,' said Sverbeev, 'and no one could help you better than Vera. She knows the ropes; she can introduce you to poets and actors; you must see everything, Kiril. Don't get the notion that the whole of Moscow is in our street or that designing bridges is the most important thing in life – that's all nonsense. Science is one thing, and life is another. I'm thinking of your own good. The more you learn of life the more you'll want to live.'

'Well, of course, I'm quite willing,' hesitated Kiril. 'After my exam I shall have time; very interesting to see Moscow, of course.' He realised at once that his words sounded insincere and provincial. But Sverbeev broke in again, and kept the ball rolling with such skill that the evening passed quickly and pleasantly. He made tea, and as they sipped it, the two men discussed various things. The girl took no further part in the conversation and did not listen. She was in the advertising department of the art school, and drew posters. Notwithstanding her air of masculinity, there was something essentially feminine and domesticated about her while the gaze of her pale blue eyes were fixed on Kiril. They agreed that she should introduce him to the Poets' Circle at their next meeting, and that Kiril should call for her the following Wednesday. She gave Kiril a vigorous handshake when she went out. Sverbeev saw her to the door.

'You pay attention to Vera,' he said on his return. 'She's a clever woman – a very modern woman. The main thing about her is that she hasn't got a woman's horizon. . . I do so want to make a real man of you, Kiril. In these times, if you're not that, life will not only pass you by, it will crumple you up. If you prove able, we can perhaps do unheard of things. And I think that you are able, I have felt so from the first.'

While he was talking, Sverbeev looked as though he were pecking with his long nose. When he reached his main point, Kiril was moved again.

'I didn't ask you to come here for nothing, Kiril. You don't really understand me at all. But the point is that Tania Agourov is coming – she'll only look in for a moment to get a book I promised to lend her, but you will be able to see her home.'

A feeling of gratitude and friendship surged up in Kiril. This man was filling his life with a strange and perturbing ferment, which, although it frightened him, he hailed with wild eagerness, regardless of its possible consequences. He spent the rest of the evening in a sort of muddled ecstasy.

Tania Agourov came, and her face, rosy from the cold, seemed beautiful to him. She sat down on the edge of the bed for a moment, barely looking at him. But her quick glance stirred him deeply, and a moment later, full of emotion, he went out into the street with her.

'Do you go to the right or to the left?' she said.

'To the right,' he answered, and added at once, though frightened by his own daring, 'that is, I'm going your way, I'll see you home.'

Tania made no reply, and they walked along together. The grim dark street seemed to Kiril to be magnificent and brilliantly illuminated. After passing down some side streets, they emerged at the Patriarch's Pond. The pond was steaming as though some engine was at work beneath its surface. Limp branches of desolate trees hung over the water like the tresses of an abandoned girl. Tania slowed her pace. At a turn in the road, under a street lamp, she peeped at him out of the corner of her eye as they walked side by side. The look, as he caught it, seemed sad and somehow expectant. Kiril took off his cap, and went on with uncovered

26

head. She gave him another glance, a sad, soft look, and said, 'Put it on, you'll catch cold.'

But he did not put it on.

Golden gleams from the street lamps pierced the dusky mist with what seemed to him an unusual brightness. Gazing at the shining yellow light, he said 'Sverbeev told me that you would look in to-night. It seems a trifle, doesn't it – you came, and you went away, and I am walking by your side? And you don't even speak to me. I might be non-existent. But this morning I thought that I should see you, and the thought gladdened my whole day.'

'But you don't know me at all,' she said with a little frown.

He answered with his utmost sincerity, 'Need one know a person to be glad of her? I was glad of you from the first moment I saw you, though we had not spoken a word.'

She listened in silence, making no attempt to reply. When they had gone down a few more streets, at the corner of a *cul-de-sac* near a little squat church, she said shortly 'Here I am.' It seemed to him that she wanted to say something more, but she left him there, standing alone in front of the dark cavern of the front door, still feeling the light pressure of her warm hand on his palm. Then he turned and went on his way, full of self pity and the pain of a sadness such as he had never known before, except once, long ago, when, as a boy, he had been with his girl friend Varinka. He went along Garden Street, and Garden Street seemed to flow towards him like a great, misty river. But he no longer felt lonely in the deserted street. And, perhaps because it was all a dream that he himself had invented, his sensations were the most vivid and acute that he had ever had.

CHAPTER III

FROM the early days of his orphaned childhood, Kiril had had a secret refuge which he kept hidden from everyone. A plain, pockmarked woman, singing to him as a baby, had sown in him a longing for rhythmic forms in which ordinary, simple words fall into marching ranks. He wrote verses in secret, and more than anything in his life he treasured the exercise-books in which he buried himself at all times of childish trouble or loneliness. In the little riverside town where he was bred and born – a little town typical of so many in Russia – very few persons knew anything of the sweet poison of poetry, and Kiril, in after years, remembered as his earliest guides in life those who had first given him the longing for song and the flow of human language.

He had been born in the little town in that wretched season when winter is reluctantly taking leave of the earth. There must have been the usual melting snow, soiled by the thaw, the usual Lenten smells in the air, and that riverside gloom which is always among the first tokens of spring.

He was born in a lying-in hospital where they killed his mother, and from which his father awkwardly carried away a small bundle on a cold March morning. The bundle contained all that his wife had left him as a farewell gift after she had lost her life through official carelessness and indifference to suffering in that yellow building. It was from his father's stories that Kiril knew so well all about that first morning journey from the hospital, and knew all the details of his early life so fully that he might have been a disinterested onlooker. Probably a good deal of it was wrong, probably his childish imagination had amplified it, but perhaps his first poetic fancies were awakened by the yearning for a woman, the longing for a mother he had never known.

His father took him home in a cab, bundled up in a shawl. The steep streets were greasy with brownish snow, because, as always in Lent, the muck was beginning to show through. Boys in the market-place were selling the first snowdrops with their pallid air of sadness. His father was silent all the way. His downcast eyes were like the cages from which birds have flown – bereft of their warm living tenants, disordered with the spilt food and the floor flecked with down from breasts beating against the bars. Under the bridge, the river was flooded, but on its banks were women rinsing their linen in its icy waters, and rooks were pecking about not far away. The cab went slowly through the town, drawn by its steaming horse, but his father did not urge the driver to go faster. When they got home to the bare, untidy room on the third floor with windows staring out at a great expanse of sad Northern sky, he put the bundle on the bed and untied it. Was his son alive, or had the shawl smothered him? No, the little brown creature was alive. It had nails on its fingers, fine hair on its temples, and a navel tied with cotton.

Then his father knelt down and sobbed in the hoarse, croaking voice characteristic of men unaccustomed to weeping. He sobbed beside the bed, and his tears fell on the baby's foot and waked him, and the baby began to wail in sympathy. It was a strange sound in that cold room roughly tidied by a man. The voice of a human creature that had cost a woman's blood and life and was her legacy to the misty, thawing earth. His father rose to his full height, dark, tousled, with bent shoulders, and looked wildly at his little son. Nodding his head, he said in a grim, broken voice, 'I won't neglect you; no, I won't neglect you, my son.'

And from that moment the little riverside dwelling became the scene of the man's ardent struggle in his determination that the child should live. Next day he took his wife's body to the cemetery, and when he returned in the dusk, his strong workman's hands hung listlessly at his sides, and his eyes were red-rimmed. So these two, the father and the son, to whom he had already given the name Kiril, were alone together. Out of doors the keen spring winds rushed over the town with devastating, thundrous noise. His father often told him about those days of sadness, when he used to sit alone with a bottle and a crust, choking back his tears. Kiril would lie on the bed, solemn and contented; for a neighbour, Arina Ivanovna, fed him from one of her huge yellow breasts with its brown nipple, the other being his foster-brother's. He lay there listening while his father talked about life, or, tired of talking, lifted his glass to the light to examine it with peering eyes as he broke into song. But he did not know how to sing, and would soon lay his head on his arms and fall asleep.

Arina fed Kiril with her left breast. He was her thirteenth nurseling, and she had the same sort of pity for him that she might have felt for a blind puppy. Like everyone else she thought that it would be better for the motherless babe to die; but he opened his mouth, he was hungry, he had the primeval desire to live, and the warm milk of this stranger was a substitute for his mother's. He was thin and ugly, with a big head, and very greedy. He took far more than his foster-brother.

Taking the breast from him Arina would say 'You're never satisfied, you greedy little thing. You're barely alive yet, and there you go sucking away, always in such a hurry. I never saw such a thing.'

30

She was a kind woman, he owed the essential foundations of his life to her, and he always thought gratefully of her. In the mornings his father went to the factory. The siren roared at dawn as though the factory's iron throat were sore, and Kiril was left alone in the empty flat. He got used to solitude. He was patient, and learned his routine. Arina Ivanovna came in at intervals to change his napkins or to put her blessed nipple in his mouth. Then she took it out, naturally feeling that it was more important for his foster-brother to live than for him. He began to drink milk, though it upset him; for he would take anything that he could get. Kiril soon learnt to get out of his wraps. He had an orphan's vitality, and he crawled about the floor when Arina put him down. When his father came home from work, he would pick him up like a kitten, and gently breathe on his eyes. The boy would blink and frown. He was pitiful and ugly, but his father thought him beautiful, and would breathe on his eyes and gaze at him with admiration. It was his son, who would some day take his place. He was alive, and he needed a mother.

'You want a mammy, Kiril, that's what you want. I shall never raise you without a mammy.'

A year later, he married a raw, untidy woman, a stocking-maker who lived in the next yard. She came to their flat with her thread and her wool and her needles. She seemed to fill the room with a smell of dampness. She took an immediate dislike to her stepson. Childless herself, she loved her ease, and she saw no reason why she should bother to look after another woman's pale-faced child.

Kiril developed quickly. An orphan's childhood is short, for there is no one to spoil or admire him. He learned to walk alone, and at four years old was more like a child of ten. In the evening he used to wait for his father on the landing, by the window from which he could see the river

31

half hidden by smoke and brushwood. He knew when it was time for his father to return, and crept out on to the stairway near the window. There he would hug his father's legs, and his father would kiss the nape of his neck and say 'my little son' in such a thrilled tone that both of them got tears in their eyes. Then his father would carry him upstairs, pressing him close to his heart, and in those moments they both knew that they belonged to each other completely. His father never caressed him at other times.

The new wife was a heavy, sluggish woman who moved slowly about the room, and her husband certainly did not find his lost ideal in her. When Kiril was six years old, he learned of the terrible act of human sin. A stranger came to visit his stepmother, a tall man with a narrow head and full red lips. He was a tanner living in a neighbouring house. He smelt of leather, and Kiril hated his lips. 'Oh ho,' said the tanner, 'the boy has grown. You can say what you like, he's a wiry little thing.'

His stepmother was wearing a new shawl with pink flowers on it, and she had put pomade on her hair in the morning. The tanner had brought some biscuits for tea, and one of them was given to Kiril, who was always hungry and greedy. He went out on to the stairs, and sat there nibbling his biscuit and its caraway seeds. When he had finished his biscuit he went out to watch the ice grinding in the river. There was a cold, damp wind. The thaw had cracked the ice so that it was moving down in heavy blocks which crashed together so that they made the first song of spring while glasslike splinters showered round them. Kiril watched the river for a long time in a crowd of other small boys, though he never made friends with any of them, and then, having got thoroughly cold, he went home. He went upstairs, opened the door, and saw something so dreadful that he nearly screamed. It looked as if the tanner

32

were suffocating his stepmother on the bed. He was in a frenzy, and Kiril suddenly heard her laugh and moan, but her head was thrown back and her eyes closed so that she did not see the boy. Was this the first instinct of life, the primal mystery that lurks in the blood?

But he did not cry out. He stepped back slowly on to the landing. His heart was racing, he did not understand what he had seen, but he felt that his stepmother had done something shameful, and that the red-lipped tanner was his father's enemy. His shoulders heaved, and he burst into tears. He did not know why he was crying, but he knew that his stepmother had defiled their home, that something dreadful and evil had happened in that room, and he was overwhelmed by such grief as he had never experienced. It was a grief of bitterness, like wormwood, and Kiril remembered it all his life. Sitting on the windowsill in the dusk, he saw the tanner come out and go downstairs. On the landing he lit a cigarette, and Kiril caught a glimpse of his full, red lips and his wide-spaced hateful teeth. What could he tell his father? What did he know? Only that the tanner had hurt him.

When his father returned, there, in the dark, he clasped his legs, and pressing his head against his knees, sobbing with pain and grief, he told him what he had seen. His father listened in silence, and when the story came to an end, took the boy's hand and led him away to Arina Ivanovna.

'The child is not to know anything about it,' he said to Arina, and he went away, promising to fetch Kiril later. Arina gave the boy a piece of carrot pie, and he sat there with his foster-brother Valerian, both munching pie and dangling their legs. They were only children, not yet seven years old.

His father did not return for a long time. His face was

33

dark and terrible as he took his son by the hand to go back to their room. There was a smell of vinegar in it, and his stepmother's head was bound up in a handkerchief, and her lower lip was swollen. She was tying up some things in a bundle, and she did not raise her round, catlike eyes when they entered. Next morning his father carried her things downstairs, she returned to her old home in the next yard, and they were once more alone in their large grim room. The red spring sun was bright. During the night the ice had gone, except for a few blocks floating down the river and blocking it near the bridge. Cold spring rivulets were trickling everywhere. Kiril did not ask any questions about his stepmother. They were alone.

His father tied up some bread, salt and eggs in a parcel, put a new cap on Kiril's head, and took him out into the street. For the second time in his life, Kiril was driven in a cab. A flock of startled mauve-grey pigeons were circling overhead, and rooks were cawing loudly round their tangled black nests. The driver did not hurry his horse, which slowly ambled on with its ears drooping like a turnip-top. Then they walked for a long time in the dank cemetery until they reached the wall in the shadow of which lay Kiril's mother. There was a white cross on the grave, and puddles round it. His father took off his cap, and knelt on the wet clay of the grave, and Kiril knelt near him. There lay she who had given him his life. In the distance he heard cocks crowing. He knew that he ought to be sad, to cry; but it was spring, and there was a white angel on the next grave. He stared at the angel, and wondered how it could move such heavy wings. It probably flew like a heron, he thought, as he bowed his head to the ground in imitation of his father. His thoughts wandered to his stepmother. She had gone, and now he would be able to build forts out of chairs again, and to run about the room,

34

and to draw a wet finger over the windowpanes to make them squeak. At last his father got up, and Kiril too. They sat side by side on a bench, and his father said, 'It's no good, Kiril, I can't find you a second mother – we'll have to get along as best we can without a woman.'

They ate their food in the open air, and bread had never tasted so delicious. Then they both kissed the cold, wet soil that covered his mother, and, hand in hand, they set forth together – this time to a world of spring.

CHAPTER IV

KIRIL never forgot those who had given the first impetus to the dreams of his early childhood, dreams that would know no repetition. One of them was Katka-the-street-walker, the first creature to bring human warmth into his lonely life. Katka was standing at her doorway one day, holding her shawl to her breast with her thick fingers, when she looked at Kiril with kind blue eyes that had a very slight cast, and said 'Whose little boy are you? Are you Bessonov's son? Your knickers'll fall off in a minute if you don't look out, you poor little orphan.'

He felt ashamed of being pitied by Katka-the-street-walker. Other boys had told him that none of the grownups would speak to her in the daytime, and he said something rude to her. Still, she followed him home, mended his knickers, that were falling to pieces, and fixed her heart on him, that heart which had found no resting place; he was so glum, hungry, and lonely, and she loved him because nobody wanted him. She, too, was lonely and unwanted. Her childless life was spent in solitude and vice. This woman with the pink face (he knew nothing then of cosmetics) and not unattractively pockmarked, was the first to tame his wild, rebellious heart. She used to come in the morning, when she had slept off the fatigue of her hard night life, sit down in front of the boy, and folding her thick hands on her lap would say:

'In the beginning was the word. Do you understand, you little graven image? The word – that means that everybody must know how to read and write. Writing doesn't matter so much, because you can always get somebody or other to write a letter for you,— but the main thing is to be able to read books. When you feel lonely, and your heart is full of misery, you take a book and read about some foreign land, a land of bright colours with bright lives in it, and you yourself get bright, see little chap? And it's easier to live if you are bright.'

He remembered all his life that girl whom nobody wanted. She came and mended his clothes, and washed his dirty ears, instilling him with a great belief in a beautiful life in which all was easy and man was free and sang songs, and where nobody had such fearfully torn knickers as his. In spite of all the disorder of her night life, she had a craving for tidiness and cleanliness. She had the quick, adroit hands of a sempstress, and she talked to him while she sewed.

'If you're not clean, you're like a clock without a glass. Dust gets in and clogs the wheels, and then the clock begins to lose, and at last it stops altogether.'

And all the time that she was mending his rags or sweeping the room, she sang her sad country village songs. Kiril never told his father that Katka came there. He knew that grownups avoided her; and his father thought that Arina was helping them. Katka came in every morning to do the room. She could not live without tidying something and taking care of someone. She taught Kiril his letters, and eventually to read, and so it was she who first introduced him to the sweet poison that opens a door of escape from men and trouble, and it was her hands, made to nurse babies but used for deceptive seduction, that fondled him in his bereft childhood.

Kiril Bessonov knew that nothing could ever make him forget the cruel day on which this unselfish and sinful companion passed out of his life. She went as simply as she had sung her village songs, and a bottle of ammonia took her

37

to rest. What shame, what ineffaceable insults she had borne in this world. But she had character, and her hands did not falter as she opened the ammonia. An ambulance, with a red cross painted on its side, came to fetch her. And it had a bell that the driver could ring. Kiril saw her thick legs, with unbuttoned boots, and a torn fur coat thrown over her swollen body, when they carried her out on a canvas stretcher. She never returned, and he was once more alone. But now he knew the sweet poison of dreams, and when he sat on the faded coverlet he could talk to Prince Charming about the friend whom he had known for such a little time.

Sometimes his father gave him money, and he spent it all on books at old Makar's wonderful shop under the archway of some wide gates. Makar's chin was so rough that it had rubbed all the hairs off his fur collar; he had a short, harsh grey beard, and his lungs wheezed in an amazingly fine fashion. He must be a thousand years old. He always sat in an enormous highbacked chair in the middle of his shop, and his teapot always stood in front of him. The half dark shop smelt of damp books and old bindings, and had the indescribable scent of printed paper. Makar would rub his prickly chin against his fur collar and talk aloud to his teapot. The teapot was his truest gossip.

'Books – they are the pearls of life. A man rots with all his sins, but a book is eternal. A book covered with mildew is stronger than wine. Everybody thinks that he is doing great things in life, but the only really great things are those that endure in books – the rest is only the folly of man.'

Kiril was afraid at first when Makar began to talk to his teapot with its steaming spout. But he found later that Makar talked to his teapot because he could not talk to people unless they loved the everlasting damp smell of his books. It was in the dimness of this shop that Kiril supple-

38

mented his dreams as the seed germinated which had been sown by Katka-the-street-walker. He got to like the damp silence of this world. He would clamber up the unsteady steps that reached almost to the ceiling, and sitting on the top one he would bewail the sad fate of the unhappy Estelle and the passionate Mnemorin, repeating to himself the lines

'The fragile elm aspires and grows tall,
Winds batter it, and rains prepare its fall:
Prone, in the end, it wins enduring peace;
May you, my soul, at last find like release.'

Which he found fascinating, though he could not extract much meaning from them.

'Find the sea voyages of Admiral Nahimov,' Makar would say from below. 'You read that book about Admiral Nahimov, and you'll learn what a man is capable of when he is ready to give his life for his country. Do you realise the significance of men like that?'

Kiril sat up aloft, looking down on the yellow bald disc fringed with pearly hair.

'Their significance,' continued Makar, raising his bony finger to Kiril's foot, 'is that they are the precious nuggets of the earth, as "Shakepeàr" says,' and his lung whistled like a bird for quite a minute.

Sitting on the top of the rickety steps, Kiril lost his sense of loneliness. He was a ten-year-old bookworm, and ardent listener, and Makar could talk to him about everything and wheeze with his lungs as much as he liked.

He read many books during the next three years, and was no longer excited over the fate of the unhappy Estelle or the sea adventures of Admiral Nahimov. He read Pushkin's story of *The Fisherman and the Fish*, and his *Caucasian Prisoner*, and through the broken-down doors of this damp-smelling cell that wonderful world opened before him about which Katka-the-street-walker had dreamed.

One day he went to the shop when the midday sun was shining, the silver river shimmering in the dazzling light, and the bright crosses on the embankment churches were gleaming against the deep blue sky like doves hovering in the air. The shop was cool and dark, and Makar was sitting as usual talking to the teapot in front of him.

'What is the wealth of man? Have you ever thought about that my friend?' Kiril climbed up and seated himself on the top of the ladder. 'The wealth of man consists of desiring no wealth. Melchisedek was an example of that. . .'

Kiril reached a volume of Baron Brambeus from the top shelf, while Makar went on down below, 'Do you remember the ancient Melchisedek's words when he was taking leave of life, as told in Mr. Batushkov's poem? "Man was born a slave; a slave will he go to his grave, and death will scarcely tell him why he passed through the valley".' Then Makar began to wheeze, and the wheezing was louder, and went on longer, than usual. He did not resume his monologue, but sat on in his armchair staring at the teapot. Kiril sat on the ladder absorbed in Baron Brambeus. There was a long silence; even the teapot ceased steaming. Suddenly the door opened, and a stranger in a peaked cap entered the shop.

'Have you got an algebra?' he asked.

Makar did not answer, he must be asleep. The man gave his coatsleeve a pull:

'Have you got an algebra?'

Kiril raised his head from his book, as the man below said calmly, in a very quiet voice, 'The old man is dead.'

Kiril flew down the steps. He saw one blue eye half open, staring past him, the cheeks a waxen yellow – his friend and teacher Makar had died there in his chair, with his teapot in front of him, and two days later he saw him to his last resting place. Few came to the funeral. Though he had befriended and taught so many who had become students and even professors, none of them came to see him off on his last voyage. Golden spring was bringing out the first shoots on the bushes. There were flowers in the town gardens, and the rooks were hovering about their last year's nests.

CHAPTER V

ARINA IVANOVNA's niece Varinka came to stay with her that spring. Some days after her arrival, Kiril met her on the stairs, where, quite at home, she was running down with a pail. She was slender, with thin legs, but her eyes were as big as saucers, and there surely was no one else with eyes like that. She was not quite fifteen.

Looking at her, Kiril said 'Are you Varinka?'

'Yes,' she answered.

'And I am Kiril Bessonov,' he went on.

She looked at him in surprise, and he added, 'I am Valerian's foster brother, Kiril.'

The she broke into a smile. He must have looked very funny in a cap which was much too small for him, from which his curls were escaping all round. But he stood his ground, and there they stayed on the landing, staring at each other. At last he said, 'I'm fourteen, how old are you?'

'I'm nearly fifteen,' she replied.

Then he burst forth, his words coming in a rush, 'Valerian can't read; he hasn't read anything, but I've got lots of books, and I've read them all – Do you read books?'

Varinka liked reading, and they agreed that he should lend her all the books that he had. Their new friendship dated from that day.

Arina Ivanovna had not had anyone to send on errands, or to wash Valerian's clothes, but now Varinka went out to do the shopping, minded the little ones, and washed Valerian's linen – She had quick hands. She, too, was an orphan.

Just behind the house there was a quiet, shady little garden. It had a fence round it, and there were some wild apple trees in it that were covered in autumn with the cocoons of caterpillars. The garden had run wild with neglect, and no one went there. It was a good place to think in, to recall memories of old Makar, and to meet Varinka. She would run into the garden for half an hour in the afternoon, when Arina Ivanovna had gone out. She brought a smell of the kitchen with her. The birch catkins used to get tangled in her silken hair. He brought his books, and, shoulder to shoulder, they read Pushkin's fairy tale of *The Fisherman and the Fish*, or, trembling with excitement, the story of *Prince Serebreni*.

The sun poured its light on them through the cobwebs, and turned Varinka's cheeks to gold, with the delicate colouring of an autumn apple. They read many lovely books together, and it was Kiril's last chance of leisurely reading, for his boyish freedom was nearing its end; because his father was going to send him to the factory next year. Everything went on in this garden just as things did in books. Did they realise that their childish meetings, the memory of the stories of heroes or of fairy fish would leave a lifelong impression, and would fill their hearts with a bitter yearning?

Summer was ending, the wild apples were ripening, and in the evening the moon hung above the garden like a huge yellow button sewn to the sky. One day, Varinka did not come. He waited with his books in vain, and in the evening he went back to the garden to think and brood. It was cool, and the air was full of the fragrance of tobacco plants from a neighbouring garden. Kiril sat on a bench, wondering why Varinka had failed to come – probably Arina Ivanovna had not let her go out. A silly little dog was yapping near the gate. Suddenly he saw Varinka coming towards him.

She was walking slowly, not having expected to find him there. She sat down silently beside him, and he asked bitterly, 'Why didn't you come to-day, Varinka?'

Then her thin shoulders heaved, and she suddenly burst into tears. His heart was heavy with despair and horrified pity as she wept with her palms pressed against her face. He seized her wet hands, but she snatched them away and they talked through their tears in disjointed phrases, glad and miserable, swearing that they would never forget one another. Then, as they sat side by side with their wet cheeks, Varinka said,

'I love you, too. I shall always read books as you do. But Auntie is going away to Kazan, and I have to go with her. If you were grown up, you could marry me. . . I would do everything for you. . . and we could live together and read together. . .'

He told her that he would be apprenticed at the factory next year, but that he would never love anyone but her whatever might happen, that she would only have to wait four years, because at eighteen a man could marry, and then he would go to Kazan to fetch her, and would keep her with him for ever. His heart was bursting with joy and pain as the tear drops dried on their cheeks, and the rays of the pale primrose moon poured down on them.

That autumn, Arina Ivanovna moved to Kazan, with all her chests and her feather-beds and her birdcages. And his little summer friend had to go too, as though she, poor orphan, were also a caged bird. Her departure brought his first adolescent sorrow, and he found no solace in his books. But when he thought of the time when he would go to Kazan for her, and they would always be together, the twilight was filled with delicious dreams.

New tenants came to live in Arina Ivanovna's flat – a master cooper and his wife. They had no children, but

44

masses of furniture, cupboards and big chests of drawers had to be carried up the stairs.

The cooper was a little, rubicund man with red hair. He went off to his workshop every morning, wearing an alpaca coat, and his wife was left at home. A tall, pale-faced woman, she sat at her window, bored to death. She often sang in a high-pitched voice, and a warbler with a crimson breast chirruped in unison while it sprinkled her hair with seed scattered through the bars of its cage.

There was a hemp-mill in a courtyard close by, and Kiril often watched the hemp breakers in the dusty sheds as they teased the fibres which women then carded with long wooden combs, before it was taken to the presses to be squeezed and mangled into bales. The sheds where the bales were kept were very quiet and dusky. In the hot, midday sun of the dinner hour, the women went to rest on the bales, and the men used to creep up there to them. Tired and relaxed, the women would give little half-hearted cries and slap the men's hands. Then everything became still, while the sun poured down its heat, the fowls lay motionless in the dust, and Kiril wondered what was going on in the sheds. But his heart was strained, and a warm flame seemed to glow in him, filling him with an unholy joy.

After Varinka had gone away, Kiril gave up peeping into the sheds. Varinka was like a transparent crystal, but there was something dark and heavy about the shed that stirred his fourteen year old blood, something that made his heart beat in a way that he felt was wrong.

He usually had his dinner by himself now, in a cabmen's teashop near the landing stage. It was in a cellar, the air was heavy and full of smoke, and the place was crowded with drivers sitting in their blue coats with the belts unfastened. Each of them had hung up his hat with its badge

45

close to where he sat. They drank endless glasses of tea, wiping their sweating foreheads, while waiters in dirty linen trousers carried trays of fat teapots raised well above their heads. Kiril ate the modest dinner costing threepence, which his father gave him, while he listened to the serious talk of the cabmen. He was full of admiration for these men who knew the town like the palms of their hands – every house and many notable people. Their fares were doctors and merchants and actors. They knew all the love intrigues, who was kept by whom, and their tangled beards were full of wisdom.

Sometimes he only took a bowl of cabbage soup that cost a penny, and spent the remaining twopence on cigarettes; and then he would walk home slowly, spitting out bitter saliva like a grown man. The cooper's wife would be at her window, leaning her chin on her hand, with her eyes just slightly lowered under their thick, arched brows, as though the sunlight and the heat hurt them. Once he stared up at her window, at her bare pink elbows. Then she raised her eyes, caught his, and smiled. She stared at him smiling, and he suddenly felt the same quivering sadness surge up in him as he had experienced when he watched the women lying on the hemp bales. Her eyes stared and smiled mysteriously, she bent her head, and her lips moved as though she were talking to him. Then, sweating with shame and perturbation, he knocked himself painfully in the doorway as he ran off to the garden. He sat there trying to think of Varinka, and of how he would go to Kazan for her; but his thoughts would turn to the cooper's wife, while his heart beat fast, and beads of perspiration ran down his forehead. Why had her lips moved? What was she saying? And why did her eyes smile, in that veiled, mysterious way?

Two days later, he saw her again. She was leaning on the

46

windowsill with her cheek resting on her hand. She glanced at him and asked 'What's your name?'

'Kiril,' he replied.

'Why do you always look up at my window? Do you like me?'

Once more he was bathed in perspiration. He felt ashamed, but unable to run away.

'Why don't you speak? How old are you?'

'Fifteen,' he answered.

'Come and help me shake my carpet,' she said. He said nothing, and she went on 'Why don't you speak? If you don't want to, I can ask someone else.'

He spoke then. 'There's no need to, I can do it alone.'

'Come up then.'

He ran up the stairs, almost suffocating. She opened the door and stood smiling at him.

'You're out of breath. . .' Her eyes peered into his, her red lips still smiling, as she took his hand and led him in. A huge oak bedstead stood in the middle of the room, and he saw in a mirror a very tall thin boy, just like himself, with dark, sunken eyes and a mass of untidy golden curls.

'Don't you ever do your hair,' said the woman suddenly, putting her hand on his head. And she took a comb from the table and combed his matted curls for a long time while he stood in front of her, seeing her neck, but not daring to raise his eyes. A strange warmth came from her.

'There,' she said at last, and looking in the mirror he saw another youth with his hair parted and a woman's hand on his shoulder. The youth in the mirror raised his hand and touched hers. He touched the warm, dry skin, and the woman's hot breath seemed to burn his ear. Then he turned his back to the glass and saw smouldering eyes close to him fixed on his chin. He did what he had seen the hemp

47

workers do: he put his arms round her and clung to her. He clung, quivering, and the woman stroked his hair and laughed softly. She did not repulse him, but laughed, and at last said quite calmly.

'Wait a minute, I'll shut the door.'

She locked it and went and stood by the bed, her hands clasped behind her head. She bent back more and more, her hands still clasped, the blood rushing to her cheeks. And then he, no some third person, ran towards her and put his arm behind her back. . .

He ran home, and lay face downward on his bed. The bed, the whole world, was in a blaze. Where was Varinka? Was there any Varinka? She had floated away for ever, like some fleecy morning cloud, and with her had floated away the youth who had dreamed boyish dreams on the bench of the little fenced-in garden. Those dreams had been ousted by the harsh, triumphant, masculine reality. And this new youth, with his parted hair, suddenly realised that his father's cast-off boots did not fit him, that one can stick a cigarette in the corner of one's mouth with a flourish, and in the silvered depths of a mirror one can boldly embrace a submissive woman in such a way as the cooper had certainly never embraced her.

That year, just before the spring, his father died. He burned out fiercely, for a passionate life-force raged in his tuberculous breast. He did not go willingly, but he went all the same, just as spring was coming. It was only then that Kiril Bessonov plumbed the full depths of his aloneness. His father had been a near and dear friend, it was his determined, manful will-power that had guarded the feeble flame of the child's life, and it was for the sake of his son that he had renounced women and marriage. It was into the mist of one of the hazy days of an early March thaw that his father disappeared. He was buried beside his wife, close to the marble angel who still strove in vain to spread his heavy wings.

Standing at his father's grave, Kiril knew that life had now seized him with her merciless hands. He returned alone to the empty flat, unable to think of the future, of what would become of him. It was just at this time that his hidden exercise-books became his most precious possession, and in those books he wrote the first musical lines expressive of his loneliness.

This lad with the curly golden hair was now fifteen, and Yagodkin, a turner who had been a friend of his father, got him apprenticed to the factory in the spring. Yagodkin had quick black eyes, and a blue shaven upper lip. He took Kiril home with him one day, and made him sit down opposite to him.

'Well, my friend, how are you going to live?' he asked after a pause. 'You've got to learn; times are different now; this war isn't raging for nothing.'

'I learn all I can,' said Kiril.

Just at that time he was working in the turning shop, where the lathes, with piercing shrieks, produced very fine work, delicate articles required for the war.

He noticed in the factory how everything had been thought out, how each bolt played its part in strengthening the whole, and he was filled with respect for what man can do. Some men thought out the design of this whirling system, others thought out the philosophy of life. He began to see what Makar had meant by his talk about the imprint of the word of man and all that it had created. He made a rough shelf in his room to hold all the books that he still had from Makar. He was utterly alone now, alone with himself and his solitude and the verses he composed for himself. He had long since tired of the cooper's wife, and, for that matter, a long-haired velvet-jacketed musician from the orchestra had come to live in the same house as she did, and tore the strings of her heart with his saxophone that made sounds like a human voice. Kiril had sulked for a short time and had then forgotten her.

'You've got to learn a lot, my lad, if you want to be a man. And being self taught isn't much good. You've got to get a thorough grounding. After that every road will be open to you, to go wherever you choose.'

This remarkable man, a simple turner, his father's friend, dwelt in Kiril's mind as one of those who had exercised an enduring influence on his life. Yagodkin was one of those rare beings who reach the very peaks of humanity by unaided intuition. One evening he brought with him an awkward long-nosed youth – a student named Lebedkin – who had been found unfit for the ranks, and was employed as an orderly in the military hospital. This young man became Kiril's tutor, and his life was now divided into three sections: the factory; the evening lessons, when Lebedkin helped him to unravel the mysteries of binomials or syntax; and the treasured hours of silent leisure and solitude, when he was lost to the world, and the music of his verses flowed so spontaneously. He did not show his poetry to anyone, not even to Lebedkin, who always came with the smell of iodoform and the atmosphere of suffering which he brought from those who had been broken by the war. This man with pimples on his face and carbuncles on his neck was a mine of knowledge. He seemed to have set himself the task of acquiring the fruits of all human learning, and could talk of Newton's calculations, the marvels of natural science or early Russian literature, as easily as about the daily happenings in his ward.

When the first agitation to stop the war began, he vanished, and he did not reappear in the town until two years later, when the revolution was in full swing. It was then that

Kiril saw for the first time a revolutionary order bearing his signature. He went to see him, and found him in the unheated building of the Municipal Archives. Kiril had to stand in a queue for two hours before his turn came, but he found Lebedkin the same as ever, with the same pimples, but the carbuncles were worse, probably as the result of continuous underfeeding. Lebedkin did for him what Yagodkin had dreamed of, what he had dreamed of for himself but had never hoped to see realised. He learned for the first time the short word *worfak*, meaning provision for a workman's university course, and Lebedkin so arranged that the factory, at which his father had worked for thirty solid years, enabled him to leave the riverside town and go to the great capital as a student.

Sadness and affection marked his farewell to Yagodkin on the familiar wooden platform, as he looked for the last time into the dark eyes behind their spectacles. He was full of a real sorrow at leaving this friend who had taken him to his heart so thoroughly. He leaned out of the window watching him for a long time. The town glided by, that town where he had spent his childhood, and where he was leaving the graves of his nearest and dearest. The train passed through riverside slums, then through the autumn fields with only bristling stubble to cover their nakedness. Struggling to overcome his wretchedness, Kiril stood at the window till night fell.

He was going away with his mind made up to work, with an absolute longing to work and make good.

Two days later, he reached the capital, and Moscow greeted him with one of her most beautiful autumn evenings, her pavements glistening after a shower. He never lost the memory of those first imperishable impressions, or his excitement when at last he entered the hostel where he was to spend the long years of his student life.

And so the improbable had become the actual, and Kiril Bessonov that autumn entered on a strange new life unlike anything he had ever known.

CHAPTER VI

Beyond the town there rose a quarter
Built on poor, marshy soil.
There poets lived. . .'
A. Blok.

ON Tuesday evening, Sverbeev reminded Kiril that Vera
Nikolsky was expecting him the next evening at eight. Why
in the world, Kiril asked himself, had he agreed to go to a
meeting of poets with a perfectly strange woman? He wrote
his verses for himself alone. He kept them secret and hidden
from everyone else, but there people would be reading aloud
to each other, unashamed, unembarrassed, things that were
to him painful confessions. Throughout Wednesday he
worked for his examination, but about six in the evening
he was overwhelmed by his excited feeling of expectancy,
and, at seven, no longer able to control it, he left the hostel.
Vera lived in a large and cold studio, the walls of which were
covered with queer red and yellow posters – all her own
work. On her little iron stove stood a teapot, so begrimed
with smoke that it might have been a relic of past ages.

'Come in, Bessonov,' she said with a free and easy, man-
to-man manner. 'Take off your coat, it will be time enough
to go to the poets at nine. Did you bring some of your
verses? They'll make you read some, they always do,
all newcomers have to. What are you frightened at? I
don't bite, I assure you. I'm not overmodest and I have
nothing to hide, but I don't throw myself at people.' She
said all this as though she were smoothing him down, with a
quiet, somewhat quizzical look in her screwed up eyes.

53

Kiril felt suddenly that her coarse masculinity no longer shocked him, and that he was listening to her words with excited curiosity. There was something bold and shameless about her and her whole complex being that subtly stirred him, and, to distract his mind from this feeling which was repugnant to him, he made himself think of Tania. He thought of her as he had seen her when they had met at Sverbeev's, her girlish profile, a pretty lock of hair escaping a little untidily from under her fur cap, and her charmingly uneven teeth.

How he wished that she would appear in this room; but it was another woman that was near him in this studio smelling of wet plaster and paints, one whom he neither knew nor understood although she stirred his feelings.

Vera did not go on teasing him. She dressed quickly, and they went out. The dark street enveloped them in a grimy fog, and the gas jets of its wet lamps shed a pale, greenish light through the mist. They walked abreast, and with a sidelong glance he saw that Vera was staring straight in front of her, mysteriously smiling and screwing up her eyes as though laughing at all that he was feeling and think-ing. A quarter of an hour later they arrived. At the top of the stairs they found an untidy, wild-looking man in a linen coat, with a butterfly tie and the morose eyes of one who has had too much, or not quite enough, to drink. He stood there, with his lips made purple by an indelible pencil which he was sucking as though it were a sweetmeat.

'Good evening, Vera,' he said abstractedly, absorbed in his own reflections. 'Whom have you brought? What's your name, comrade? You can't recite for more than five minutes, we've got twelve people reciting to-night.'

'I have no intention of reciting,' said Kiril, thoroughly perturbed. 'I only came to listen.' But the unkempt man glanced at him with vacant, indifferent eyes. 'You can't refuse; it wouldn't be sociable.' And then, utterly ignoring their presence, he began to make notes on a sheet of paper that he held against his knee. The room was full of people. Poetesses, with beads on flat chests, shingled, or with bobbed hair brushed in a crescent over their cheeks; girls whom he knew by sight, in vivid jumpers, green or scarlet, and with bright-coloured socks worn over their stockings, wandered to and fro, their painted lips droning verses. There were young things, pupils from the poetry studios, who listened dreamily to the droning voices, their eyes staring as though they were drugged. There were thin, dignified young men in horn-rimmed spectacles, who were most of them the leaders and masters, moving among the crowd of disciples with the stately slowness of the consecrated. All these young creatures – in furs or cloaks or wretched coats lined with dogskin – all were under the magic spell of fame and the idea that poetry might be made the basis of a career. They seemed to Kiril to be like moths fluttering in the glare of the footlights.

The room became more and more packed, and some of the crowd found seats on the windowsills. Vera led him through the crush with assurance, and they sat down in a corner on a wooden bench against the wall. Deliberately, or by chance, Vera sat very close to him, and, to his surprise, he found that this vaguely excited him, and that he no longer had a feeling of revulsion. The room was soon so crowded that it became impossible to move from one place to another. The masters took their places at a round table on a raised dais, and the unkempt man rang a bell violently. The session had opened.

A languishing youth, frail as a reed, in rather short, turned-up trousers and grey spats, stepped forward, and clasped his hands, writhing like an Antigone in agony. Then he suddenly began to chant, clipping his words, wringing

55

his hands and contorting his body in a very paroxysm of despair. Two girls near Kiril gazed at him in ecstatic admiration as they childishly patted stray strands of their hair into place. At last the poet, having poured out all that was torturing him, modestly lowered his eyes and was silent. The two girls clapped violently, but the bell rang, and the chairman put a stop to the ovation. A moment later the youth began a poem on hunger. Some of the audience moved their lips, silently repeating the words. It was very hot. The masters sat rigid in their semi-circle, with solemn faces, just like doctors at a consultation.

A grim, red-haired young man, with disdainfully curving lips, took the place of the reed-like youth. He turned sideways to the audience, and contemptuously, as though spitting out his words, hissed out his verses about low drinking places, thieves and *souteneurs*, the title of his medley being 'The ballad of the Finnish Knife.' Having hissed out his ballad, the young man stepped down without bowing, although there was a great deal of applause at the back of the room, and even the masters tapped their palms with the tips of their fingers.

He was followed by a poetess with shingled hair and eyes as translucent as crystal. Gazing over the heads of the audience into some far distant cosmic space, she proceeded to tear verses out of herself with as much agony as though she were uttering prophecies or making the most intricate calculations.

Poets and poetesses followed one another, simple creatures who intoned their verses in a sing-song in provincial accents, tossing back their hair, which was cut round in peasant-fashion; girls who minced their words as though they were chewing a caramel; and the alert, smart young men always to be seen at fashionable gatherings, well-groomed and accompanied by beautiful women, who do no work but are regarded as poets and whose means of livelihood is a mystery.

And next to Kiril, while he listened to all these chants and crooning lamentations, sat a woman, practically a stranger, a casual acquaintance, who was now openly leaning on his shoulder. All this was in striking contrast to the formulas and calculations and parabolas which usually occupied his mind, but at this moment plans and tracings seemed infinitely far away, while all that was going on round him took on an extraordinary importance and significance. What stirred him most was the thought that all these people possessed the miraculous gift of word and song for which he had struggled so long. He was so absorbed that he did not notice when his name was called until Vera nudged him and the unkempt man clapped his hands and called to him across the crowd: 'Your turn, Bessonov.'

He rose in confusion, and, pressing his hands to his breast, tried with pleading tones to prove something to them; but they would not listen, and they clapped, and the unkempt man, pushing his way through the crowd, dragged him on to the platform. Kiril saw a sea of human faces in front of him, dozens of women's eyes staring at him from a dark abyss, and he at once became wet with perspiration in his overwhelming fear and agitation. Someone behind him hissed angrily: 'Damn it all, say something. Don't make such a fuss.'

He stood there in confusion, rubbing his damp palms together, and realised that he must say something, anything he could remember, or they would laugh him to scorn. Straining his memory with a painful effort, he could not at first recall a single thing. Then something came back to him: verses about his own people, the town in which he had been born and spent his childhood, and about the growth of corn, all strange to city life. With his eyes almost shut, so

57

frightened that he could not hear his own words, he recited the lines. The sad poem captured the audience, and there was loud applause. It was probably just because he was so nervous that he had recited it so well and with such intense feeling. He wanted to resume his seat, but was prevented, and again he heard the voice behind him whispering loudly 'Give an encore,' and he remembered some more verses. Wet with perspiration, his hair glued to his forehead, he stood there in agony for ten minutes. Then he stepped down, blind to all around him. And immediately a woman's hand, firm and warm, pressed his as though some intimate tie united them. Then, still oblivious of the crowd, he left the room with Vera, and plunged into the fog. The darkness, the very damp, were comforting. He raised his burning face with joy in the cold caress of the air. A gentle rain was bathing the already drowsy town.

The poets, too, were dispersing to all the various parts and suburbs of the city, as though they were lighting up the ghostly dampness with the inextinguishable brightness of verse and dreams.

up the Commandant remembered the suppliant and her
nervous anxious face, and so Stromec had got his liberty.

Soon after she had finished school, Tania, finding herself
at the cross-roads, determined to live her own life. Her
brother was at the front, her mother were living in
great poverty, and realising that she could do nothing

CHAPTER VII

Vera took his arm as he walked awkwardly by her side.

'What I recited was awful,' he said, feeling really shocked
at his own daring.

But Vera pressed against his elbow, and looked up at him
from beneath her little fur cap with a warm, bright, womanly
glance. 'You did it beautifully, so sincerely and unaffectedly,'
she said with a drawl, and the fact that she not only did not
find fault with him, but expressed her approval, made her
seem much nearer, much more attractive, to him. And,
indeed, what was there to be ashamed of? He had never read
any of his poetry to anyone before, but now that he had done,
his verses had not been inferior to the others, he had been
applauded, and the woman beside him praised his talent.
What if he really had talent, a brilliant talent that would
lift him high above the rut of tracings and calculations? He
remembered the hostel, the weekday feeling of the long dark
hours of hard work. Sverbeev was right. What did that
future hold for him? Over production, starting trains at a
wayside halt, a canary – while here was talent which would
perhaps make his name famous, so that instead of being a
railway engineer like hundreds of others, a mere rivet lost
in the great structure of the city, he would be a poet, one in
a thousand, a brilliant factor in his country's glory! These
thoughts were by no means defined, but they intoxicated
him as they passed vaguely and hazily through his mind.

They went down the boulevard into Strastnoi Street,
and stopped at the tram halt, standing shoulder to shoulder.
It was raining, and there was a cold wind, so that the rain-

drops clung to their eyelashes. In a few moments Kiril followed the girl into the tram automatically, and it was only when they were rolling through familiar streets that he asked, in astonishment, 'Where are we going?'

Vera was slyly silent for a minute, and then she said slowly, 'You'll see. I want you to meet a cinema man named Cooperov. While you were reading your verses, I had an idea. . . I suppose you need money? Well, try to get on the films. Lots of the students do. I help to paint some of the scenery. They're just staging a historical film; you might come in as a young nobleman. Cooperov will be able to tell at a glance.'

Kiril might have asked himself what it mattered to this woman whether or not he needed money, and, in any case, why she was dragging him, late at night, to Petrov Park, to introduce him to a cinema man. But he was, at the moment, incapable of thinking anything out clearly, his feelings were confused as though that evening had torn his life from its orbit so that everything in the future would naturally be more and more magnificent.

The tram gradually emptied. They were passing through green avenues now, trees looming vaguely on either side of them. At last they reached a stopping place, and got out near a solitary lamp. The unfamiliar street was quite empty. With calm assurance, Vera rang the bell of a huge building, with a multitude of windows, which appeared to be unoccupied. A moment later, the door opened, and they entered an enormous barrack-like hall, through the casements of which a greenish light gleamed dimly from outside. It was a cinema studio. The man who let them in turned on a thousand candle power lamp, and blaze of brightness lit up the network of windows, the pasteboard scenery, the gilt furniture, and various properties – a heap of *boyar**

Boyar – Russian noble of the middle ages.

60

costumes, desks with reading lamps, and electric wires trailing like snakes from the lighting apparatus – in a word, all the appliances of this mysterious workshop. Until such time as a flat could be found for him, Cooperov was sleeping on an old leather divan in the studio that looked like the seat of an omnibus. He was a little man with a big head and Mongolian eyes, and was wearing a short coat of some indescribable mustard colour, and had rust-coloured puttees wound round his skinny calves. He was not in the least surprised by the late visit. He gave Kiril a rapid glance which seemed to sum him up in a second, and led the way past an ornate old mansion knocked up out of planks covered with an appropriate shell. Kiril picked his way carefully through the tangle of wires, feeling somewhat excited at this unaccustomed scene, and suddenly, behind the mansion, he caught sight of Sverbeev.

Sverbeev moved towards them with an embarrassed smile, as though confused at being found in such a place. 'Splendid of you, Vera, to bring him here,' he said, and put his arm round Kiril's shoulder. 'You ought to see everything in life, old man, and something may come of it; you never know. Here's a Russian nobleman for you, Cooperov, you'll never find a better.'

Cooperov once more sized Kiril up, half closing his narrow eyes. 'If he grows a beard, the producer will take him like a shot. . . He'll do all right.'

They sat down behind the mansion, at a table littered with gilded papier-maché goblets and tankards. Cooperov swept them all aside, and a moment later the cardboard properties were replaced by a real bottle of Russian spirits. Then he produced a German sausage, cut into slices, brought a dish of salted cucumbers, and supper was ready.

'Don't you be afraid, Kiril,' said Sverbeev coolly and slowly winking at his friend. 'It all seems very strange at

61

first, I know, but you cultivate Cooperov, he's the producer's right-hand man.'

Cooperov poured some vodka into the squat round wineglasses, and they all clinked. 'Well, *boyar*,' said Cooperov genially, 'here's to our better acquaintance. And when the *boyar* film is finished, something better may turn up. We've got a dozen students here who make a living at it, and those who show any talent get parts.'

The vodka was harsh and tasted dreadful, the first gulp making one shudder. But an instant later one was suffused by a pleasant warmth. Sverbeev talked as he tackled his cucumber: 'We ought to meet like this oftener. We live in our lairs like bears, lectures, examinations – with never a touch of human intercourse. Five years learning, and another five before you can make any sort of position – that means starting life at about thirty-five: not for me, thank you. Drawing plans is all very well in its place, but life is life.'

Cooperov eagerly backed him up: 'If you don't see life, you've got no horizon, and what's an engineer without a horizon?'

They drank again, and this time it was to engineers and horizons. Kiril suddenly felt that he, too, wanted to live like that, on a big scale, triumphantly. The vodka began to make his knees feel pleasantly weak. Sverbeev's smile seemed expansive and full of wonderful promise, Cooperov predicted fame, and Vera had a look on her face which seemed to indicate that the question of his gifts, his fame, and everything after which he was then dimly groping was a foregone conclusion. He drank more, and there was no shudder now, and the enormous hall seemed to become infinite, while its roof appeared to be the sky, the cloudy dome of which showed through the glass as though it were bearing down on them. Sverbeev kept on nodding to him, and at his side, touching his elbow with hers, was this woman with ardent eyes – everyone was being so kind to him, so very kind. Then Sverbeev rose, put an arm round him affectionately, and led him to a sofa that stood in another part of the room.

'Lie down for a bit, Kiril,' whispered Sverbeev, and Bessonov was wrapped in a glow of blissful peace as he sank on the springy, slightly heaving sofa. Everything spun round him, but his mind was at peace, undisturbed by memories, and everything seemed strange, so delicious that he gave a sad little laugh. Through a thick haze, he heard Sverbeev singing, while someone, probably Vera, strummed an accompaniment on a guitar; and then, after what seemed to him to have been only a few seconds, the huge lamp was extinguished, and the pallid sky dimly lit the roof. And beside him on the divan was something familiar, something indescribably warm. He stretched out his hand, and met other hands, dry, with nervously grasping fingers. Arms twined round his neck, and a woman was hurriedly murmuring disjointed words close to his dry lips. He could not resist that passionate, tremulous voice. Incredulous, horrified, he strained to understand what she was saying . . . and then the voice was silent, and all was darkness.

About six o'clock in the morning, Kiril, probably awakened by the grinding noise of the first tram, rose and wandered to the glass wall. Day had broken, showing a garden outside. It was raining, and in the pale dawn the fading autumn leaves hung above the muddy paths in sickly green. He stood for a long time, staring out at the garden and the misty rain. The morning wore a sort of dying smile. Behind him, in the now cold studio, Vera lay asleep on the divan – Vera whom he had seen only twice in his life, but who had come into the closest touch with him though he had not planned it and had felt not the slightest passion, not even any attraction. Well, it was just one of the incidents in the life of a man, to which one need not give a second thought – something like the cooper's wife when he was a boy. But the cooper's wife had not been the only one; there was Varinka, and now, now there was that wonderful creature with whom he had walked along the Bronni two days ago, on whom he longed so ardently to concentrate his whole being. How could he approach her with an unblemished heart after what had happened in the night?

He was like all the others, or worse. And then he suddenly imagined how Sverbeev would laugh at him if he could know of this morning repentance. Well, everyone has different feelings. As for himself, he had, from childhood, always dreamed his dreams alone, written his poetry in secret, and revealed his secret to no one.

Then he remembered his triumph of the evening before, the new call from life which he had heard for the first time, and his repentance faded away. This real life, of which he had known nothing hitherto, was full of new thrills, excitement and amusement. Noiselessly he went back to the divan. Vera slept the impassive sleep of dawn. He gazed down at her relaxed mouth with feverish eyes, marvelling at the spontaneity and facility of her surrender. Vera opened her eyes and sighed, and, still under the spell of her night dreams, gave him a long, mysterious look.

CHAPTER VIII

THREE days after that night, which dwelt in his memory as a sort of chasm, an abyss in which a feeling of burning shame mingled with a strange exultation, Kiril went back alone to the cinema studio. They were shooting a scene, and enormous mercury lamps shone like violet suns, while a crowd of boyars in long coats, like those worn by choirboys in Russian churches, were resting on sofas, munching sandwiches out of paper bags. Cooperov, who had sent him a message to come by Sverbeev, was dressed in a workman's blue blouse. He rushed at him excitedly, and dragged him to the producer.

The producer was standing on a chair, shouting instructions to a group of supers who represented *oprichniks** being entertained by a musician playing a sort of bagpipe. These *oprichniks* should have been a lot of dare-devil youths, but they were miserably huddled together and looked utterly incapable of any sort of gaiety. The producer, wearing a weird grey coat with patch pockets, and green golfing stockings right up to his knees, was directing the scene in a frenzy. After storming at the *oprichniks* for a time, he sprang from his chair and very theatrically seized Kiril's hand, and drew him towards the light. Then he stepped back a few paces, carefully sized him up, and rushed away to break the supers up into groups.

'It's all right, I think; I congratulate you,' whispered Cooperov as he passed him.

Happy and excited, Kiril remained alone. On the way to

*A special regiment instituted by John the Terrible and used chiefly for punitive expeditions.

the studio, he had tried to convince himself that it was only his poverty and the necessity for finding work that were driving him to this, and he did not wish to own, even to himself, that something quite different, something stronger than money, something more important than work, was urging him: that is, the extraordinary craving which had been roused so unexpectedly, with such enchantment, at the poets' meeting three days ago. . . . He had tried to resume his work during these last three days, had stubbornly forced himself to make drawings and to prepare for his examination, and he had succeeded. But new songs of victory rang within him all the time, and the sound of those songs overwhelmed him and drowned the thoughts of his drawings and his examination.

Old Makar had talked to him, when he was a child, about the omnipotence of man's word, and perhaps it was his mission in life to interpret that unique word, to bear aloft the banner of high ideals, and not to be a mere railway engineer, nameless, and leaving no memory of noble effort.

Standing aloof, he gazed at the insupportable violet lamps, listening to their droning, and he was filled with joy at the thought that, from now on, he was to be a part of this new world.

This new world spread before him, luring and enchanting him. He made up his mind that his work at the studio should not interfere with his preparation for the examination; but the hours fixed for rehearsing and photographing dragged out into whole days, and when he was able to return to the hostel, it was only to find himself drunk with excitement and fatigue. He liked the rehearsals, he liked strutting about in costume and make-up including a beard, he liked to study in the mirror his face so changed by its paint, to wander about in the soft theatrical boots of coloured leather, to look so different, to play a part – although there were dozens doing what he was, and the real actors did not know them even by sight. But to him it seemed that he was their equal, and, meeting Vera at a rehearsal, he was delighted to be able to drive away with her, just as the actors drove away with the artistes.

His relations with Vera continued from that day. They drove away together and from that time forward everything went as he wished. Then he noticed a man's overcoat in her attic, and he blazed up in a fury. Vera gazed calmly at him with her washed-out eyes, and knocking the ash off her cigarette, she queried:

'What business is it of yours, Kiril? Other men come to see me here. Please don't imagine, I don't in the least want you to think, that you are the only one. . . Otherwise you'll begin to make scenes. I'm not meant for domesticity. It's dull. I have never understood how some women can carry on an eternal duet with the same man, meeting him, waiting for him, suffering, writing letters. . .'

She spoke roughly, was perhaps challenging him with her roughness. But she went on: 'Please don't get wrought up. I took a fancy to you because there is still a sort of freshness about you, and if you can dispense with this masculine pride of yours, we can get along very well together. There's plenty of time yet for me to settle down for life with one man, and to bear children.'

She said all this like a man, dangling her foot and knocking the ash off her cigarette. And all this – her bachelor attic, his illicit intercourse with the unloved woman to whom nothing was forbidden – stretched out in front of him like a huge frozen desert.

Vera went on smoking and talking at her ease: 'It's very stupid to take it all so dramatically. There's no necessity for me to give an account of myself to you, I might say nothing. I'm only telling you because I never dreamed that, as a

67

student, and therefore emancipated, you could look at things in any other way. But the peasant in you is still alive; you must possess a woman, bully her . . . what you need in addition to the woman is a field and a cow. . .'

Suddenly, behind this hostile woman, now hateful, perhaps by reason of their inexcusable intimacy, there arose in his imagination the image of that bright-eyed, wonderful creature to whom, during these last few days, he had been unfaithful, and to whom he would so gladly, so joyfully, dedicate his future fame and the new life to which he had been called. He could tell her everything, she would understand everything, because she, Tania, was the intangible, perhaps the imagined, ideal for whom he had been keeping himself since childhood.

He made no response to Vera, and a quarter of an hour later he left her, full of his resuscitated dream, and firmly determined never to go back to her. For the last week rain had given place to frost which had dried the streets, and now the autumn wind was raising columns of the stinging town dust on the boulevards. As Kiril Bessonov made his way along the boulevard the cold wind seemed to cleanse his soul.

Near the Pushkin monument, he saw two men sitting on a bench, and he thought that he recognised one of them. Looking more closely, he saw that it was the unkempt man of the linen coat whom he had seen at the poets' meeting. He now had on a round cap of dogskin. He waved his hand from afar, inviting Kiril to come and sit by him.

'Don't forget it's the regular meeting on Wednesday,' he said in a confidential tone, as though Kiril were an old member. Kiril was on the point of thanking him warmly, but was prevented by the unkempt man introducing him to his companion.

'Meet Dontsev, Bessonov, I'm sure you're heard of the critic Dontsev.'

Dontsev had a bushy beard which enveloped him like a sheepskin, and an old camel's hair coat completed his slavonic aspect and seemed to emphasise the incongruity of his appearance with his setting.

'Peasant poet?' he said in a gracious voice. 'Have you been long in Moscow?'

'No, I'm a factory hand. At least my father was,' said Kiril hurriedly, for some reason feeling confused.

'Well, come and see me, my good man – We'll have a talk. If you have talent, we'll help your first footsteps. Everyone passes through Dontsev's hands, my good man, everyone.'

Small, pale, turquoise-blue eyes gazed at him out of the forest of curly beard; but those eyes seemed beautiful to Kiril. Dontsev took a notebook from his pocket, and scribbled his address in pencil. And there, on a street bench, in the cold November wind, Kiril's fate was sealed, and a fresh path opened in front of him in which new and wonderful flowers blossomed.

CHAPTER IX

KIRIL overcame his shyness sufficiently to go and see
Dontsev on the Friday evening. He lived in a big, untidy
house – an immense building which housed about a
thousand people. There were a dozen perambulators in the
courtyard where small boys were trundling their hoops and
a lot of Tartar pedlars were crying their wares in heavy,
raucous voices.

Dontsev's room, too, was huge and untidy; bookshelves
crammed with tattered, much befingered volumes covered
walls from floor to ceiling, and dog-eared manuscripts
littered the dusty table. Dontsev, wearing an embroidered
Turkish smoking jacket, looked like a ragman. His wife
was rocking a baby in the adjoining room, while a five-year-
old boy, with the air of a grown-up and looking the image
of his father, stood in the doorway.

In his usual gracious voice, sounding as though every
word was well oiled, Dontsev invited Kiril to sit down.
'Well, well,' he said, with the bedside manner of a doctor,
'have you brought it? Read it, my good man. Don't be shy,
read. We'll talk afterwards.'

Although this was just what Kiril had come for, he was
overwhelmed with bashfulness as he took his notebook from
his pocket. He was actually doing deliberately what had
seemed to him a week ago to be impossible. But since that
meeting at the poets' circle it all seemed not only possible
but inevitable, and he began to read awkwardly and with
unnecessary gestures. Dontsev rested his head on his
hand, and his thick nose seemed to be following every line.

Then he gave a deep sigh, shook some crumbs from his beard, and said 'Go on.'

Kiril read on, and when at last he had finished, Dontsev removed his hand from his chin, and staring with his doll-like turquoise eyes, exclaimed "Talent, my good man. On my honour. You'll have to work at the form, but you may conquer a place in literature. Wait a minute, I'll enter you in my index.'

He pulled out a long drawer, full of index cards, and, after rummaging for a time, found a clean one, and proceeded to write down Kiril's name, age, and place of birth. Then he put the card in an index case, and, once for all, Kiril was enrolled among the immortals. But that did not end the visit. His host took off his embroidered jacket, put on a deer-skin coat, and said with solemn decision: 'And now let us go to our literary circle. I take a new talent there every Friday. This Russia of ours is full of talent.'

He pulled on an enormous pair of old-fashioned goloshes, took his hat, and, in response to an enquiring look from his wan and miserable wife, said majestically: 'We are going out.'

They were in the street a moment later, and Dontsev talked loudly all the way about Russia, so that passers-by could hear and turn to look at him, guessing him to be a man of importance. He patted Kiril on the back as he shuffled along like an old man in his ill-fitting goloshes.

The circle to which Kiril was introduced met in the flat of a certain Varvara Nikolaevna Dolev, who wrote novels and plays. She was a heavily built woman who had attracted the attention of pre-revolutionary critics. When they entered she was sitting, like a statue of Buddha with the smile of a sphinx, at a long table on which masses of documents were scattered in studied disorder, with innumerable copies of her own novels and plays among them as though by accident. Near this moustachioed lady sat the committee of the society, old and young, with stolid faces, turning over business papers as though at an economic conference. All round the talents crowded, poets and poetesses, the many talents brought by Dontsev every Friday, a fresh talent every Friday. This Friday the talent was Bessonov.

Madam Dolev was the centre of this human flowerbed, and, like an overblown rose, she scattered smiles as though she were shedding petals. Her fat, faded cheeks, puffed up to her narrow, Japanese eyes, and her upper lip, almost as hairy as that of a grenadier, made a striking example of the evanescence of woman's charm. The room was very hot, and Kiril's head began to swim as soon as he entered its smoke-laden mixture of human exhalations and odours. With accustomed quickness and address, the company were snatching cups of tea and little cakes called *baisers*, which were as fluffy outside and as empty within as the human variety of kiss.

Within ten minutes Kiril was sitting under the wing of the hostess, to her left, as a new member. He was surrounded by women and the overpowering smells of scent and powder. The hostess rang a bell, declared the meeting open, and then gave a few particulars about the new poet who was to read his verses that afternoon. Dontsev was sitting at the other end of the table, triumphantly winking and nodding encouragement, treating him as his own personal creation. After the hostess's short introductory remarks, it was Kiril's turn.

He rose, feeling crushed by the multitude of eyes, the stuffy nearness of Madam Dolev, and his own self-conscious shyness. He read a first thing, then a second and a third. From time to time, he glanced pleadingly at Dontsev or his hostess, but they were obdurate and merely nodded, so he went on. At last, he finished. Applause was forbidden here,

72

lest it should mar the unity of an impression, a notice to that effect being posted on the wall.

A neat, ashen old man, with a high-pitched girlish voice was the first speaker. He analysed Kiril's poems very ably from the point of view of phonetics, their sound, so to speak. He hinted at classical influences, and then dwelt on classical poetry in general, till it became obvious that he could then and there have rolled off a professorial two hour lecture if the time allotted to each speaker had not been limited.

Next came a red-haired man covered with freckles, who asserted with passionate heat that this poetry was decadent, that such poetry was not wanted and must be eliminated.

Not less heated were the arguments of a homely, depressed man in a pince-nez, who looked like an ugly duckling, who proved beyond a doubt that Kiril's verses were in harmony with the age.

Then a woman professor spoke, a remarkably sensible creature with short hair and high cheekbones, not unlike Plevako. She found fault with the purely technical aspects – such careless assonances. Then five or six others spoke. Kiril was too dazed to remember them all, but one thing at least was clear; they all treated him as a real poet.

In the interval, Dontsev looked at him with the eyes of a conqueror, and passed him a note containing one word – 'Congratulations.' All this was more intoxicating than that first evening at the poets' circle. Then the young man like an ugly duckling came up to him and demanded insistently that he should inscribe himself as a member of the Romantic-Classical group.

That night Kiril returned alone. Moscow, on that autumn night, swept by snowless wind, seemed immense and flaming. For a moment the horrible thought seized him that he had an examination in a week, that he was on his way to the hostel where everyone was sleeping the sleep of the weary, but he thrust back the unwelcome intruder with careless ease. The night accepted him as a guest and a companion.

CHAPTER X

THE production of the film in which Kiril was taking part was nearing its end. The last scenes were laid in Pskov, and as he did not appear in them he did not go there with the company. During the last days of his work at the studio he was bitterly conscious of the void which would ensue when his visits to the familiar glass pavilion ceased. He had grown accustomed to the brightness which contrasted so vividly with the dull monotony and darkness of the hostel, with its hard work, its lectures, and its preparation for the examination. A few years ago, the possibility of becoming a student in the capital had seemed like a dream, but now it had somehow lost its glamour since he had experienced the excitement of the poets' circle and the glass studio. The general view, the accepted idea, was that he was called upon to serve Art. His technical drawings now seemed to be merely a confused attempt to find solutions of problems which were of no use to anyone, and he was inattentive at the lectures and failed to take in their meaning.

He realised with horror one day how much he had missed. He had been absent for three weeks and had irretrievably lost track of much that was quite clear to his fellow-students but utterly incomprehensible to him. He felt alarmed and ashamed, and decided to catch up with the others. He flung himself at his books, but somehow he felt boneless, unable to concentrate – he must be going to pieces. There were three sides to his life – one was his poetry that dimly beckoned and promised, the second was the orderly student life which now seemed alien, and the

75

third was Petrov Park with its violet lamps, its actors, the grease-painted faces, the ephemeral properties.

On the last day of the production, Cooperov whispered, as he passed by, that Kiril should stay on after they had finished. For the last time, Kiril took off his blond beard and sat down on a sofa to wait. He had not seen Vera for some days, but at that moment he would have been willing to make it up with her if only he could have retained her as a connecting link with the studio. What if he did not love her? People came together without love; indeed, love was the rarest of the bonds of union. A liaison was a liaison, an ordinary episode imposing no responsibility on either side, and could be broken off as easily as begun. Tania might be his love, but he had not seen Tania since the day he had walked home with her, and she seemed to recede farther and farther from him as the days went by, as though he had merely dreamed that she existed. And because his life was physically connected with Vera the vision of Tania seemed to evoke more sadness as it became more ethereal and exalted. He might have found in her all that he had searched for since boyhood, and in his mind Varinka, barely retained in the placid memory of a child, had somehow merged into Tania, the new love. She was not lowered in his eyes by her affair with Chelishev; that only draped her in a cloud of sadness, femininity and dreamy inaccessibility. Yes, if only he were with her! She might actually merge in that lodestar which had been his guide since boyhood, beckoning toward a promised realisation of all that was best and highest in him. But there was no Tania; the only woman with whom he was intimate was Vera. Well, what if she were coarse? What if she were accessible to all men? It was not as though he were going to entangle his life with hers; their relations entailed no responsibility, no consideration, on either side; simply take her, after the manner of a man, smoke a cigarette,

76

and go away, just as he might call in at a bar on his way home.

He waited until the photographer had finished, and then Cooperov came and sat down by him, crossing his bony legs in their rusty puttees, and sticking a cigarette between his lips with a sigh of relief and relaxation: 'We're finishing the film, old man. I wonder when we shall have another one to do? But that's not the point. The point is that it is very often the least gifted people who make the most brilliant careers. You seem to think that it is enough if you have talent; that all the rest will happen of itself. Well, it won't.

'Above all, you've got to know how to play your cards. That, and a reserve of resourcefulness in your brain are what matter most. Without that, talent is no good. Why should I be telling you all this? Why, because at this moment you hold your life in your own hands, like a bird, and it's the easiest thing in the world to loosen your grip and let it go. It's not everyone who gets the chance, but once it flies into your hands, hold tight.'

Kiril thought of his recent good luck. It had indeed flown into his hands as unexpectedly as a bird.

'I began all this,' went on Cooperov, 'because I've seen plenty of your sort sucked into the quicksand. You've got to stand firm on your two legs, Bessonov, and you've got to have skill and a pair of fists. But, above all you've got to have money. How do you suppose Professor Chelishev first roused Tania? With his handsome face, or his lectures? Much she cares for his lectures. No, by his manner of life, by having the means to live lavishly, and you can only live lavishly if you have money. Perhaps I've taken pity on your youth. It is pitiful to see a man with down on his wings who can't grow feathers. I'm only saying all this to make you think things out. Don't sell yourself for twopence, and

77

drop all those dreams. In these hard times, dreaming will only make a turnip of you. You must feel life between your fingers as if it were a piece of material' – Cooperov quickly and greedily rubbed his thick fingers together, yellow with nicotine, as though sampling a piece of stuff – 'If you want advice, you can trust me, don't make any mistake about that; I know life in all three dimensions.'

Cooperov talked a good deal to him that day, all in the same muddled strain about life in general, but the only thing that impressed itself deeply on his mind was what he said about Tania. It was only later that the thought struck him 'How did Cooperov know about Tania?' Perhaps Sverbeev had told him, but why did Cooperov talk as though he knew her personally? And Tania's image, magnified, immense, once more rose before him. These men, whom he hardly knew, kept on talking about her and dragging him into the side paths which he was exploring, away from the torment and agitation of that road on which he might perhaps remain true to himself to the end. Was it all imagination? Even if it were, he felt that in all that had happened that autumn in Moscow, with its mud, the greenish light of its lamps, its strange ever-surging crowds, in all that grim, callous city, there had been one lodestar, a heart that was dear, but inaccessible, closed to him. With her he might give himself up to the work of which he had dreamed in his narrow provincial town, and the chaos of the last month would drift away, leaving him untouched; whereas, now he felt that he was being burnt up by all this uncertainty, this muddle, this talk of joy, and the dozens of new acquaintanceships. And Tania's image took on a new aspect. To what could he look forward in his poverty, in his wretched provincial coat with its ridiculous pockets – Yagodkin's parting gift – in his shabby, cheap, mass production shoes, in his big-peaked imitation English cap? The

78

very gold of his hair was fading thanks to the miserable sixpenny dinners he got at the students' cheap restaurant, where other youths as young as he was looked like the withered officials out of some place of archives. And the future? What was his future to be after five years of underfeeding and overwork, after five years of study, of sordid life in the huge hostel where even elementary cleanliness was wanting, where all lived, not as though at home but, as mere temporary lodgers in barracks or in some building still under construction? Perhaps if he had some corner of his own, with his own books and his own dreams, as he had had after his father's death, perhaps then he might have concentrated, analysed himself, torn himself away from all that was false in his present surroundings, might have returned to the only things which had any real value, and have thought matters out to their logical conclusion, and so have become more simple, more genuine, more human.

But that was impossible, and Cooperov was right in saying that you must bestride the stubborn, prancing steed, or it would trample you under its hooves. With money and fame (Oh how bitterly that hitherto unknown word hurt him!) one might obtain many of the means for softening the most recalcitrant of hearts. For a moment he was astonished at the ease with which, in the absence of anything to encourage them, his thoughts ran on triumphantly on those lines, and how far, far behind him had dropped his earliest ideals, as though separated from him by scores of years; while those best of men, Makar, Yagodkin, seemed to have melted away as melts in spring the ice of winter.

Next day, believing that he had really reached a final decision, Kiril Bessonov set out determined to find the ugly duckling whose acquaintance he had made at Mdme. Dolev's. In a large red house, with a coat of arms emblazoned over its entrance, he found a crowd of young men in fur

79

caps, their collars turned up, with bulging portfolios under their arms. There was much busy running up and down stairs, meetings were going on amid a cloud of smoke in the rooms which flanked the corridor on both sides, and from time to time, young men of important mien, kept emerging from the smoke to dash off to some destination undisclosed. In one room someone was reciting poetry in a sing-song, and in another, someone else was reciting poetry in peasant accents. It was into a third room, where a dignified group was seated in a semi-circle, that Bessonov made his way. But a man in horn spectacles said 'This is private.' At last, in a little room at the very end of the corridor, Kiril ran the ugly duckling to earth. Surrounded by people in overcoats, smoking, the duckling was sitting at a table. The duckling recognised him, shook hands without rising (he behaved like a cabinet minister) and said in a businesslike tone 'Have you come to put your name down?' Then he opened a drawer, got out a book of members' tickets, wrote in Kiril's name, signed his own with a flourish, blew the dust off the official stamp, impressed the ticket with a purple circle – and Kiril was a member of the Romantic-Classical group.

He left the room with the ticket in his hand, and in the corridor he unfolded it and examined it with a beating heart. Perhaps this would actually determine his aim in life? But, at that moment, the unkempt man of the linen coat rushed up to him; reeking of tobacco and shouting excitedly, 'Why have you joined them? Anyhow, we regard you as one of us. The true poets are all with us.'

Shrugging his shoulders, as tense as though an electric current were drawing sparks from him, he seized Kiril and dragged him away.

CHAPTER XI

IT was only a week before his examination that Kiril definitely realised that he could not make up for his lost time. He made the strongest resolutions that he would bury himself in lectures and books, but his books mocked him, incomprehensible formulas and calculations flitted before him, and he saw that he had missed too much. His studies in the past had followed a logical sequence, layer on layer, but now there was too much for him to retrieve. The impossibility of catching up enfeebled him, crushed him; but he was determined to overcome his weakness by sheer will-power. Three other students occupied broken-down cots in the same room. They, like himself, had been absent for whole days, looking for work, selling books, unloading waggons, and now, late into the night, they poured over their hastily scribbled pencil notes. Kiril had never become intimate with them. The first place in his interest had been taken by Sverbeev, with whom his life had become interwoven.

Kiril's thoughts, while he was working for his examination, frequently turned to the man whom he was beginning to hate. His dread of the examination had for some time mingled with a vision of Chelishev, the magnificent and detested professor. For a second time that man was standing in his way, and Kiril foresaw that he would fade away into nothingness this second time before this famous and self-satisfied master. His name was linked with that of Tania Agourov, and what had at first seemed to Kiril to be only a slender, mysterious thread in the girl's life, now took on proportions that awakened a grim hatred within him. Yet, what wrong had Chelishev done him? Of what had he been

81

guilty? Of having been through the school of life, of having become a successful inventor, of having a charming voice and being attractive to women? But there was nothing base or vicious in that. Those were merely the traits of a man who had mastered the stubborn horse, who had done exactly what Cooperov had urged him to do himself. Was he envious? He had never been conscious of envy. He had only wanted to study. He had come to the city to devote himself whole-heartedly to work, and suddenly the city had called to him in wild and stirring tones. Whose fault was it? Certainly not the professor's, and yet he could not overcome his hatred. Sverbeev often talked about him, Cooperov talked of him, for his name came up every time they discussed a refined and agreeable life. And what was there in store for him, Kiril? Days of hard study, nights in a cot with broken strings, and the degrading certainty of failure in his exam.

The day of that examination came at last. He had hardly given himself time to eat or sleep for the last week, and he had, up to a point, mastered the intricacies that had at first so much alarmed him. He had not assimilated everything, but he could find his way through the entanglements. He went to the examination with the feelings of a winner. The auditorium was nearly empty, only on the front bench were a score of students who were also taking this examination. The daylight in the high dim windows was wan and dejected.

In a few minutes, Chelishev carelessly called the first students to the blackboard. The chalk tapped, and the blackboard was soon filled with a maze of lines. Kiril watched every movement of his fellow-students' hands with rapt attention. He could follow everything, the mysterious signs held no mystery for him, and he felt once more surge up in him the triumphant glow of the successful hunter.

The first batch of students returned to their places with pleased, perspiring faces, and began to collect their books and papers. Kiril had calculated that he would be in the third group, but suddenly heard his name called with two others. He thought that he must have been mistaken, but Chelishev repeated his name in a clear, toneless voice. Kiril moved to the blackboard in a quiver of excitement. He found himself quite close to Chelishev for the first time. The curve of the brushed back hair greying at the temples, the shaved, youthful lips, the arched, somewhat haughty nose, the lines from the nostrils, like an actor's, the air of listening to himself – everything about him, from his well-cut coat to his plump well manicured hands – spoke of a well organised manner of life perfect in every detail. Kiril stood before him abashed, conscious of his own inferiority, and awaited his problem. And suddenly, much of what he had striven so hard to acquire slipped from his mind.

Chelishev, not looking at him, seemed to be seeking for the most complicated question, and then asked him to calculate the rotations of the gyroscopic governor of a steam engine. An intense joy filled Kiril. It was exactly what he knew best; for some reason, he had worked that out again and again. He approached the blackboard, picked up the paper-wrapped chalk, and began to sketch out his formula. With broad strokes he developed his scheme, carefully drawing his lines, enthusiastically working out his calculations, carried away by his success, almost exultantly complicating the labyrinth of his figures, and gradually working out the solution. He went on feverishly for a quarter of an hour, and then, with a last stroke of the chalk, turned to the professor. Chelishev, standing behind him, had been watching his work. He approached the blackboard, took up the chalk, and, in the same clear and indifferent tone in which he had called his name, said 'Your calculation is wrong – The

pressure of the left socket is exerted above, not below –'
And he quickly drew a line through the calculations on the
board. 'And you have not allowed for the increase of strain
due to impact.' Again, offensively and contemptuously, he
drew the chalk through Kiril's figures, and, suddenly,
looking him straight in the face with his slightly protruding
eyes, he said:

'You had better admit, Bessonov, that you are not properly prepared for this examination. I cannot tolerate such
an attitude to work. I can understand mistakes, they are
always possible, but not a complete absence of knowledge.
I cannot pass you.'

He went back to his desk, and marked something on a
sheet of paper. Kiril saw the serious faces of his comrades
in the front row as though through a haze. His had been the
first failure. Some of them were feverishly turning over
pages, looking for the calculations of the gyroscopic governor.
Then, as though nothing had happened, as though this
irreparable, this horrible, calamity had not befallen him,
Kiril, Chelishev called the names of the next group.

With unseeing eyes, Kiril gathered up his books, and left
the auditorium. Never in his life had he experienced such
a feeling of loneliness and desertion as now. He did not
know which way to turn, and, oblivious of all his surroundings, he wandered out into the street. There was a sharp
frost, but only a few snowflakes were slanting down, and
horses were slipping on the frozen stones. He walked about
aimlessly for a long time, almost devoid of thought, and even
without any feeling of hatred for Chelishev. If at that
moment he had met someone to take him by the hand and
make him turn and analyse his life in the light of truth,
he might eagerly have followed him and, without hesitation.
But no one took him by the hand; he had no one. He found
his way to the noisy thoroughfares, and, instinctively,

without a thought, made his way to Sverbeev, as to the
only friend he had. Sverbeev opened the door himself, and
once more Kiril followed him down the passage full of cupboards. Other lodgers peeped out through their half-opened
doors, the Primus stoves in the kitchens sounded like a
waterfall.

'What in the world brings you here at this time of day?'
asked Sverbeev, opening the door of his room, 'business?'

'Yes . . . that is, no,' answered Kiril. 'It's nothing much;
I've been ploughed.'

As he said this, he stared past Sverbeev, the confession
was too humiliating for him to look at him.

'So that's it?' Sverbeev raised his eyebrows. 'Chelishev
ploughed you. Well, he's true to himself. What do we matter
to him? Did he ever have to work in the conditions we work
in? I should like to see him in the hostel preparing for an
exam. with one book among three of us. There's no such
thing as justice, never has been, never will be. Chelishev
is going abroad; he saves money, he's making a fortune.
What does it matter to him what you, student Bessonov,
suffer? He got ten thousand for two patents, enough to
keep us in comfort for five years. He's a rock, Kiril.'

Sverbeev stretched out his arms with a strange movement,
as though spreading his wings. 'But I should like to topple
that rock over, for spoiling our girls, for his riches, for his
indifference to us. And I wouldn't be afraid to do it.'
Having poured all this out, Sverbeev stopped abruptly,
and his fire seemed to be extinguished. 'However, I only
mean - I'm sorry for you, and for Tania. That's why I have
those feelings about him. Is it long since you saw Tania?'
he said suddenly, as though in passing. 'She was asking
about you.' The words fell heavily on Kiril's unhappy and
aching heart. Tania! With her, even this failure, his wretched
examination, would have been easy to bear. To look into

85

her serious eyes would banish all sad thoughts, all doubts.

Passionately, exultantly, he exclaimed: 'Look here, Sverbeev, fix up a meeting with her. I don't believe all that about her and Chelishev, and, even if it were true, how am I to judge her?'

Sverbeev paused a moment before answering: 'The Chelishev affair is only froth of course, and it can't be serious. He's a married man, and he has a reputation to maintain. If he has a little romance with a pretty student it's only a passing intrigue. All right, Kiril, I'll fix it. And if you prove yourself a man, you can trip Chelishev up far more effectually than he tripped you up to-day. It all depends on you, I know. Tania is looking for a quiet corner for herself, not a muddy hole, and, of course, she doesn't want his money; she's not that sort. If only I had his money.' Sverbeev languidly stretched out his legs and inflated his chest. 'If only I had his money, or if we were both rich, we would have a be-e-e-eautiful time.'

Kiril was surprised that Sverbeev should be saying the same thing, and in almost the same words, as Cooperov.

'Be-e-e-eautiful, Kiril. Well, never mind. By hook or crook we'll find the money, we'll get it. As for your exam., don't worry, it's all rot, and it isn't worth a single sigh. Perhaps in a month from now we'll fix up a failure for Chelishev, and a far more serious one than yours. Only, you've got to keep your will power on edge, sharp, like a pocket knife, and always ready to hand.'

Kiril listened, staring at the thin, long-nosed face, and the thoughts of his exam., which had seemed such a catastrophe a few minutes ago, receded farther and farther, became dim and a minor consideration in comparison with what was opening up before him. He was attracted and excited by the thought of meeting Tania in the near future.

Sverbeev took two glases out of a cupboard. There was a demijon of vodka on the floor in a corner of the room, and Kiril greedily took a gulp of the blessed, burning liquor. It came at just the right moment, and seemed to fill up the black chasm inside him.

'You think over what I've said to-day,' said Sverbeev, seizing the hand that held the glass. 'We can't tolerate injustice of that sort in these days. Everything for one, and only crumbs and charity for others. You and I grew up on factory soil, Kiril. Chelishev's arms are short. Do you understand?'

And although Kiril did not understand in the least, he nodded a quick assent. An hour later, comforted and warmed, he left Sverbeev, walked down Bronni Street, and, with a smile that was almost happy, turned into the courtyard, and climbed the stairs to Vera.

CHAPTER XII

IN accordance with instructions received from Chelishev that morning, Tania Agourov made her way at half past one to the large clock near the tram terminus. There had been a heavy snowfall during the night, and the town was now a downy white, pervaded by the dim winter fancies induced by the cessation of the noise of traffic when only the silvery ring of carefree children's skates was heard in the comparative silence. The minute hand of the clock showed that it still wanted five minutes to the half hour, and Tania stood below it, watching it move downward in jerks. She hid her frozen chin in her fur collar, staring at the glittering white snow, the bright runners of the sledges gliding down the boulevard, and at the fluffy nodules hanging on the trees. And in these minutes of waiting and reflection, it was brought home to her how incredible, how irreparable, were the happenings which she was passing in review as the cause of her presence here at this busy weekday hour.

Sometimes it comes about like that, and the busy town life is interrupted while one stops for a moment waiting for a tram or a friend, and the crowd surges round like a river as one stands alone with one's thoughts. And at such moments, one's thoughts are extraordinarily clear and one gets a vision of one's life as in a daydream. How had her intimacy with Chelishev arisen? What was it that had attracted this stranger, so much older than herself and of such an utterly different station? And what had drawn her to him with such terrible, indomitable force?

Years ago, her brother had sent for her from the provinces in order that she might continue her studies in Moscow.

Dmitri Agourov, finishing his course at the military academy, was living alone as a bachelor soldier. After the years of war and bloodshed, of which he had had his full share, he had felt a passionate longing to acquire knowledge, to reconstruct his life. He had early made up his mind to help his sister to study in Moscow. She had finished at school, and was merely marking time in the provinces. So now, after the quiet, familiar streets of the small town where she had grown up under her mother's wing in the little white house with its painted floors, she was in Moscow, with the right of entry to the huge white building in front of which stood the statue of Lomonosov, in place of all the surroundings which had moulded her childhood. Dmitri Agourov arranged for her to take the social science course, and they lived together, for they had always been on terms of intimacy, and it was his wish to be her guide and counsellor.

The determination to achieve all that she had set herself to do, with which she had come to Moscow, was characteristic of both brother and sister. . . . She wanted to make a new life for herself, and in order to do so she must take her studies seriously. She was just as Dmitri had known her in childhood, except that the long years of privation had given grown-up lines to her brow and her grave mouth. He was delighted to have his sister with him, but soon grew accustomed to it, and as he was very busy Tania led her own independent life. The days were filled with work, and they dined in public restaurants. In the evenings they went to meetings, rarely staying in, but occasionally going to a theatre with cheap tickets obtained at students' lotteries.

At thirteen, Tania had fallen in love with her drawing-master, an artist named Cherimoushkin, a sinewy, somewhat unattractive man of the semi-artist type, at whom the other schoolgirls laughed good-naturedly. Perhaps that was why he seemed to Tania to be a martyr, a hero, and why she wanted to tell him that she, Tania Agourov, was always, and whatever might happen, drawn to those who were lonely and not very happy. She thought all this out quite seriously, and then went to his flat.

The artist was in, and very surprised to see her. He listened to all that she had to say, and then began to laugh, slapping his thigh as his long legs stalked about the room. Then he went away, and returned with a plain girl with two plaits, very like himself. She was a little younger than Tania, and he introduced her as his daughter. The artist wanted them to make friends, but they sat facing each other with nothing to say until Tania went home. That was the end of her first love.

The second time it was a Hungarian prisoner, Stromec, who was pining for his own country, and whom she made up her mind to liberate. Stromec was billeted in their house, and in the evenings he played his guitar while he sang melancholy songs. They were mainly about Hungary, which he was certain that he would never see again. Tania felt convinced that if the extent of his sufferings were known, Stromec would be sent home; so she went to interview the Commandant of the town at his official reception hour. The Commandant received her in his study, asked her to sit down, and listened to all that this girl with a delicate, boyish face poured out so collectedly, and with such an air of determination. Then he politely enquired who this Stromec was, and why she was so much interested in him. Tania replied that Stromec was simply living in their house and that he was a complete stranger, but that he would die if he could not return to his own country. The Commandant then told her, again with politeness, that it really had nothing to do with him; so Tania went away in despair. Stromec, nevertheless, was in the first batch of exchanged prisoners; so it was obvious that when Stromec's name came up the Commandant remembered the suppliant and her nervous anxious face, and so Stromec had got his liberty.

Soon after she had finished school, Tania, finding herself at the cross-roads, determined to live her own life. Her brother was at the front, she and her mother were living in great poverty, and realising that she could do nothing unaided, she went to the president of the town committee. She was not allowed to see him, but she waited in the passage till he came out, stopped him, and told him, looking straight into his eyes with her own beautiful blue ones, that she needed work, that she had to support her mother and herself, that she knew several languages and was willing to do anything that she was told. The request, expressed with so much, and such unchildlike dignity, the whole appearance of the courageous little thing, were so extraordinary that, contrary to all rules, the president led her to his room, and two days later she was taken on as a clerk in the administration.

It was later that her brother suggested that she should study in Moscow, and she changed her whole life with the same straightforward determination. She decided to live on the student's stipend, depriving herself of everything, and to help her mother by doing any work she could find. She soon found work; a newspaper offered to take her notes on student life. She made the round of the university hostels, collected information, talked to professors, and all who met this girl in her leather coat with her stray locks of chestnut hair and her charmingly uneven teeth, this wonderful little reporter – all were glad to talk to her while her yellow pencil travelled rapidly over the pages of her notebook.

In the students' hostel, Tania one day ran across Sverbeev. She recognised the wiry long-nosed man, although he had aged very much in the last few years, as the son of

91

a telegraph clerk in her native town who had lived in the house next door. The telegraph clerk had had five sons, all long-nosed, tall and pimply, and Theodore was the eldest. And Theodore Sverbeev, on his side, recognised in this girl the proud, bright-eyed little Tania. She was glad to see him because he was a link with the dear, unforgettable years, because he was Theodore Sverbeev who had worn a shabby schoolcap, as shabby as the students' cap he was wearing now. He, too, was glad. He promised to help her, and he had helped her in many ways. He collected information for her, and Tania would call in at his room in all simplicity and friendliness. Tania told her brother about seeing Sverbeev, and he was surprised, and they talked over much of their childhood together. Sverbeev furnished her with details of their life at the Institute, and one day he told her that she really must interview Professor Chelishev about his inventions, as he was very much in the public eye at the moment. And Sverbeev arranged that he should see Tania at his private apartment to tell her about his new projects and his latest discoveries. Chelishev, who naturally expected a typical journalist, was prepared to go into great detail about his work, and was greatly astonished when he was suddenly confronted by this courageous little girl who confidently informed him that she had come to interview him for a newspaper. He took her into his study, where Tania found herself face to face with the man about whom everyone was talking, a man with a fresh, almost young, face, whose greying temples seemed rather to add to his appearance of youthfulness than to suggest age, and with bright, clear eyes that looked quizzically at the somewhat abashed little reporter. He told her everything that she wanted to know, he even wrote down for her some of the complicated details which it would be difficult for her to remember; he made sketches for her, indeed, he treated

92

her as simply as though she were a real, full grown journalist, and Tania went away, touched and charmed by his beautiful, caressive voice and the way in which he had facilitated the interview. Her long report was printed without a cut, it had been her first real test, and from that day the newspaper gave her responsible work. Always resolute and business-like, with her attaché case and notebook, she would go where reporters were not wanted, but neither admission nor information was ever refused to her.

The most important thing about all this, however, was that she never forgot the cause of her first success; she thought of Chelishev often and with warmth. And, strangely enough, Sverbeev did his utmost to stimulate her memory, to make her impression indelible. He kept the recollections of this man stirred up in her mind until Chelishev became even more eminent and important to her than he had seemed at their first meeting.

It was just at this time that Chelishev brought to a suc-cessful termination his experiments on the automatic coupling of railway trucks which would mean the dismissal of a whole army of railway workers and an enormous change in railway management. The final experiments were splen-did, and once again this fortunate, indefatigable worker had achieved success. And once more, just when public attention was fixed on the subject, Sverbeev arranged for an interview with him.

'You want to send that young reporter again?' Chelishev said gaily, as he agreed to receive Tania.

She went to him at seven o'clock on a Friday evening. She was excited, but repressed her excitement with the same firmness that she showed in all things. He lived in a small two-storied house in one of the narrow streets off the Arbat, little streets which were like those of a country town with their gardens and their fences, behind which autumn leaves

93

were falling from the trees and cocks were crowing at one another in rural tones. Chelishev opened the door himself, and let her in. A smile hovered on his lips, but Tania felt that the smile lacked ease, and that he was not unmoved by her visit. He led her to his study, and she sat down on his huge divan. It was the study of a savant, books lined the walls to the ceiling and the floor was strewn with plans and drawings. It was very quiet. Tania took out her notebook, but was too agitated to open it. Chelishev sat opposite to her, staring at her and gently rubbing his chin. When they began to talk, he answered her questions with his eyes narrowed as though his thoughts were elsewhere. She wrote down what he said mechanically, and the letters sprawled pitifully over the ruled sheets of her notebook. She suddenly raised her eyes, and looked at him pleadingly. If there was not to be any dissimulation or embarrassment between them, something must be said, and Tania's eyes could not but say it, for she was incapable of concealment or deceit. She knew that she ought to go away, because otherwise she would, in a moment, reveal all her thoughts, all that feeling for this man which she had carried in her heart, helplessly and hopelessly, for months.

Chelishev rose, as though on impulse, and picked up the notebook which had slid from her lap. Instead of going back to his chair, he sat down beside her. She sat quite still, staring desperately straight in front of her. His large hand gently touched her hand with a caress. He bent down and looked keenly into her eyes as a doctor looks at his patient. And she answered with a long look that was a complete avowal, that hid nothing. And they sat so, side by side, and the notebook slipped to the floor again, but neither of them picked it up. The look in her eyes moved him to the depths of his heart. Though all this was foolish, futile, and might perhaps ruin her life, she could not, she would not, at that moment pause to think. And perhaps it was the truthfulness of her blue eyes, the enchantment of her youthful appeal, the unawakened, passionate forces in her that caught Chelishev and overwhelmed him with a long-forgotten madness. . . . Slowly, losing his usual self-restraint, he took her hand in his. . . .

And thus came about her first encounter, her first nearness, with this man who had seemed to belong to another planet. Tania went away without any regret in her heart. She went over it all again in her hours of solitude, and it was as though a storm continually raged within her.

She was drawn to him more and more, and made no effort to curb her longing. What though these terrible forces which she felt within herself were but the madness of a dream? When life called, one must give one's uttermost. Her heart was overflowing with unrestrained tenderness and agitation when she reached home that night full of indomitable resolution.

CHAPTER XIII

IN Chelishev's distinguished and conspicuous life, so brilliant and well regulated in its appearance, there was a certain incompleteness, which he would not admit even to himself. He had long ago organised the even tenour of his days; for, like most busy people, he put a high value on routine. Any disturbance in the rhythm of one's life involves the expenditure of a good deal of strength and energy, and he had none to spare from his scientific work and his inventions. With his tall, clever and brilliant wife, he was on those terms of ordinary, somewhat casual, friendliness, which are so characteristic of couples who are no longer young and have settled down to domesticity. There are big gaps, but they are bridged by children or by business or the little details of family life. Yet, below the surface, in the deepest recesses of the soul, smoulders a desperate longing for the dreams that are lost, the visions now fled for ever which had throbbed in youth with such irresistible strength. And moments arise when the smouldering embers break into a blaze, and a devouring fire, terrible in its intensity, consumes old roots as well as new growths. On such occasions, the whole course of one's life is changed. Chelishev's meeting with Tania, did not, of course, alter the whole direction of his life, nothing was changed in his routine. But the breath of youth was breathed into it, enchanting, intoxicating, reminding him of his still unspent strength, and his busy working days blossomed into that yearning for the beloved which he had forgotten for so long. Had he behaved badly toward this passionate, confiding child? He suffered, for a time, in thinking of the frivolity and sinfulness

96

of his behaviour. But that feeling faded away, ousted by a suggestion of masculine triumph. He was accustomed to making an impression; he knew, up to a point, the sort of glamour cast by his name, so that nothing seemed more natural than the pleasant, easily-explained conquests that served as complements to the triumphs of his scientific work. But he avoided chance episodes of that kind because of the agitation which they always entailed and sequels which were always certain to disturb the even tenour of his days in one way or another. And whenever he had overcome a temptation of that sort he plunged into a perfect orgy of work, loading up his desk, writing far into the night, and finding his sole relaxation in dining out with his wife or taking her to a theatre – which made a good impression, but which he inwardly felt to be intolerable and a poor substitute for the bud which he had allowed to slip by without blossoming. This mode of life was characteristic of most of the professorial houses. Once a week – on Fridays – they were 'at home,' and they generally went once a week to the theatre, his wife always looking her best, the homeward journey at night usually silent, each of them engrossed in his or her own thoughts, for they had long ago said all that they had to say to each other.

And now, all of a sudden, the very thing against which he had always striven had come to pass, and what made it worse was that it had happened with a girl who might very well have been his pupil. He felt disgusted, indignant with himself, but on the morrow, the daily round obliterated those feelings. And, a day later, he realised that he wanted to see her again, that he was being stormed by forces which he had forgotten, that she had come into his life like the spring wind which bursts open the window, shatters the panes, blows out the candle and scatters one's papers.

When a week had gone by, he asked Sverbeev to send

97

the girl to him again, as he had promised to give her further details as soon as he had worked them out for himself. Tania came – with the same determined line between her brows – to his room in the Institute this time, and they stayed in his official study till late that evening.

Chelishev was to go to America on a scientific mission in the spring of next year. He meant to visit Germany and France on his way, and to leave his wife in Paris to await his return. He had been saving money with this object in view for more than a year. He had not been abroad since the beginning of the war, though he was a member of many learned societies and had many foreign connections, and he did not want to be pinched but to be able to enter thoroughly into American and European life. He and his wife had planned out the whole tour with great care – they had selected the watering-place in France at which she was to stay for a time – and he was ready to spend freely, both his money and himself, on this tour. After all, everything was due to his own earnings, he had worked as a hand in a Belgian factory, he had obtained his diplomas, and only then returned to Russia, where he studied, invented, taught, studied further – until he had reached his present position. His inventions brought money and celebrity and the possibility of living comfortably, if not luxuriously. He wanted, above all things, to keep the position which he had won with so much effort.

He had married just before the war, and pined for his wife while he was at the front; but passion, as in the case of most married couples, had soon given way to ordinary affection, and at last to habit, a dull accustomed path with no winged flights.

Yes, habit had taken the place of love, and the revolution, those terrible years of separation, increased the tendency to weave their lives in separate strands. Then, when success

98

came, his wife had very quickly become accustomed to the new comforts of life, the money, and the position which it brought. When she expressed annoyance at his lateness for meals, at the dust and disorder of his heaped up desk, Chelishev's masculine pride was often hurt: 'Couldn't the woman realise what a fearful effort, what hard work, all this cost him?'

He was fond of his lecture room and his semi-circle of students with their tousled heads, hurriedly scribbling in their notebooks; but, just as his own work was unremitting, he demanded hard work from his pupils, and they were all a little afraid of this versatile man who belonged to a different social stratum.

Work on one of the State Economic Committees had been offered to him a few months earlier. His advice was wanted in regard to an extensive scheme for the manufacture of machinery in Russia, and his prospective visit to America was in connection with that undertaking. And suddenly, his whole serious, well-considered career, the steady progress of his research, his well-based ambition – all these were shattered: and by what? Wrought up, yielding to an irresistible temptation, a sudden impulse had plunged him into an incredible liaison with a girl of half his own age, the one thing in life of which he had been most afraid. And perhaps the most intolerable aspect of the whole situation was that the girl asked nothing for herself, that he could not find any excuse for himself in any grasping or shamelessness on her part. No; she was chaste, she was delicious in the first awakening of her womanly tenderness, and she asked for nothing, she expected nothing, she uttered no word of reproach. That was why he had to be doubly solicitous on her behalf. They must meet, but it was indescribably difficult for him to find time for their trysts in his busy life. Their meetings must be secret lest their

99

liaison should become the subject of gossip, and Chelishev's life became gradually filled with those petty, irritating, and tiresome details which are always the accompaniment of a secret love affair. They usually met in his room at the Institute. She would arrive with her portfolio and note-book, looking very businesslike, and no one, of course, could guess that it was a lovers' meeting. Twice, when her brother had been away, he had gone in the afternoon to her flat near the Patriarch's Pond – for just an hour, snatched between a lecture and a committee. He, Professor Chelishev, known to so many friends and students, had crept furtively upstairs and rung the bell with an apprehension that re-minded him of the thoughtless escapades of his youth. Timid, lovely as a wild flower in the frame of her own surroundings, radiant with happiness, Tania had let him in. 'The lover Professor Chelishev,' he thought to himself ironically, as he plunged once more into his hard-working, everyday life, coldly and cynically trying to convince himself that there was nothing unusual about all this, that it was merely a quiet spot in the seething vortex of his existence, and his uneasiness gave place to some extent to an agreeable consciousness of his reserve of strength. But the uneasiness persisted, renewing its attacks until it made him realise that he had strayed from the path of safety.

CHAPTER XIV

THREE stages could be clearly traced in Chelishev's relations
with Tania. The first was a period of perplexity, a sense of
having tangled the thread of his well-ordered life with the
growth of his new love; the second was characterised by a
certain cynical, masculine pride and self-justification,
mingled, however, with the disquieting unrest that was now
complicating matters; and the third, the period in which,
his first infatuation satisfied, the novelty outworn, he fully
realised that he must gradually break with Tania, to obviate
the risk of such complications as might arise from any
chance coincidence and, attaining undue proportions,
jeopardise important interests.

He was at first alarmed by this inner feeling. How could
he, regarding himself as a man far above the common herd,
how could he take precautions such as would degrade his
love to the level of a chance liaison, a vulgar intrigue? The
course of one's life should not be changed by every threshold
which one crossed; one should not have to consider and
measure every step one took. The romance of town life,
prudence – everything had its own time and place. But
what about Tania, who gave herself so lavishly and with
such happiness? Was it just a casual threshold that she was
crossing, or was it something that was to alter the whole
course of her life? What frightened Chelishev was his
realisation of Tania's sincerity, her utter renunciation of
self, her dangerous, her fatal passion. Tania loved him
with all that rare fullness which, for a woman, means
happiness, but, for a man, so often means the beginning of
the end. He decided to break with her. But how was he to

do it without lowering himself in his own eyes, without marring the ideal which she had created? There was need for inventiveness here, but the faculty for invention in matters of science is by no means the same as that required in the conduct of human affairs.

He began by trying to diminish the number of their meetings. Perhaps they might be made so infrequent that she would gradually forget, so that she might be caught up in some new interest while still thinking of him with sadness, but kindly, until their meetings became nothing but a melancholy and tender memory haloed in the mystery of romance. Things so often did happen like that, so that no one was able to say whose fault the separation was or how it came about.

The number of their meetings was reduced, reduced to such an extent that he might have thought that everything was going as he wished, if Tania, on the rare occasions when they did meet, had not poured out so lavishly all the emotion dammed up by the pain of waiting.

At their first meeting in his study, Tania had been convinced that she had met her fate, that she had found that haven, that refuge, for which she had been seeking with such steadfast hopefulness. Her first confusion had given way to an exalted, though bitter, ecstasy. Was not this great man, so distant to others, intimately close to her, Tania Agourov? Going about her daily tasks – lectures, newspaper interviews – this secret inner life was always present, always agitating and absorbing her. The joyous restlessness of the first days was gradually succeeded by a feeling of attachment, of devotion to, of adoration for, this man. He wished their meetings to be fewer? Very well; that must be so. He was abstracted, he seemed worried rather than happy – very well, she understood, she would not interfere with his life. But she had realised the dream of her adolescence – her naive, provincial, perhaps silly, dream – she had met a man who had conquered her by his talent, his strength of will, who had given her the proud sense of being his comrade. And her life was secretly illumined by a light glowing within her which she jealously concealed from everyone.

Meanwhile, she often wondered about Sverbeev. There was a protective air about him, as though he knew what was going on and approved of it. He often talked about Chelishev and had arranged several of their meetings – ostensibly, of course, so that Chelishev might provide her with material for her articles.

The sultry autumn had dragged on endlessly, mist and damp had continued till November, and then, in one night, a sharp frost had dried up the the streets, turned the puddles to glass, and covered the pavements with thin ice. And then a fierce north wind had brought down the snow. The storm raged for three days, and winter emerged from the chaos of ice and snow.

Tania's last meeting with Chelishev had been in her flat a month ago. She had sat at the window, waiting for him, clasping and unclasping her cold hands. It had been three weeks since she had seen him, and the blood rushed to her face and she felt faint with excitement and happiness when his car stopped at their door. A moment later the bell rang. Breathless, she ran to let him in: his familiar brown portfolio, the fur cap which added to his height, and his dear, dear face, now ruddy from the frost. . . . Yes, he was older than she was, to others he was distant, indifferent, haughty – but he was hers, hers. . . .

The intensity of her passion, the soft arms twined round his neck as this sweet, mad child stood on tiptoe to reach him – all this turned his head once more and dimmed and thrust into the background the purpose with which he had come. For he had come to put an end to the whole affair,

103

to explain gently, very kindly, that their liaison was impossible – he had not meant to say that this was the end; he had intended only to say that that winter he was too busy, that he had to prepare for his visit to America, and that therefore, for the time being, they must cease to see each other. But everything happened in just the way that he had wanted to avoid. How could he begin to say things like that when she greeted him as she did. His passion spent, Chelishev sat suffering from a sense of his own weakness and the thought of the time which was being hopelessly lost from his crowded hours, and his inability to straighten out the crooked course that his life had taken. He went away tortured by self-reproaches, full of gloomy presentiments, after she had seen him off with her love-radiant face for what she felt would probably again be a long absence.

Chelishev was going to the theatre with his wife that evening, and at half-past seven he laid aside his work, and went to her room to dress. A faint scent of spilt powder pervaded the room as he looked at his wife standing in front of the mirror, her tall figure still beautiful, a string of pearls round her somewhat full throat, her lips slightly touched up: of course it was not youth, she lacked the untouched freshness of that, but he saw in her the stability of existence, the many years of their life together, and he was frightened at the thought that he was risking the loss of it. No, here were the bonds that held life together, the cement, and if a crack should appear in it, the whole thing might crumble. He must take himself firmly in hand tomorrow, and with cold determination put an end to his romance.

At the theatre, and later at their *tête-à-tête* supper, he was unusually attentive to his wife, just as he had been at the beginning of their married life. They had had wine, and as they drove home, pressed close to one another in the cab, there was a look of promise in the still young eyes, that had once cast a magic spell on him, now slightly dimmed by the wine as they peered at him from the face nestling in her furs. In the morning, faced by his usual full and busy day, Chelishev was more than ever determined to finish with Tania.

A month after their last meeting, Tania, tortured by his coldness and neglect, became aware of something that filled her with horror. She had telephoned three times to Chelishev, but each time he had answered in a bored, displeased voice that he was too busy to see her. Meanwhile her suspicions had been confirmed. Without yet fully realising all that it meant, but full of dread in her lonely helplessness, and not knowing how she could see him in order to tell him, she decided to write. The letter said nothing about her fears, it merely said in a few lines that she must see him – for the last time, if he so wished – but an urgent and imperative reason made a meeting indispensable. She sent her letter, and, nearly dead with grief and despair, awaited his reply. He answered her letter, saying that though his days were full to overflowing, he would meet her on Monday at half-past one. He had to attend a committee meeting but ought to be able to get off at about that time. He could give her ten minutes, not more, because he had another meeting at half past two. It was a cold, business letter. He gave her a rendezvous in the street, not even in some private room, probably to make the meeting as short as possible; and he even fixed a time limit. With staring, unbelieving eyes, Tania read this letter from the man who had recently been so close to her. And at half-past one on Monday she made her way to the spot named, and stood beneath the clock, whose hand, as though jeering, jerked down to the bottom of the dial, where VI was marked.

CHAPTER XV

A LIGHT wind was blowing across the town from those open spaces into which the trams disappeared on their curved rails. The snow glistened with a bluish glint, and the horizon was soft with a smoky, blue haze in which the glass of the street lamps shone like crystals. Rooks flew across the boulevard through the spacious winter expanse, and settled on the snow-laden branches in irregular groups. There was a scent of snow and horse droppings, that definite though indescribable smell of Moscow in the first days of winter.

Standing under the clock, idly watching the peach-rose clouds above the housetops, Tania caught sight of a man approaching her slowly, very dignified, as though trying to look as if he were not going to a rendezvous. She was amazed at the remote, cold look which Chelishev gave her. They shook hands and strolled along the boulevard. They were both silent, and Tania had not courage enough to be the first to speak. At last Chelishev began in a businesslike tone: 'I got your letter. It was very difficult for me to meet you. I am so fearfully busy just now. Let's talk.'

'Yes,' answered Tania, nodding.

'You wanted to tell me something important,' he began again.

She nodded again; but he felt rather than saw the gesture, because she was walking with her head bowed. It was difficult to talk because there were so many people about, following them, pushing past them. At last they came to the square, crossed it, and walked up the slope of the boulevard till they reached an empty bench and sat down.

'Let's talk,' he said again, looking anxiously at his watch.

'I had to see you,' said Tania, speaking with difficulty and without raising her head. 'I should think that you would understand yourself why I had to see you.'

He suddenly flushed a deep crimson, his face was suffused in a moment, and, to cover his confusion, he fumbled in his pocket for a handkerchief.

'No, I must confess that I do not understand,' he said quickly. 'Has anything happened?'

'Yes.'

'What exactly?' His voice sounded unfamiliar and insincere.

Tania raised her face to his, and looked him in the eyes. Then, simply, in a whisper that was like a sigh, 'Constantine Petrovitch, what happens to a woman when she lives with a man? You know better than I do; why do you make me tell you?'

'How . . .? But is it possible?' he asked almost soundlessly and unable to conceal his horror.

'Why not?' asked Tania sternly. 'It is obviously possible, because it has happened.'

He sat on the bench dazed, crushed by this unexpected, this incredible, confession that wrought havoc in him. Just as he had straightened out his life, this came with irony and broke and hideously crushed everything. They sat on without speaking or moving. Below them, on the boulevard, urchins were rushing about on skates, for it was the lunch hour and the streets were not crowded. Businesslike trams were hurrying down or toiling heavily up hill.

Chelishev stared at the urchins, at the blue haziness of the already darkening town. His steadfast, immovable assurance had gone. So, that was the sort of casual and unforeseen incident that could trip up a man's life. For a moment, he was lost in reflection, barely conscious of the boulevards, the hurrying life of the town.

107

Then he realised that he was thinking only of himself, of his own position, and was forgetting Tania, He was behaving as though the full burden of their misfortune fell on him alone, leaving unscathed this silent, suffering, and now hated, creature beside him, who was, he could not help feeling, to blame for the catastrophe. He struggled to throw off this paralysis; he pulled himself together, and came to a rapid decision. He must speak, convince, act. . . . Softened by the self-pity which he had just experienced, he spoke gently, persuasively, confidently.

'Of course this is most unfortunate. I never dreamed that such a thing would happen' (he was making full use of the deep notes of his beautiful voice). 'But there is no trouble that one cannot get out of. Of course it must be liquidated as soon as possible.' He was becoming convinced by his own eloquence. 'You realise, Tania, that in our position such a thing would be impossible. Life must preserve its course; it is difficult enough at the best. I have a deep, a sincere, regard for you; but I cannot lie about it, I cannot talk to you of love; you will admit that I never have done so, will you not? It just happened – and now we must get rid of the consequences as quickly as we can.'

Tania raised her eyes to his. She looked at him almost as though she pitied him. So, that was all he had to say to her? He was just like any other, any ordinary, man.

'There is no need for you to worry,' she said. 'I never dreamed of endangering your peace of mind or your way of living.'

He was horrified that she could place him on so low a level. 'No, let me speak. I am older, more experienced, than you. I know more of life. It is only natural that I should speak first of all about the necessity for extricating ourselves. Don't be angry with me, Tania; but one must talk rationally about such vital matters. Money will be needed, and you must let me, as a friend, do all that is necessary.' He was moved by his own words, by the assertions of his care for her with which he was trying to cover his determination. He fumbled in his pocket, took out his notecase and counted fifty roubles – clean new notes received as salary that very morning. Tania let him put them in her bag without a word, her eyes fixed on the snow. He felt reassured, and, speaking in his accustomed, intimate voice, the voice that had been so dear to her, he said, 'You will do all that is necessary? You promise?'

'Of course I will,' she replied quietly.

He had expected her to be offended, to say something, to reproach him. But she was silent.

He was, naturally, sorry for this charming, self-willed girl; but, after all, was he responsible for the morality which had led to such awful consequences? It would have been much more complicated before the revolution, but it was now a comparatively simple and straightforward matter . . . and, since everything could be arranged without any fuss, why make a tragedy of it?

'I should like you to let me have news in due course,' he continued. 'You will understand how anxious I shall be.' But still Tania said nothing as she sat on the bench staring at the unblemished, untrampled blue-white snow. She had expected that his first thoughts would be about what all this must mean for her, how her whole being must be shattered by this tremendous, supremely important event in the life of a woman, of what must be her sufferings in the complications of her plight. But all that worried him was the thought that she might go back on her word so that complications would be brought into *his* life.

He was uneasy under her silence, and went on talking, trying to assume a bold front as he smoked a cigarette.

Snow slid, whispering, from the trees overhead. Pale

lemon-coloured specks of light began to dot the distant, frosty, purple haze of the great town. It was the gentle, quiet hour in which the twilight silently, imperceptibily, comes down, embracing the world in its mantle of blue.

Chelishev was annoyed. This silence was tactless and insufferable, and the girl was ignoring the fact that his time-table left him very little leisure.

He sighed, looked at his watch, and rose – he certainly could not stay any longer. They walked a few yards along the boulevard, and then Tania spoke:

'I expect your way lies down the hill – I have to turn off here.'

'You're not angry with me Tania? Truly, I never wanted this to happen.' He spoke with as much tenderness and sincerity as he could muster.

'There is nothing to be angry about,' she replied. And though her dryness was mortifying, Chelishev felt glad that it saved him from further tedious explanations. There, on the boulevard, they said good-bye. He walked slowly down the hill, fearing lest he should appear to be in a hurry. He looked back in a minute, but Tania was no longer in sight, and he gave a sigh of relief, feeling that he had left all his burdens on the boulevard.

When he reached the square, the street lamps were being lighted, the trams went thundering by – it was the old, safe, familiar life which suddenly seemed precious, as though someone had been trying to take it from him a moment ago. He called a cab, and the merry jingling of the harness on the shaggy horse seemed to promise that everything would turn out all right.

Tania made her way to the end of the boulevard, and then sat down on a bench again. She might to all intents and purposes have been alone in the dreary street. The lamps there were still unlit. Rooks were fussing about overhead as though finding it difficult to settle down for the night, and they were the nearest approach to companionship. How simple things were, after all, these things which had moved her so deeply. He had put some money into her purse – the masculine solution – and there was no further problem, just a business transaction. But had he asked her, had he even thought, about the tragic effect of all this on her? Perhaps it was true that she had no right to expect love from him; that it was only a fantastic dream; and, of course, in this savage, driving life there was no room for dreams, and Chelishev would be the first to laugh at her for thinking otherwise. Still, she had dreamed, and he should have understood; yet he, who should have caught the first notes of her soul's music, brought nothing to bear on their relations but frigid reasoning. Well, that was how things went in these hurried, hustling times. Dreams were swept aside, and the only survivors were those who knew how to order the work and pleasure of their lot.

The lamps were suddenly turned on, and the shop-windows were lit up. Evening as it crept in had been met with bright lights on all sides. Void of all emotion, as though all her feelings had been blown away in the last hour, Tania moved slowly toward her home. Reaching the green sign of the halt, she boarded a tram and was whirled down the boulevard. Her brother had already returned, and she told him that she had been detained at the newspaper office. Then she glanced calmly through the evening paper, and began to get tea.

CHAPTER XVI

THE bright days, full of new promise, which had followed
Kiril's examination, had soon obliterated all memory of his
failure to pass it. To begin with, Dontsev had not only
accepted some of his poems, but had actually published them.
Kiril was overwhelmed by the joy of seeing his name printed
as the author of verses which thousands were now reading.
As he went by the newspaper kiosks his eye would catch
a glimpse of the blue cover of the review that contained his
work. For the first time in his life he went to a publisher's
offices, and found the right room after passing through what
seemed to be the endless corridors of a vast palace. An
unconcerned young woman with bobbed hair looked up his
name in a book, and tore out a printed order for him to
take to the cashier from whom he received payment for his
poems.

He went out, with the money in his hands, and paused
on the quay. The Moskva River was already frozen over,
and rooks were hovering about the holes in the ice. A cold
wind brought a breath of woods and fields and wide open
spaces from the distant winter horizon which stretched far
beyond the palaces, the crenellated walls of the Kremlin,
and the town itself. Staring at the frozen water, Kiril stood
by the railing, intoxicated by the strange, proud thoughts
that filled his mind. If he had failed in his examination, if
he had fallen behind the others, what did that matter? The
world was full of plodding mediocrities who satisfied tests
and passed exams. One needed no special cleverness, to
say nothing of talent, to be one of them; the world was full
of them. But the creation of something original, the writing

of poetry; that was something to be proud of, that was something really worth while. First steps are always difficult, but fame would reward effort, and then one would realise that one's nights of thought and labour had not been in vain. On those lines, life was wonderful, magnificent. He turned with a beating heart to meet the full force of the wind which was carrying with it the scent of all the roads of Russia's faraway immensity.

From the evening on which he had gone back to Vera, he had resumed the relations which he had earlier thought of putting an end to, and which, by imperceptible transition, he had ceased to hate or fear.

'You can wriggle as much as you like,' she had said, 'but you will be drawn to me all the same. Only, don't come back if you want to be melodramatic. So long as we suit one another, well and good. We shall see what happens later.'

It came to him suddenly that their relations were convenient. They were so easy, one could break them at any moment, and in their crude coarseness there was nothing to obscure Tania Agourov, the one and only creature to whom he felt really attracted.

Sverbeev arranged a meeting with Tania for him. They met in his room, as though by chance, and for a short half hour Sverbeev left them alone. Very little was said in that half hour. Tania was silent, though self-possessed, and in her silence he was reminded of his dreams in the past, of his native town, where he had spent his motherless childhood, where he had sat in the little enclosed garden with Varinka, who, like Tania, had tiny curls clustering on her temples. And in that silence he recalled the first bitter-sweet ecstasy of his life, when his heart had been filled with the proud promise of the future. There seemed to be so much of the past in Tania that though little was said, it was as though they were bound together by a strong, invisible cord. Then Sverbeev returned, and Tania went. She would not let him see her home. And Sverbeev's room had immediately become empty and desolate.

'Well, what about it, Kiril? Are you getting her away from Chelishev?' asked Sverbeev, and somehow Kiril was not shocked by his coarseness, so strong was the hatred and jealousy of Chelishev that burned in him. The first feelings with which he had heard of Tania's relations with the Professor had long ago turned into a dark, sullen hatred of the man who had not only deprived him of Tania, but had ploughed him at his examination with such cold indifference.

'Tania's a splendid creature if only Chelishev doesn't spoil her,' said Sverbeev, sitting down by Kiril and putting his hand on his knee. 'But you wait a bit, your turn will come. I'm not just talking through my hat.' And, just as happened before, Sverbeev seemed in some strange way to strengthen Kiril's unspoken and inexplicable relations with Tania.

It was some days after that before Kiril saw her again, and meantime Vera had once more begun to play a part in his life. She was no longer repellant to him, she was even becoming a habit. He could not bear to stay alone in the hostel listening to men discussing the lectures or watching them trace their plans with inky fingers. It bored him terribly. A year ago all that had seemed to be an impossible, unattainable ideal, the very prospect of hard work had excited him, but in the actuality of the present, the vision had all faded away into nothingness. So Vera became a necessity, very much as his cigarette is a necessity to a smoker.

Although the film had been finished, Vera took him one day to the studio, and he had gone eagerly, because it was there that one learnt the great art of graceful movement, of controlling one's body. Students were having a riding lesson that day. The riding school, dark, and strewn with sand and sawdust like the ring of a circus, was redolent of ammonia and horsedung. Pallid young men and over-ripe damsels were cantering timidly with faces as expressionless as cameos. Here, in this quiet corner, potential cowboys, intrepid athletes, fateful heroines – the Russian brand of the great stars of America and Europe – were being prepared for fame and glory with a riding school as the laboratory for their transmutation. The only sounds were the snorting of the steeds and the cracking of the whip of the man in an officer's cast-off cloak who was directing the paces of the broken-down cavalry mounts. Pale young men in check caps, their trousers tightened round their ankles with safety-pins, showed a reckless disregard for danger in urging on their listless chestnut or white horses, while the girls, in similar caps, held their hands to their full breasts while they jogged up and down in the saddle with the rhythm of the trotting of their mounts. No one but an outsider, indifferent to the methods by which fame is achieved, would have viewed the scene with such flippancy; and Kiril found excitement in the dim, mysterious riding school, the smell of the horses, the persons careering on them, and they were all making an indelible impression on his mind.

These men and women knew how to use their bodies; they would become artists, and he was, for the first time, seeing the laboratory of that art with which he had so recently come into contact.

Two paths lay before him, offering ways out of the labyrinth of calculations, the monotony of his poverty-stricken student's life with its lectures and its hostel. Two dazzling, enchanting paths were open to him: to one of them the sign-post was the blue cover of the review which contained his poems; the other was the screen with its magical reincarnation of his personality. And the screen, in spite of its voicelessness, had become the greatest, the most powerful of leaders, drawing huge crowds, dazzled by its creations of imagination, and it could make one's name, and give riches and glory. He sat on a wooden box, inhaling the smell of stables, while Vera sat smoking at his side.

'Listen, Kiril,' she said at last. 'If you want to be in the swim you've got to mix with these people. I've talked to Cooperov, and he's promised to put you on in the next picture.'

He nodded hurriedly, like a schoolboy. This girl always talked cynically and coarsely, but she knew what was what in life, and she was teaching him. He was ready to follow her anywhere, because he had been horrified and dismayed lately to feel that the ground was slipping away from under his feet. How had it all started? When had he begun to slide? Not so long ago he had known his own mind, had known what he wanted, and how to organise his life to achieve the results he desired. But now, all his former ideals seemed to be out of date, countrified, and he had lost faith in them and was blindly groping after new ones. Life had called to him and been kind to him; how was he to return to a past which he had outlived? The presence of Vera with her self-assurance, was evidence that he would never go back.

They sat in the riding school for about an hour. When they got outside, Vera stamped her feet and swung her arms like a cabman, and said:

'It's silly of you to have so little money; if you had some we could go to one of their evenings in the "garret". You've heard of the garret, haven't you? You'd meet the real thing there.'

About once in two months, though not regularly, Yagodkin sent money to Kiril, not much, about fifteen or twenty roubles. It was literally the pay of sweated labour. And he had received twenty roubles in that way the day before. He was always extremely careful with money, spending it only on what was strictly necessary, but when Vera began to talk about some 'garret' where he could meet the people with whom he wanted to throw in his lot, all thought of economy vanished, and, without any hesitation, he said:

'I've got some money if it's needed.'

She was agreeably surprised. 'Splendid. It's for your own good. You've got to mix with them to become one of their set; so will you go to the garret with me?'

'I'll go,' he said.

'You've got to take your drinks with you. Fetch me at nine, and we'll buy the stuff on our way.'

He saw her shameless, grey eyes close to his face, and he was, as always, stirred by their shamelessness. They agreed to go to the garret together that evening.

CHAPTER XVII

KIRIL called for her at nine. He had already spent four of his twenty roubles on a new apache shirt, open at the neck, like one that he had seen one of the actors wearing. Vera ked the shirt. Her primus stove was roaring; she was heating her curling-tongs in its violet flame. As he sat watching, on a chair by the wall, Kiril saw, as though for the first time, how untidily Vera lived. It was not like a woman's room: there were cobwebs in the corners near the ceiling, which was as smoke-blackened as a forge; just swept away from the middle of the room were heaps of rubbish, greasy paper and cigarette ends; the floor had spots of paint all over it; a dirty towel with red cotton embroidery at its ends hung over the sink, where there was an incessant gurgle of water from the tap. No, it was not a woman's room, and, indeed was Vera really a woman? She dressed mannishly, she smoked, and her attitude towards life was that of a man, stopping at nothing, grabbing, as she passed, anything that she wanted, anything that took her fancy. He, for example, had caught her fancy – a man of ideas and habits quite foreign to hers – and she had taken him, and obtained his submission. How crude it all was. And once more the image of Tania rose before him, putting this creature to shame.

They left the house half an hour later. The cold moon was encircled by an icy halo, and the runners of the sledges made music as they slid over the frozen snow. Through the window of a delicatessen shop they saw a salesman, dressed in spotless white like a surgeon, operating on a large ham. There were all sorts of appetising aromas, and the many bottles ranged along the shelves seemed to be a polite reminder that life could be made very pleasant if one so desired. Vera chose three bottles of cheap wine, and they left the shop. When they had reached the chemist's shop at the corner, agreeably conscious of their burden, they hired a cab to take them to Sivtsev Vrajek. The horse was fresh and drew the narrow sledge along at a good pace. The cold wind stung their faces, the driver shouted warnings to pedestrians – life seemed to Kiril to be really full of nebulous hopes on the very verge of fulfilment. They soon passed the flat-chested statue of Timiriasev, so like a bishop, and found themselves on the slope of the boulevard with its trees salted by winter. They crossed the Arbat. Trams and cars dashed about helter skelter, chauffeurs wildly hooting passers-by out of their way, and vanishing in a cloud of snowflakes of their own raising. Chauffeurs, in orange belts indicating that they plied for hire, stood near their taxis on the ranks, stamping their feet. Small urchins shrilly shouted *Moscow Evening News*, while the long-nosed statue of Gogol looked down on the scene with utter condemnation.

Vera stopped the cab at the frame house in the Sivtsev Vrajek that had survived from the fire of 1812. They entered a countrified courtyard in which there was an empty dog-kennel, and began to climb an unusually creaky staircase which smelt insufferably of cats. The staircase led to a very long corridor through which one had to grope one's way, feeling for each plank with one's feet. At the end of the corridor, from behind an almost imperceptible door, came the hubbub of voices. Overcoats, caps and goloshes were piled in a heap on the floor of a tiny vestibule partitioned off from the passage, and through the chinks of a curtain one caught a glimpse of girls in bright, fantastic costumes making up their faces in front of a mirror. A strong smell of beer and spirits met the newcomers, as the host, Ignatka

Surgouchov, in an unbuttoned blouse, sprang into the passage for a moment crying 'How d'you do, Vera?' and disappeared behind the curtain where the girls were putting on their makeup.

All round the walls of the attic were long tables at which young men and women were seated. All the tables were covered with bottles. A small square had been left free in the middle of the room for dancing or performances. Kiril and Vera were squeezed on to a bench at one of the tables. Ignatka Surgouchov instantly dived into the room from under the curtain, opened the bottles they had brought, and passed them down the room. Someone poured vodka into someone else's wineglass for Kiril. The food provided stood on the tables in huge tureen-like bowls. It was a mayonnaise of cabbage, sprinkled with cranberries: one stuck a fork in the bowl, and carried the cabbage across the table to one's mouth.

As Kiril began to distinguish the faces of the men and women seated in the long rows, all slightly under the influence of alcohol, he recognised Sverbeev with his long nose, nodding and winking at him. As he caught Kiril's eye he shouted something inaudible through the deafening din of voices.

Next to Kiril was a young man with the face of a drunkard, deeply lined and looking very dignified and bored. He hardly drank at all, but sat staring in front of him with torpid haughtiness.

Kiril's head began to swim very pleasantly after he had drunk two large glasses of vodka. He saw the young man beside him shake a pinch of white powder from a paper on to his thumb nail, and supposed that he must be taking something for a headache. Then the young man hastily sniffed the powder first up one nostril and then the other. After that he resumed his haughty, vacant stare.

Kiril gradually recognised several of the cinema actors whom he had casually met. There were girls with bobbed hair combed over their cheeks, with glassy dreamy eyes, and among them sat the producer Barnoulov himself in a smoking-jacket, with a fat nose, and a pipe that looked as though it were a growth on his face.

All the noises combined to make the uproar of a waterfall, and nobody could possibly understand what anybody else was saying.

Ignatka Surgouchov suddenly dived from under the curtain again, this time without his blouse, which he had taken off because of the intolerable heat, and, wiping his face with his handkerchief, yelled:

'Attention. Artists from the school of burlesque and grotesque will perform the latest Parisian novelty, "The Charleston".'

A wave of excitement immediately swept over the room. Girls took powder-puffs out of their vanity-bags, and powdered their noses so that they could witness this new European show with becoming dignity. Two girls who had been making up fluttered out from behind the curtain like wood-nymphs. One had on a black silk garment like a man's dress coat, and the other was wearing lengths of various coloured ribbons caught together by a few stitches and suspended from shoulder straps. A young man began to play the piano which stood in a corner of the room, or, rather, not to play but to smash it, crashing on the notes and ruthlessly extracting a series of noises like the neighing of horses mingled with groans and yells. From time to time, he varied this by thumping on the woodwork with his fist, or callously dragging his elbow from top to bottom of the keyboard, springing up from his seat at least half a yard as he did so. To the accompaniment of this elemental lunacy, the two girls, linked together, began to twitch their legs as though palsied, and to stamp convulsively in one spot, their knees knocking, and their calves slanting outwards. Then, still linked together, their hands clasped and raised high in the air, with cheek pressed against cheek, they began with meticulous exactitude to measure with tiny footsteps the small square that had been kept open for dancing.

There was a burst of applause, chairs and benches were noisily pushed back, women placed their hands on their partners' shoulders, and moved into the middle of the room. The pianist struck up a foxtrot, and the square became a heaving mass of colliding couples. The women put their hands on the men's backs, palms outward, and, barely moving their feet, stared vacantly into space. The men, pressing their cheeks against those of their transient partners, swung them to and fro as though trying to shake their last doubts out of them.

The wine-stained tables were deserted, except for a few non-dancing men who were finishing the cabbage salad, spilling the dressing as they ate. Slightly drunk, Kiril looked at the unfamiliar scene, at the swaying oscillations of the dancers which hitherto he had seen only on the screen, and everything – his new apache shirt, he himself, chained down by this timid shyness because he had not acquired any of these charming social accomplishments – seemed so pitiful, so unutterably primitive, that in sheer despair he drank another glass of vodka.

A very stout, dough-faced woman with white eyelashes, languishing somewhat under the effects of wine, was leaning on his left shoulder with all her enormous weight. He searched the haze for Vera, and discovered her at last, seated between two men, laughing it appeared to him at his expense, nudging, with her shoulder, first one and then the other of the two men, both of whom were leaning too close to her. And there came over him a feeling of complete indifference to anything that she might do. His bemused mind was full of a great bitterness over the frustration, the incompleteness, of his life. His feelings had the poignancy characteristic of the experiences of men unaccustomed to drinking. He had come here, to this town, in order to make a career; a lodestar had seemed to guide him unerringly on toward wide spaces in which hard work confronted him, and where there appeared to be many paths open to him, and there, a creature different from all these women had passed by him, so near and yet so inaccessible. . . . She was utterly indifferent to him, and her fate was linked with that of a man whom Kiril felt that he hated. He was companionless, and he could not hope that any of his dreams would be realised. If only he had money, a lot of money, so that he could grip life firmly in his hands, instead of spending four roubles on an apache shirt. . . .

All these thoughts, drifting in a haze of alcohol, were suddenly interrupted by Sverbeev, who pushed his way to Kiril through the throng, and put a hot hand on his knee.

'Why so melancholy, Kiril?' he said in what seemed to Kiril to be the voice of an only friend. 'Looking at life? Well, look at it, look at it. But there's a far finer life for the man who knows how to grasp it.'

Sverbeev talked on in a whisper. Kiril could feel his hot breath in his ear. He was becoming more and more dazed, and more and more conscious of the garret's acrid smell, the smell of human bodies, and therefore sinful, because it only made the men and women cling closer to each other. And Sverbeev went on whispering:

'What could not one make of life, if one only knew how to grasp it? But it's not so much knowledge that's wanting as audacity. If you had courage enough, my boy, we could get a devil of a lot of money. You could provide yourself with a fine apartment, you could throw the hostel to the

123

pigs, and Tania would come to you like a human being, instead of your meeting once a month in my hovel.'

Almost faint at this vision, excited by this warm, insidious voice, Kiril asked eagerly:

'But how . . .? How . . .? Tell me, Sverbeev. Am I so incompetent in what matters in life? I want to do so much, I want a full life, I realise now that I can never return to my former narrow existence. I shall write poetry; my poems will be published; they are being published already, and everybody is talking about my talent. And once there is talent, there is fame. . . .'

Unconsciously, Kiril had raised his voice to a shout. Sverbeev put his hand on his mouth, and almost harshly whispered in his ear:

'Wait a minute, don't yell so that everyone can hear. If you want really to live and to achieve fame without spadework, you've got to have money. That first and foremost. Do you understand?'

'Yes, I understand,' he nodded.

'A lot of money, and how are you to get it? Do you know? I do.'

'How?' asked Kiril hurriedly, suddenly going hot all over 'How, tell me.'

'You won't give me away? You'll die rather than betray me? Swear by Tania.'

'I swear.'

'Well then, listen. Let them go on kicking up a row, but you listen. There is money, plenty of money, and it can be got without any risk, four thousand at least. Do you know who's got it?'

'Who?' asked Kiril with dry lips.

'Chelishev; he's been saving it up for his trip abroad.'

'But how?' Kiril was nearly choking.

'How? It's as simple as simple can be, Kiril. I'll tell you

the whole plan and you'll say: "Sverbeev is a genius; not a rascal, but a real man. Chelishev is the rascal" – and we'll curb his rascality a bit, that's all. Let's get out of this, and I'll tell you all about it. I'll tell you something . . .'

But at that moment, Ignatka Surgouchov sprang on to a bench, the long ends of his silk tie floating like a butterfly. He nearly shouted at the crowd: 'Artists of the school of the grotesque,' and like a winged angel he began to pass along the pathway of linked hands the men raised for him. The women dived out of his way with little shrieks, and the two dancers, who had performed before, ran into the centre, this time in yellow camisoles, as if carried away by their passion.

Taking Kiril's hand, Sverbeev forced his way through the crowd with him to the door. In a corner, seated on a pile of coats, a couple were frozen in a kiss, utterly oblivious of their surroundings.

After great difficulty in finding their coats, the two men went down the corridor, Kiril swaying so that he had to hang on tightly to Sverbeev, as they stumbled over the planks. They groped their way to the creaking stairs, and went down into the sharp, cold air. And there, in the courtyard, as the result of weakness, mixed drinks, and cabbage mayonnaise, Kiril was sick.

CHAPTER XVIII

THEY walked together along quiet, sobering back streets. Fresh snow had fallen and the trees bent under its weight in the gardens of the little, old-fashioned frame houses. There was an almost rural peace and quietude in these lanes, the snow scrunched under foot, and overhead the great, cold constellation of Capella shone in a sky left clear by the emptying of its snowladen clouds.

'I didn't begin talking to you like this because I was drunk,' said Sverbeev, 'and when you have come round a bit, I'll go on. You just fill your lungs with fresh air to get all that poisonous stuff out of them. . . .'

They walked on without seeing anyone but the muffled figures of night porters keeping watch at doors and gateways. In the winter night the town had an air of purity and sinlessness. They reached the boulevard, and went on down its snowy road. It lay deserted in its broad whiteness, looking like a huge counterpane.

'Are you all right now?' asked Sverbeev. 'Very well then, listen while I tell you all about it. First of all I must tell you about myself. We've knocked about together for a year, but you don't really know anything about me. Were you ever aware of the fact that I was in the party for four years? That I fought on seven fronts? That I was a Divisional Commander? . . . I've been through fire and water. I ought to be taking part in the Government now, instead of being at the Institute. But it all bored me Kiril. I was so bored that I let myself go. I neglected the party; so of course they cleared me out. And, I'll tell you why. There are thousands like me. We rushed to every danger-point, we fought, we never spared ourselves, we tossed hither and thither like thistledown in the wind. . . . Then the horizon cleared and we were taken straight from the firing line to do book-keeping. "Learn to keep accounts, comrades, and wear out the seats of your trousers at work in a government bureau." No, thank you. Once you've had a taste of freedom, you're not going to let anyone shut you up in an office. It's too stuffy. But if you don't like office work you can get out; we manage all that very simply. Very well, I say to myself, I fought for you and now you kick my backside and turn me out if I stick to my own principles.

'You know what our generation went through; from the schoolroom straight to the war, and from the war – into the revolution. What did we know? So long as I had the party ticket in my pocket and they had a job for me to do – I was a man. But when they took away the ticket and took away my job – I was left stranded. I made up my mind to educate myself so as to be independent. There was the Institute – I'm good at mechanics, so I thought that I could keep pace with the others. But my head was like a coffee-mill. And what good would it all be? Over-production. The sort of life that includes a canary in a cage! Was that what I fought at the front for? Was that all that my varied experience was going to give me? I wanted life. And if you want life, you've got to struggle for it. Very well; I began to observe life, and I saw that justice is merely an abstraction that people boast and bluster about, and that in reality there is no such thing. Everything is just as it always has been – one leads an easy life – the other, a hard one. Life comes to one with full hands, while the other can hardly touch her skirts as she passes by, no matter how hard he tries.

'At the Institute we are biting granite, we have to live on twenty roubles a month, we go to the railway sidings to unload trucks; but Professor Chelishev, for example, goes jaunting off on his travels abroad. A rouble is a fortune for you; he will spend a hundred without turning a hair. I have a great grudge against Chelishev, mainly on account of Tania. As for you and me, just as we are trudging now, so we shall still go on trudging. See . . .?'

As Kiril walked beside Sverbeev, listening to him, the frosty wind blew away all his intoxication.

'So that's that. To improve our own lot, we must have money, money above all things. Without money we are nothing – the proletariat may be freed from its chains, but it has nothing left to lose now that its chains have gone. But Chelishev has money. Please don't think that I want to steal; not in the least; I'm not going to soil my hands over him. But if justice is to reign, then let it reign. It's true that I loathe him; I loathe his grand airs; but I don't want to crush a reptile in the name of justice. I am no Raskolnikov.* Let the reptiles live. If there were no rogues in the world there would be nothing to recognise honest men by. No, I'm thinking of another kind of justice. Chelishev used Tania, to put it bluntly, and, setting aside all cant, that is not the sort of thing for a professor to do. If it became known, he could be turned out, lose his job. Forcing a student to be his mistress – we could make a fine story of it; so that he would be ruined in half an hour. Well, then; you are engaged to Tania Agourov – wait a minute, don't interrupt. You are engaged. Wouldn't you marry her if she consented?'

Sverbeev's hot breath brushed his cheek.

'Why, you'd jump for joy – I know you through and through! You are engaged; I am your friend, the student Sverbeev, there's no spoof about it; it's all gospel truth. You find out about Tania's affair, and you want to expose Chelishev, to shame him through the press. That's easy,

*The hero of Dostoievsky's novel *Crime and Punishment*

128

because the newspapers will take Tania's part. That being so, let him take his choice: he pays three thousand and you and she give up your studies and go to the provinces . . .'

They stopped in the middle of the path. Kiril felt hot, and his heart was beating fast. He drew his hand across his forehead, panting like an overstrained dray-horse.

'Buck up, Kiril,' said Sverbeev, straightening Kiril's cap. 'If you're any sort of a man, this is the time for action, not for trembling. And, if you're not a man, it's no use wasting words on you.'

'No, I'm a man,' said Kiril as firmly as he could.

'Then, if you're a man you can't refuse to do as I suggest. Two thousand for you and Tania, and a thousand for me. You and she will go south, say to Batoum, and life will begin all over again for you on the coast.'

Sverbeev said all this as though they already had the money, and were dividing it up.

It was not that he approved of the proposal, or was ready to carry it out, that Kiril seized Sverbeev's hand while staring at the face which he could hardly see in the dim light, but because he was suffused with a warm glow at the thought of being with Tania for ever, of looking into her clear blue eyes, so wonderfully clear, her delightful smile.

'I knew you were the real thing,' said Sverbeev, taking his hand, 'Don't ever give life the go-by, especially if it comes to your hand of its own accord. As it is, life is waiting for you; you can take it, or leave it. There's another fellow you've got to cultivate; that's Cooperov. There's a man with a head on his shoulders, and if he takes a fancy to you he'll put you on to things that will bring in other money besides Chelishev's. I'm only telling you this, because you mustn't miss anything in life; but must spread your fingers out – so – to wind the thread on your hands. And Tania will be yours; she's only got to get out of this entanglement.'

129

They had reached the square, crossed it, and begun to walk up the boulevard on the other side.

'Not a word to a soul about our plan; you understand that, don't you?' said Sverbeev. 'We've got to work it out in detail.'

They went on in silence; one could just distinguish the dark masses of the rooks' nests on the white branches. The stars were now hidden by long clouds, and it began to snow again. Soft and thick, bringing peace, intensifying the silence, the flakes fell from the low clouds as though a thousand swans were shedding their downy feathers. Some of the whirling flakes fell on Kiril's lips as he walked beside Sverbeev on this unforgettable night. And so, in the cold winter air, his imagination heated and ablaze, Kiril was being caught by fate in new meshes.

CHAPTER XIX

Tania made her way, at about eight o'clock in the evening of December the second, to a white house standing in a court-yard in one of the side streets off the Povarskoi. A garden stretching far back behind it, full of snowladen trees, was the only thing that differentiated it from the general run of houses. The door was opened by a nurse, in a white overall that was none too clean. The yellow wooden bench in the vestibule looked as though it had been infected by the wretchedness of the patients who had waited on it with gloomy forebodings. There were a few forlorn coats hanging on a rack.

'For an operation?' asked the nurse casually. 'Please take off your wraps and come to the waiting room.'

The nurse helped her off with her coat, and Tania then went down a dull, blue-painted passage to the waiting-room, where she sat down on a hard sofa covered with American cloth. The very quick ticking of a little clock on the table was the only sound to break the silence of the empty room. Tania folded her hands in her lap, and waited. Her mind was a blank, all the defiant forces of rebellion having died within her, leaving only a dazed apathy If things were fated to be so; so they would be. She could not imagine how she would be able to go on living after it; but, at the moment, it was the only thing to do. So she had come here. . . .

A small woman doctor, wearing high heels to lessen her appearance of shortness, with very smooth black hair and a large, kind Jewish nose, came in after a few minutes, and sat down at the table. She produced a big ledger and entered Tania's name and the nature of the operation required.

'You'll sleep here to-night, my dear,' she said very maternally. 'Your operation will be at half-past eight in the morning. I've put you at the head of the list. Now come with me, and I'll take you to your room.'

She led Tania up some stairs, along empty corridors of the same blue tint as that through which she had already passed. They passed the open door of a ward, and Tania saw a row of beds with white-gowned women lying in them. Somewhere, behind another door, a newborn baby was grunting like a little pig. In this vast house, thousands of new lives made their entrance into the world, and thousands made their exit. Birth? Death? They are such near neighbours.

The small doctor, her high heels tapping, led the way to a private ward.

'You'll be here, my dear,' she said in the same motherly tone adding in a more businesslike manner 'Is this your first abortion?'

'The first,' Tania answered in a dead voice.

Notwithstanding the motherliness and the businesslikeness of the little doctor, Tania felt that she was examining her with curiosity, woman to woman. A moment later she was alone in the bare, isolated ward with its white walls with a frieze, a high hanging yellow lamp, a white cupboard, a white table, a bed with a net curtain, and nothing more.

Outside were clumps of trees in the cold; inside, the dry heat from the metal radiator. For the first time, she was overcome by her terrible loneliness, by unbearable sadness.

She had not even said good-bye to her brother, though perhaps she would never see him again. She had told him that the newspaper was sending her to Orehovo for a few days.

She got out the book which she had brought with her in her bag, and tried to read, but the letters swam before her eyes and conveyed no meaning. She must simply wait till morning. Yes, dazed and benumbed, with all her dreams shattered, she must wait, listening to internal voices, which she might never hear again, and to the silence. . . . But the silence in this house was not an empty silence: in fact, it was full of mysterious sounds if one listened attentively. There were babies crying in different tones just under her feet; little lives that had begun to-day or yesterday or a week ago. Hundreds of women have the right to become mothers, to have a child; and thousands are deprived of it, and she, Tania, was one of them.

Folding her numbed hands she sat motionless, her book lying open in front of her. Was her youth really and truly of no value? Were all her dreams worthy of no better ending than this wretched nursing-home? She strained her ears to catch other sounds: Yes, somewhere in the distance, someone was moaning slow, intermittent, muffled moans – it was a woman. Perhaps she was suffering the first pangs of her labour, perhaps she had been mutilated by an operation?

Men who calmly created lives, and walked the earth with so much assurance, were afraid of any illness, scared by the slightest scratch. But here . . . here women bellowed like animals in giving birth to those lives, tearing out their very entrails, baring their innermost beings before strangers. Here they were cut, cut as one cuts a melon, to help them to give birth to a child, or, if need be, to kill it. Beyond her walls, she could now hear another woman. She, too, was moaning, but in a high-pitched tone, and screaming from time to time in her pain. There was the sound of pails being carried along the passage, and the drone of electric bells and she could catch the sound of the nurse shuffling along in soft slippers to readjust the indicator. Yes, the house was full of life.

A nurse came in at half-past nine, rattling the utensils she carried, and by ten o'clock Tania was in bed.

Everything was strange and lonely in this bare room, and, as always when one is on a journey or in a strange room, it is in bed that one is most conscious of one's loneliness and has to shift about before one finds a comfortable position, and wants to nestle down with one's hand under one's cheek, so Tania at last fell asleep, like a child, with her cheek pillowed on her hand. And the nursing home was asleep, but, in the next ward, the woman who was unable to forget her pain, went on moaning.

Tania was called at half-past seven. It was some time before she could realise where she was or who was calling her, and then she was troubled by the cold grimness of the room. Nurses were busy with her for half an hour, making all the necessary preparations. Then they took her downstairs to the operating theatre. The work of the day had already begun. Pans were being carried from the wards. A man on the stairs was busy polishing brass. When they had gone down, Tania found in the operating theatre the surgeon whom she had consulted a week ago, but she hardly recognised him in his white garments, looking like a chef. He was busy sterilising his instruments. His white linen cap did not suit his fat, thick-lipped face, and looked funny. He really did look like an old chef. The nurses undressed Tania, and put a clean nightgown and weird long white stockings on her. It was warm in the operating theatre, but one was conscious of the winter, the frost, behind the windows. There was a soft clink of instruments and the gurgle of boiling water.

'Well, ready?' said the surgeon, turning away again while the nurses led her to the high operating table with its steps to help one to climb up on it. Tania's heart was beating very loud and fast. She gave a last look at the frosty windows, the white walls, the nurses . . . and then she sank down, throwing her head back.

A hand holding a large piece of wadding was suddenly pressed against her face. A sticky, sweetish, suffocating smell filled her nose and mouth – it was disgusting. Long sheets seemed to be enshrouding her, coming one after the other, wrapping themselves round her tighter and tighter. She tried to struggle, to free herself; but the hands that held her hands prevented her. She felt more and more suffocated, but she ceased to care – nothing mattered. She heard a voice very close to her say 'the mask,' and then a voice, which she immediately recognised as that of the surgeon who was like an old chef, said to her: 'Count up to ten; one, two, three . . .' She was surprised, but she began to count. She got as far as four, stumbled, tried to begin again, and could not. She sank deeper and deeper into an abyss, and in that abyss she remained.

It was half-past ten when Tania came to herself on her own bed in the private ward to which the woman doctor had taken her the night before. A dull, blunt pain reminded her of what the chloroform had made her forget. It was all over, and one more unwanted life had been brought to an end. Chelishev need not worry any more; he would learn the news with a sigh of relief, and would be sure to swear to himself that he would be more careful in future. And she? He had finished with her; he would never again be what he had been to her. She must reconstruct her life as best she could; he had never made any promises. Oh, the misery of it! She lay on her back, her forehead damp with perspiration, and visions floated before her wide-open eyes . . . her pale, almost childish, hands fingered the frill of her night-gown. Great, scalding tears filled her eyes for the first time, and ran down her cheeks, tears wrung from her by thoughts of her irreparable injuries.

A nurse came very soon, bringing some tea in a china mug, and with a deft movement put an unpleasantly cold thermometer under her armpit.

CHAPTER XX

AFTER his evening at the garret and his wintry night walk with Sverbeev, Kiril began to look at life from a new angle. So, all things were permissible, nothing was forbidden, in the struggle for a richer, fuller life. Hundreds of thousands of drab creatures, incapable of rising in the slightest degree above the drudgery of the daily round, plodded on and on in the dull monotony of unceasing toil. Sverbeev was right; better not to live at all than to live a life of that sort.

Thoughts about Chelishev terrified him at first, but he fairly soon accustomed himself to them. One man had no right to everything, to be greedy, and to grab too large a slice of life. Again Sverbeev was right: if a man did grab too much for himself, then it was right and proper to snatch from him the loot which he had so inequitably misappropriated.

But an unexpected encounter stirred him deeply, and was later to enable Sverbeev to define and intensify the vague promises for the future that he had been dangling in front of him.

He had met Lebedkin one day in Mohovoi Street, just in front of Soviet House. Kiril was strolling aimlessly and absent-mindedly along the street in the late afternoon when a black automobile dashed up to the door and he collided with the man who sprang out of it. With glad surprise, they recognised each other in a moment. It was the same Lebedkin, somewhat aged, in a grey English cap, as thin and pimply as ever. It was like some dim apparition from the forgotten past. Both men, each in his own way, were moved by the encounter, and, after a warm handshake,

137

agreed to meet again that evening. Kiril went to keep the appointment full of excitement and pleasure at the thought of once more seeing the man who had sown in him the first seeds of knowledge, and had helped to get him to Moscow.

Thick carpets muffled all sound in the entrance hall of Soviet House, but in Lebedkin's room reigned the old, familiar, bachelor disorder. The table was littered with newspapers, a bag of sugar, and bread, and portfolios bulging with papers loomed up like a huge breakwater. They sat down close together and eagerly began to talk.

'Well, how are you getting on, Kiril?' asked Lebedkin very affectionately, 'Climbing up the hill?'

Kiril was embarrassed, and answered vaguely 'I'm trying to,' but at once remembered his failure to pass the examination, and thought of the way in which he was utterly neglecting the Institute. Wanting to divert the talk from this painful subject, he added that he had taken to writing verse, and a moment later was pouring out views on life in general – about over-production, and about new paths which his poetry might open up for him.

Lebedkin listened in perplexed silence to his incoherent babble, until, at a pause, he said sadly 'Who has been stuffing you with ideas of that sort? Or have you arrived at them for yourself?'

At that Kiril feverishly began to try to demonstrate the ideas which Sverbeev had inculcated. Lebedkin paced up and down his bare room as he listened.

'None of those ideas is worth much, Kiril, we are very familiar with them.' He stopped, his hands in his pockets, and spoke sharply, almost angrily, as he always did when he was moved. 'Now, listen to me, while I tell you how I look at the matter. For every hundred mentally sound persons there is, in our times, at least one unsound, insane. Their disease in most cases is shell-shock, you ought to

138

know the word, shell-shock, due to the war or to the revolution. They are the first to go under. The stronger, saner ones survive – selection of the fittest, so to say.'

As Lebedkin talked, with his hands in his pockets, he swayed gently to and fro on his toes, and his narrow, greyish face was radiant with that light of inspiration which Kiril had always associated with him.

'This selection was carried out by our revolution. The feeble disappeared; the strong remained. But it is not everybody, even among the strong, that is capable of accepting the new laws of life, and what you have just been telling me, once more reminds me forcibly of the fearful dangers with which you of the younger generation are faced. We, the older ones, can maintain our hold, we can, when necessary, strike out on new lines, we have at our backs the traditions of the old culture which will never let us rush down the steep gradient to the bottomless pit – but that danger is there for you, and I am afraid that you are in that very danger now. When life is moving in leaps – and life with us makes a fresh leap every year – you must learn to adjust yourself to those leaps, or you will fall so far that not a trace of you will remain. Listen while I tell you what I mean. Lots of you went to the war in the spirit of romance, and it was for the romance of it that you went through the revolution. When the revolution overflowed, like a river bursting its banks and deluging the fields, you still remained romantics. That is where you are out of touch with reality. You remain filled with the old dare-devil romanticism, so that the actualities of to-day seem dull. What the devil is there of romance in the rise of prices day by day and politics filled with bitter workaday problems? And yet, as a matter of fact, old fellow, there is romance there too. I had just as much fighting as any of you. I fought from the Don to Archangel, but I've hung up my rifle now, and I don't regret it. You see what I'm doing now? You see those piles of papers, those portfolios? We are struggling, calculating, getting prices down – You say to yourself "Lebedkin is tied up in Soviet red tape." No, Kiril, there is romance here, too. Lowering the cost of production, putting up new electric power stations, there is romance in that, and anyone who wants to survive must understand that it is so. You can't go on living antiquated heroics – that way lies ruin. You think that I don't understand your mood? I understand it perfectly. You say to yourselves that the times are dull; life is uninteresting, so let's find heroes in the bars, let's slobber over our ideals, let's weep, let's bow down to hysterical epileptics.

'What we need is a new romanticism, a new heroism, not the elevation of Bohemianism on a pedestal. I'm watching the younger generation, Kiril, and unless you realise that you can find poetry in calculating prices, unless you consent to acquire culture . . . we . . . you . . . the whole of our benighted Russia . . . everything, is doomed. Mark my words, Kiril, such an end would be inglorious, ignominious. Far better to have met one's fate during the revolution than now, when a new life is emerging into being.'

Lebedkin said all this while he walked about the room or swayed on his toes, his thin shadow falling on the wall. Kiril spoke at last, spoke with pain, dragging every word from his innermost being.

'But what if I see happiness in something quite different? What if I am incapable of building, am unable to carry bricks, don't know how, haven't got the necessary patience? Life may unexpectedly open out in other directions. It may be that I have got talent and should only bury it under bricks, get nothing out of life, fail to develop myself fully.'

'Who has been telling you that you've got talent?' said Lebedkin, coming close to him. 'Who's been shovelling

140

empty husks over you and filling your head with rubbish? And you've believed it all; you've started down that path and will soon lose your real self, lose every scrap of it. Chuck it, my friend. It was not for that that I got you to Moscow. You'd have done a thousand times better to stay in your factory in the provinces. Factory work is real work, after all. You've had a taste of Bohemianism here, and have filled your head with nihilistic ideas – Soviet Nihilism. Oh, it doesn't take the big towns long to ruin men.'

Putting his arm round his shoulder, Lebedkin went on:

'Look here, Kiril, I'm sorry for you; I don't want you to get off the track. You've got to learn, to learn a lot, because you can't get anywhere without culture. If you stand in need of help, I'll help you. You've got to earn; I know you can't live on the allowance, and I'll find work for you, only give me your word that you will go on with your studies. It is time that we became real men, it is time that we ceased to be Asiatics. Our ethics are no better than they were in Tartar days ² and time will not wait.'

Lebedkin sank into an armchair, and Kiril realised how terribly he had aged in the last few years, how dull his turquoise-blue eyes had become. Gazing at his former tutor, there surged up in him memories of that remote childhood which had been crowded with dreams . . . dreams. Yes, Lebedkin was right; one must study. He must catch up all that he had lost while it was still possible, while there was yet time. Yes, perhaps he ought to go to-morrow to ask Chelishev for permission to take his term examination again.

This meeting with Lebedkin moved him deeply and brought him into an entirely different frame of mind. He felt with his whole being that what Lebedkin had said about life was on the right lines, whereas his unwarrantable ambitions were all wrong, evil. . . .

He longed to impart to Sverbeev all that he had felt that night. He wanted to tell him that he had met an old friend, a good man, his first guide, that they had exhaustively analysed the meaning of life together, and that he knew now, with absolute finality, that one could only build up life, as he had always wanted to, by study, hard work, toil, not by verses and dreams. And he did tell Sverbeev all this the very next day at the Institute, when, at the end of the lecture, the students gathered up their papers and went away, leaving the two of them alone in the empty lecture hall. They sat down on the steps of the professor's raised desk. Kiril talked, while Sverbeev listened, thinking his own thoughts. At last, sighing, he said:

'Government patter, Kiril. And a jolly fool you'll be if you swallow that Government bait. As for your Lebedkin, or whatever his name is, he is working on the problem of production, and a very good job he's got. Splendid! Looking after number one! That's a much better proposition than listening with all your ears to lectures as you and I have just been doing.'

Exactly why it was splendid to be working on the problem of production, Sverbeev did not explain. And Kiril decided that, no matter what Sverbeev thought of his new attitude, he would go next day to ask Chelishev to let him take the examination before the Christmas vacation.

CHAPTER XXI

IT was nearly six o'clock when Kiril, feeling overwhelmed with shyness as usual, approached Chelishev's house. It was not only this man's superiority as a professor that affected him, but his offensive social superiority. The servant who let him in eyed him askance before going to announce him. Kiril was left in the hall, standing in the attitude of a petitioner, while he listened to the chink of china. After several minutes a door opened, and Chelishev appeared standing on its threshold. He did not ask Kiril to come in, but, with chilly politeness said:

'You have come on business, comrade?'

'I have come to ask you something professor,' said Kiril in a choking voice that he hated. 'I failed in an examination last month . . .'

'Well, what about it?' asked Chelishev, in the same cold tone, after a short pause.

'I realise now that I had not prepared properly, and that I had not worked as I ought to have done.' Kiril said this in a dead voice, while he stared into a corner where a bronze Atlas on a tall pedestal was holding up a globe. 'I want to take the examination again, before the Christmas vacation.'

Chelishev looked at him with an air of great astonishment: 'That is to say . . . how?' he said at last. 'How can I make an exception for your special benefit?'

'I did not think that it would upset the regular scheme,' said Kiril, now brazening it out.

The shyness, which had at first had such a hold on him, had been ousted by his earlier hatred for this man with his self-assured frigidity. What if he were to tell him that he knew all about his intrigue with Tania, to tell him and watch his face all the time intently and eagerly? Ah, that would undoubtedly destroy his self-assurance and drive the indifference from his face. But that must come later, later – for the moment he must stick to his tone of quiet supplication.

'No, of course I shall not make an exception for you. You will please take your usual place next session.'

He rubbed the palms of his hands together. So far as he was concerned, the interview was at an end; there was nothing more to be said. A minute later, he led Kiril to the door, where he hurried out, fumbling awkwardly in getting his feet into his overshoes. It was only when he was on the steps that he realised that he still had his cap in his hand as though he were coming out of church.

Feeling deeply injured, and full of hopeless despair and hatred, he went down the steps into the twilight quiet of the street. A pale lemon light came through the curtains of Chelishev's windows. Kiril could not concentrate his thoughts, and had no idea where he was going when he plunged into the narrow thoroughfare. It had seemed so simple to make up his mind to rid himself of his evil associations and compel himself to resume his work. . . . But now he had come up against a stone wall of indifference to his fate and distrust in the sincerity of his newly formed resolutions. Yesterday Lebedkin had talked in lofty tones about life, and to-day life had vouchsafed only a bitter response to his appeals, and, if such was indeed her voice, surely Sveerbeev was right in refusing to indulge in any illusions as to the future, and forcibly moulding the recalcitrant clay in accordance with his own desires.

But what was his next step to be? Whether he should return to his past did not, of course, depend solely upon Chelishev. Chelishev was merely a detail, merely the point from which he had proposed to start. It was true that

Chelishev had shown nothing but cold indifference as to his desire to retrace his steps, but obviously the thing to do was to shake off the feeling of humiliation caused by his interview, and to follow his own course with unfaltering resolution. Kiril felt, however, that he not only lacked the necessary will power, but that he lacked even the desire.

While he listened to Lebedkin the night before, so much of the past had come back to him, recalling the voices by which he had been first initiated; but Sverbeev was right, Kiril had to-day come face to face with life, and her voice had held nothing but unconcern and hostility.

There was a lot that was stirring in what Lebedkin had said, but all it came to in the end was that one must slave like a labourer digging in the stiff clay in the hope that some day it might yield a harvest. But would it?

Of course there was a good deal in Sverbeev's theories that was muddled and vague, much that was shameless in its callous cynicism, but at least they promised that life should soar like a brilliant rocket, and then – well, it did not matter what became of the ashes after the bright flight had finished. No, one ought to live ardently, avidly, in the present.

Enjoying these thoughts, Kiril quickened his pace, and soon emerged on the Arbat, which was full of the noise and movement of the hurrying evening crowds. Everyone who knows Moscow, even slightly, knows that the Arbat has a physiognomy of its own and is not to be confused with any other street. Its heels are planted in the Smolensk market, and its head is thrust into the irregular Arbat Square, where, in the spring, the sale of flowers is at its liveliest, snowdrops, or mimosa with its downy little balls. It is there that the carts stick worst in the thaws, and the carters urge on their horses with blows and stentorian shouts. Between the market and the square, the Arbat flings out streets on both sides like some gigantic heraldic tree. And in those side-streets, one is straightway in the provinces. Here there are houses with French windows, and here churches, with names like 'The Assumption on the Grave' or 'Nicholas on the Strand,' ring the Angelus in the peaceful dusk. The residents in these side-streets are mainly retired officers or professors, men who live in the past, and when one emerges from them and finds oneself in the bustling noise of the Arbat, one's country mood of meditation is swept away, and life resumes its urban aspect.

And, so it was with Kiril. No sooner was he on the Arbat than all desire to think or reflect left him, and he began to wonder where he should go, what he should do with his evening. He did not want to go to Vera – a few days with her so sated him that he did not want even to remember her. He had a craving for some distraction to obliterate the painful impression left by his visit to Chelishev, and it flashed into his mind that a week ago he had given some of his verses for one of the journals to Dontsev, verses in which he had sounded a new note. His name was already familiar to them in the offices of that periodical whose windows were adorned with attractive advertisements. The first steps might be difficult, but he had already made them, so he expected everything there to go smoothly and triumphantly.

The menacing cyclopean eye of the clock in Arbat Square showed that it was a quarter-past six, and, having carefully memorised them, he remembered that the publishers' office hours were from five to seven. So he made his way to their building.

He wanted to confirm his faith in his success as a corrective to Chelishev. Somewhat excited by the thought, he dived through several alleys, crunching the crisp snow under his feet, past a huge building with a rotating globe on its roof bearing the words Sovietic Shop, went down Herzen street and then Ogarav street, and quickly found himself on the doorstep of a big, handsome building. As he mounted the stairs, the clicking of typewriters came to him through closed doors. He found a young man in sports clothes, plus-fours and a shooting jacket, smoking a pipe as he sat at an American roller-top desk, behind a wooden partition. He had a cleanshaven face, but grew a short Norwegian skipper's beard under his chin, which looked like a black bandage over a cut. Indeed, the partitioned office, its window plastered over with bright posters suggestive of trans-atlantic travel, had something of the air of a ship's cabin, and the young man might well have been the skipper of some magic ship to carry passengers away to life and glory.

Glancing up at Kiril, the young man moved his pipe from one side of his mouth to the other, and at that moment the telephone bell rang. As though anxious not to lose a moment of his invaluable time, he turned enquiring eyes toward Kiril while beginning to speak into the receiver. Having at last finished his telephone conversation, he said: 'Your name is Bessonov?' Then, reflecting for an instant, he added 'I don't know it, I don't remember it, will you enquire of the business secretary, second door on your left.'

The business secretary turned out to be a girl with a milk-white skin, profusely and evenly sprinkled with freckles, as though with confetti. Her crown of flaming red, curly hair was done with studied carelessness.

'What number was your contribution entered under? You don't remember?' She spoke in a bored tone, and began to rummage through a pile of written and typed manu-scripts. Her search proved fruitless, and she started looking through a long, funereal ledger where the hopes and dreams of provincial youths were grimly inscribed.

'When was it?' she asked at last.

'A week ago,' said Kiril quickly.

'It's too soon to come for an answer, comrade.' She was just shutting the book when her eye caught what she was looking for.

'Your name is Bessonov? The verses are rejected.' She said this in a tone almost of enjoyment, and promptly returned to the work which she had been doing when he had interrupted her – the very careful mounting on cardboard of a picture of Mary Pickford taken in an elegant negligée on one of the mornings of her visit to Moscow.

When he had remained standing there for a time, she raised her blasé eyes to his again, and said:

'The verses are rejected, comrade. The editors do not give any reasons.'

'But Dontsev said that they would certainly be accepted,' said Kiril, filled with despair by the thought that nobody here knew him or cared a rap about his fate or his success.

'Dontsev is not the editor,' said the girl haughtily.

With an indescribable sense of humiliation, even deeper than that which he had experienced on leaving Chelishev, Kiril went away. In the partitioned cabin the young man sat smoking his pipe and reading his newspaper with an air of calm indifference – the youth who skippered this unboardable ship. Kiril went downstairs as quickly as possible, so that the young man should not notice him, and he carried with him the grim vision of that pile of rejected manuscripts among which of course were his own, though the secretary had failed to find them.

Had he not lent too ready an ear to those who so easily invited youths like him – unknown, tousled boys who had come to Moscow to study – to take the path which was to lead them to literary success ? He had seen so many boys of that sort in the last few months, wearing short jackets, carrying notebooks filled with verses under their arms, who had given up work and study to spend their evenings in chanting their peasant ballads. And in return for their long hours of thoughtful meditation, the expert theorists vouchsafed a few lukewarm handclaps valued by the authors above bread or blood. They slept on office tables, wandered all day from one publisher to another, trying everywhere to place their poems, and took their pleasures in the bohemianism of drinking places, finding a warrant for their manner of life in the classical precedents of Russian writers. He had seen all that, and been horrified by their lot, and to-day his own verses had been rejected. He walked the streets feeling that life was empty, bitter with frustrated aspirations. He looked neither to left nor right, and his misery deepened and enveloped him as he turned back toward the hostel.

He found Tarasik, his room-mate, a little man with a large head, sitting on his bunk with his cheeks cupped in his hands, buried in a book. There was a tin teapot on a chair in front of him. As Kiril entered, Tarasik, glad to be no longer alone, raised his yellow, old-looking face, and said:

'Will you have some tea? I can heat it up in a minute.'

He fussily poured out a mugful, and Kiril felt gratefully glad that he had found a warm, living soul in this desert. He sat down on the bunk beside Tarasik and scalded his throat as he took his first gulp of the comforting weak tea.

CHAPTER XXII

TARASIK began to pace the room, rubbing the back of his neck, which was covered with short, prickly hair. From time to time he glanced at Kiril, who was sitting like a man completely exhausted, with his eyes fixed on a corner of the walls. The tea did not seem to have warmed him at all, and he looked cold and wretched. After a few minutes Tarasik sat down beside him.

'I've been watching you for a long time, Bessonov,' he said softly, as though afraid of startling this man who, generally so reserved with his fellow-students, was now so openly showing his weariness and misery. 'And I've wanted to have a friendly, heart to heart, talk with you.'

Kiril looked listlessly at Tarasik with his close-cropped hair, his pale blue eyes with dark lines under them, and his general air of youth devoid of youthfulness. There had never been any intimacy between them, yet he saw a friend in him, and found a warm, human sympathy in the blue eyes.

'Say anything you like,' he said with sincerity.

'I want to talk about you, if I may; I mean, what I feel about you.' Tarasik clasped his knees with his yellow hands, and hesitated, as though trying to find the best words to express what he had long thought out.

'You see, don't be annoyed, Bessonov, please, you see, you have seemed lately to be bored and restless, as though you didn't know what to do with yourself, or where to go. I know exactly how it feels when one gets bored. It's just when one feels like that that one is apt to do something fatal.'

Kiril listened in dejection to Tarasik's impulsive beginning.

'And it seems to me,' went on Tarasik, with growing excitement, 'that you are bored because you haven't fully understood, you haven't assimilated, the real basis of the life that we are living. It's a hard, dreary life, Bessonov, many have wearied of it, have found it too much for them. But if you reflect a little, if you look at it in its true light, you will see that it is wonderfully spacious, and not merely a dull existence containing nothing but privations.'

Tarasik's colourless, un-young eyes lit up the whole of his sallow, sexless face. 'Wonderfully spacious, Bessonov. Here we are, living side by side, a joyless, workaday life. Vacations are for the future; the present is all drab toil. But that drab toil is worth considering. Take an example – I live so far off that you can't get there with seven-league boots. I come from Pechorsk, far away in the north, where steamers put in only five times in the whole of the summer. Oust Tsilma, my village, is still in the sixteenth century. The men are trappers, and the way they live – It's a dying province – scurvy – syphilis – my father never dreamed of my being an engineer: we had been trappers or fishermen for generations, so I must be one too. But things turned out differently. The civil war rolled up to Pechorsk, the waves of the revolution beat on our wild coast, and one of the waves washed me away; so that here I am . . . in Moscow at the university.'

Tarasik, looking as though lit up by the ecstatic flame of his own thoughts, laid his hand on Kiril's knee. It was as if he were at last, in this midnight talk, pouring out in low, passionate whispers all the feverish dreams that had so long been pent up in him.

'It would seem that I ought to be out trapping in the barren frozen wastes, to be following in my grandfather's footsteps, yet here I am in Moscow, learning about unheard of things. Just think, our province is full of wealth – oil –

coal – untouched by human hands. My dream is to go back as an engineer, to bring my native soil to life by giving it all I know. Roads and irrigation will bring it to life. I want to fight syphilis and scurvy. How could anybody like me have dared to dream such dreams – I a trapper's son – a Pechorsk lad – if the revolution had not awakened me, had not caught me up, and flung me into Moscow?'

He moved nearer to Kiril. 'And I'll tell you something more, Bessonov. In the Children's Village* they've opened a school for non-Russians. Ostiasks, Lopars, Samoeds, can go through a university course, and they are all longing, burning, to return with culture, to spread enlightenment, to bring healing, to construct. Isn't it wonderful to think that those poverty-stricken races, which were quickly dying out, are, for the first time, sending their trappers to trap culture? My father let me go, but he had no faith, he thought that I was going to my ruin. When I return as an engineer, I'll teach him the new faith, and although he's an old man and an Old Believer, he's no fool, and he'll understand. Well, that being so, how can one be dull? The thing is to keep up with life, to keep in step with it.'

'But what if I don't want to live in the future, but in the present, to-day?' said Kiril tonelessly. 'I don't want to see life slip by me while others enjoy it. If that is what matters most to me, Tarasik, and if I can't catch hold of life . . . well, that tears it.'

Tarasik stared silently as though weighing his words, his sallow face, with the flat nose which was his racial heritage, looking very thoughtful. At last, he spoke: 'That can't be the true aim of life, Bessonov. I'm afraid you're off the track, that you're missing what is most important. There's a lot to be learnt from our student life, a lot in it to interest

* The name the Bolsheviks have given to Tsarskoe Selo, which meant the Tsar's Village and was his country residence near St. Petersburg.

us. It is a poor and unenviable existence on the surface; but it has living roots, real roots. . . .

'It's a pity you never come to our group meetings, Bessonov. They seethe with life, because our youth longs for life and knowledge. It's not all slack morals as people write; there's plenty of dogged hard work. I belong to the inventors' group; we're all students, and each one of us is busy with some scheme, each of us has a whole plan of life mapped out. That's what makes our time so remarkable, there is a shoot breaking from every pore, stretching out towards life and knowledge. Even in Pechorsk they can understand that much, I'm sure, Bessonov.'

The tea in the mug standing in front of Kiril was getting cold, while Tarasik incessantly paced the students' cell-like room, rubbing the prickly nape of his neck and puckering his face into wrinkles as he gave expression to the foundations of the faith so firmly established within him.

'I should like to go with you,' said Kiril impulsively, 'but lately my life has so shaped itself . . . so much has got entangled in it, that I might perhaps be glad to get rid of . . . only I don't know how, and I don't even dare . . .'

He thought of his life with pain and sadness. He was only on its threshold, yet how much he had already lost, and how many alluring and dangerous calls it was making on him. He felt with his whole being the truth of the ideals Tarasik expressed and to which he was urging him to return. But he lacked the will and the strength to return, and even if the path lay open before him, he would have been horrified at so simple and straightforward a solution of all new doubts and ideas.

'Well, I shall be sorry if life draws you off in another direction,' said Tarasik feelingly. 'It seems to me that you and I might not only reach an understanding, but might go hand in hand. . . .'

Kiril rose from the bunk and went up to his comrade, and as though in obedience to an inner voice and not of his own accord, firmly clasped Tarasik's small, hard hand, and said in a sort of exultation of despair:

'In any case, thank you for believing, Tarasik, for believing in me, and asking me to join you.'

Tarasik hastily drew him back to the bunk, and they sat down, facing each other. Their passionate, intimate, heart to heart talk lasted far into the night. It was well past midnight when Kolotilov, the third inmate of the room, returned. He was a sickly, dried up young man, the son of a mechanic who had been killed in 1905. And it was as though that night the lives of those three were intertwined, lives of toil, but full of companionship with common ideals and aspirations. The time passed quickly in hurried conversation, till the drab dawn brought with it the old, harassing cares. Kiril remembered that he had to see Sverbeev that day, and once more he became immersed in his poverty-stricken student life.

The young men washed in haste, gulped down some tea, and hurried off, each of them to his own affairs.

The daylight showed dimly through the begrimed windows of the workhouse rooms. The talk of the night hours was submerged in the worry and work of the opening day, and an hour later each of the three was living his own life in his own way, following his own path. But in the unhappy soul of Kiril Bessonov, more agitated than ever, that night had left a lasting memory like a painful scar.

154

CHAPTER XXIII

BITING winter winds were driving massive clouds across the skies in a heavy snowstorm when Kiril met Tania Agourov, three days after his talk with Tarasik.

The meeting was unexpected, but it was to mark an extraordinary, a fatal change in his whole life.

It was a fortnight after Tania's operation, and her pain seemed to have lessened somewhat; but it only seemed so, for in reality, deep within her, her sufferings were terrible, and she was aghast at the blank emptiness that faced her after this, her first, catastrophe. It was as though all the colour had been washed out of her being, as though all the magic hues had faded from days that were once so bright, as though the promise of her youth had lost its flames and left her bereft of all but the ashes of her dreams. It was as though all zest in life had perished in that white house with its garden of snowladen trees.

She had resumed her interrupted occupations; she had gone to her lectures and to her newspaper, trying to pick up again the threads of her former existence, but she could not do it. Her grief grew steadily heavier and more desperate.

It was in this frame of mind that she met Kiril at the post-office. She was posting a letter to her mother, a very calm letter which reflected nothing of her real life. Kiril felt, for the first time, that she was glad to see him. They posted their letters and went away from the post-office together. Tania's face was more boyish and thin than ever, and the blue of her sapphire eyes was deeper. The narrow street along which they were walking was quiet at that hour of the wintry December afternoon.

155

'I've been wanting to talk to you for a long time,' said Kiril timidly, afraid of her characteristic coldness. But after a moment's pause she said softly:

'And I'm glad to see you, Bessonov.'

He was so overwhelmed by happiness at her words and at being once more beside this most dear and distant of creatures that his lips trembled so that he could not speak. He gazed at the profile of her bent head as they walked on in silence.

'Where are you going, Bessonov?' she said at last.

'Nowhere; I'm going with you, if I may,' he said hurriedly, and then added 'If only you would let me tell you everything.'

'Tell me,' and she nodded.

'I want to tell you about the unattainable,' he said quickly, 'about you, I mean. Every man can have his dreams, Tania – it may be that everything around him is coarse, sordid, shameful; but his dream is like a candle, and he protects it lest anything should put it out.'

'I understand, Bessonov,' she said quickly, 'I understand perfectly. But what if the candle does go out? What if one has not succeeded in protecting it? Then, what is one to do?'

'I never thought of that,' said Kiril, puzzled. 'But I suppose that life is hardly worth living if that happens.'

'That's just what I think,' she said in a pleased tone. 'It's splendid that we think alike. The very first time that I saw you at Sverbeev's I thought that it would be easy to talk frankly to you – to walk along with you and talk. But somehow it never happened.'

'But now, Tania?' he asked, as he bent down and looked into her face. 'If I might hope to meet you now, not like this, not accidentally, a great deal might – no, it certainly would – be altered in my life.'

He said this with the utmost sincerity, looking at her in

an agony of hope. But she walked on without answering. They reached the Patriarch's Pond, the frozen surface of which was black with skaters. Small boys were perched like rooks on the lower branches of the trees. Then the orchestra in the bandstand struck up a tender, dreamy, happy waltz, and the skaters paired off and floated over the ice in time to the melody. It all seemed like a vision under a frozen spell. The various metallic tones of the instruments, some high, some low, rang out and rose toward the wintry sky which looked like a quilt of swansdown. And Kiril and Tania, tongue-tied by their cares and their frustrated desires, seemed to float upward with the music.

Kiril reached out to grasp her elbow, and she let him hold her thin, girlish arm as, side by side, they walked away from the Patriarch's Pond, away from this icebound enchantment, as silent as though they had said everything that it was possible to say to one another, and the spell was not broken until he recognised the entrance to the house to which he had brought her once before.

Tania went up the steps, and stood there, lost in her own thoughts, her chin buried in her furs, and her eyes gazing straight in front of her. Kiril realised that she was standing like that because she did not want to leave him, so he too mounted the steps, and then opened the heavy front door. It swung back, closing of itself, and they found themselves in the dark entrance. Kiril's heart was beating fast as he stood close to her, and, after a moment, he took her hand. It lay in his hand, so small, so cold, and twice he kissed the narrow palm which touched his face with soft tenderness. He could not speak for some time; he wanted to conceal the tremor in his voice. But he could not control it, and he began to speak.

'I wanted to tell you, Tania; my life has been going down hill terribly; terribly, and I'm afraid if it goes on I shall soon reach the bottom. And it seems to me that it is only with you that I could go back, because I have thought of you from the beginning, from our first meeting. You never even noticed me, I know. But I created an ideal, and the farther that ideal was withdrawn – and you have been far away lately, Tania – the easier it was for me to be untrue to myself.'

She listened to him, standing in the darkness, her hand still in his.

'Don't talk about ideals, Bessonov,' she said suddenly. 'An ideal is a terrible thing, because, when one's life is utterly devoted to a dream, things may so happen that one discovers that there is nothing left to live for. But listen – I want you to think kindly of me, if you can – if you know of anything against me, remember that it was due to an ideal, and not to my wickedness.'

'I know of nothing,' he said trembling, 'and if I did it would only make you better and purer in my eyes. I used to think of you at one time in the way that a man thinks of a woman, I admit it, but that is all past and done with, it's not that sort of thing that I want, I assure you. I must have a guiding star of my own, toward which I can reach out, and, having which I shall not fear anything in life. I have dropped my studies, Tania, I have done nothing for three months. I'm not working, and I don't know what to do with myself – they told me that I might become a poet, but the day before yesterday my verses were rejected, and I am convinced that they are very poor, and I have resolved never to write any more. It seems to me now that I only started writing poetry to try to brighten my existence, so – well, if you were with me I should know that I could not build my life on verses – if we were together, it would not matter how hard things were – if only we were together. . . . '

Suddenly her little hand quivered in his, as though she

158

were trembling. In a whisper, scarcely above her breath, she said:

'It's splendid that you are like that, Bessonov. It may all be impossible; but that does not matter, what matters is that you feel like that, too. Because you will understand, you will understand how it happened that my life took the course it did.'

She said all this in a quavering whisper in the dark, cold entrance lobby. She was finding a last refuge in the soothing breath of familiar words from a man whom she knew so little, but to whom, in some strange way, she had felt attracted ever since their first meeting. He was using the very words to her which she might have used to another, with the same emotional unrest, and they re-enforced and justified the terrible thought which had filled her mind since her catastrophe. His arm encircled her as she leant against his shoulder feeling crushed under the burden of her remembered emotions, and with the fleeting illusion that she could recapture them, she pressed her lips to his with a passionate moan, in a long, yearning kiss. Moments, hours, months, passed in that dark hall. Then, with a cry of despair, which seemed to him to combine a call and a promise, she tore herself away, and fled up the stairs. He heard her groping with the key at her lock, heard the door slam to, and then all was quiet. He stood there in the silence with his hands clenched.

He became aware that his face was wet, that his coat was wet. Then she had been weeping? Why? Oh, why? He had an ardent longing to run up those decrepit stairs to ask her, to comfort her, to know. But it was all so still up there. And then the stillness was shattered, when someone in the flat on the ground floor, just behind the wall against which he was leaning, struck up a quick, lively two-step on a piano.

He left the house, and returned to the street. He did not wipe his face, trying to retain as long as he could the moisture of those tears with the extraordinary feeling of her nearness that they gave him. He walked aimlessly, not knowing whither or why, feeling only that from to-day his whole life had taken a new turn. He found himself back at the Pond. The band was still playing, the trombones with their deep satisfied voices, the horns in luring, promising, flattering, high-pitched tones, floating up to the violet-tinted sky, which had already begun to shed its down again.

CHAPTER XXIV

WHEN Tania entered her flat, she went straight to her room without turning on the light. The frosty windows showed a dark blue. She could see her frozen breath in the air, the Dutch-tiled stove having gone out in the morning. She went to the window in her coat and overshoes, her collar and the front of her coat still wet with tears. A moment ago she had parted from a man who had said good-bye to her in the very words and with the inexpressible tenderness with which she herself longed to say good-bye to all she loved. If only she could bring herself to hate Chelishev. But it had not been his fault that she had created an illusory image, had endowed him with qualities which he had never possessed. Once more there arose before her the white ward, the glitter of steel instruments, the stifling chloroform mask, and again she was reminded that her dearest hopes lay in ruins, and that she would never be able to resume her former life.

So be it. But she did not wish to live otherwise. She neither would nor could. Thousands, doubtless, were able to master their fate, finding an ennobling satisfaction in fighting the good fight, toiling, discharging their social functions, ever gaining new strength to carry on. They were free to do so. They were strong souls, with strong wills, and had the right to live. They could control life, and need not fear the failures, the suffering, it held. They could meet disappointment with dogged resistance. But there were others; weak souls for whom the first disillusionment was fatal, like those materials in which the first tear leads to the ruin of the whole piece. That was what had happened to her.

She had carefully analysed her feelings, tried to weigh things up, and, wholeheartedly, almost without hesitation, had reached the conclusion that she could not go on living. She could not easily give again her priceless, her unique gift, nor had she any wish to do so. There, in the hospital ward, she had been shamelessly crucified on the operating table and sobbed out her moans as she made her great sacrifice. The week after she had returned, alike at home, at the university, at her newspaper office, meeting people, attending lectures, making notes for her journalistic work, she had been conscious that all the colours had faded, that all this human rushing and struggling, no longer warmed and vivified by her dreams, had become grey and cold. It was as though one terrible blast of wind had swept away the golden pollen without which all fruition was impossible, the fruit could not even begin to form. She felt that she was lost, her life a void.

She had no wish to see Chelishev again, nor did he seek a meeting.

This, then, was what life was like, in violent contrast to all that her imagination had pictured. She could not live, if this was the reality. Kiril Bessonov, whose feeling for her she realised, was the last man she would ever meet, and it was through him, through his unspoken love, that she had taken leave of all that was dearest to her. In that prolonged, bitter kiss in the cold entrance hall, she had expressed her final tenderness, her final gratitude to life in spite of everything, for all that it had given to her.

Her eyes were dry as she gazed through the frosty panes of the dark window. Her brother was not at home, and, as usual in the evening, the rooms were cold. The old woman who came in to clean the flat had gone away. Some days before, Tania had found in the middle drawer of her brother's writing table, a small black revolver that looked like an expensive toy. With its short barrel, its butt grooved in criss-crossed lines, it slipped easily into one's hand and clung to the palm without feeling at all heavy.

Her brother lived his own life of ascetic abstinence, full of proud ambition, and working hard with the determination to finish as soon as possible at the Military Academy. On the left lapel of his coat he wore a small enamel decoration, bearing a red flag, the badge of the Communist Party. His walls were hung with maps, swords, belts, Zeiss fieldglasses in their leather case, and steel hooks for boots. The whole room, table, chairs, floor, was littered with papers.

How terribly she would upset his orderly routine. . . . But he would understand; he was a man of courage, and he would understand. She had written a letter for him, explaining everything.

But in order to do what she had to do, she must go away from here. She must say good-bye to these rooms, just as, a little before, she had said good-bye downstairs to the man who would perhaps remember her.

She gazed round her brother's darkening room very calmly, almost with exultation. The letter that she had written yesterday she put in the drawer of his desk in exchange for the smart little revolver. A minute later she had left the room, her heart wildly racing, as though stumbling in its uneven beats. Her brother's green cloth military cap was hanging in the vestibule, and as she went out, she raised herself on tiptoe to kiss its surface, and then resolutely clicked the Yale lock as she closed the door behind her.

As she went down the stairs, listening to their familiar creaking, she was thinking that it was for the last time. The only thing she feared was that she might see Kiril again, but he was nowhere in sight. Except for two women

163

rattling their pails as they drew water from the tap at the corner, the street was silent. Tania hurried forward without a backward glance. She was soon in the busy streets, and hurried on, mingling in the crowd, until she reached a yellow board fastened to a post. The board was covered with squares, like a chessboard, each of the squares bore a number, and under each number was a tiny motor bus bearing the same number and an indication of its route. Tania stood there waiting in the usual afternoon crowd. Red trams, with frost-covered window-panes, and looking like huge caterpillars, went clanging along, and sledges drawn by shaggy, unclipt horses passed her in a never-ending stream.

At last, scaring foot-passengers out of its way with its deep, triumphant rumble, and the dazzling light gleaming from its apocalyptic eyes, a bus came to a standstill, rocking slightly on its tyres. Tania got in and sat down on the front seat, looking through the wide window which framed the winter landscape that seemed, a minute later, to be rushing towards her. The purple shadows of the evening lay over the town. Wide streets with curving lines of tram posts, kiosks covered with gay advertisements, the distant, lofty opening of the Triumphal Arch, approached with increasing rapidity.

Here and there lights appeared like children playing at hide and seek, but they were too faint to make any impression on the darkness which was quickly enfolding the city. The motor bus drew up at the stopping places, stood throbbing while passengers got on or off, and then rolled on again. It soon passed the railway station, rumbled under the viaduct with its row of emerald green lights, and emerged in the broad, airy avenues of Petrovsk Park. Small, detached houses and cottages sped by them on either side. The entrance to the racecourse, lit up by tall, moonlike lamps, was guarded by prancing bronze steeds, and, beyond the steeds and the race track were trees and snow and the white plains of Hodinka Fields, over which an aeroplane was flying low, like some bird of prey.

Tania was the last passenger, no one but herself alighted at this halt, no one boarded the bus, which, now quite empty, rushed away toward Petrovsk Razoumovsk, smothering her in fumes and bespattering her with snowdust. She breathed the freshness of open spaces as her eye was caught by the sombre silhouettes of the trees against the snowy expanse. She took a well-trodden side path, and soon found herself in a thick plantation. Overhead rooks cawed in sepulchral tone as they selected their roosting places for the night. Sitting down on a snow-covered bench in the deserted alley, lost in thought, she stared for a minute or two at the snow glistening in the dusk with bluish glints, and beautiful in its unsullied purity. In spite of her desire to put an end to everything quickly, as she had planned, she could not tear herself away from this immaculate purity, and the encounters, the loves, the sorrows, and all the episodes of her short life seemed to beckon to her as they passed through her mind. There in the little town where she had spent her childhood, she was leaving her mother to die of grief in just such snowy stillness. But what else could she do since things had turned out as they had, since she had settled her fate in that way? She put her hand into her bag and stroked the butt of the revolver with her finger.

With scarcely a feeling of regret or remorse, she drew the revolver from her bag, and unfastened her coat with her left hand, still staring at the snow with eyes which did not see.

Yes, so, just there, against the little breast which, unashamed, she had once laid bare for Chelishev. She must feel for her ribs, the fifth and sixth, just between them, that was the place.

She frowned, tense in the anticipation of pain, her

mouth open to cry out her horror and suffering. She pressed the muzzle firmly to her left breast, and pulled the trigger. A moment later, her eyes filled with terror, tortured by unbearable anguish, she removed the revolver from her breast. There had been no shot. Wasn't it loaded then? Fumbling with icy fingers, she opened the breech, and there, in the little chambers. she could see the yellow metal rim of the cartridges. She closed the breach again, examined the revolver, and saw the tiny plate of the safety catch. The catch moved easily from 'sure' to 'feu.' 'Feu' means fire, she thought to herself, and, without a second of delay, thrust the revolver inside her coat again, pressed it to her breast, and her face drawn, pulled the trigger again with all her might. At that moment someone struck her a violent blow in the back. She wanted to look round, but remained motionless amid an unearthly screeching from the startled birds in the trees overhead and the snow thickly falling from the branches. Its soft, feathery flakes whirling round her brought a fleeting memory of childhood, and then oblivion.

An hour later, a red-cross ambulance, through the windows of which one caught a glimpse of a white cot, filling foot-passengers with fear and trembling, roared through the town and sped along the broad, deserted highroad.

CHAPTER XXV

IT was nine o'clock next morning when Kiril and Sverbeev left the tram which had brought them to Soucharev Square, usually so busy, but now deserted. A few lonely men hurried down the steps of an underground lavatory, obviously perishing in the violent, sweeping wind which drove the falling snow before it in sheets. Kiril, shrivelled up into an icy mass, and hardly able to face the wind, followed Sverbeev without question.

The hospital to which Tania had been brought the evening before, and where she had died in the night after an unsuccessful operation, was in an enormous palace, the curved, colonnaded façade of which extended round half the square.

They went through the gates into the courtyard. It was hither that the opaque-windowed ambulances brought from every quarter of the great town all those men and women who had been torn from life, victims of accidents or crimes or catastrophes, or of their own hands. From one end of it to the other, the great city was full of the living, busy with their human affairs and activities; but the scrap, the cast-off material, the failures, the lifeweary, those whom the town had macerated in its iron jaws, all of them were brought to this hospital.

Sverbeev had heard the evening before the news of what had happened to Tania. A reporter whom he knew had rushed from the newspaper office to tell him, and together they had hurried to Tania's flat, to Dmitri Agourov. He had reached his sister two hours before her death. He was staggered by his grief and horror when he saw her anguished eyes, her delicate little face already death-like in its pallor. Sitting beside her bed, hardly able to breathe, he stared at the small open mouth from which clots of black blood oozed at intervals, with a sound of gurgling in the throat. Her chestnut hair was lying spread over the pillow. Yes, it was his own darling Tania, so quiet, to whom he was so accustomed that there were many things about her which he had never noticed, and now, she was so aloof, no longer of the earth, conscious only of the voices within her, of her own agony.

He had read her letter, and he knew her story. As he sat beside her, their childhood, all their life, came back to him; and here was this fragile soul, this tender plant, trodden down by the city. But how was it that he – a full grown man, clearsighted and priding himself on his knowledge of the world – how was it that he had allowed all this to happen? How was it that he had seen nothing, guessed nothing, understood nothing? Dmitri Agourov spent those two hours there full of dark and tragic thoughts, full of contempt for himself for his carelessness in regard to the being whom he loved best in all the world.

Her breath came in shorter and shorter gasps; she seemed to soar farther and farther away; her transparent hands, cold as marble, were turning blue. The death rattle no longer tortured her little throat; the pulse which had been still feebly discernible on her slender wrist stopped, gave a few more beats, like the painful flickerings of a candle before it goes out, and then – all was over; the candle had gone out. The hands of the big oak clock showed a quarter to three when Dmitri went out of the ward into the corridor. He compared his wrist watch with the big hospital clock, but the movement was automatic, for he was too dazed to know what he was doing. He must have started in the wrong direction, because a hospital attendant in a white overall hastened after him and touched him on the arm. Agourov

168

found his cloak and his military cap, buttoned his collar, and went out into the starless wintry night.

Sverbeev and Kiril went to the enquiry window, and asked a young doctor how Tatiana Agourov was. The doctor looked them over, and in his turn asked 'What relation are you to her?'

'We are her comrades,' answered Sverbeev.

'She died in the night; her body is in the mortuary.' And having said that, the doctor turned again to the tabulated foolscap sheets with which he had been occupied.

Following Sverbeev out, Kiril sat down on the steps. He took off his cap, letting the icy wind tear through his hair. He wanted to sob, to scream, to stamp his feet and curse; but he sat in silence, crushing his cap in his hand. Sverbeev took it from him and put it back on his head.

'That'll do, Kiril,' he said in a tone that was almost hostile. 'It's no good letting yourself go. The thing to do is to think out some way of making the fellow who caused this death drink vinegar. We shall have to talk about that. Get up and come along; we must have a last look at Tania.'

He led the way again. What was now the hospital mortuary, and had once been a chapel, stood in the middle of the courtyard. There was a padlock hanging on its closed iron door. A dray on sledge runners was standing near the door, and a militia man was sitting in it beside its driver, and they were both smoking with a businesslike air. From the doorway came a faint, sweetish smell, the awful smell of the human body's decay.

The town, after its night of rest, was already resuming its busy life of buying and selling and working. Thousands of beasts were being killed in the slaughterhouses to feed the monster. The streets had been swept at dawn, and the rubbish bins had been emptied of the trash which had filled them. Motor dustcarts had collected and carried away

169

the refuse, and here, in the courtyard, the mortuary was also being emptied of its rubbish and refuse – the dead. Failures, out-of-works, bandits shot in skirmishes, suicides, women dead of grief or jealousy, careless creatures who had been run over by trams or burnt or crushed or mangled – the dregs of humanity, the city's daily sacrifice, the steam from its exhaust pipes. An attendant in a waterproof apron smeared with blood like that of a butcher, removed the padlock and opened the door, and the ominous smell became stronger. The driver of the dray took a last puff at his cigar, and went inside. Directly afterwards, with the help of an assistant, he brought out the naked body of a man, one of them holding its shoulders and the other its feet. The corpse was placed in the sledge face downwards, and covered with a tarpaulin. The militiaman and the driver sat down on each side of their gruesome burden, and the sledge drove off.

'Let's go inside, Kiril,' said Sverbeev. 'You're not afraid? Oh, we must live, Kiril, live at any cost, anything, everything, but that,' and he nodded in the direction of the mortuary. 'That is the end, there, nothingness. Life! We must live! And we must be revenged on the man who is guilty of all this. . . . '

He took Kiril by the hand, and they went together into the terrible darkness. Five, six, ten – It seemed to Kiril that there must be at least twenty bodies on the tables. Side by side with a huge man with a protruding black beard, lay the innocent, nude body of Tania, almost childlike in its slenderness. Her head was thrown back as if she were listening in wonderment. Just under her left breast was a dark spot plugged with a brown wad. But most awful, most heartrending of all, were her childish feet which were never again to tread the earth. Covering his face with his hands, and barely conscious what he was

170

doing, Kiril ran out into the courtyard, flung himself on the ground, and buried his face in a snowdrift.

There had been no real mingling of their lives except in his feverish dreams and in that last kiss which they had exchanged in the dark hall; yet he felt with his whole being that all that was best and highest and most disciplined in his life had gone with Tania as irrevocably as the spring-broken ice is swept away by the rivers. After this death, now that Tania had gone, there was no need for any self-restraint, everything was permissible, all roads lay open, and the darker, the more tangled, the more shameful they were, the better.

Sverbeev began rubbing Kiril's temples with snow. 'Now you must above all things be a man, old fellow. You must give Agourov all the help he needs,' he said in a hard, businesslike voice. He brushed the snow from Kiril's clothes and firmly led him away.

Tania was buried next morning. Snow had been falling since dawn from the low purple clouds which hung heavily over the town, and was still coming down, wrapping the world in its mantle of white. About a dozen university friends, and one or two newspaper colleagues followed the little red coffin that looked like that of a child. Dmitri Agourov felt the icy burden of death on his broad shoulders for the first time. Kiril walked at his side, his feet floundering in the deep snow. There was a likeness between Dmitri and Tania, something in his courageous face recalled her sweet, dreamy features, and Kiril watched him as they went along, trying to catch the elusive resemblance.

The little procession made its way across the snowbound town, past tramlines, through squares, it followed many roads into the broad white Pressnia Street, and beyond that to the Vagankova Cemetery with its white trees and the icy breath of country snow. There the little red coffin was

171

lifted from the sledge at the gates. It was a light load. Kiril took one end of the coffin, and his face was only separated from Tania's face by a thin board while he and the others carried the precious burden.

As he walked the short distance to the grave, Kiril's thoughts turned to his own life, and he recalled the dear ones who had gone. He remembered how his father had taken him to his mother's grave, that mother whom he had never known. Now, Tania had joined the group of those he mourned as lost for ever. They did not take long to reach the snow-covered mound on which the little red coffin was laid with the lurid look of a poisonous flower, in its white setting, and the heavy white flakes went on falling as though they would cover up forever beneath the weary waste of winter days, all the infinity of human grief and suffering. From that little mound Tania was saying her never-to-be-forgotten last farewell to them all.

Sverbeev took Kiril back to his own room, buying food and a bottle of vodka on the way. Vodka, vodka, to drink, to get drunk, to lose consciousness of everything, that was what Kiril longed for. With one gulp he swallowed half a glass; the cold green bottle promised warmth and peace and indeed, almost at once after that terrible day, he was wrapped in the blessed oblivion of intoxication.

'Well,' said Sverbeev, 'may Tania's soul rest in peace. Let's drink to that and to the hope that we may never turn away from life, never give in, like Tania, but always keep our fists clenched. Will you drink to that, Kiril?'

Kiril sighed. Overcome by self-pity and horror at the prospect of a life ruthlessly bereft of hope, he gazed at Sverbeev through the haze of memories which suffused him.

'I'll drink to that,' he said with a shudder. 'I want to live a real life, not to go downhill, not to be knocked out;

172

but I've missed so much at the Institute that I shall never be able to catch up, never. . . . '

He rested his head on the table and wept weak, tipsy tears that brought no relief. He felt that he was not sober, that he was acting like a drunken man, but he could not control himself.

Sverbeev sat down by him, and put his arm round his shoulder, so that his long nose almost touched Kiril's face.

'Stop grieving, you silly chap; we'll make such a life for ourselves as the others have never dreamed of. We'll have money, and perhaps you will have fame as well.'

He turned Kiril towards himself, and twice kissed him on those lips which were salt with tears.

CHAPTER XXVI

TANIA AGOUROV'S death was, as a matter of fact, a favourable factor in the complicated plans which Sverbeev was making for his great coup. He had, of course, not counted on that fatal issue, but since things had turned out in that way (and it was beyond his power to affect the course of such events) he must make the most of her death as a means for the furtherance of his ends.

His first aim was to get complete control over Bessonov, and he expected that aim to be facilitated by the grief and remorse under which he was labouring. He was not mistaken; for, full of despair over the irreparable catastrophe, Kiril never went anywhere except to Sverbeev, in whose room he had first met Tania and who was the only person to whom he could talk about her for hours. Sverbeev gained complete domination over him in those days. Kiril, of course, had not the slightest idea that it had been Sverbeev who had so subtly and persistently brought Tania and Chelishev together. He did not know that it was he who had arranged their first meeting and unobtrusively fanned Tania's interest in the professor. He had done it all deliberately though with no thought of its having so terribly tragic an end, and now that Tania was dead, he had to straighten out the threads which had become too tangled a skein even for him.

What had been his object in bringing Tania and Chelishev together? It was all very complicated, but he had not lost sight of his reason in all the tangle. His idea had been to rouse Kiril's jealousy and hatred by bringing Tania into her relations with Chelishev, his aim in stirring up those dangerous feelings was due to his intuition at the very beginning that the *naif* lad, still bearing the stamp of the province from which he had emerged, still capable of dreaming, was the safest and best accomplice he could find. He and his secret schemes could remain hidden behind the downright straightforwardness and rebelliousness which Kiril expressed so freely. If he could once be persuaded to take the road toward which Sverbeev had been leading him during the last months with such careful cunning, he would go forward to the bitter end without flinching.

Sverbeev had worked out his plan almost like an architectural design. He had brought Chelishev and Tania together in order that Kiril might become the girl's defender, in order to rouse a dangerous romantic passion to provide a motive for threatening disclosure, so that he, Sverbeev, as an older man and Kiril's best friend, could intervene to avert a scandal by obtaining a settlement on a pecuniary basis, so that he could approach Chelishev, not as a blackmailer, but with the avowed object of helping him. The lines of the design had become more complicated by reason of Tania's death, since threats of exposure were no longer possible, and the girl whose defender Kiril was to have been was no longer alive. All that he could do now was to show that Chelishev was responsible for her death, and to make this youth – with his dreams and his actions all muddled up – accept the idea that, since Chelishev had ruined Tania, all things were permissible in regard to him and that any punishment which they could inflict would be too small and insignificant for his crime.

Yes; he must rouse a passionate longing for revenge in Kiril, and, with a careful hand, he rubbed out some of the lines in his design and inserted new ones. These new lines would provide a solution for the still unsolved problem – how to get money out of Chelishev. There could, of course, be no question of robbery, or of any sort of scandal. It must be done skilfully, insidiously, in some way that would be far worse for Chelishev than any mere theft.

Kiril, with his shattered dream, his sense of injury, his grief, was essential to the carrying out of the new plan. That was the basis, the outline, of what Sverbeev proposed. The details and further ramifications of the still undesigned means were another matter. He had not forgotten what Kiril had told him about his interview with Lebedkin, who, he remembered perfectly, had a lot to do with manufactured goods. That inspired him with new ideas which, though wholly pacific, were highly exciting.

There had long been a dearth of manufactured goods in the Co-operative Store which supplied the needs of the students. If he could obtain a consignment of such articles for the Students' Co-operative, he could easily manage so that the store would receive only a part of the goods (they would be only too glad to get anything they could) and there would be no difficulty or risk for him in disposing of the rest through other channels. That was where Cooperov came in. He knew everybody and had connections on all sides, and the two had long ago put their heads together, and arrived at an understanding.

Sverbeev must above all else get money, money for a bigger, broader life, money to enable him to give up the Institute, to leave his stinking hovel with its perpetual buzz of primus stoves which no door could shut out. In order to obtain money without working for it, it was necessary to think out every move, as if in a game at chess. Riches do not roll their muddy waves up to the feet of the genius, or to those of the world's great creators, but to those of the most ordinary of men if only they are cunning and relentless. And, that being so, why should not he, Sverbeev, be in the first rank of the triumphant?

176

The idea of making use of Kiril's connection with Lebedkin began to modify and define the outline of his design. But it was still first of all imperative to get Kiril, in his despair, to go along the desired path to a point at which he would realise where he was and the impossibility of his return; for, when once he had found it impossible to go back, he would rush forward headlong to the goal which Sverbeev had marked out for him.

With the approach of the new year, Kiril became more and more acutely conscious how far behindhand he was with his studies. If things went on like that, if he did not recover his lost ground before the spring, he would be expelled. What would he do with himself then? Return to his native town as a disgraced failure? Perhaps get Yagodkin to find him a job at the factory? Was that to be the finish of his hopes and his dreams – to return to the factory as an apprentice? Long before Tania's tragedy, he had had hours of anguish in the night when he had felt that he had lost his grip on his work and could never recover his grasp of it.

Sverbeev had correctly calculated all this in the designs which he was framing. He let Kiril indulge his grief and his restlessness for a time. Indeed, it was very sad about Tania, but what a lot of weaklings were swept away by the wind in these days. Weaklings were swept away; the strong remained. And the sight of the weaklings' ruin only intensified Sverbeev's ardent, avid will to live. The gap, the hiatus, between the revolution and the dull work of reconstruction, with its terrible plague of fatigue and disillusionment, brought grim determination to some; but to others only the fear that they might become stranded in the dreary transition period, to be horrified later by the discovery that the fleeting years had sped by unnoticed and were irrecoverably lost. Sverbeev felt like that with every nerve of his being. Some might pause to chant their requiems, but others meanwhile manipulated the hands on the dial of life, turning minutes into hours or hours into minutes, as they chose.

How had it happened that he had followed Chelishёv's trail so closely? How was it that he knew about the money he had saved? It had happened in this way: He had gone to the State Bank one day with Cooperov, and sat down on a wooden bench, bored, smoking idly, and watching the busy scene while his companion attended to his business. Masses of men carrying portfolios were crowding round the grilled windows of the cashiers, and one heard the clicking of abacuses through the steady hum of voices rising to the domed roof, while tellers behind a barred partition were counting money – millions of roubles – and tying it up into packets which they labelled. There was untold wealth behind that partition, while on this side were busy, hardworking folk, shabby cashiers, clerks receiving or paying out with supreme indifference the money which did not belong to them. Sitting on the bench, amid the hubbub of the bank, Sverbeev indulged in vague thoughts about all this wealth.

There were two windows close to him, labelled 'Purchase and Sale of Foreign Money.' Beside them several foreigners, wearing soft felt hats and coats with large kangaroo-skin collars, stood somewhat awkwardly changing their money, while a group of self-confident patrons, wanting to buy it, pressed up against them. There were several fat, well-dressed women, a red-haired broker, a dried-up, bewhiskered old man looking like a statesman, and suddenly Sverbeev caught sight of Chelishev among them. He stood in the queue awaiting his turn, with a portfolio under his arm. Sverbeev quickly rose and took up a position just behind the professor, leaning his arm on the edge of the oak counter, and watched him with keen interest.

When Chelishev's turn at last came, he took out his

pocketbook, opened it, and extracted a sheaf of white notes. The girl cashier in a green knitted jumper deftly spread them out, and, removing the notes which had obviously been placed crosswise to mark the hundreds, arranged them all in an ordered pile. Then she moistened her thumb on a small sponge and rapidly counted the corners. When she had finished her count, she made a memorandum of her total, and passed the packet to another girl sitting beside her, who also counted the notes, and, finding that their counts tallied, took out a few notes from a package of very soiled, long, greenish bills, and handed them to Chelishev, while Sverbeev heard her say 'A thousand dollars.' Chelishev put the money in his pocketbook, slowly buttoned up his coat, and walked away.

Sverbeev was astounded. How had such an enormous sum come to be in Chelishev's possession? Doubtless there were others who had more; but what struck him was that Chelishev should have so much. He went to the bank with Cooperov on several other occasions, and caught sight of Chelishev again three or four times. Vague ideas began to float in his mind almost imperceptibly until they gradually took form as hazy projects, though he did not at the moment dream of putting them into action. And thus it was through a mere coincidence that the first conception of his plan arose.

Kiril spent the first few days after Tania's death in a fever of pity, misery, horror and love. As always happens, he now attributed the highest, most inimitable, and unique qualities to her, and their last meeting became for him a source of unending anguish, awakening feelings hitherto unknown. He had, in reality, seen Tania only casually and on rare occasions, and she had not played any active part in his existence. But it seemed now that all was emptiness and chaos, and that life had lost all purpose. But Sverbeev came to his aid, assured, calm, understanding. He let the

179

first paroxysm of grief spend itself, and, as it waned, real life, with its daily cares and encounters, proceeded to plaster up the wounds with its usual rapidity. It always is so, and so it was with Kiril. Then, as he became calmer, Sverbeev stealthily began to stir up a vague, dull hatred of Chelishev which Kiril could not fully explain to himself.

Chelishev had caused Tania's death. Chelishev was going abroad in the spring to enjoy himself, to have a good time, without a thought for Tania or a twinge of remorse. Chelishev had saved up a lot of money for his journey. These were all different threads, but Sverbeev twisted them together into one cord, and, when that cord was firmly twisted, it became evident that if Chelishev went abroad, he, Kiril, would be to blame for his failure to avenge Tania. For, had not her last farewell in the dark hall perhaps meant that she bequeathed to him the task of avenging her? Sverbeev added the rest: They were alone in their knowledge of Chelishev's crime, they might expose it, Chelishev must pay for their silence. No, that was not trading on Tania's memory, it was punishing Chelishev. And though Kiril could not, for the life of him, see how he would be avenging Tania by taking money from Chelishev, he accepted the proposal readily, passionately, exactly as Sverbeev had anticipated.

But, at just this time, Chelishev finished his lectures at the Institute, and went to Leningrad for a month to deliver a course there. Sverbeev was rather pleased than otherwise by this, as it gave him more time to work out a plan of action.

Meanwhile he took Kiril to the studio one evening just before Christmas. Cooperov was still living there pending the finding of a flat.

Kiril sat down at one end of the wide divan where Vera had so resolutely and purposefully made him take her on that faraway, unforgettable night. Sverbeev flung himself down at the other end, while Cooperov, his hands in the pockets of his smart velvet knickerbockers, smoking his everlasting pipe, paced up and down past the canvas walls on which ancestral portraits hung crookedly, and among the gilt furniture with its tarnished gold.

Sverbeev, rumpling his thin hair, then told them all that he had so far planned in regard to the Students' Co-operative Stores, Lebedkin, and the consignment of goods.

CHAPTER XXVII

THE rest followed with a rush for Kiril, though somewhat against his inclination, because the real affection which he felt for Lebedkin made him shrink from utilising his friendship so shamelessly. However, he gradually persuaded himself that there could not be any harm in making use of the connection for his own benefit. It only took Cooperov a few days to ascertain exactly what part Lebedkin played in the distribution of manufactured articles, and meanwhile Sverbeev threw out hints in the Students' Co-operative Store that it might be possible to get a consignment, and he offered to take the necessary steps to find out how to do it, and to obtain the goods. The whole business was readily entrusted to him under a formal authorisation bearing the official stamp, and after that everything went smoothly.

On Sunday Cooperov invited his two friends to dine with one Naoum Robertovitch, a great authority on all matters concerning factories and their output. He was to tell them exactly what goods were now in most demand, was, if necessary, to lend money for a deposit, and in general do all he could to help. He had recently bought a handsome residence on the Solianka, which, as his wife and children were abroad, was at the moment a bachelor establishment where he entertained the prettiest girls in Moscow, even including actresses. Sverbeev explained all this in great detail on their way to the Solianka. Kiril was sick at heart, but full of determination as they rode to the home of their mysterious host. If he had happened to meet Lebedkin at that moment he would have clung to him to free himself for ever from his entanglements. But there was no Lebedkin, there was no one on earth to make him return to his former life, and the new, the fascinating and alluring unknown, was gradually emerging from the mist and taking shape. No, there was no other way; the old life was too empty since the loss of Tania. The tram ran quickly and gaily past the boulevard with the guns captured from the enemy at Plevna and the grey memorial chapel to the heroes of the Turkish war, past the buttressed Kremlin walls, and down to the Solianka. Sverbeev sat opposite to Kiril, his long nose buried in his fur collar, staring with unseeing eyes, immersed in his own thoughts. They left the tram when it reached the Solianka.

Christmas had come with heavy snowfalls, and the sky was dark with clouds, so that the grey daylight began to fade soon after midday.

The small detached house occupied by Naoum Robertovitch stood in a quiet courtyard, isolated from the outer world. The door was opened by a vivacious and smart maid with curled hair, wearing an English starched cap and apron such as Kiril had only seen on the films. It was clear that she was used to all sorts and conditions of visitors. A gramophone was playing a wild, gay foxtrot in an adjoining room, the sounds of the instruments being interrupted at intervals by caterwauling and the squeaks of children's trumpets, or the clash of cymbals, and it was all so bright and jolly that Kiril became pleasantly excited straightaway.

Naoum Robertovitch was standing in the doorway of the room in a wonderful crimson striped pullover. His hands in his pockets, he called with ponderous affability:

'Come in, young men, come in.'

He was so pleased with life that satisfaction oozed from the man's whole being, from his nostrils, from his beautifully parted, greying hair with curls so tight that it looked like astrakhan, from his short red neck looking as though it

183

had just been rubbed with a Turkish towel, from his big head with its prominent forehead that he lowered like a bull. It was probably with just that bull-like movement of the head that he pushed from success to success. Kiril felt at ease with him at once. The man made no secret of his wealth, his success or the cleverness with which he twisted life round his hairy fingers.

'Well, young men, we'll listen to the foxtrot till the ladies arrive, and, to give us an appetite, Nura will bring us each a cocktail.'

Nura, the smart maid who had opened the door to them, handed round the cocktails on a tray. She did it with cool assurance, not in the least like a girl in service, giving each of the men a pert look as he took his drink. At that moment, Cooperov suddenly emerged from the kitchen, gay and very red, suffused with the heat of the stove. He was cooking a goose according to some wonderful recipe.

'Ah, Kiril, old man,' he boomed with unnatural loudness, 'I'm busy . . .' Snatching a bottle of vinegar from a cupboard, he waved his hand, and rushed back to the kitchen. Everything somehow seemed very pleasant and unconstrained. It was as though a curtain had been drawn aside to give a glimpse of another – a wonderful life – carefree, fascinating, such a life as Kiril had never known. These people had every comfort, every pleasure, simply because they were rich. Money was at the root of it all, and the very gramophone, making enough din to bring the house down, seemed to be shouting that with money you could have a marvellous, ecstatic, inimitable life. . . .

Could it be possible that to achieve some semblance of this for himself, all he had to do was to hold his tongue, not tell Lebedkin everything? It was not even necessary for him to lie; he only had to hold his tongue. What was there to be ashamed of in the desire to have a little happiness, to be free from sordid cares, to enjoy the exquisite pleasure of a success won by one's own wits?

Naoum Robertovitch appeared to be an exceptional and remarkable man who knew exactly what to do with life, and how to bring variety into days which resembled each other with deadly monotony.

He would go to Lebedkin the next day if they told him to, he would lie if need be, he would do anything to extricate himself from the morass in which he seemed to have been floundering for the last few months.

His spirits rose as he looked forward to the future. Naoum Robertovitch had taken no particular notice of Kiril at first, but he went and sat by him before long, and nodding his head in time to the mad foxtrot, laid a hairy hand on the young man's knee.

'So Comrade Lebedkin is a friend of yours, I hear?' He asked, still nodding his head.

Kiril was delighted that he could answer boldly in the affirmative. Yes, Lebedkin was his friend, he had been the first to hold out a helping hand to him, and would do anything for him. He was a little excited by the feeling that this answer of his, showing that he was not without connections, somehow put him, the student Bessonov, on a level with this man of wealth.

Naoum Robertovitch patted Kiril's knee, and nodded with satisfaction, as he said: 'Good, splendid, my dear comrade.'

He did not ask anything else, but Kiril felt that he was no longer a mere, obscure student in his eyes, but a man of interest worth noticing. Soon afterwards the lively Nura ran to the front door, and the hum of merry women's voices and the fragrance of cold air and scent filled the hall. Naoum Robertovitch went out to greet his guests. Sverbeev sat down by Kiril and whispered with awe: 'Artistes from the Ballet!'

There were three artistes from the Ballet; two young

185

things with bobbed hair, one of them small and dark, looking like a good little boy, and the other fair-haired with extraordinarily limpid green eyes; and the third was an older woman, thin and as muscular as a horse, who lit a cigarette the moment she entered the room, her example being quickly followed by the other two. The women were rosy from the frosty air. They sat down, crossing slender legs encased in wonderful sheeny grey silk stockings, and looked appraisingly at the students.

A short, awkward silence was ended when the familiar tones of the gramophone put them at their ease, not with a foxtrot this time, but with the strains of a Charleston which made the women smile. Cooperov again dashed in a few minutes later and seized a pepperpot. Naoum Robertovitch then led the way to the dining-room.

Kiril stopped short on the threshold, dazzled by the display which met his eyes. Highly polished china, crystal tumblers, various wineglasses of emerald and ruby, were gleaming under an enormous, low-hanging lamp with a yellow silk shade. The table was laden with *hors d'oeuvre*, pale pink slices of smoked salmon, a great slab of cheese under a glass cover, a dish of black caviar surrounded by cracked ice that glittered like diamonds, and bottles showing gold or crimson in the light stood in stately dignity among the eatables, adding to the medley of colour and brightness.

'Please be seated, dear comrades,' said Naoum Robertovitch with ceremony in a solemn bass voice.

After a few seconds of confusion, while they were taking their places, Kiril found himself between Sverbeev and the thin dark girl who reminded him vaguely of Tania. Then he noticed, among the winebottles, short, squat, transparent decanters of vodka, the vanguard, the infantry, so to speak, of the feast.

'Look after your lady, comrade,' said his host from the

186

other side of the table, frowning significantly with his thick, beetling eyebrows in a way that made Kiril seize one of the decanters which were bedewed by the moisture condensed from the atmosphere. He filled a glass each for the girl, Sverbeev and himself, and the festive meal began to fulfil its promise of entertainment.

The vodka made him drunk at once, and he could never clearly remember the details of that amazing dinner-party. Everybody talked very loudly, there was an incessant clatter of knives and forks, dishes were emptied, the caviar was handed round for the tenth time, the delicate salmon disappeared, decanters were drained, but reserves were quickly brought up, and then Cooperov, in his jolliest mood, appeared from the kitchen, carrying on uplifted hands the uncrowned king, a fifteen-pound goose, stuffed with apples in accordance with some special recipe of his own. All this was lavishly washed down with wine from the slim-stemmed glasses, the women keeping pace with the men.

The smells of goose, of wine and of scent, all intermingled with the booming of the gramophone, seemed to be rising to the ceiling in spirals, while the curly-headed Nura stood in the doorway viewing the scene with a smile. Kiril had a very hazy memory of how they all got up, pushed back their chairs, and went into the next room. He followed, and found that the room in which the gramophone had just been playing was now nearly dark in the dimness of only one yellow-shaded lamp in the uplifted hand of a bronze bacchante. He sat down on a chair near the window, suddenly feeling miserably unhappy. Sverbeev, on a sofa, was whispering to the dark girl who reminded him of Tania. On another sofa, just under the moonlight rays of the lamp, his host was sitting by the thin woman, and there was something shameless about their immobility.

Utterly wretched, Kiril got up and went back to the dining room. But there he found Cooperov making the fair-haired dancer's large, pale green eyes stare and blink at something that he was whispering into her ear. He felt lonely amid the debris of the feast – the crumpled napkins, overturned glasses, orange-hued skins of tangerines. All the others were preoccupied with each other, and, still feeling miserable, he went into the passage. Through the open kitchen door he saw Nura, her curls showing beneath her goffered white cap. She seemed to him to be the only really distinguished person among them.

Scarcely conscious of what he was doing, he went into the kitchen. He did not want anything from her, he was simply terrified by the sense of isolation, and felt an urgent need for human intercourse. He shuddered suddenly as he stood before her, moved by memories which surged up in him, bringing tears to his eyes, and he began to talk disconnectedly about his life, about Tania, about the horrible new path that he had begun to follow. Nura listened for a time, and then with a meekness which was amazing, took his hand and led him into a little dark room opening out of the kitchen, where her bed stood and her black-framed photographs hung on the walls.

'You lie down on my bed,' she said. 'I'll be back in a minute.'

She helped him on to the bed, and he laid his cheek on the cool pillow. Then she slipped out of the room, saying that she would return directly. Happy now, though his cheeks were still wet with tears, he lay on her bed and waited. Then the bed rose and began to float away, carrying him with it, then it dipped horribly and began to sink. He clutched at the sides, afraid of falling off, and longed for Nura to return. She did come back very soon, and sat down by his side. In a blissful semi-consciousness, full of vague yearning, he stretched out his hand to touch her, and Nura said in a familiar, solemn low bass:

'Get up, comrade, we're going to drive out of town in taxis. You'll damned soon get rid of all this in the fresh air.'

He opened his eyes and saw the wonderful crimson pullover quite close to him. Naoum Robertovitch was sitting on Nura's bed beside him, shaking his shoulder. When he had roused him, he made him sit on the bed at his side for a moment, and then, drawing the beetling eyebrows together into his characteristic frown, he said:

'Dowse your head in cold water, and let's get out.'

He raised him quickly from the bed, and took him to the kitchen sink. He turned on the tap, and Kiril was almost choked and numbed by the jet of ice-cold water. He struggled to free himself, but Naoum Robertovitch held him firmly by the collar until he had come round completely. Still unsteady on his feet, but now fully conscious, Kiril wiped his forehead, and while he was doing so, Naoum Robertovitch pressed his little red-brown eyes and his hairy nostrils close to his face, and asked abruptly:

'Well, are we going to do business together, comrade? I hope you are up to the job, eh?'

Refreshed and revived, Kiril answered 'Of course we're going to do business.'

The others were already getting into their coats in the hall, and Nura with her inextinguishable smile, was helping the ladies to put on their overshoes. Kiril was ashamed to meet her eyes and took his coat into a corner. Naoum Robertovitch took him by the arm and led him out. Nura stood on the top step smiling her farewells to them. Going through the courtyard, they found a large black taxi throbbing at its gate. Six of them merrily crowded into it, while Kiril took the place next to the chauffeur. The whistling, frosty wind brought complete sobriety as it beat into his face. With hoots like the quacking of some monstrous duck, the car rushed rapidly through dim town thoroughfares, where men and women, huddled up in their wraps, were passing along or standing in groups at the brightly illuminated entrances of cinemas where gaudy posters promised to distract them, to take them out of themselves into the life of fairyland. The poorer and more shabby of the wayfarers were seeking their fairyland in beershops hazy with tobacco smoke.

Sobering more and more, Kiril looked at the familiar scenes filled with dread lest he should have to go back to all that to-morrow, resuming the dreariness of his existence. No, what he wanted was to go on careering in this carnival frolic, in this mad black car, out of town, to the gay night of light and glitter and music that Naoum Robertovitch had promised them. And he made up his mind that he would do whatever might be necessary, no matter what it was, with a feeling of satisfaction that his magnificent desires would be fulfilled.

At last, leaving the confinement of the town streets, the car, hooting triumphantly, rushed into the vast and mysterious snowy spaces of the beyond. Kiril was becoming cold, and a feeling of intoxication was returning to him in the bitter wind which blew into his face. He stared straight in front of him into a blackness scarcely touched by the few lamps of the suburb but seeming to him to be ablaze with blinding lights.

CHAPTER XXVIII

Birdie mine, birdie mine, pretty little birdie,
Blue are your eyes, beloved little birdie.
Apolon Gregoriev.

ON the outskirts of the village of Allsaints, they stopped at
a frame house which was to all appearances dead and deserted.
The wind was whistling round it in the telegraph wires, and
its unlit timber façade looked shabby and uninviting. Its
ill-smelling entrance was hardly distinguishable in the icy-
cold darkness. Holding on to each other, the whole party
tiptoed up an unusually creaky flight of steps. It was all
very mysterious and exciting. Cooperov gave two gentle
knocks at a feltbound door, and a formidable bearded face
appeared almost at once, its eyes gleaming so brightly that
their whites were discernible even in the dark. The man
admitted them, one by one, to a bare, formal room with an
air of never having been inhabited. When he turned up
the oil lamp, they saw that he was a Tzigan in a red cotton
shirt and velveteen breeches which hung over his topboots
like plus fours. Without saying a word, he led his guests,
still in hats and coats, through a dusty green curtain, and
they found themselves in another room, brightly lit by an
incandescent oil lamp which hung from the ceiling, with low
divans round the walls.

Coming towards them from another door, they saw a
group of Tzigan women with heavy eyebrows, wearing bright
silk dresses and shawls, followed by their cavaliers, whose
hair was well oiled, and whose cheeks were blue with harsh
stubble.

Naoum Robertovitch, still in hat and coat and with a

191

green muffler round his neck, threw a kiss toward the Tzigan women with his hairy fingers, and said:

'We've come to see you, dear comrades.'

The room at once became filled with the birdlike chatter of the women's throaty voices and the smell of scent and powder. So far as Kiril was concerned, the rest of the evening was a confused medley of silk shawls and thrumming guitars accompanying first Stesha, then Nastia, then Koucherov, and, finally, the whole choir together. Vodka was produced in great flagons, and the secretive little house very soon became the scene of such a noisy carousal of drinking merriment and mad excitement that it seemed as though its decrepit walls must give way, and eject the whole wild human crowd like lava to roll farther on its unchecked career, shattering the quiet of the night with its seething unrest.

Quite fuddled, and with his neck so red that it looked as though one could light a match at it, Naoum Robertovitch danced out into the middle of the room, and one of the women, with a long, expressionless white face, glided towards him. The loud thrumming of the guitar gave off bubbles of sound as though the strings were breaking. Kiril, becoming more and more drunk, was inexpressibly glad to be taking part in this jollification which need never come to an end if he would only take a little trouble.

As though in response to his thoughts, Sverbeev took a seat beside him, and, his eyes dull with vodka, his long nose shining, his breath reeking of alcohol, said:

'This is life, my boy, d'you see? Not your flypaper existence. Do you see how you ought to live? And it's all in your own hands, old chap, if you don't weaken or break down at the last moment. Come into the passage, and I'll show you something that will make you stare.'

He led Kiril into the cold room where the Tzigan had met

192

them when they arrived, and under its dim oil lamp he dragged a weird-looking dirty package from his pocket. He tapped the wad, and opened it to show Kiril a sheaf of white notes with numerals in their right hand top corner to indicate their values. Kiril was almost blinded by his amazement at the sight.

'You see?' whispered Sverbeev right into his ear. 'You see?' he repeated. 'That's the deposit from Naoum Robertovitch. If you don't funk it, you and I will go to-morrow and ask Lebedkin for a consignment of goods for the students, and we shall get good pickings out of the deal.'

He quickly thrust the wad back into his pocket. Overwhelmed, and with all his ideas about Lebedkin in confusion, Kiril stared at the spot where he had just seen the banknotes, and muttered almost mechanically, 'I shan't funk it – Lebedkin will give us anything I ask for.'

'Splendid! Meanwhile, enjoy yourself – some of the Tzigans are pretty, or would you like me to let you have the dark girl? Here, wait a minute, take these on account, you may have to see her home,' and, fumbling in his pocket, Sverbeev gave him two notes. Then they returned to the hot, crowded, smoke-laden room. The drunken merriment went on late into the night. The Tzigans sang their songs well, rustling their silks and rattling their bangles, and a sort of menagerie atmosphere added to the revelry that made one's head swim. About two o'clock they decided to go out for a drive in the park, the whole crowd, guitars and songs and all. Ruddy-cheeked drivers appeared as if by magic, and Naoum Robertovitch poured out vodka for them, while the Tzigans formed a ring round him, and clapping their hands sang in his honour:

'Let's drink to Naoum, to Naoum, our dearest,
And till we have drunk to him, we'll drink no more.'

Naoum Robertovitch himself took another glass of vodka

193

with the drivers, and then there was a bustling confusion as they sorted out their wraps. Kiril put on his coat and went down the steps. The air was cold on the dark porch. The brunette actress, whom Kiril did not at first recognise in her cloak and hood, was standing at the edge of the porch, holding on to the balustrade and obviously feeling very ill. Taking her by the shoulders, he helped her down the steps. Low sledges were standing in front of the gate, their shaggy horses jingling the silver-toned bells of their harness. The drivers were scrunching the snow as they stamped their feet. The starry, frosty night seemed to be making pure melody in contrast with the debauch which had been going on inside.

'I'm ill,' said the actress, leaning all her weight on Kiril's arm. He took her to the sleigh, and laid her carefully on the rugs. There was something childish about her low moans, and in her helplessness she reminded him of Tania. He got in beside her, gently pillowing her thin shoulder, and looking into her dark eyes to which the starlight gave an appearance of immensity. The rest of the party crowded noisily out of the house and took their places. The ancient song of the road tinkled out as the shaggy horses sped along the highway which was deserted at that hour of the night. The faint lamps of the village flickered like tiny specks, while the sky glowed in the distance from the reflection of the many lights of the great slumbering city.

A woman's voice broke into a sad, monotonous little song, and the voices of the other women took it up in its sadness. Then the deep tones of the men mingled with it, as though to provide a foundation for the high notes, while the stars swam on and on in all their winter brightness, and Kiril found a reflection of their limpid gleam in the dark eyes at which he was gazing with tender solicitude – eyes that recalled Tania and his vanished dream, eyes full of mystery,

194

thrilling him with their sad charm as he looked into their depths. Then, as the sleigh skidded, the frightened woman pressed close to him, and after that there was nothing – nothing but the creaking of the sledges, the jingle of the bells, and the moving strains of the Tzigan songs – as they made their way back to the town.

They drove round the park, and finally reached the barrier. Kiril woke up to find the Tzigans saying good-bye before going back. He left the sledge, and, still with his silent partner, got into a cab. Standing up in another sledge, Naoum Robertovitch was waving his beaver cap and shouting 'So long, dear comrades.'

Moscow came towards them through the night. An engine was shrieking under the viaduct, demanding right of way. Kiril's chance companion swayed to and fro in silence, leaning against his shoulder. His thoughts wandered. All sorts of ideas came and went, and he could not concentrate. The cab stopped eventually in front of a large six-storied house, and Kiril got out and paid the driver.

'The front door is locked, we shall have to go up the back way,' the girl said. Excited and full of longing, he led her through the gates, across the courtyard and up the service stairs which smelt of cats.

'Which floor do you live on?' he asked carelessly. He moved as though to embrace her, but she pushed him away from her with violence, and said in a tired voice that was full of hatred:

'Get out – can't you see that I'm ill? I hate you.' Leaning over the bannister, she began to moan convulsively.

Kiril went out into the courtyard, took off his cap, rubbed his temples with snow, and, still uncovered, his hair silvered by the snow, he stumbled into the street, into the night, sick with pain and misery.

Still limp from the orgy of the night and vaguely conscious of the nightmares which had filled his few hours of broken sleep, Kiril went with Sverbeev to the enormous building in which Lebedkin worked. He had not seen Lebedkin since the day of their first meeting. He still felt twinges of remorse, but he knew now that nothing would turn him from the course upon which he had decided the day before.

Two lifts in the hall were speeding up and down like enormous gilded birdcages. A man in uniform turned a silver wheel, and the lift glided up, carrying them to the fifth floor. In the long white corridor with its doors of frosted glass, it was as quiet as a hospital. In Lebedkin's office, the complicated pattern of the parquet floor was brilliant with polish. Two men carrying portfolios were waiting there, and a typist near the window was vigorously tapping her machine.

Diagrams consisting of columns and squares of red, yellow and white covered the walls. Life here seemed to be governed by time-tables, and that perhaps was why everyone spoke in whispers.

A secretary came in from an inner room in a few minutes, with a folio of official papers. He took down the names of the students on a memorandum form as a preliminary to their interview with Lebedkin.

Kiril entered his study with a faint sense of uneasiness. He and Sverbeev had long ago agreed what each of them should say, but whatever he said would be false, and he was about to lie for the first time to the man who had opened life's doors for him.

Lebedkin looked very forlorn and lost in the huge room where everything was arranged in such order that one had to lower one's voice still more. He was just as bony as ever, and his neck was bandaged because of his perpetual carbuncles. He sat sideways on his chair in front of a table on which there was a telephone standard with two receivers.

He gave the students a warm welcome, and looked at Kiril with friendly eyes while he listened to them. He looked at their petition, and made a mark in one corner of it with a blue pencil.

'Take this to the third floor, and they'll tell you what to do,' he said kindly; and then, leaning back in his chair, he asked Kiril in a searching tone:

'Well, how are you getting on? Given up those ideas of yours?'

If Lebedkin had looked at him more intimately at that moment, if he had put his hand on his shoulder as he had done before, if he had questioned him further, perhaps Kiril would have confessed, would have burnt his boats; because here, with Lebedkin, was truth, whereas outside there was such a labyrinth of lies, such a maze, that he would never be able to find his way out.

But at that moment the telephone bell rang, and all warmth had gone from Lebedkin's tones when, picking up the receiver, he began to talk; and, the longer he talked the more bored and official became his voice as he discussed an inflated account, and the more feeble became Kiril's impulse. Lebedkin finished his telephone conversation, and turned again to them, but his face no longer had the same expression.

They said good-bye, and a moment later were on their way downstairs. There were many people running up and down with papers in their hands, and Kiril had a feeling that he was in reality descending the precarious steps of his own life. But the feeling vanished almost as quickly as it had come.

Sverbeev undertook to look after all that remained to be done. He disappeared in mystery for several days, visiting Naoum Robertovitch and dashing in and out of the volcanic headquarters of syndicates in pursuit of his consignment.

197

Just how it was all done, Kiril never knew, but he met Sverbeev and Cooperov in the studio one evening when the whole scheme had been carried out.

'Well,' said Sverbeev, winking at Cooperov, 'it's done. I'm jolly glad you didn't play the fool, Kiril. Let's count up what we've made.'

His hand dived into his pocket with a familiar movement, and drew out a thick wad of mauve and white notes which he spread out on the table like a fan. Kiril gazed at all this wealth with uncomprehending, unbelieving eyes. Cooperov shuffled the notes together like a pack of cards, tapped their edges on the table to straighten them, and began to count. He went on counting for some time, but finished at last, and Sverbeev asked under his breath:

'How much?'

'Twelve hundred,' answered Cooperov, and moving quickly close to Kiril gripped his knee firmly and said 'Well, what are you going to do with all that money? We've skimmed off four hundred each, like cream. It is cream. Four hundred for you, Kiril Bessonov. Twenty months' allowance at one go – and no questions asked. Sverbeev managed the deal very cleverly.'

Rapidly counting out a dozen notes, he handed them to Kiril. 'Take them, citizen, take them, and count them. And if you don't want to prove yourself a born fool, Cooperov will show you how to double, to treble, them, perhaps how to increase them tenfold. You understand, don't you? I'll teach you all about it, and I won't charge you anything for the lessons. See?'

Through a haze of mingled shame and ecstasy, Kiril looked first at Cooperov's triumphant expression, and then at the notes which he held in his hand. Cooperov let him fold them and put them in his pocket, and then continued to instruct him in the noble art of living beautifully.

CHAPTER XXIX

FOUR years before, when he had done with war, Lebedkin had been horrified by the monotony and hatefulness of the life which confronted him.

The great capital had lived a normal life, its residents had gone on surrounding themselves with children and household chattels, while tempests raged on steppes and highroads. They went about their business, came home, passed on rumours, quarrelled over promotions, and nursed the infants that came in such numbers just in those terrible years. When Lebedkin had to return from the front to make a report or take part in a conference, he lived anyhow, anywhere, like a soldier on campaign, and he felt no craving for the comforts of home life.

Yes: four years earlier he had returned to Moscow, having done with war, and had to live that hard, drab life which was the lot of everyone: in the morning he went to his work, in the evening he returned to his solitude in order to escape from the gossip, the grousing, the quarrels that surrounded him. He devoted himself to his new work calmly and rationally with his characteristic earnestness. The task of reconstruction involved a great deal of drudgery. The whole immense country was beggared, homeless, brutalised. But after a time, little by little, a few factory chimneys began to smoke here and there. The maps and diagrams produced at economic conferences seemed to have been prepared for an unattainable Utopia. But, year by year, the diagrams showed an increase of smoking chimneys: ruined walls were being re-erected, machinery was being installed, and new centres of production began to make their appearance. How great is man's capacity for faith! Typhus had raged, nay, was still raging, all over the land, laying low the herds of human beings who were transported in railway trucks which were virulent with germs. And yet here were these beautiful maps showing prospective electric power-stations which would harness the latent and hitherto untamed forces of the great rivers. The whole scheme seemed phantasmagorial.

Meanwhile the incessant drudgery dragged on: book-keeping, making accounts balance, estimates, appropriations – figures, figures, dull statistics which he began by hating. Steadfastly and systematically he studied the columns of figures until he got caught up in the romance of it before he was aware of it.

Just as it was a visionary ideal on the battlefield that had made the daily sacrifice of human blood seem worth while, not too great a price to pay for achievement, so here, within these prosaic walls, confronted by nothing more dangerous than columns of figures, Lebedkin was sustained by his inspired dreams of the future. There, for the sake of an ideal, man had wrought cruel destruction; here, for the sake of an ideal, man must labour without flinching. Planning, calculating, estimating costs in his office, he had always before him the new vision that provided the incentive for all his toil.

It was just a year since the Textile Syndicate had laid their plans and proposals before him. They were so complicated, such a bewildering structure of costs and prices, that it was like besieging a paper fortress to attack them. But he set to work with method. How was it that while these fine paper fortresses were being erected with such success there was still a dearth of textiles? Why were the shops beset by long queues of eager men and women? Why was it that every yard of calico produced cost so much before it reached the peasant? How was it that the raw materials never arrived on time, with the consequence that the whole routine of the factories was disorganised?

Step by step, line by line, he unravelled the tangle. He found lack of co-ordination everywhere, and on all sides corruption, carelessness, and a low standard of output. He tackled the problem with enthusiastic ardour. To achieve a reduction of half a farthing in the production cost of a yard of cotton gave him the same feeling that he had experienced over every step forward gained when he was at the front.

Within a year he had been able to introduce new measures involving a very accurate plan of campaign for the lowering of costs, a perpetual warfare waged from within the walls of the paper fortress. Firmly, patiently, stubbornly, he fought on to achieve the ends which he had set for himself. In a year he reduced prices, improved quality, and nearly doubled the output. It looked as though success was to crown his hours and days of fruitful toil.

But something strange and incomprehensible was happening, something which, to his horror, seemed to nullify all his gigantic efforts, something stupid and irrational. There were the same queues outside the shops, prices on articles sold by private traders continued to rise, and there was the same smouldering discontent over the lack of goods. Some hidden hand was ruining his work. In spite of all the figures he could show on paper, he was being beautifully tricked by mysterious dealers. Lebedkin felt that he was being overreached, losing his grip on his new task. He began to lose his self-confidence, no longer felt certain that all that he had done during the year was wise and well-considered, that he had taken the only possible course. Life seemed to be teaching him that he had been wrong.

After the students had left him, his mind became full of the vicious circle from which he could see no way of escape.

He worked on in his study, receiving petitions and talking incessantly over the telephone that stood in front of him. He had a conference at five o'clock, and in the half hour interval which he allowed himself between that and his day's work, he looked through the newspapers and hurriedly swallowed the dinner brought to his room by a girl messenger from the dining-room downstairs.

The Director of Syndicates was to read a paper at the conference on 'Methods of Production and the Depreciation of Machinery.' On entering the conference room, Lebedkin immediately began to make notes on a large memorandum pad. He must obtain a licence for the importation of new machinery; he must persuade the Transport Commission to lower the freight rates on raw materials; he must organise the inspection of private traders; he must make arrangements to enable the network of co-operative stores to become centres of distribution, and to co-ordinate the needs of individual districts with the general scheme; five truckloads of goods must be sent to Turkestan and measures must be taken for that. He wrote on and on. The whole of the vast country was included in his notes. Russia was alive, she must go on living, and every yard of material which reached a workman at Penza or a Sard in Tashkend would help her a little on the long and difficult path which she must tread.

It was thus that Lebedkin buried himself in the work which had at first seemed so repellant, concentrating all his energies on overcoming the many obstacles by which he was confronted.

CHAPTER XXX

NAOUM ROBERTOVITCH spent his days in a very different fashion. He woke at about eight o'clock, and then lay luxuriating for a quarter of an hour under his blue satin bedcovers. At half-past eight, still in his pyjamas and slippers, he went to his dressing room, where he stayed till nine scheming and thinking out how best to organise his programme. Nura laid breakfast in the dining-room and brought the morning papers to him – *The News*, *Truth*, *Economic Life* and *The Moscow Labour Gazette*. His favourite reading was found in the crime columns. He had just finished shaving his left cheek with a safety razor, when the telephone bell rang. Still stroking his cheek with the steel blade, he went to the 'phone. The laconic conversation which ensued would have seemed to any outsider to be of a purely domestic nature.

'Aunt Mary?' repeated Naoum Robertovitch. 'Oh yes; Aunt Mary is due to-day. The price of a ticket from Minsk? Well, with hard seats it's thirty-four and with upholstered seats about forty; Ha, ha – ' And he began to laugh. 'It's not I who fix the prices, you now, it's the Railway Commission. All right, give me the address. Aunt Mary arrives about five. How much luggage will she have? Well, how much can you take in without inconveniencing yourself? Five or six boxes? Very well, I'll tell her. So long.'

He was obviously pleased as he put down the receiver, and, humming to himself, returned to the mirror to finish shaving.

At ten he was in the dining-room, eating a ham omelet and reading the newspapers, but all the while he was pressing the receiver to his ear with his shoulder. 'More defalcations, more defalcations, what a country!' he exclaimed, as he took a piece of ham on his fork with one hand, while he rattled the telephone receiver with the other.

'Citizeness, will you put me through? Yes, yes, I want central – '

There were so many things to be done before he began his real business day at eleven: there were various people to ring up, there were the papers to be read, there were his opinions on the misappropriations and various trials to be given to Nura.

All his telephone conversations were concerned with domestic matters. They were either about the arrival of Aunt Mary, who was ill, or with someone who asked him for the loan of thirty gramophone records, or some intimate friend who rang up to say that he was bringing a complete file of 'Fire,' to amuse Aunt Mary in her illness. The names given were 'Seeme' or 'Ready,' or the like, and one merry jester said that he was an inspector of audits and that his name was 'Baitman.'

Naoum Robertovitch laughed and gurgled into the telephone while he talked to them and read his newspapers. At last he finished, changed his slippers for rubber-soled boots, breathing heavily with the exertion of lacing them, his neck at that moment looking the colour of raspberry syrup. Then he put on a well-tailored suit which very considerably masked the defects of his figure. Thus arrayed and very pleased with himself, he stood for a moment before the mirror arranging the bow of his butterfly tie before he went into the hall. Nura helped him on with a somewhat shabby khaki overcoat and handed him an Astrakan cap, and in them he looked so ordinary that he would not attract any attention.

Then he left the house, and waited for a tram. He got into the rear coach, buried his face in his collar, and sat hunched up throughout the journey. Now and then he breathed on the frost-covered window, scratched off a bit of ice about the size of a halfpenny, and peered at the streets through the peephole. There was a queue outside a draper's shop over-flowing from the pavement into the road. There was a militiaman guarding the door to prevent the crowd from rushing it, and now and again mounted militiamen pushed their way through to clear a passage for ordinary pedestrians, or thrust back the queue when it impeded the traffic.

Naoum Robertovitch buried his face again. He got off at Sverdlov Square. The Great Theatre was covered with hoarfrost, its brown pillars a glittering white, its four green bronze horses rearing towards the winter sky. There was a bluish haze over everything, and in the distance, beyond the Kremlin walls, was the pale disc of the sickly sun. The large plate glass window of a general store was already being lit up. A few yards farther along there was a dense black crowd in front of two drapers' shops.

He cast a passing glance at the familiar picture, and made his way to a little café in a side street, which temptingly displayed in its window a row of glasses heaped high with whipped cream. A printed notice announced with biblical simplicity 'All the Children of Moscow Come to Eat our Cream.'

In this haven, Naoum Robertovitch made a pause in his journey. He sat down at a little table near the window and ordered a glass of whipped cream; for the most serious, the busiest of men may surely sometimes indulge in dainties. Every spoonful seemed to soothe his stomach as it spread over it.

It happened that an acquaintance came in before long. He, too, was wearing an unostentatious overcoat and cap. His expressionless face was slightly pockmarked. He sat down, putting his thick despatch case on a chair by his side, and ordered a proletarian cup of tea. When his tea had been brought by a girl in an apron, he propped his head on his hands, and, with an air rather of listening than of talking, said:

'What is the commission?'

'Ten per cent. all round,' said Naoum Robertovitch, licking his spoon on both sides. 'You'd better tell me how many of them there are waiting.'

'About four hundred altogether, I should say, in the city as a whole: two hundred invalided soldiers, and the rest women with babies.'

'They'd better take the thin materials; it's a bit late in the season for the thick ones; time to think about spring.'

The shabby man began to implore Naoum Robertovitch to raise the percentage to fifteen – it was cold, the woman had their babies with them, even the maimed ex-service men had to wait for their turn now. But Naoum was in-exorable: 'I should be giving it away at fifteen,' he said, and it was obvious that he was disinclined to discuss the matter further.

The shabby man finished his tea, and said 'It's a sheer loss,' and, with a gesture that seemed to wave Naoum aside, got up, and left the café.

Naoum Robertovitch ate his last spoonful of cream, paid at the desk with the air of one who is annoyed at having dealings with low acquaintances, and went out.

He walked down the street, pleasantly aware of the recurring flavour of the cream, paused for a moment at a shop window full of quaint bric-à-brac, and went into a café with a beautiful signboard, bearing the words 'Des Gourmets.'

He ordered a cup of Warsaw coffee, and while he was sipping it, again it happened that an acquaintance entered. This time it was a dark-eyed, admirably shaven young man in a monkey-skin cap, and a smart short coat trimmed with the same fur.

'Naoum Robertovitch!' He exclaimed in pleased surprise, as he sat down at the same table. The young man was obviously a well-known customer in the caéf, for he was called away to the telephone several times during their conversation.

'What's the price, Naoum Robertovitch?' he asked, 'and how much can you supply?' He spoke softly, and stuck his little finger out gracefully while he stirred his coffee. He was obviously a well-bred young man.

'I can offer you six lots to-day, all heavy cotton goods, c.o.d.,' said Naoum, puckering up his forehead as though calculating.

The six lots were what Sverbeev had obtained. The goods had already been broken up into small packets that could be sent by parcels post. They were only waiting to be addressed. Other consignments were also ready for despatch to the provinces, or even to the Caucasus or Siberia, week by week. Nothing was retained for retailing in Moscow. That was a basic principle in the whole business.

Purchasing agents, girls, women with babies, wounded soldiers, stood in a dozen queues in the intense cold, and all that they obtained went through Naoum Robertovitch, to private traders in the provinces. Those who stood in the queues were paid ten per cent. on the purchase price; Naoum Robertovitch got five per cent., and the private traders raised the prices as much as they could get their customers to give. Enormous consignments put on the market in Moscow thus disappeared with incredible rapidity.

Lebedkin had tried in vain to discover what was at the bottom of all the jobbery over the manufactured goods which were being turned out in quantities. What he had estimated and calculated as sufficient yesterday, was swept up by the insatiable human avalanche of to-morrow; and, for the first time, he began to lose confidence in himself.

The young man sitting opposite to Naoum Robertovitch was the representative of the private traders. In various inconspicuous back premises, large fortunes were being made at this game.

'We must all eat,' said Naoum to the young man, 'and so must I. The seller may add another fifteen per cent.: that's no business of mine. I only take five, and I won't take a farthing less. You know my terms.'

With much play of his eyebrows, and with the graceful air of discussing the latest theatrical production, the young man tried flattery and cajolery. He used every conceivable argument in vain. At last he took out his handkerchief, wiped his damp forehead, and leant back in his chair. This man was a rock, and he was only wasting his time.

In ten minutes, they had concluded an agreement by which the parcels should be sent c.o.d. through the Moscow post office. The young man gave the addresses of the provincial middlemen, and left the café with an air of disappointment. Naoum Robertovitch finished his coffee, and looked at the square dial of his wrist watch. It was a quarter to one. He must hurry if he did not want to be too late for the bank. On reaching it, he took off his overcoat and his new fashioned overshoes, and went upstairs. On one of the broad tables he filled in a transfer form: every month he sent to a certain Mr. Friedland in Esthonia the equivalent of fifty dollars, the amount permitted by the government.

The rest of his day was varied. In a café in Ilinkla Street he met three contractors who proposed to build a large five-story house on the Novinsk Boulevard, the flats of which were to be sold on very profitable terms. First of all he demanded the estimates, and then the matter was discussed.

At half-past three, he dined with two journalists at the Authors' Dining Club, took some vodka, felt drowsy, and went home to have a nap. Nura, alone and bored, was singing in the kitchen to her own accompaniment on a guitar. He gave her a paternal squeeze as he took off his scarf. Nura drew down the blinds, switched off the telephone, and the cosy house was soon trembling with deep snores. Naoum Robertovitch was renewing his strength for the evening.

He slept till six. Then Nura woke him up, switched on the telephone, and brought him a glass of hot tea. His cheek bore the imprint of the pattern embroidered on his pillow, as he sat drinking the first and then a second glass of tea. By that time he was fully awake.

Then the telephone began to ring: more enquiries about Aunt Mary, this time concerning the sort of cigarettes she smoked. Naoum Robertovitch chortled with content; a successful day was ending well.

Then all kinds of women's voices called him up, and so amused him that at last it could not be said that he was speaking, but spluttering or purring into the telephone; and he even snapped his fingers once or twice. None of this was in any way serious, of course, but mere chatter for his amusement. He only talked seriously to the thin ballet dancer who had been at the party. He promised to fetch her at a quarter to eight to take her to a comic opera. Then he rang up the theatre and asked for two seats, but not too near, about the seventh row of the stalls. He was always discreet.

He left the house early enough to give himself time to go to the ballet dancer by motor bus, and stood in the street long and patiently waiting for it.

The day's work was over; now he could rest, amuse himself, listen to some jolly music; and the huge-eyed bus carried him back to real life.

CHAPTER XXXI

Then and there, in the studio, sitting beside Kiril and affectionately patting his knee, Cooperov proceeded to teach him how to double, to treble, or perhaps even increase tenfold the cream which they had skimmed off.

'Ever tried to play?' he said.

'How do you mean, "play"?' asked Kiril in puzzled surprise.

'Well, obviously I don't mean the piano. I mean the real thing; can't you understand? Chemin-de-fer or baccarat? Do you know how to play chemin-de-fer?'

'Look here,' Sverbeev interrupted him, 'that's a two-edged tool. You'd better not start that sort of thing. You go in a prince, and come out a pauper.'

'You're a fool, Sverbeev,' said Cooperov contemptuously. 'Do you suppose that if I take him in hand I shan't look after him? I never play unless I'm certain to win. It's not a simple game by any means, and you have to be pretty smart and clever to make your two beat an eight; but there isn't a point in it that I don't know.

'Don't you listen to that long-nosed fellow, but just take my advice. Come here to-morrow or any other evening, and we'll go to the Monte Carlo Casino. You'll find all the animals in two's and two's there: an embezzler who has come for a change of air, and a detective watching him in the interests of the people he's robbed. It's crowded with all sorts and conditions of men, and every single one of them wants to win, not to win just a trifle and then bow and go away, but a fortune straight off, twenty thousand or so. And that can't be done. But if you make it a hard and fast rule to go away the moment you have skimmed off a spoonful of cream – you can go every night, and every night can make a bit.'

Cooperov's nonsense amused Kiril. He had a large sum of money in his pocket, he had never had anything like it before, and he was eager for fun, for the sort of life he had never known. Even if any thought of the Institute, with its lectures and examinations, had crossed his mind, he would have dismissed it as beneath consideration. His thoughts of Tania were fading, he was losing that vision, just as he had lost so many others by the wayside. No, there could be no turning back, he had done with visions; Sverbeev was right, there was no room for visionaries nowadays. He would be expelled as a failure in the spring – well, by that time, with Cooperov's assistance and a bit of luck, he might be rich, so that he could publish his first book of poems and make himself famous.

Stimulated by thoughts of that sort, he lent a ready ear to Cooperov. Cooperov talked well, and if only a tenth of what he said was true, he would have funds enough for a lifetime. If one went out looking for happiness, one must look for it everywhere, alike in the highways and the byways, one must not ignore the narrowest of lanes.

Cooperov's lesson went on and on –

Kiril felt unusually elated next day as he walked about the streets, pressing his elbow against the protuberance in his pocket which was the earnest of his success and happiness. He had awakened early, and had lain for a long time thinking of the coming day with its promise of new and strange experiences.

The students, after a cup of tea, or perhaps of only hot water, had scattered in every direction: some to lectures, some to the laboratories, some to look for employment, hurrying to the Labour Exchanges to hire themselves out to unload trains or to clean streets, working and slaving just to keep themselves alive. Life was no easy thing for the inmates of the hostel, where every dawn saw the renewal of a bitter struggle for existence. It was full of dogged young peasants who had flocked to it from all parts of the country, moved by ambition and hope, who were now wrinkling their brows in their efforts to lay, stone by stone, the foundations of their futures. There was not one of them who had so much as an inkling of the life of which Kiril had had a glimpse, a life in which nobody worked like a slave, an easy life spreading out its arms to those who knew how to seize and hold them. A little knowledge, a little cunning, a bit of luck – he would, indeed, have startled his fellow-students if he had shown them what he had in his left hand pocket; but to-morrow he might double it, next day he might treble it – Yes, if the Blue Bird flies in at your door, you must know how to keep it.

He left the hostel early, and wandered tirelessly about the town. He stopped for a long time in front of the windows of shops into which he could now go to buy what he liked, rejoicing in the sensation that he had become one of those who have made good.

He called for Cooperov at half-past nine as they had agreed. They drank three glasses of vodka each before leaving the studio, just to buck them up, and indeed, they both felt very full of dash when they started. The night was much less cold, winter was breaking up, and through the clear windows of their tram they could see the town beneath its heavy burden of melting snow. They had to change trams before they could get to the Casino, the brilliantly illuminated entrance of which offered a hospitable welcome to all devotees of the goddess of fortune. Provincial embezzlers who, as Cooperov had put it, had come to Moscow for a change of air, stopped entranced at the sight of the dazzling blue grey light of the spherical lamps, and were under a spell as they made their awe-stricken way into the building.

Cooperov and Kiril handed their wraps to black-coated attendants, paid a rouble each to a venerable old man at the foot of the staircase, and mounted the broad stone steps. Kiril was struck by his first sight of the real thing, which hitherto he had seen only as pictured on the films. Enormous oval tables, so thickly strewn with bright-hued playing cards that they looked like green lawns studded with flower beds, were surrounded by seated players. At each table, on a chair somewhat higher than the others, sat an extremely polite and elegant young man. Some of these young men were clean-shaven, like actors, and some had short-clipped military moustaches. They might have been the conductors of some strange silent orchestra of odd musicians. The long-handled flat scoops which they held were like living limbs in the dexterity with which they passed cards round to those who required them. With extraordinary agility, the young men caught the cards on their thin scoops, passing them round, and depositing them on the table in front of those who wanted to try their luck, and, in like manner gathering up the cards at the end of the deal and pushing them through slotted openings in the table. From time to time, mysterious lights of varied hues shone down on the table, bells tinkled as though to signal the departure of a train, and the wooden tray with the cards began another journey of enchanting danger, passing round from player to player.

The young men, in colourless voices, devoid of emotion or sympathy, would announce 'Baccarat,' or 'Put on your stakes, gentlemen,' or 'Your card, citizen.'

And all round, packed closely together, but each of them shunning his neighbours as though they were wolves, sat men who had come to this weird roundabout, with its cries, its cards, its bells and its green and red lamps, in pursuit of happiness. Other men were standing behind the seated players, full of sympathy, suffering with them, and always ready with advice. They could not go on playing themselves, but they could not tear themselves away from the sight of the defeats and victories of others, which were the replicas of their own losses and winnings. With an ingratiating air, they offered brotherly counsel to anyone who was in doubt as to taking a risk. They felt that they must get the confidence of the players, must, as it were, become members of their circle and take a vicarious part in the game though no longer having any material stake in it.

Piles of paper money kept changing hands – slumbering, latent forces, which, to-morrow, might awaken in mighty activity.

Somewhat mystified by the scene, Kiril approached one of the tables. It was still early, so there were not many players, and Cooperov took a hawk-eyed survey of the room to find an advantageous place. He wanted a seat where the player on his left, who would be holding the bank, would not be likely to demand high bids for the cards, and the player on his right would be an eager buyer. It was on considerations of that kind that his system was based. At last he found what suited him, between an elderly man with ruddy cheeks who played carefully and cautiously, and a nervous, shabby Armenian who was constantly counting his money under the table He took his place, and Kiril stood behind him, watching Cooperov's tobacco-stained fingers with their promise of good luck.

Cooperov began to play unostentatiously, and with caution, winning very small stakes, pending broader and more daring action. He did not let Kiril take any part in the game until it was his own turn to hold the bank. Then

he gave him a ten rouble share, and prepared for the attack.
The twenty roubles in the bank were covered by two players
on his right. Cooperov drew the cards from the wooden
case. Holding his first card close to his near-sighted eyes,
the Armenian murmured in a stifled voice:

'I want a card.'

Cooperov looked at his own card, gave the Armenian
a red king, and the twenty roubles of his adversaries came to
the bank.

Cooperov dealt again, and again the Armenian and
another shabby man in a worn coat punted and lost. He
only dealt three times, and then sold the bank. He had won
nearly a hundred and sixty roubles in his three deals. Kiril's
one white note had become eighty roubles. He was filled
with exultant confidence in success, with the certainty
that here and now he had found a basis for his future.
He was suffused with a delicious, warm glow. Gambling,
gambling – that would waft one lightly over the abyss!
Fortunes were probably made here by thousands. Of course
what he was doing now was not the way, he must take his
place at the oval table, decide for himself, try his own luck,
instead of simply standing behind Cooperov.

Cooperov, however, would not allow him to play that
night. He himself let three full rounds go by, holding the
bank twice more and making another two hundred and
forty roubles. Then, rising as though only for a moment,
he winked at Kiril, and they left the room together.

'How much have you made?' asked Cooperov. 'Two
hundred? I've made the same amount, and now we're off.
You can stay here just five minutes too long, lose all you've
won and some of your own besides. The whole point in
playing is to know when to stop. I've learnt the trick
now; but I paid a pretty big price for the lesson, see?'

He led Kiril down the stairs exultantly. From there they

went and had some beer at an underground place on the Arbat where there was a Tzigan choir.

The street lights had become torches marching in a triumphal procession. What had seemed to Kiril to be utterly unattainable a week ago had now all the glorious reality of actual achievement.

The café closed at half-past one, and Kiril took leave of Cooperov, overflowing with sentiment which was considerably enhanced by alcohol. He did not want to go back to the hostel, but could not think of any other place. Then Vera suddenly came into his mind, filling him with feelings of tender joy.

He had not seen her for a month, not since Tania's death but that did not matter. They were quite used to not meeting. They did not mind, and made no effort to see each other until some special urge arose. Then they would resume their relations without asking any questions, and with no great expectation that their next separation would be any shorter.

Vera was at home, mounting some photographs which she had just been colouring to serve as posters for a cinema.

'Hallo, is that you, Kiril?' she said, looking at him haughtily with her shameless grey eyes. 'I'd given you up; you can't expect me to play the widow.'

But she was not serious, only joking, and she delighted him by the familiar gesture with which she raised her hand and took off his cap.

CHAPTER XXXII

In the New Year, after severe January frosts, the winter showed distinct signs of breaking up. The days gradually lengthened, and the February sun was already warm enough to bring the icicles tinkling down from gutters and pipes and the slithering of the snow down the roofs in great rolls that looked like huge bolsters.

Kiril had been three times to the Casino with Cooperov in three weeks, but he had not once been allowed to play, and he had been carried off as soon as Cooperov had made a few winnings. Added to what he had begun with, Kiril's capital had now increased to seven hundred and thirty roubles. He spent two hundred on clothes. The future seemed to hold nothing but good fortune, yet he grew more and more gloomy day by day. Why should he be feeling so miserable now that he was already on the road to success?

Everything at the Institute was going on as usual. The students were busily getting ready for their examinations or for the practical work of the summer vacation. But Kiril had torn himself away from all these activities of his recent associates. He felt that he was a stranger within the gates, and he was horrified now by the thought that he would be expelled, though the first prospect of that probability had not in the least disturbed him. How was he going to live? How could he face Lebedkin and Yagodkin, those friends who had had such faith in his capacity for work and success in his desire to acquire knowledge. If he had already obtained recognition as a poet, not merely in the house where the Poets' Circle met but by the general public, it might have been possible for him to plead that he had

217

relinquished his studies for the sake of his talent. But he hardly ever wrote poetry now. He had no inspiration, it was just stringing words together. Had he really exhausted all he had to say? Had Lebedkin been right when he warned him against the devastating influences of the big city? But there were thousands of his kind at the universities, at the Institute, building their future, full of hope and faith, creating, giving lessons, unloading trucks of firewood: they were not exhausted, their strength was not undermined by such thoughts as began more and more insistently to assail him.

Tania had not had the courage to go on living when her life had gone wrong. She was weak, and how many such fragile blossoms had been blown away by the harsh winds of Moscow? If it was really impossible for him to extricate himself from the meshes in which he had become entangled, would not that be the simplest way out, to find the solution of everything in one stroke? He thought of this very often for it seemed to offer the only means of escape and to obviate all fears for the future, no matter what disasters it might hold.

He must, in any case, have money to prevent him from being left in the hopelessly degrading position of the man who finds himself penniless. This thought was his constant obsession, and it was that which made him, one memorable evening, take the decision which drove him along the road that led him to disaster. He made up his mind to try his luck by himself, without anyone's advice. Cooperov was away, making a film at some distance from Moscow, so that Kiril had no fear of meeting him on the fatal evening. He decided that he would play with the same cautious cunning as his master. He set fifty roubles aside from his other money, in a separate pocket, to determine his fate. Either, if he began by winning, it would enable him to increase his stakes, or, he would lose just that much. In either case, he would leave the Casino never to return to it.

He tingled to his very fingertips with the excitement of anticipation which always assailed him when he entered the gaming room. He would go alone that night without any mentor, and would take his place at the table as a competent player handling his own money, and not just fidgeting from foot to foot behind someone else's chair.

He was so excited, so obsessed by his one idea, that he could hardly get through the day, and by half past ten he was already in the Casino. It welcomed him with its bright lights and its mirrors and the promising rustle of bank notes.

A young man with the noble face of a well-fed Caesar, wearing a remarkably fashionable collar and a striped bow tie, gave him a sharp look, and then, in tones which were like those of a parrot and yet alluring and respectful, waving his hand toward one of the tables, he said: 'There is a free place there, monsieur; on your right, the second bank.'

He had not enough courage to refuse, and sat down on the oak chair, trembling. There were about a dozen men playing at this table, and Kiril took them in at a glance. Next to him on his right was the shabby Armenian with whom Cooperov had played on the first evening. He came every night. Farther on was a timid young man in a neat beige lounge suit, who was handling big money. He punted at random, and bought all the banko that were offered, all of them immediately breaking in his unlucky hands. In all probability he was an official sent on some special mission to Moscow from the provinces, who had been using government money and was now doing his best in his ineptitude to rid himself of all there was left.

With a look of terror on his childish pink face, he kept turning to his neighbour, a sombre and concentrated man whose artificial metal left hand clinked when he used it, making one think of mediaeval armour. He was winning gloomily, with never a gleam to brighten his solemnity, as though he had made up his mind to wipe this pink creature ruthlessly from the face of the earth.

Beyond them was a Chinaman with an effeminate yellow face, probably one of the pedlars who sell silk belts and little bags in the Loubiansk market. He often showed his yellow teeth as though rejoicing in his participation in this gay life, in spite of the fact that he was losing as hopelessly as the provincial embezzler. Farther down, near the sharper curve of the egg-shaped table, were others, most of them looking shabby and tired, the only conspicuous figures among them being a Sard with a handsome face, who looked exotic in his pale blue robe, handling the cards with reverence, and an old forester, with a beard like a bear-skin, gnarled as an old tree, and with the appearance of having been roughly carved out of wood with an axe. How had the woodman got here? Had he come as a warning to all this urban scum? However that might be, he had plenty of money tucked away in his topboots, and from time to time he pulled out a rag with one of his hairy hands, untied it, and flung down his offering on the altar of this pagan temple.

All these men round Kiril looked at him cautiously, as though watching to see how the newcomer would behave. The well-fed Caesar, however, was all graciousness from the first, and seemed to be promising good luck. The wooden scoop, like a boat sailing steadily over the green sea of passion, reached Kiril.

'Your bank, Monsieur,' cried the croupier in his pleasant though parrot-like voice.

Trembling, Kiril laid down ten roubles, and dealt the first cards. With omnious slyness, the Armenian raised his cards to his very nose, and then flung them down as if they burnt his eyebrows. A mocking nine of spades lay on the table beside a mournful queen. There was no hope for Kiril; the bank had been broken at the first shot, and, with unseemly haste, the Armenian took the ten rouble note and added it to his little heap of money. Once more the case made a move on its way round the table.

The Chinaman held the bank. With a faint smile that revealed his lemon-coloured teeth, he dealt out the cards a second time and a third time. His original ten roubles had now grown to eighty. The forester plunged in with the force of his heavy weight. Smiling his stereotyped, lifeless smile, the Chinaman turned up an eight. The forester, freely perspiring, dipped into his boot and dug out his rag of money. Five players had a hundred and sixty roubles staked. All eyes were watching the battle.

Cards were again drawn from the case, and again the Chinaman turned up an eight. Surely he would sell the bank after that, as the next card was bound to break it. The croupier was all ready for him, but with Buddhistic fatalism, as though unable to realise that he was on the road to ruin, the Chinaman held on. Did he think that he had struck a vein of luck and hope to make a fortune out of it?

Whatever were his thoughts, he went on with his fifth deal, eagerly awaited by the onlookers. His stake was covered in a moment by the players who were now keyed up to make fun of him.

'Place your stakes, Messieurs,' cried the croupier, with an expectant look at Kiril.

Scarcely conscious of what he was doing, Kiril flung down the forty roubles remaining from what he had set aside for the whole evening. It was the pink young man's turn to take the first card, and he was feverishly playing banco. This was unpleasant for the other players in view of the young man's bad luck. Kiril watched the embezzler's hand with a sinking heart. He picked up his two cards, looked at them, flushed, and showed his hand to the Chinaman: a knave of hearts with an eight. The Chinaman, maintaining his everlasting smile, turned over the cards in front of him, and a black nine and ten lay threateningly on the table.

'The bank has a nine; the punts are lost,' called the croupier, and scooped up all the notes on the table with one dexterous movement, Kiril's forty roubles being included in the anonymous pile.

'Do you wish to continue, Monsieur?' the croupier said, turning towards the Chinaman. And the Chinaman, as though awaking from a blissful dream, merely shook his head, and put both his yellow hands round the rich pile in front of him.

Kiril did not, for a minute, understand what had happened. But then he realised, with a feeling of hopelessness, that the fifty roubles which he had set aside for play had all disappeared. The croupier's scoop had licked them up unnoticed in a second. Pearls of perspiration covered his forehead. This was the moment at which to get up and go away in accordance with his programme. But he could not go away after having wasted fifty roubles when the next coup might retrieve them. No, he would stop a little longer, just to look on, to watch for an opportunity.

And he did not go away; but stayed on.

The game continued, somewhat dull now, lacking startling incidents such as the coup made by the Chinaman. Not realising what he was doing, Kiril took another fifty roubles from the pocket of his new suit. He punted three times unsuccessfully, barely retaining the ten roubles necessary for his bank. He paid them down, and began his deal. The Armenian picked up his cards with avidity, and asked for one. Kiril turned his up and found a six jealously guarded

222

by an ace. He gave the Armenian a card, so that he then held three knaves.

'Baccarat,' cried the croupier, and, with an air of astonishment, the Armenian paid in two of his dirtiest five rouble notes, as though it were less painful to part with them than with cleaner ones.

On the next deal, Kiril gave him a ten, and the Armenian looked at him with hatred, bitterly regretting the money he had lost. Hastily consulting the number of one of his bank notes as an augury, he made another effort to retrieve his losses. Kiril drew the cards breathlessly, and the Armenian would not buy another card. A seven was the best card in Kiril's hand. The Armenian breathed with a hiss, turning crimson, and began to unbutton his waistcoat.

'Eighty roubles in the bank,' chanted the croupier genially. 'Are you selling, Monsieur, or are you going on?'

Kiril looked round helplessly. Everyone was tensely waiting. There was no movement of sympathy or encouragement. He made a rapid calculation. If he got one more lucky card, he would take a hundred and sixty; Fate was perhaps hovering over him, dangling success before his eyes, an easy success, so much to be preferred to stingy caution. In a second, as though afraid of changing his mind, he seized the cards.

Full of ardour, as though wings were uplifting him, the provincial in the beige suit again went banco. With his usual ill luck he would lose and have to pay eighty roubles. He felt sure of this as he frowned and wiped his forehead while preparing to ask for a card. Then suddenly, his eyes round with amazement, he cried like an excited child:

'A nine.'

Flinging down his cards, he looked round with a broad smile to share his joy with the others.

'A nine. . . . And I thought it was a ten. It was a good thing I didn't buy.'

He was hugging himself with a delight which no one shared. Smiling with happiness, he drew his first winnings towards him. Kiril was overwhelmed by annoyance with himself. Why had he gone after that uncertain eighty roubles and lost everything? He should have taken his eighty roubles and gone on playing with them as Cooperov had taught him. Now he was again left with nothing, and a hundred roubles had vanished and left no trace. No; at the end of the next round he would be wiser, he would only deal three times, and not a single one more. He waited impatiently, hating the other players for being so slow.

But the bank stuck with the man with the iron hand. Rattling his ominous mediaeval forearm, he began to devastate the now silent table. He lifted his heavy hand with a noise that sounded like the clanking of chains. The first to fall a prey to this weapon was the simple-looking forester. Twice he covered the whole bank, and twice he had to dive into his boot for his precious rag. The shabby-looking player lost small stakes, and excitedly tried to win them back. The Sard's turn came in due course. With Eastern dignity, he measured himself against this relic of the war. He examined his cards slowly with his almond eyes, under their heavy brows, and the iron-handed foe charged with a nine like an armoured car or a tank. The Sard put his hand into the breast of his embroidered robe, and drew out a European pocketbook.

Having rid himself of his other insignificant opponents, the tank moved towards Kiril. The man gave him a long, morose look, and, in that look Kiril read the mortal fear of the dealer in producing that last card in spite of all his efforts to appear calm and indifferent. He had made a mistake a second or two ago in the heat of the moment, and wished now that he had taken his winnings and decided to put fate no more to the test.

There were four hundred and twenty roubles in the bank, and the last word, of which the iron man was so much afraid, rested with Kiril, who again made a rapid calculation. He had had five hundred roubles when he came; he had lost a hundred; so four hundred still remained.

Supposing he covered half? He wouldn't soon get another chance as sure as that a sixth, or even a seventh, card would give him. 'Two hundred roubles,'– at one stroke, and the pink provincial embezzler at once asked with eager anticipation:

'Halves?'

Kiril nodded, and stretched his hand toward the case.

'Put your money down,' said the iron-handed man in a deep bass that sounded like the chiming of a clock.

Kiril convulsively unbuttoned his coat, and counted out two hundred precious roubles with tremulous fingers.

The iron man gave him a card. Two kings with broad, bearded Falstaffian faces, were grinning at him from beneath their clownish crowns.

'A card.'

'No more cards,' said his opponent with gloomy triumph, 'I have an eight.'

The iron hand had rattled, as though drawing a bolt on his success.

'The bank is for sale, what offers, messieurs?' the croupier cried.

'Thirty'–'forty'–'sixty' offered various players.

'I buy,' said Kiril suddenly in a voice which he did not even recognise as his own.

With a slow movement, his icy fingers drew out his last two hundred. The croupier at once pushed the case of cards towards him. There was a deep silence. With flushed faces, the players were anxiously and greedily counting their money.

'Give me a card *au rebours*,' said the iron man, his dreaded, hateful voice coming from far gone ages.

Kiril gave the card.

'Nine.' The voice was as incisive as a guillotine.

Kiril looked at him without seeing him.

The croupier's rake at once pushed Kiril's two white notes towards the iron man. A hand moved away the case of cards. Kiril sat there a moment longer, his head bent, lest anyone should think that he had no more money. Then he rose, went out on to the landing, and paused at the top of the stairs. Just in front of him was a mirror, and he saw a young man in it, wearing a useless new costume and pitifully like himself, staring out at him. They moved towards each other with a smile of such bitterness that his heart was near to breaking for pity of himself and that young man.

The pink provincial caught him up almost directly, his hands in the pockets of his beige suit. He looked at Kiril, and with puerile anguish said:

'I've lost everything. . . . It's terrible. You and I comrade, I see. . . . I beg your pardon,' and he hurried down the steps.

Kiril followed him, put on his coat, and left the building. The town, busy with its night life, had no use for him. The trams were coming up Garden Street with phosphorescent flashes which lit up the road with fantastic brightness. It was thawing, and even in the cold wind there were vague promises of spring.

Devoid of all faith, all hope, feeling as though he had already lost two lives, Kiril was as purposeless as the wind which met him.

CHAPTER XXXIII

AND now Kiril realised with horror the magnitude of the catastrophe as the result of which all his hopes lay shattered at his feet, like so much dust.

To what had he been pinning his faith? How could he have been so blind, how could he have been so disloyal to his ideals?

It was not merely the loss of the money or the humiliation of the fatuous stupidity with which he had lost it in one night; there had been equal stupidity in the manner of its acquisition by treachery and mendacity as contrasted with honest work. The most terrible loss had been the loss of himself. He could not resume his studies at the Institute, where he was now completely out of touch with everybody and everything.

He could picture to himself the reproachful astonishment with which Lebedkin would look at him if he should tell him of his dreams of riches and ease. When had he, Kiril Bessonov, the son of a factory hand, begun to entertain notions of that sort? Whose hand had led him into the path which he was treading? Everything that had formed the basis of his existence – work – books – had been erased from his mind as though by a piece of indiarubber. Was he simply weak? Or had he really been convinced by Sverbeev that it was dull and futile to build up his life on the lines which he had marked out for himself, that there were means by which he could make life easy, bright, and free from care?

Yes, he had been weak. There were hundreds who plodded on, studied, worked out plans, became engineers – he had not followed in their footsteps; bored, he had fallen out by the way, duping himself with impossible fantasies, and now, one night at the Casino had brought a vivid, terror-stricken realisation that he had been utterly wrong and had cut himself off from all that was real. How was he to go on living?

Thus it was that, after a night of misery, he rose with a different outlook, as though he had been cured of blindness.

Perhaps Yagodkin would send him twenty roubles next month? Meanwhile he could sell his new suit. He would resume his old life, take his meals in the students' dining-room – but no, that would be impossible. He could not resume his old life, he had lost too much time, and could not possibly make it up. He would be expelled in the spring for inefficiency. There were plenty of candidates only too eager to fill the vacancy. He was in a blind alley. He had failed all along the line. He had failed as a student, he had achieved nothing as a poet, and he had not even had sense enough to keep the big sum of money which he had come by so casually.

In the far off days, Makar had talked of wonderful far off lands – so too, had Katka-the-street-walker; but he had not reached any wonderland; all that he had found was the smoke-laden atmosphere of a Casino, where the dishonest and the unsuccessful hunted for happiness. Tania, lost in the void, had faded away into the haze as dreams fade when the dreamer awakens – Tania, who had filled his soul with hope. And in her stead had appeared Vera Nikolsky, with all her brazen self-assurance.

Sverbeev had been right, then, a thousand times right, in his practical cynicism, when he said that there was no time nowadays for idealists. And, since he was not to be allowed to dream, since he did not know how to live as others live, would it not be better simply to go away, to go quite simply, as Tania Agourov had gone?

228

Suicide suggested itself as desirable and as the sole solution of his problem.

In these days of bitter reflection, when he was reconsidering the whole problem of life, he found himself writing verses in an entirely new vein. He hardly went out at all now. He hurried to the dining-room with other students; he attended lectures which he could not follow intelligently, and he became more and more convinced that it was impossible to pick up the threads of his old life. It was only when his room-mates were out and he was alone that it was possible for him to write his poems. He wrote a good deal, and it seemed to him that all the emotions through which he had lived were reproduced in what he wrote.

Spring would soon be here. The February days, though stormy, were touched by the warmth of the pallid sun, and the grey snow was becoming slushy. The birds were beginning to sing. The sun would vanquish the storms before long, dissolve the miry slush, and enfold the earth in a mantle of gold.

It is on such days that the joy of living reaches its zenith, and, listening to the merry crowing of the cocks, one dreams of lands which, in all probability, one will never see.

Filled with fresh hopes, Kiril made his way one Sunday morning to Dontsev's flat, carrying a manuscript book of verses under his arm. For the last fortnight he had avoided Sverbeev, and Sverbeev, on his side, had made no effort to see him, because he had at the moment no immediate need for his services. But Sverbeev knew through and through this golden-haired youth with the clear grey eyes, knew that he had mastered him and could count on his obedience to his wishes whenever he chose.

Kiril found Dontsev, wearing an old dressing gown, in his study full of dusty books, talking aloud to himself as he paced up and down. He was preparing a lecture. His

229

beard was, as usual, untidy and filled with all sorts of crumbs.

'Ah, sit down, Bessonov . . . you see I'm getting a lecture ready.'

He made Kiril take a seat; while he put down his lecture notes.

'I suppose you've brought some new verse? Well, well, read it.'

Slowly and shyly, Kiril produced his book. He had already acquired the proud tremolo which was the usual manner of the poets at the circles which he had frequented. Dontsev listened with his head bowed. 'You've got to work more over your verses, much more,' he said at last with a deep sigh. 'You ought to work at least six hours a day. Talent is not enough by itself, my dear fellow; a knowledge of technique is required as well. . . . '

'Help me to become a real poet, Lodi Petrovitch,' said Kiril, quivering with the intensity of his feelings. 'My life has gone all wrong. This may be the only thing that can save me and set me right.'

It was with tremulous, anxious hope that he fixed imploring eyes on this man who might get his life back on to the right track. If the question of direction could be decided once for all, he would know how to concentrate his efforts, how to restore his ideal; and how to find again some purpose in his life.

'Well, that's not impossible,' said Dontsev with thoughtful hesitation. 'I've helped a good many. . . . '

Kiril brought to mind all those country lads to whom he had listened while they recited their verses in febrile ecstasy. They had been torn from their normal work, and they soon lost their country freshness, sleeping on boulevard benches and creeping into beershops to mourn over the lot of the poet in the stupor produced by the fumes of alcohol.

230

'I mean a real poet; the real thing, or nothing. There are probably a thousand writing verse, and less than a hundred who get into print. I don't want to be one of the thousand.'

'No, of course not,' answered Dontsev in a tone of boredom. 'If there is talent, the rest will follow naturally.'

There was no note of enthusiasm in his tone, and just as he seemed about to develop his theme, a small boy half opened the door, and said in a deep voice: 'Come to dinner, father. It is getting cold.'

'I've called at an inconvenient moment,' said Kiril with bitter despair. 'I'd better come again some other day.'

'Oh no. That's merely, so to speak, the prose of life . . . however, come whenever you like. I'm always glad to help with advice.'

To the roaring accompaniment of a primus stove on which meat was obviously being cooked, Dontsev saw Kiril to the door. He descended the stairs in a state of deep depression. So, that was what was in store for him. He was to be the thousand and first aspirant, to wander from publisher to publisher with sheaves of rejected verses; to sleep on the boulevards an unrecognised genius, while life passed him by in all its brilliance, brushing aside the refuse of unsuccess. No: if that was the situation, he would break with Dontsev as he had decided to break with Sverbeev: he would isolate himself, pull himself together, and start afresh to build up his life, brick by brick.

He went back to the hostel torn by new, burning hopes, listening to new inner voices. He must have silence and solitude for the requisite searching of the very depths of his soul, so sadly neglected of late, silence and solitude to make it possible to bring to blossom again the bright hopes of the past. But at the very moment when, all alone, he was trying to recover his peace of mind, Sverbeev rushed in like a

231

flash of lightning, vehement, his long-nosed face distorted, no longer smooth and persuasive but crushed, and in an instant he had crushed Kiril, and had relentlessly trampled on all his new formed resolutions.

CHAPTER XXXIV

'WHAT are you moping about?' Sverbeev cried, spluttering through his wide-spaced front teeth. 'You started the whole business, and now you go and hide, like a monk in his cell, as though you had nothing to do with it. No, my lad, things have taken such a turn that unless we can put them straight we're done for, and you can order a requiem service at your favourite shrine. Let's get out of this; we can't talk in here . . . I'll tell you all about it outside.'

He had never seen Sverbeev so upset. He spoke harshly, indeed, he was obviously exaggerating his harshness, but it was equally obvious that he was utterly disconcerted.

In five minutes they had left the hostel and were hurrying along the streets toward the café where Sverbeev had first spoken about Tania. They took a seat well away from the window, and the waiter brought two thick mugs of ale. Sverbeev gulped down some of it, and, without waiting to wipe the froth off his lips, bending his head to bring his sharp face close to Kiril's, he began to speak:

'I don't want to meddle with the workings of your soul, Kiril; perhaps you mean to enter one of the monasteries that have been abolished, or to become a second Pushkin and write a masterpiece like "Ruslan and Ludmila" – that's your own private business. But you and I did a bit of business together that was not private but concerns others as well as yourself . . . haven't you heard anything?'

'No, nothing,' said Kiril, giving Sverbeev a look of frightened surprise.

'Well then, listen. Last night Naoum Robertovitch was

taken; taken away, and it wasn't to the Tsigans, either. And now he'll ruin the lot of us to save his own crocodile hide. You understand? He'll ruin you and me, and that means not only disgrace, not only being expelled from the Institute . . . it means a trial, and they'll make an example of students who have gone wrong, you can bet anything you like on that. And we shall get two years each, and your Lebedkin will be reprimanded for having trusted swindlers. You understand, Kiril?'

It was as though some icy blast had leapt up and shattered his whole being. With horror in his voice, Kiril asked this terrible messenger, who was once again smashing his whole life, and this time with every aspect of finality:

'What is to be done, Sverbeev?'

'That 'is exactly what we have got to discuss. That's just what I've brought you here for. I've got a plan, Kiril, and I'll stick to it through thick and thin. Please don't interrupt, but listen.'

Sverbeev swallowed some more beer, and paused for a second, squinting down at his long nose, his cigarette smouldering in his curved fingers.

'We've got to make good the deficit before Naoum has time to give us away; that is, we've got to tell the Students' Co-operative that there was a mistake in the bill of lading, and that a second consignment is coming along. See? We've got to make up that second consignment and deliver it. Then let Naoum do his worst; we shall have duly delivered all that we received.'

'But where are we to get the stuff?' asked the horrified Kiril. 'Are we to go and ask Lebedkin again?'

'Lebedkin will have nothing to do with it. We shall have to buy what we need in the open market – we've got to look sharp about it, too – before Naoum is questioned and gives the whole show away. We've got to buy, and to do that we shall need at least fifteen hundred roubles – have you got any money?'

'No,' said Kiril, bitterly ashamed at having to make the confession. 'No, I haven't got any money.'

'Blown it already?' said Sverbeev, with a contemptuous snort. 'Like some fine Hussar? Well, I haven't got any either, nor has Cooperov, I know. So, what about it? A trial, the dock, a test case? Not if I know it! Never surrender is my motto, and I shall fight as long as I can find a weapon or a loophole. And that brings me to the main point.'

On the other side of the window, beyond the lobster, red as a cardinal, which it displayed, busy people could be seen passing to and fro. It was a warm February day, the roofs were dripping, and golden sunbeams, penetrating even here, emphasised the daylight dinginess of the cafe, which, with all its sordid ugliness, could not wholly shut out the joyful promise of spring. Filled with apprehension and misery, Kiril listened to Sverbeev's main point, while he watched the passers-by who were carefree, innocent, and not involved in this terrible business.

'I've come to the main point,' repeated Sverbeev, 'and you ought to know what I'm driving at. We've discussed Chelishev all through the winter . . . that's our only hope, our only salvation.'

Kiril did not understand in the least. He frowned painfully.

'It's no good frowning. I'm not here to discuss noble ideals, but something quite different, perhaps something pretty shady . . . Chelishev has got money; we both know that; plenty of money. Chelishev dishonoured Tania, and was probably the real cause of her death. When she died we made up our minds that we would threaten him with exposure. Well, I have thought the whole thing out again,

235

and it's obviously too late for any exposure. One would have to have proofs for that, and what proofs have we got? Who can prove that he had an intrigue with Tania, and even if we could prove it, who would care now? If we had followed the thing up then and there, while the scent was hot, we might perhaps have frightened him so that he would have accepted any terms, but the scent is cold now, and he would sue us for slander, and win his case, too. No, we've got to take rougher measures, measures that are not exactly to my liking; but remember this, without Chelishev's money we can't save ourselves, we shall both go into the dock, and we shall get two years, you can be quite certain of that.'

'But what are we to do?' asked Kiril, in a miserable whisper.

'Exactly: what are we to do? If Chelishev won't give us the money, we must make him.'

Dry-lipped, Kiril interrupted him: 'If he won't?'

'Take it,' said Sverbeev, after a second's pause, looking away from Kiril.

'Take it? How do you mean, take it?' And, with increasing horror, Kiril clutched the marble top of the table.

Sverbeev turned carelessly toward the window, puffing at his cigarette: 'How does one take anything?' He asked calmly after a moment of silence, and now looking at Kiril with angry eyes. 'How does one do such things, dear comrade Bessonov, dear rosy-cheeked, golden-haired poet, whose virginal innocence so appealed to Vera Nikolsky? It is perfectly simple. One goes to a man and says "give and if you won't give, I'll take." '

'But that is robbery,' said Kiril faintly.

'What does it matter to you whether you are tried for swindling or for robbery? Of course, you may get it in the neck for both. But there is a chance that Chelishev will come to terms for fear of scandal. We should be delighted

236

to hush up the whole matter, I'm sure, we don't in the least desire to cause any unpleasantness. Still, he's not going to get off for Tania scot free.'

'Listen, Sverbeev,' said Kiril, trembling. 'Leave Tania out of it. Her name shall not be brought into this disgusting business, and we are not going to use it to save ourselves.'

Sverbeev put out the stub of his cigarette in a little pool of beer on the table: 'In the first place, it is not a disgusting affair, but quite ordinary, though unpleasant, I admit. In the second place, we don't want to use Tania's name for our own benefit, but as a reminder to Chelishev that he can't do just what he likes and get away with it. If you care to know my opinion, I consider that it's your duty. However, perhaps you were lying when you talked about your love for Tania.'

Outside, drop by crystal drop, the melted snow was falling from the eaves through the golden sunlight of the afternoon. The promise of spring filled the air in the slush-sodden, sun-bathed Moscow streets. But Kiril felt himself imprisoned in this cafe which suggested nothing better than man's stupidity and intemperance, while close to him sat this man who looked at him with relentless eyes, relentlessly urging him on to a hideous, irreparable task.

He paused for an instant in the effort to recover his self-control, and then said: 'Listen, Sverbeev. What if I tell you, as man to man, and in all friendship, that I've finished, that I'm tired out, that I am hopelessly at sea, and beg you to let me go. Perhaps I can straighten out my life again, maybe I can find my way back to the right path – otherwise, I shall go downhill, down to the very depths. I want to write poetry, and if I can't do that, I shall go back to the provinces and work in a factory. I've got friends who would help me; only, let me go now!'

He spoke with intense feeling while he looked imploringly at Sverbeev, with the thought that perhaps his ultimate destiny lay in the hands of this man.

But Sverbeev returned his look with one of unutterable contempt, and answered in a tone of cold fury which filled Kiril with despair:

'You're a slippery customer, you are. You want to slip away and write poetry – but where's the money for the goods? Put up the money, and then indulge in poetry by all means. I'll let you go then. But you want to wriggle out of danger like an eel. Well, I'll tell you what I think about it, and I don't care how you take it. To my mind there are no degrees of dishonesty; you can't say that one thing is more dishonest than another. You went to your friend Lebedkin and lied to him, didn't you? Answer me, did you, or didn't you? Why then these sudden qualms over Chelishev? By means of Chelishev you may be able to conceal your treachery to Lebedkin. You might be able to plaster up the crack, and that would be all to the good. I'm speaking of the spiritual aspect, so to say. From the point of view of actual facts – oh, what's the use of talking? If we don't get Chelishev's money, we're done for. In another week or two, Naoum Robertovitch will drown us like pups. You may not want to put up a fight? Well, I do.'

'Anyhow, what will happen if we agree about Chelishev?' asked Kiril.

He suddenly saw with terrible vividness what lay before him if his share in the fraud should become known. Lebedkin would discover that he, Kiril Bessonov, had lied to him and betrayed him. Was he to drink the cup of shame to the dregs while Chelishev continued to live at his ease, going from triumph to triumph? Was he to be allowed to enjoy that foreign tour that he intended to take as soon as the spring examinations were over?

Somewhere in the Vagankov cemetery lay Tania unaveng-
ed, and with the first approach of spring her little grave
would be overgrown with the grass of oblivion. And was he,
Kiril, to refuse to compel Chelishev to make even the
slightest atonement? Sverbeev was right; he had wanted
to wriggle away like an eel; he had been averse to soiling
his delicate hands, and all the time the past lay behind him
full of wickedness – his own wickedness towards Lebedkin,
and Chelishev's wickedness towards Tania. Crime? Was
not all that he had done to himself that winter a crime?
Was it not a crime to forsake one's ideals, to lower oneself,
to let oneself become intoxicated by the lying allurements
of the city? With temples throbbing as though he were
drunk, he turned toward Sverbeev, his eyes burning, exulting
in his baseness.

'However that may be, Sverbeev,' he drained his mug
and spoke somewhat breathlessly, 'however that may be,
why should we be sentenced while Chelishev goes off to
Paris to amuse himself?'

'That's just what I say,' Sverbeev answered hurriedly.
'I'm not asking you to kill Chelishev, but just to make a
wise use of our rights. And, do you know what would be
the wisest way?' And he pressed up as close to Kiril as he
could. 'We must get a plan of Chelishev's flat,' he whispered
in a voice that was not his own. 'I'll explain afterwards –
everything will explain itself. We'll work out the details,
arrange how and where to begin. You'll get the plan; you'll
go to the flat and ask Chelishev to let you take in the spring
term the exam. at which you were ploughed. You understand? It's not a crime; it's our sole salvation, don't forget
that. It is a crime for people to go under, but not to save
themselves.'

The terrible conversation was over, but Kiril had not
really grasped all that it involved. They agreed to meet

again next day at the same place, Sverbeev bringing Cooperov along. They parted at the door. Flushed and dazed, Kiril passed along the gay, sunlit street, but there was no joy for him in the foretaste of spring. There was a trickling of melted snow, March would soon be here, and then the ice would break, the snow would vanish. 'In March, spring will be here,' he said to himself, and he went hot all over at the thought that in March all the dread and menacing happenings of which he had had a fleeting vision would lie behind him. Perhaps this was the decisive, the final, turn that he was to take. He found relief in that thought as he walked along the sun-bathed street.

CHAPTER XXXV

Tania Agourov's terrible death had stirred Chelishev deeply, destroying the peace of mind in which he had sought to wrap himself after their last meeting. How was it, he asked himself, that a man so eminent, so sincere, so sensitive, had so superficially passed by the tragedy of that young soul without giving it any adequate consideration? Perhaps she was abnormal, hysterical – still, he had not been free from blame. He felt humiliated for many a long day, remorseful, horrified. But, like every healthy, self-assured and successful man, he quickly developed an anti-toxin: after all, he could not be held responsible for all the complications of a woman's lot. He had not pursued Tania, rather it had been she who had sought him out, and had it not been of her own free will that she had reached her decision in the matter which they had discussed on the boulevard? That being so, how could he have foreseen such a sequel – such a senseless, impossible, nerve-shattering catastrophe?

Chelishev wanted a life firmly built on solid foundations, he wanted a life which should run smoothly and one in which he could play his part sure of his health, his muscles, and the unruffled, undisturbed activity of his practical, well-balanced mind.

He worked out self-justifications and excuses for his conduct in the same way that, as an inventor, he worked out in minutest detail every small pivot and tiny wheel to ensure the smooth functioning of the machine as a whole. His affair with Tania had not only been unnecessary, but impracticable for a man in his position. He had felt that it was a flaw in the mechanism of his life which had to be remedied as quickly as possible. So he had remedied it. Perhaps he had dealt with it too lightly, too much in the manner of a man, giving too little thought to it in his busy pre-occupation with new ideas, new ambitions and the consciousness that he was establishing himself more and more firmly. The question of his mission to Europe and America had been definitely settled. As soon as the spring examinations were over, at the end of May, he was to go away for nearly six months, to supplement familiar experiences with new impressions, to see with his own eyes the life and the technical marvels of two continents.

In the spring, his latest invention, the automatic coupler for railway trucks, was to be put into operation on the Caucasian lines. Life lay before him unrestricted, full of promise.

He had never had the slightest wish to hurt Tania or to make her unhappy. Least of all had he wished to seduce her; but it had all just happened somehow, and then it had become imperative that a speedy end should be put to the whole affair.

Thus, having produced for himself the anti-toxin of unanswerably rational excuses, having convinced himself that he had not been in any way to blame for the tragedy, Chelishev devoted himself to his pursuits with redoubled energy.

After the shock which he had sustained, he felt particularly glad and grateful for the solid stability of his home, where everything was in its right place, everything was smooth, thorough, systematised, and comfortable. And, over it all, reigned with accustomed ease, the woman who was his real mate. She fully appreciated the part which her husband played in the community, and she bore his name with pride and dignity. Self-assured and beautiful in her maturity, she helped to steer their ship on the ocean of life. It was here, in this haven of safety, that he had eagerly sought refuge after his renunciation of Tania. There was as it were, a re-union between him and his wife, as though after a period of separation. He found it pleasant and not in the least dull to stay at home in the evening, to work in his study till eleven o'clock and then to join her for tea, to watch affectionately and gratefully, her slow graceful movements as she poured out or leaned on the table, a little heavily perhaps, smiling her slow, tranquil smile, or, later, in the bedroom, to look at her, in her boudoir cap, like a ripe and mature Slavonic Phryne, sitting up in bed to nibble an apple and read by the pleasant, steady, rosy light of the porcelain lamp. It was as though they had rediscovered each other, as during these evenings they discussed their plans and talked of Europe, thrilled by the exciting promises held out by far away Paris.

Chelishev had been saving up ever since the autumn for their journey. Whenever he could get a little money together he bought the necessary greenbacks wherever he could obtain them, at the bank, or from chance acquaintances. He began by keeping the money in his desk, but later he entrusted it to his wife, who put it away in some secret hiding place of her own. He wanted to make the sum a round two thousand dollars before their start. He had every right to it; he had earned it by working hard as professor, lecturer and inventor. There was not a penny which he had obtained otherwise than by his own fertile brain, his knowledge and research.

Tania's terrible end had brought him up with a turn, and he devoted himself to his work with renewed force and passion. Work, work, that was the sole essential, he had achieved position by work, his whole life had been his built up by work. He hated idlers, wasters, lazy students, above all things, and with them he was implacable.

Kiril went to call on him again. Regarding this golden-haired lad as a slacker, Chelishev had taken a dislike to him from the first without fully realising it himself. There were a lot of men like him; who came to Moscow to study, went wrong, and became a hindrance to the serious workers, and then, after knocking about for a year or two, were expelled for inefficiency. They were the dross of their generation, wisely skimmed off to leave only the true metal, capable of being tempered to meet danger and resist temptation. They were the autumn leaves which life in its ruthlessness sweeps up into heaps, and it was from them that most of the wretched failures, the criminals, and the suicides, were drawn. Chelishev's healthy, full-blooded appreciation of life made him regard them as useless, and foredoomed. Perhaps Tania Agourov had been one of them? He had not had time, perhaps he had lacked inclination, to analyse her character. Did he regret his omission? But why should he? It was impossible for anyone to relive the past, and he was less capable of retrospection than most men. That was a closed chapter, closed with all its madness, all his sorrow for the misguided, though charming, girl.

His domestic relations, and the systematising of his useful life, the value of which was universally recognised, were the only things of real importance to him. And, having arrived at that conclusion, he dismissed the complex and painful subject from his mind.

On the immense drawing table in Chelishev's study, lay a map of the Union of Republics. Yellow patches indicated the steppes, green showed the vast forests, mountains were marked brown – here was a sixth of the globe, thinly populated and still including immense waste tracts, with sand, marshes, and frozen areas. But, year by year, there emerged more and more clearly, what were, so to speak, to be the sinews of the future, schemes in process of gradual execution. In the State Commission of which he was a member, a scheme for the development of the whole country was evolving step by step. Here, in an arid desert, a railroad was to be built which would replace camel caravans; there the shoals which rendered a great river useless were to be dredged, and, in accordance with the Five Year Plan, measures were to be taken to make it navigable. Electric power stations were to be built. Many rivers were to be increased in depth to carry vessels which would then bring life to endless towns and villages. Dotted black lines on the map showed the railways of the future. The red spots were the power-stations yet to be, and the red splashes round them were the factories which would be driven by power taken from the harnessed rivers. Here, this geographical map spoke in silence of all that was real. Engineers of the future, graduated from the Institute, his pupils, would build the railways and the bridges and bring the schemes to completion. It was to this task of development that Chelishev wanted to devote all his energies. Had he then not been right when he refused to stop on his way to indulge in despair over the loss of one of these little ones? Thus it was that he tried to stifle the rebellious voice of his conscience.

Perhaps it was because of all this that he felt particularly annoyed and ruffled by Kiril Bessonov's visit. He was irritated by this hesitant, wavering student who never knew his own mind. He had called three times in Chelishev's absence, according to the maid's description.

'I believe you undertook to take your examination in January,' he began coldly. 'So far as I can remember you did not do so.'

'I had not time,' answered Kiril, at once losing countenance and feeling abashed and confused as he always did with Chelishev.

245

'In that case, what do you want to know?' asked Chelishev irritably.

'I want you to allow me to take the exam. in the spring term . . .'

'Why not in the autumn? Will you kindly tell me, Comrade Bessonov, what it is that prevents you from working as other students do?'

Kiril was silent. He stood with his head bowed, like a little boy, before this devastating man. He could barely catch a glimpse of the greying hair, the clean-shaven, obstinate chin, and the particularly hateful grey silk bow so exquisitely tied.

Speaking with growing annoyance, Chelishev said: 'You come to my home time after time, although you know that I interview students only at the Institute. You don't want to work. You, yourself, don't know what you do want. Excuse me, Comrade, I have no time to waste on idle chatter. If you want to take your examination in the spring term, do so by all means. I have no objection; but spare me any more of these useless interviews. And, above all, understand that you must work, and that you must work hard.'

Kiril left the house crushed and humiliated by Chelishev's tone. But that feeling quickly gave place to a burst of fury such as Chelishev always roused in him, a fury which he welcomed because it seemed to sanction and justify whatever he might do. Crossing the road, he looked up at the yellow-curtained windows, clenched his fists, and muttered:

'Wait and see, Professor Chelishev. If that's how you feel, everything is permissible.'

Sverbeev had been right, and, that being so, Kiril would be able to draw on hidden forces in himself of which he had never suspected the existence. His eyes burning with excitement, and his heart filled with hatred and a craving or revenge, Kiril passed on his way.

CHAPTER XXXVI

THERE were five rooms in Chelishev's apartment, and at one time his own household had used them all. But the two rooms nearest the kitchen were now occupied by an old aunt of his wife and by a student at the Conservatoire, who was the daughter of a friend. The Chelishevs had crowded up in that way so as to avoid having strangers thrust upon them.

On the three or four occasions when Kiril had visited the flat, he had been able to get a fairly clear idea of its topography. The small, detached house contained only two flats; the upper one occupied by Chelishev, while in the lower, lived Prince Ourousov, the former owner of the house, and a shoemaker name Feskin. At the back were a small garden and a courtyard containing a garage, which was now converted into a dwelling for a family from South Russia.

At the door of Chelishev's flat, a notice instructed one to ring once for him, twice for the old aunt, and three times for the Conservatoire girl. Immediately on the left as one entered, was Chelishev's now familiar study, and, beyond that, the dining-room, of which Kiril had once caught a glimpse when he had gone through the kitchen and along a passage to take the back stairs. The bedroom was next to the dining-room and also opened on the passage, as did the two rooms occupied by the lodgers. There was a little room off the kitchen for the well-trained and unpleasant maid who had displayed so much reluctance and suspicion when she let Kiril in.

With the assistance of Sverbeev, he had recently found

out a good deal about the routine of the Chelishev household. The Chelishevs, for example, never went out on
Saturday evenings, because the maid was allowed out for
twenty-four hours at that time. The Conservatoire student
played at a cinema, and had to be there by six o'clock for
the first show, never getting back before one. As for the
old aunt, she was deaf, very devout, shut herself up in her
room at an early hour, and played no part in the life of the
house.

Sverbeev had learned many of these details from the
shoemaker Feskin, whose friendship he had cultivated for
the purpose. Feskin, a bachelor with a head of curly hair
which was so woolly as to look negroid, was a rakish youth
devoted to women, with whom, however, he never had the
least success. He made beautiful boots for himself, had a
fine concertina, put on side, and was very generous in treating his friends. But there was something repulsive about
his tight curls, his sinewy, awkward figure, and in the way
in which he showed his wounded pride when his addresses
were rejected. It was because of that that the girls disliked
and were afraid of him. Because, whenever his attentions
were repulsed he would get drunk, make a row, and shout
insults at the woman in the open street. He was feared and
disliked in the house, and Ourousov had felt that his life
might as well be over from the first moment that he was
domiciled in his flat.

On his first visit to Feskin, Sverbeev had taken a pair of
leggings to be repaired. Then he took a pair of shooting
boots which needed patching, and they led to talk about
sport, and the distances at which each of them could hit a
bulls-eye. Feskin boasted that he could smash a raw egg
thrown into the air, explaining that he had learnt to shoot
while he was fighting with the Greens for two years in the
forests of the Ukraine. Sverbeev then told him that his

248

division had been given the job of clearing the Greens out of the forests, and their acquaintance promised to be so interesting that they decided to develop it outside the shoemaker's workshop. They agreed to meet at a little Georgian restaurant in Bronni Street, and spent a very pleasant, sociable evening there together. Feskin was wearing a new fur-lined jacket that reeked of sheepskin, and ostentatiously flung it open to display the fur as he sat down opposite Sverbeev. Being a regular customer, he nodded to the proprietor to take his order, and he approached them with an air of great dignity, a blue-cheeked Georgian, wearing an astrakan cap, a leather belt showing off his girlishly slender waist.

'I've brought along a chum as my guest to-night,' said Feskin, delighted to have a companion whose conversation was so entertaining. 'Make his acquaintance, Sergo, he's a sort of compatriot, because he and I may have fought one another while I was with the Greens and he with the Reds. . . . We've got a lot of yarns to swap, so now, old chap, get us some pepper vodka and pickled herrings, to start with. . . .'

'The *shashlik** is very good, the meat is tender,' said the Caucasian, hospitably offering his best to his honoured guests.

'Well, let's have some *shashlik*; only, see that the onion is chopped fine . . . however, you know all about that better than I do.'

All these preliminaries had put Feskin into high good humour.

'Ah, comrade, comrade,' he said, shaking his head, 'we're just where we were before the war. I can tell by your boots; you wouldn't wear things of that sort if you could help it, any more than I should be sewing leather and

* *Shashlik*, chunks of mutton cooked and served on skewers.

patching shoes if I were not so poor. I ask you, what did we fight for? What did we spill our blood for? The rich are on top again, and the lower classes are just where they were.'

'The rich are always on top,' said Sverbeev bitterly. 'There are you, downstairs, while you have Professor Chelishev above you, and I bet he lives a bit better than you do.'

'Chelishev?' And Feskin raised his eyebrows significantly. 'Chelishev lives in a style that anyone might envy; first class. He doesn't have his boots mended five times; he throws them into the dustbin. An eagle, that's what he is. They tried to squeeze him a bit in his flat, he was living so grandly, better than anyone . . . Well, he took the matter to the Kremlin; he's got influence everywhere.'

'Never mind, he's going abroad in the spring . . . That's what he's been hoarding money for . . . He's got about four thousand, but that's not enough for him.' Sverbeev was talking in a casual tone, but Feskin looked at him shrewdly, expectantly.

'How do you come to know so much about Chelishev?' he asked suspiciously.

'If I didn't know, I shouldn't tell you. I saw him buying dollars at the bank,' said Sverbeev carelessly. He changed the conversation at once by beginning to tell Feskin about his campaign against the Greens. But the idea he had thrown out had evidently penetrated Feskin's thick skull, and remained there to germinate.

They ate some of the pickled herring, and were feeling genially warm with the vodka they had drunk, when the chef appeared in a filthy white overall and cap but with Asiatic pomposity and all the pride of an artist, carrying the *shashlik*. He brought the little chunks of meat in on the skewers, and proceeded to push them off the slender

250

sticks on to their plates, smothering them with chopped onions. Sverbeev and Feskin meanwhile went on with the talk which interested them.

'We were fighting on different sides, so to say,' Feskin continued as he chewed the mutton which was anything but tender, 'but here we are, sitting at the same table, with nothing to quarrel about. You're a beggar, and I'm a beggar. The time has gone by when they all based their hopes on the poor and there was therefore someone always ready to look after their interests. It's the middleman that makes the weather now. The middlemen, indeed, they're only *kourlaks** under another name. Where is there room for the likes of us? Who's going to look after us if we don't look after ourselves? Am I right, comrade? Put your trust in Karl Marx, but look after Number One.'

Feskin had kept on drinking vodka that burnt his throat all the time he was talking.

'Here we are, you and I, talking about Chelishev – If you'll excuse me for saying so, Chelishev hoards up thousands – you saw it with your own eyes – while we are among the underdogs. We killed off bourgeois without end, yet the bourgeois has jumped on to our backs again and is riding us just as he did before the war, so to say. And whose fault is it? It's our own fault. We're slackers, and we're to blame for it. Take this Chelishev, for example: I'd like to take him and shake all his learning out of him. Wait a bit, mister Intellectual Worker. You're the salt of the earth, they send motor cars from the Kremlin to fetch you, while I'm only a low-down cobbler. You've got thousands, while I work twenty-six hours a day and have worn my fingers to the bone with waxed thread. What have you got to say about it? What's yours is your own, and what's mine is yours, too? No, wait a bit Citizen Intellectual Worker.

Kourlak=Fist: The name given to rich peasants.

251

Did you fight at the front? Did you shed any of your blood? Were you wounded? Not at all, you hid in the rear behind a wall of books. . . . Well then, now go and mend shoes, and hand over your thousands to me. Am I right, comrade student? You have a merry life; I have a sad one; I am wretched, there's nothing left in life for me, it's all over. We did have some fun, and we did have hopes, but now it's back to your basement to make shoes with French heels for the wife of the Intellectual Worker. . . . '

Well,' said Sverbeev significantly, raising his glass to the light, 'if you shake Chelishev, you'll only be doing an act of justice. You're quite right, Feskin. The money belongs to us, to the people; we work day and night to produce it, and then it's taken abroad to be spent.'

Something flashed between them at that momentous instant. The veins swelled on Feskin's narrow forehead while he stared at Sverbeev as though trying to penetrate to his innermost being. Sverbeev gave a chuckle, and seasoned a piece of mutton with pepper and onion before putting it into his mouth.

'One man by himself can't go very far,' began Feskin again with a cryptic air. 'I'm wretched and you're wretched, our interests may be the same, if I understand what you mean?'

'Quite right,' answered Sverbeev, he, too, having a mysterious air as he added 'If the two of us twist our strings together, the result may be a rope to tie up the boat without anyone being the wiser.'

Feskin was quite delighted with Sverbeev. He would not let him pay, and even threatened to take offence at his offering to do so. It was agreed that Sverbeev should take to Feskin any boots that he had to be mended. The Georgian accepted Feskin's money with the bearing of a disinterested and hospitable host. The vodka had warmed them and the mutton had given them a genial feeling of repletion.

252

Bronni Street seemed jolly to them, full of jolly people and jolly things. There was, for example, a Caucasian shop with a sign over it reading 'Vartan's sandals are beest.' And the lamps were bright, although the lamp-posts were drunk.

'I found out all about you before I brought my boots for you to mend.' said Sverbeev in a tone full of meaning. 'And I came to the conclusion that you were the right sort of person.'

'You can rely on me. My nickname at the front was "Feskin the Grave," because I was pitiless – there isn't, and there never has been a scrap of pity in me – and because I could be as silent as the grave when necessary.'

It had not taken Sverbeev long to size Feskin up. There were plenty of indications that he was the right sort of man for the job, and, besides, there was no time to lose because news had reached him that Naoum Robertovitch had begun to squeal. Later on, Feskin turned out to be the pivot of the whole affair. He furnished Sverbeev with a lot of details about the house, such as the hour at which Chelishev generally went to bed, and the days when the Ourousovs went to visit their married daughter who lived out of town. The Ourousovs had only the status of lodgers in the flat, of which Feskin was the registered occupant. They generally went out for the day on Saturdays. It was for these reasons that a Saturday was definitely chosen.

There were several inconsistencies and missing links in Sverbeev's scheme, as a whole. Why had he dragged in Bessonov from the first? He had a ready answer for that; he had suggested to Kiril from the beginning that he should be the avenger of Tania Agourov's wrongs and he had stirred up his jealousy of Chelishev because that would give a romantic aspect to the whole affair, and enable him to plead that the avenger, carried away by passion, had acted on impulse without stopping to consider what was lawful

253

and what was not. He counted very much on Bessonov, who, if there should be any mishap, might provide an excellent cover for himself, whose defence, indeed, he might even undertake, laying all the blame on Chelishev. Cooperov might also prove useful at that point. Then, too, Bessonov was young, he had a clean record, and was too guileless to give anyone away. Sverbeev had gone into the whole thing very thoroughly with Cooperov, reasoning it out with practical shrewdness, and now Feskin was the first of the links needed to complete the intricate scheme which might prove to be a very successful undertaking. It could not be said that he thought lightly of crime; he simply did not give it a thought. He was accustomed to acting wholly in accordance with his own plans, and there were no such things as right and wrong in his opinion. At the very beginning of the revolution he had seized upon and assimilated the idea that everything was permissible, and that was doubly so in dealing with a man who had taken so much from life as Chelishev had. The only important thing was to put the business through with the least possible risk and injury.

Feskin's help was invaluable. Wonderful schemes sprang up in his narrow, criminal mind, and at their subsequent meetings, Sverbeev and he needed no words to make them understand each other. What was the first step to take? What should be done and who should do it? Those were points which Sverbeev thought it best to leave for decision at the last moment. But one thing was absolutely certain: the whole business must be finished before Naoum Robertovitch had time to ruin them all. Of course, the examining magistrate would at first be busy tracking his big business confederates; the small fry would only be considered later, but they had only a fortnight at the outside in which to do what they had to. During the last week Sverbeev had become thin with the consuming fire of his anxiety.

The first days of March were damp, and the ice was breaking on the Moskva Rover. Since his last meeting with Sverbeev, Kiril Bessonov had spent much of his time wandering along its bank and past Our Saviour's. His mind was no longer filled with hatred of Chelishev, but with fear and remorse. How had he become involved in this dangerous business? Who was he that he should set himself up as Chelishev's judge? At the thought of Chelishev he was overwhelmed by a feeling of emptiness, nothingness. He was like a rudderless boat at the mercy of the current. He had, as it were, been torn from the bank, like one of the ice blocks which were floating down the river, being dashed against the piers of the bridges, melting, disappearing, being hopelessly carried away to the wide beyond.

The crenelated walls of the Kremlin were sharply silhouetted against the low-hung, cold, grey sky. The transpontine quarter of Moscow lay broad and grim in the hazy mist. Kiril went down the granite steps of the cathedral, and leant against the iron railings of the quay. If one looked long enough at the water, one got the sensation of being on a ship. The high wind held a chilling moisture, notwithstanding its promise of spring. As a little boy, he had stood watching just such a scene while his stepmother was with the tanner being unfaithful to his father.

What great prospects life had held for him then, and how soon he had forgotten everything, how disloyal to himself he had been, how readily he had strayed up every divergent path only to find himself now on this desperate, ill-omened road which boded nothing but evil.

Tears caused either by the wind or his misery filled his eyes as he watched the icepacks floating by him, some of them like white swans, some of the little floating islands having their snowy surface patterned with designs of plants and trees. Away they drifted, away to far off happy spaces.

CHAPTER XXXVII

IN March the whole Institute was absorbed in final preparations for the spring examinations. Dozens of young heads – dark, fair, auburn – were bent over books, drawing-boards, or notes. The corridors, usually so dim, were penetrated by golden rays which made bright rectangular patches on the unpolished floors. The commission which organised the practical summer work of the students was already busy. They would be sent off to help in the building of new lines, to work in railway shops, to become smiths, fitters, or stokers, for the time being. They would be brought face to face with manual work – practical, physical work, as distinguished from theoretical, mental work. They would board the trains by which they travelled, not as passengers, but as engine-drivers.

All the two or three hundred students were hard at work, but bubbling over with excitement, like young animals, at the prospect of the summer vacation with its promise of space and freedom. Kiril felt isolated and lonelier than ever in the hostel amid the sound of rustling papers which was constantly in his ears as the students rapidly turned over the pages of their text-books or their notes in cramming for the coming tests. The faculty had already had the question of his expulsion for inefficiency under their consideration, and his fate now depended entirely upon the degree of success which he achieved in the examinations.

Kiril, however, entertained no doubts on the subject. He knew that he would be expelled, because, however much he might try, he could never catch up with the others, having completely lost touch by wasting so much time.

Yet he was irresistibly drawn to his fellow students. Was it that he was instinctively saying good-bye? Among them he found himself breathing once again that atmosphere of book-learning and study in which he had originally found his ideal. They were all determined, energetic young men, who, only a little while ago, before they had devoted themselves wholeheartedly to the fascinating pursuit of knowledge had been under arms and fighting, or working in factories. The lines which had already furrowed their foreheads were indicative of that very resolve to conquer life which had so recently inspired Kiril. And now? He was no longer one of them; he had become an apostate. His fate was being determined by the inflexible will of another. How was he to go on with life, now that he had lost all hope, now that life had become a desert? His wasted time was irretrievable, just as his one bitter meeting with Tania could never be repeated, and the course of his life was being ruthlessly and unalterably laid down by Sverbeev in whose hands his fate was firmly grasped. Things were happening which concerned him in which he took no part, about which he was not even consulted, and others were reaching decisions, solely in accordance with their own desires, which would determine the part that he was to play.

Sverbeev had finally decided the date on which Chelishev was to be robbed. They had always talked about it in hints, and had never yet called the thing by its true name. They had persuaded themselves that it was a simple and straightforward transaction, as though Chelishev would remain passive, offer no resistance, and meekly acquiesce. They always spoke of 'the affair,' though they all understood that 'the affair' meant 'the robbery.'

After the snowstorms of February, after the wet thaws of March, after the freshets had filled the rivers, spring seemed to have arrived suddenly, as though riding on

257

horseback. The partly thawed brown masses from the roadways were being carted out of the town on lorries. Near the Arbat Gate, close to the Strastnoi Monastery, small boys were selling pungent, pollen-laden mimosa and the first snowdrops in all their swan-like, white purity. The monastery quivered in the purplish haze of the sunlit air and its cupolas reflected the golden rays. Beyond the town, beyond Petrovsk Park, a broad, gleaming expanse absorbed the last beams of the lengthening spring day.

On March 11th, two days before 'the affair' was to be carried out – Sverbeev having finally decided on the thirteenth – Kiril, Sverbeev and Cooperov met in the refreshment room of the Baltic Railway Station. That had been chosen as the most neutral place and the one in which they would be least conspicuous. The room was full of people, all pre-occupied with their own affairs: their tickets, their porters, or the friends who had come to say good-bye. No one noticed the three young men who sat down at a little table – they were probably there to see someone off or to meet an in-coming train. Watching with keen eye lest anyone should appear to be interested in, or curious about them, Sverbeev sipped his beer, and outlined the final arrangements.

According to the latest information, obtained from Feskin only that morning, the Ourousovs were going out of town on Saturday. Chelishev's stupid, stuck-up maid had boasted that she was going on Saturday night to dance the foxtrot and various other fashionable dances at a party which the Caterers' Club was giving. Everyone knew that her lover was employed in a bakery. A point of great importance was that the pianist who lived in Chelishev's flat was to play the dance music at the party, so that she, too, would be away till the small hours of the morning. In addition to all this, Feskin had discovered that Chelishev's wife had been ill for the last three days, and that medicine had been sent for from the chemist's on several occasions. It was essential to take all these details into most careful consideration.

This was Sverbeev's plan: On Saturday night, a little after one o'clock, all three were to go to the house. Feskin's window was visible from the street; if it showed a red light, it would mean that everything was as had been expected, and the way was clear. If no light showed, they were to go past the house and wait for Feskin near the hoarding covered with posters at the corner of the street. If all was well, they were to act as follows: Sverbeev and Kiril were to go up the back stairs, open the kitchen door with a key which Feskin had obtained, and break the chain with wire cutters. Feskin would stay downstairs at the back entrance while Cooperov kept watch at the front door, signalling to Feskin if he noticed anything suspicious.

Kiril had found out the positions of the various rooms in the course of his visits to the flat. The room next to the kitchen was that of the pianist, who would not be at home. The next room was that of the deaf old aunt. Then came the bedroom, in which Chelishev's wife slept, and where the money was kept in a small, antique, red bureau. Feskin had very slily and cleverly managed to find this out from the silly, conceited servant without rousing her suspicions.

It was at this point that the real danger began and that great coolness and self-possession would be necessary. How were they to manage so as not to wake up the wife? Chelishev himself slept on a divan in his study, which was separated from the bedroom by the heavily curtained dining-room, so that he would not hear anything. They could tell by his window whether he had retired for the night. The important thing was that Madam Chelishev should not be waked. If they could manage that, the rest would be easy. She kept the key of the bureau in a bag which lay all night beside her bed. All that they had to do was to extract the key, open the bureau, take the money, and slink silently and mysteriously away, leaving no trace behind them. They would then hasten along the street, take the first cab they encountered, drive to the Stone Bridge, pay off the cabman, find another cab – and, after that, anyone who liked might try to find them in the great populous city.

And, in order to make sure that Madam Chelishev should not wake up, Sverbeev had obtained a bottle of ether from a friend on whom he could rely. It looked as though every contingency had been foreseen. Careful alibis had been thought out to protect each of them from any possibility of suspicion. Sverbeev, for example, was to return to his lodgings just before one o'clock on Saturday night, and ring to be let in, pretending that he had forgotten his key. He would apologise to his fellow lodgers for having troubled them, and they would then be able to testify that he had been in before one o'clcok. About half an hour later, he would slip out unnoticed: and make his way to the agreed place of meeting on the Prechistensky Boulevard. Cooperov would go out of town on Saturday morning for the week-end because he had to look for lodgings for the summer. He would go to Podolsk, see all the persons who might be useful as witnesses later, and would then secretly return to Moscow by the eleven o'clock train.

It was more difficult to establish an alibi for Kiril than for the others, because he lived in the hostel. He was to invite his room-mates to go to a cinema with him on Saturday evening, and on from there to a party which a group of studio students were giving at the Garret. It was highly improbable that they would accept on the eve of the examinations, but he himself would really go to a cinema, and on

260

to the party, buying the necessary drink on his way. He would attract as much attention as possible, and at about one, when everyone would be drunk and the crowd all mixed up, he would leave unnoticed, and join the others on the Boulevard. In that way they would be able to prove that all of them had been at some other place, and, one of them, even out of town.

Kiril listened to Sverbeev with horror and despair. He was now entirely, hopelessly, irretrievably entangled. Sverbeev, sipping his beer, was talking as though he were telling some perfectly innocent and ordinary story, but the end of his long nose was white, as it always was when he was in danger or otherwise upset.

There was much going to and fro, porters dragged luggage about, two foreigners in enormous fur collars and felt hats, talked about their coming journey, apparently to Poland. Outside, the engines were blowing off steam as though issuing invitations to unknown, far off lands. Kiril was depressed by all the busy bustle of the station, its noises, and its gigantic clock, measuring off the minutes of meeting and parting. Beyond, lay wide, open spaces, still snow-laden villages, and country towns where thousands of obscure men and women were labouring and loving, all of them absorbed in their own narrow lives. His heart ached at the thought of all that he had lost. Should he, at this, the eleventh hour, while there was still time, turn from the terrible path which he was treading? Should he jump into a train, let the rhythm of the wheels soothe him and lull him to sleep, to find himself next morning at some unknown station, in some strange town, Russia was so big? Or, he might journey to his native town, take a rickety cab, drive along those streets that were so painfully, so desperately, familiar, enter the house in which the simple workman Yagodkin had received him like a son, fall on his neck, and tell him that he had come back for ever, to make atonement, and to begin his life anew? Ah, there, indeed, lay happiness!

Still sipping his beer, Sverbeev was going on with his dreadful story. He must listen, listen as Cooperov was listening in his absurd jockey cap. His vision faded away. They finished their beer, paid, and started to leave the station. A suburban train arrived just then, and its passengers were hurrying to the exit, a crowd of Moscow working men and women, carrying baskets, bags and suitcases. A solemn row of black taxis and a motor bus, waiting only for the signal to start, stood outside. The thawing city, still muddy with slushy snow, swallowed up the suburban crowd with indifference as it dispersed in every direction, disappearing in the maze of clammy streets. And Kiril's inconceivable fate was irrevocably sealed in the station that morning.

CHAPTER XXXVIII

KIRIL did not know what to do with himself on the morning of Saturday, March 13th. In his heavy, dreamless sleep of the night before, he had lost all sense of actualities. But now, to save himself from being alone, from going over the same ground again and again with remorse eating out his heart, he must find some place to go to. He had no other aim or purpose when he went out into the bleak, damp town about midday. Spring was not making much headway. There was a cab at the corner of the street, and its driver, with a face like a Greek icon, solemnly proffered his services: 'Come along, let me take you for a drive.'

His well-fed horse had a full nosebag, and the cabman, who was of an attractive peasant type, looked like a hard worker. Yes, it would be good to drive to his village, probably somewhere northward, to wander in the woods and smell the resinous scent of the pines, to listen to the droning of a sawmill, to go out at night to watch the heathcock's nuptial dance, to forget everything – Yes, above all, to forget everything, to purge his heart of the black blood which was stagnating within it, and to recover his health of mind.

Baskets of empty beer bottles were being carried out of the café to which he had so often been with Sverbeev. All that beer had been drunk the day before – how many dazed heads did those empty bottles represent, how much drunkenness, wickedness, and human degradation? The bottles smelt as evil as the sins of yesterday. He, too, had got drunk there, listening to the Tzigans. Naoum Robertovitch had gone to the Tzigans, and now he was in prison and was going to ruin them all. If only he had not been caught, or if the heart under that wonderful pullover had been the heart of a man, he would not have given them away, and then Kiril would have been saved from all that he had to do that night. The very thought of it made him shudder, and he at once tried to think of something else. A beggar in a brown shirt stuck to him, and refused to be shaken off:

'For Christ's sake, help us, brother. We've been at the station two days without food.'

He had to search his pockets to find a small coin for him, and the incident did serve to change the current of his thoughts. What if he could change places with that fellow, have to sleep outside the railway station, but be free from the harrowing pain that was gnawing at his heart? There were thousands who came hungry to Moscow, but they found work, adjusted themselves to their new surroundings, and took root – whereas he – he had not known how to adjust himself or to take root.

Musing to himself in that way, seeking to dodge the real issue, he came gradually to the busy, noisy streets. The hoardings round a house in process of erection were covered with bright-coloured posters. He walked past without consciously reading, or even looking at, any of them, but they refused to be ignored, and he carried away the picture of a lion-tamer with his group of wild beasts; he was aware that there was to be a Grand Comic Evening; a lecture on Sex and Marriage; and that Persimfans was to give his Fifth Concert. Persimfans, what a funny name – it might be the name of a hairwash 'Do you use Persimfans for your Hair?'

Busy, hurrying pedestrians pushed through the crowd on the narrow sidewalks. At one street corner Kiril stopped to buy cigarettes at a Sovietic shop kept by an ex-soldier in a grey military cloak with ordinary bone buttons, and wearing a fur cap with great dignity. He did not smoke, but he wanted to do something new, to get into touch with someone in his loneliness, and the stall-keeper had a pleasant way of offering his wares and was glad to discuss such exciting topics as the weather; for life at the stall was monotonous: the spring was late, and they were sure to get more frosts. Kiril's eye was caught by various attractive, multi-coloured packets in a glass case on the counter. Some were black and some were green, and many of them bore odd names like 'Hertzogovina Flor,' or 'Ambassadors,' or 'Bricklayers.' The cheapest and most proletarian of the cigarettes were called 'Tchervonets.' For some reason or other, he took a fancy to 'Hertzogovina Flor,' and, after buying a packet, asked for a box of matches.

Somehow or other he had to get through the dreary interminable hours of the day. On and on he went, till he found streets so thronged that the crowd overflowed from the pavement into the road; on past the offices of the journal which had rejected his verses, those offices in which he had been reminded of a ship skippered by a young man in horn-rimmed spectacles. Perhaps that reputation which might have been his at some future date was to be lost that night forever. He was risking it on one chance, just as he had risked everything on one card at the Casino. He looked at the expressionless windows: the ship of fame was sailing past him unconcerned. Who was there on board to care that there was a solitary swimmer struggling down here, drowning – let him drown. Not so much as a ripple on the surface of the rolling waters would mark the spot at which he went down. Away, away from those offices, away from himself – anything to get through the day.

When night came, once more in Sverbeev's hands, he would no longer be a free agent. Sverbeev would decide everything for him, and determine exactly what he was to do

He continued to wander aimlessly, trying to shorten the horrible hours, and he was confronted at various points by mocking clocks with insolent hands timing his progress through the city on their white dials.

He stopped for a while in front of a hairdresser's shop. From behind the plate-glass window, three wax women with beautiful pink shoulders and very long eyelashes gazed at him with languorous sadness. One was blonde, another had the flaming red locks of a Medusa, and the blue-black hair of the third, with its parting down the middle, gave her a madonna-like aspect. Like himself, they had nowhere to go in these busy working hours. They had a mysterious, alluring air that seemed to beckon him. Their artificial feminine beauty was fading behind the glass, as though in a hothouse. They were prisoners, just as he was a prisoner, his fate was not unlike theirs. A delicate white hand, with exquisite pink nails, lay by itself, helpless and beautiful, on a black velvet cushion. As he stood gazing at these three newly-found sisters, who shared his loneliness and sadness, he decided to go into the shop and have his hair cut. Glad of an excuse to while away half an hour of his interminable day, he entered the abode of the three wonderful women.

It was not a busy hour for barbers, and the shop was empty. The daylight was reflected in the mirrors, as though in pools of water. The bored, white-aproned assistants were reading newspapers. One of them, who looked like an Englishman, covered him with a billowy white sheet. The shop was warm, and as quiet as a Buddhist temple. A man drops into a hairdresser's in passing, worried, troubled, hurt. A quiet assistant in a white apron puts him into a chair, envelopes him in a shroud, and seems to shut off the dynamo of his mind, so that for a moment he finds forgetfulness. Beneath the mirror's silvery surface, in its very depths,

266

he sees the traits of the youth he used to be. His armour is removed, time ceases to exist, and peace descends upon his soul. Then the man in the apron says, 'will that be all?' removes the sheet, and the illusion ends. So it was that Kiril spent his half-hour at the barber's. It was good to escape from thought, restful to lean back in the chair, to look at the faces reflected in the mirror, to watch the golden hair falling on his shoulders as though he were a tree shedding its leaves.

He left the shop soothed, and feeling that he was now prepared. The long day dragged on. He wandered about, testing his luck by the numbers on the passing trams, which were now beginning to light up; by the people he met; by the signs on the shops. If he chose a four-letter word, and the next tram had a four-figure number – then all would be well, everything would happen safely, and all his fears would turn out to have been a fantasm, like the visions of the half-hour in the barber's shop. And, anyhow, by to-morrow everything would be over, behind him, and perhaps he would be able to begin a new, free life.

It was dark now, and the white dials of the clocks were illuminated. In a few minutes he would be able to go and dine. At six he would return to the hostel, lie down and read, and begin to urge his room-mates to go to the party. And, of course, neither of them would accept, and at ten he would go out alone.

So it was that Kiril carried out the programme arranged by Sverbeev. He returned to the hostel at six. He lay reading on his bed. He invited his room-mates, and they refused; they had neither time nor money – the examinations were very near.

At ten o'clock he went alone to the Garret. The place was crowded as usual. Tureens of cabbage stood on the long tables, and Ignatka Surgouchov was serving a devastating punch from a white pail with a soup ladle. Vera Nikolsky was there, by no means sober.

'The fools have made me drunk,' she said, as she leaned against him with her heavy shoulder.

Kiril watched the feet of the dancers which gave indications of the effects of the punch, and decided to make Vera quite drunk, so that she would not be able to notice when he went away. He was afraid to drink himself, but he did swallow one glass for the sake of appearances, and to screw up his courage. Vera was soon so drunk that Ignatka sent her to sleep it off on his bed behind the wooden partition. A beardless, red-faced cinema actor was already lying on it, his head pushed through the iron rail at the top.

Kiril stayed for another hour. Then he left the rowdy room with its spirals of smoke, its noises, its smells, and its Charleston which boyish girls and men in green plaid blouses were dancing, their legs shaking convulsively. At that hour, the damp, foggy town was subdued, almost silent. Kiril went out into the street, looked round, turned up his coat collar, and hurried off to meet Sverbeev on the boulevard as arranged.

CHAPTER XXXIX

Sverbeev was waiting for him on a bench of the boulevard, which was quite deserted at this hour. The black trunks of the trees were visible, but their leafless tops faded away into the darkness above them.

'Is that you, Kiril?' Sverbeev spoke in a cautious, unrecognisable voice. 'Sit down; Cooperov will be here in a minute.' Kiril sank down beside him on the bench.

'It's a good thing you've come a bit early, because there are still one or two things to discuss. First of all this – Take it and conceal it. I suppose you know how to use it?' Sverbeev drew a small black object from his pocket, and handed it to Kiril.

'What is it?' said Kiril doubtfully.

'What do you suppose it is?'

Kiril took it, and felt at once that his hand was grasping the cold steel of a pistol.

'Do you know how to use a Browning?' Sverbeev asked again.

Kiril was silent for a moment, shuddering. Then, regaining control over himself, he said: 'Tell me honestly what you are giving me this for? Do you think. . .?'

'I don't think anything – except that you don't tackle a bear unless you've got a gun. You can never tell how things will turn out – so that I – for self-defence – or perhaps we shall be up against it so hard that this will be the only way out. D'you understand?'

Kiril was suddenly filled with hope and thankfulness. What he held in his hand might prove to be his salvation, the solution of which he had so often thought. With this in his possession, he need no longer be afraid of anything; because, if the worst came to the worst, this would give him a way out. He did not say a word as he put the Browning into his pocket, but he was burning with excitement.

'We shall have to get a move on soon,' said Sverbeev anxiously.

At that very moment, a figure emerged from the gloom of the deserted boulevard, and, hurrying toward them, the third of the conspirators arrived to complete their secret nocturnal meeting. A cold wind, coming up from the river in gusts, cleared the moon from clouds for an instant or two at a time, so that it lit up the dome of Our Saviour's, and made it shine dimly in the dark haze.

'Is everything all right? Shall we be getting on?' panted Cooperov, out of breath.

Before leaving the bench they once again went over their plan of action. Then the dark street swallowed them up, while, quickly and in silence, they walked past the sleepy houses. Kiril felt that he was on the road to purgatory. When, at last, they reached their destination, the familiar house filled him with horror and remorse. Chelishev's study window showed no light, and the whole place was in darkness.

They separated. Cooperov stayed by the front door. Sverbeev and Kiril hurried to the courtyard. The low backdoor, with its stone balance weight, opened with a loud creak, and Feskin was waiting for them on the bottom step of the backstairs. The orange flame of a match flared up for a second, revealed the deathlike pallor of his face, and went out.

'Nothing new?' asked Sverbeev in a hasty, hot whisper.

'They went to bed soon after twelve,' said Feskin, 'I should think that they are asleep by now.'

Again they went over what each of them was to do in the

event of any interruption. Cooperov remained on guard at the front door. Slowly and cautiously, they went up the backstairs, step by step, and paused to listen at the door. All was silent, but the silence seemed to fill their ears with the ringing of a loud bell which prevented them from listening and made them feel as if they were submerged in some dark, viscous liquid. Kiril's heart was knocking, he had never dreamt that a heart could pound so terribly, it was like the beating of the wings of a captive bird.

Feskin groped for the keyhole, and turned the key which had been obtained in advance. The door opened an inch or two, still held by its chain. Through the narrow opening came a puff of warmth and the smell of a kitchen. A clock, apparently on the wall, was ticking very fast. Feskin put his hand through the aperture, a sharp, metallic click broke the silence, and the chain had been severed with wirecutters.

They waited, breathless and without movement. But nothing stirred in the flat, only the clock rushed on as though running a race with itself. After a moment, Sverbeev pushed the door open, and Kiril followed him into the hot kitchen. Feskin remained to keep watch on the stairs.

'You go first,' whispered Sverbeev in Kiril's ear. He flashed his torchlight for a second to show him the door, and took hold of the handle. The hateful door creaked, as though crying out for help. Again they waited, petrified. All was silent in the infinitude of the passage, except for the drip, drip of a tap in the lavatory. Again the light was flashed, showing the floor of the passage. Step by step, they crept along it, leaving the pianist's room to the right, and then passing the deaf aunt's door. The pianist would not be back before three, and the aunt, besides being deaf, was in the habit of sleeping with the bedclothes over her ears. At last they reached the door of Madam Chelishev's bedroom.

That was to be the last ordeal. If only she did not wake as they entered, a wad of cotton-wool would make her unconscious. Sverbeev was already soaking it in ether. Then, silently, it would all be over in five minutes. They would have the money and slink away without a sound, unnoticed, and leaving no trace – they needed nothing but those fatal five or ten minutes.

The bedroom door was curtained by a portière. The thick carpet, which covered the whole floor, absorbed their footsteps. A flash from the torch showed the room, and then all was again darkness. The room smelt of scent and medicine and warm femininity. The woman sleeping under the pink coverlet had been outlined for an instant.

Sverbeev moved towards her, switching his light on once or twice, and in a few seconds he felt her breath on his hand. He placed the wadding over her face; she made no movement, no sound. But Kiril's ears were ringing, as he stood waiting in the middle of the room, afraid to move or breathe. What was Sverbeev doing there, in the darkness? His forehead streamed with perspiration. Then the triumphant flash of the cold light on the ceiling filled Kiril with terror. Sverbeev was at his side, whispering, his hot breath on Kiril's ear:

'Ready. . . where's the bureau?'

What was ready? Could it be possible that he had killed her? Kiril's perspiration felt like a cold bandage round his brow as he followed Sverbeev, utterly abandoning himself to him and fearing the slightest separation from him. . .

No, he had not killed her. She was faintly moaning in her dreams under the pad of ether, as she lay, an inert mass, on the big mahogany bed. Porcelain, bric-à-brac, a lamp under a yellow silk shade, the red bureau, all characterised it as a woman's room. The key of the bureau was always in a bag on the bedside table.

'Hold the torch,' whispered Sverbeev fiercely.

He emptied the handbag in a moment – a powder puff, a gold lipstick, a handkerchief, a key – he was at the bureau almost in a stride. The top pulled open, and rested flat on its brass supports. Sverbeev quickly opened a drawer and rummaged through its neatly folded contents: little boxes, leather jewel-cases, gloves, lace, oddments of all sorts.

In a side drawer, underneath some crisp folded lottery tickets and a few other papers, he found a packet tied in a silk handkerchief. He was too excited and impatient to be able to undo it, and broke his nail in trying to untie the knot. He succeeded at last, and there was the money: the money, the green notes that he was looking for, several wads of them, and, under them, the Russian gold that Chelishev had not yet had a chance to change.

Sverbeev began to stuff the loot into his pockets on the instant, and in a very few more seconds he would have finished the operation if the whole affair had not taken a new, a terrible and unexpected turn at this last moment.

Perhaps, in their hurry and excitement, they had made a noise as they emptied the drawers, or perhaps at that very minute some instinctive presentiment had awakened Chelishev. It was probably in obedience to an imperative impulse of alarm that he had gone to the door of his study and listened. Had he heard his wife's faint moan or some other suspicious noise, or had he caught a glint of the torch? Whatever might be the explanation, he appeared before them in the doorway leading from the passage at the very moment when they were thinking that they had brought the affair to a successful issue.

Kiril could never recall whether seconds, minutes, or hours passed; but what he did recall was imprinted on his brain with such unbearable vividness that the horrible scene was like a photograph which was never to fade.

273

In a long white shirt, with tangled hair, now looking quite grey, the terrible man gave vent to what sounded like a shout of triumph. At that instant, Sverbeev put out his torch. Kiril, beside himself with terror grasped his Browning. Chelishev hesitated for a second on the threshold, and then, with another exclamation, rushed back to his study – and then it was that the horrible and irreparable thing happened which, later on, Kiril found himself unable to explain.

Instead of dashing after Sverbeev down the passage and out on to the stairs, thence to disappear into the darkness, Kiril ran in the same direction as Chelishev. At the study door, he caught up with him, and, possessed by some hitherto unsuspected and incredibly inhuman cruelty and passion for destruction, fired twice at the hated neck.

Chelishev fell on his face, straight into his study, where a green reading lamp glowed peacefully on a table beside the divan.

Then Kiril fled along the passage, without a glance behind, down the stairs, and into the courtyard. Neither Sverbeev nor Feskin was in sight. In a frenzy of horror, expecting to be arrested then and there, he went out into the street to meet his doom – but, he met no one. The street was empty, and the March fog was dense. He walked on, unconscious of his direction, the chill, damp night air gradually cooling his burning face. On and on he walked, through unfamiliar streets, till he found himself at the boulevard, its trees looming gigantic in the primeval mist. He crossed the road, pushed through a revolving gate, and began to walk along a gravel path.

There, in the fog, Sverbeev appeared at his side, out of the void, as though he had fallen from the sky.

'What have you done?' he asked, breathless, with anger and hatred.

'I've killed Chelishev,' answered Kiril with simplicity

and bitterness, while tears of horror and despair rained down his cheeks.

'You fool! You rotter! To make a bloody mess of it, like a bandit! I'm not responsible. You did it, and you'll have to answer for it. Dolt! Idiot! Why the devil did I give you the Browning?' Sverbeev pressed his palms to his forehead and groaned: 'Never mix yourself up with fools, and never try to do anything with cretins.'

He went on in a raving mutter for a minute, then pulled himself together, and shook Kiril's shoulder:

'What are you doing here? You've done it, so you'd better run. Perhaps no one has found out yet. Come with me, and don't look round.'

Holding Kiril firmly by the hand, Sverbeev dragged him along the boulevard, and, five minutes later, under cover of the protective fog, they reached the Prechistenka. There Sverbeev took a cab to the Mesnitsk Gates, and drove through the sleeping town, in the March fog, to the other end of the city, to the end of all things.

Half an hour later, they took another cab, which they found near the telegraph office with its yellow-faced clock, at the Mesnitsk Gates. All through the night they paid off one driver after another, crossing and recrossing the great city. The driver they had at dawn dropped them near a cabman's tea-house. Seated at a corner table, they ordered tea and bread, and gladly gulped down the hot stuff that was brought in two enormous flowered teapots, and ate brown bread, while cabmen sat all about them, drinking tea out of their saucers. The drivers looked almost square in the long blue, padded and skirted coats, which they wore over their sheepskin jackets. They all had their hair parted in the middle, and they looked exactly like the drivers Kiril used to see in the little place where he got his threepenny dinners as a boy. He looked at them with bitter despair. There had been a time when he felt that blue-coated drivers, just like these, were his companions. They were finishing their tea, preparatory to going back to their work through the long cold morning. But he had nowhere to go, nothing to go back to, because last night he had irrevocably ruined his life.

He looked at Sverbeev through a mist of tears, and sobbed aloud, covering his face with his hands. An old cabdriver, on his way to the door, patted him kindly on the shoulder and said: 'Oh-h-h, weakling, why do you drink? Drink costs many tears, curse it.' He went out into the yard to take the nosebag off his patient shaggy mare.

CHAPTER XL

STRANGE and inexplicable though it may seem, Sverbeev had been right when he said that no one had seen their mad rush from Chelishev's house, because the terrible affair appeared next day to be wrapped in impenetrable mystery. No one knew anything about it, there was not a single clue, and even Madam Chelishev, when she recovered from the shock, had been unable to suggest anyone as a suspect. Sverbeev and Cooperov had taken every precaution to cover up their movements and leave no trace of what they had been doing in the night. Sverbeev had gone to the Institute first thing in the morning, had done some work in the laboratory, attended a lecture, and then gone to the students' dining-room and taken his place in the queue to await his turn. He had joined the other students in the general chorus of horror over the terrible, the monstrous crime, so tragic and so senseless.

Kiril marvelled that Sverbeev should be able to exercise such iron self-control; when he, himself, felt not only that his life was ended, but had, in passionate hope and passionate despair, reached a pitch of ardent longing for expiation. He could not go on living after what and happened. It was impossible to live with the consciousness of this terrible crime burdening his soul – perhaps all the more terrible because undiscovered. Never would he be able to forget it, nor would time ever lessen the poignancy of his memories. He must go and say, simply and straightforwardly, 'I am the guilty man.' Only in that way could he obtain the right to continue his life. Failing that, the Browning still held enough cartridges to enable him to atone by making an end of himself. The carefully hidden gun was now a friend.

How had it come about? How had it happened that he, after slipping downhill, step by step, had finished by committing the worst of crimes, the murder of a fellow-creature? Was he a real criminal, or was he only a weakling who – largely through his own fault – had been entangled, and so had become an apostate? Had he realised that he was going to commit a murder when he consented to take part in the affair, to go to Chelishev's flat that night? Surely, if he had contemplated murder, his first thought would have been to provide himself with a weapon; but it was Sverbeev who had given him the Browning, had, indeed forced the pretty, lethal toy into his unwilling and reluctant hand – he lived in torture for several days after the murder.

It was while Kiril was absorbed in thoughts and doubts of that kind that Sverbeev got hold of him again. Passing him in the corridor, after a lecture, Sverbeev had whispered 'Come out and meet me near the clock at the corner, I've got something very important to say to you.'

And, as usual, Kiril had obeyed the detested voice, although his whole being protested, and he hated to go. They met under the clock, and Sverbeev led him to a tiny square, slimy with thawing snow, which was empty of people at that hour.

'You're down in the mouth, I see, Kiril,' said Sverbeev in a business-like tone. 'The thing's done, and you won't mend matters by moping. The main point is that I've got reliable information that they can't find any clue, and that means a clean bill for us. It's true that we still have to sell the dollars, but Cooperov and I can manage that; so we've decided to give you the gold. Not counting the two hundred roubles from each of us three that we promised to Feskin, exactly a quarter of the money was in gold. So your share is twenty-eight hundred roubles, and here it is, done up in this newspaper. Mind you hide it well. Do you understand?'

Sverbeev came nearer: 'I'm doing my best for you, old man; I am really, and you ought to appreciate it. I might give you up, after the way you bungled it; no one meant you to do anything so revolting. And you couldn't give us away without a single witness. There were two of us to testify against your word, to say how furious you were with Chelishev about the exam, how you went to see him at home outside working hours, and how you had felt over the Tania affair. If you put all those things together it becomes clear that you were Chelishev's worst enemy – and the deduction is obvious. But Sverbeev is not the man to leave a friend in the lurch – No, Kiril, I won't fail you. Only, we must clear things up so that not even a bit of fluff remains to give a clue.

'Cooperov went back to Podolsk early in the morning, and no one knows that he ever left it. I got back to my room safely. I waited till the girl in the room next to mine went out to buy her milk, and then I slipped in and went straight to bed. The lodger who let me in before one won't forget that I had forgotten my key, and that he opened the door for me. As for you: you were at the Garret; plenty of people saw you there, and, if the worst comes to the worst, you will be able to clear yourself. See how cleverly Sverbeev thought out every detail? But you must set my mind at rest about yourself; I can't bear to see you so downhearted.'

'Listen, Sverbeev,' said Kiril tonelessly, after a moment's silence. 'I can't go on living; I won't go on living, with this on my mind, and I'd rather go straight to the devil than sit on the water's edge till I see myself, with my own eyes, making bubbles in it.'

'Then what do you propose to do?' asked Sverbeev, anxiously alert.

'Go and confess; simply tell the truth, Sverbeev, and take the consequences, execution, prison, anything you like. But I won't go on living like this.'

'You'd better put a bullet through your head,' said Sverbeev in a hard tone. 'Do you want to drown us all like Naoum Robertovitch? You'll be drowned all right, but we shall repudiate you. We shall stick to our alibis – you know what alibi means, don't you? You can go and sink yourself, damn you, but we'll stay above ground to live well and splendidly. We'll plant daisies on your grave in the spring, if you like.' 'I shall die in the spring and be buried,' he hummed softly.

'No, Kiril, I've learnt the rules of life. Pay no heed to anything outside yourself, don't let anything upset you. No one will appreciate your sorrow, and no one wants it. Snap your fingers and enjoy yourself so that you may feel compensated for everything that you have had to suffer – the dangers, the lice – so that you may realise that all that you have gone through has bought you the right to do anything you want, yes, Kiril, everything, and if you have to shove a man out of your way, don't think of it as a crime, but as the normal struggle for survival. Remember that in 1919 you would push a man off a railway truck without a qualm and with never a thought as to whether he would be killed by the fall or be frozen to death – the only thing of importance in those days was to manage to reach your destination with the sack of flour you had got hold of. . .'

'But what if I can't live like that, if, with this on my conscience, I am no longer a man? You can live like that, because you are built that way, but I should be lost, I should lose my soul, I am losing it. . .' Kiril was speaking with obvious sincerity, and with an almost frenzied horror.

'If you're lost, then you're not worth a copper on a market day. . . Go to hell by all means. No one will care a damn. But you are choosing a queer time to go just when life is beckoning and calling. If you're making all this fuss about the other night – well, that was just civil war; to-day it's you, to-morrow it's me. Of course, it would have been better if it had not happened, but what's done is done, and can't be undone. . .'

Sverbeev spoke rapidly, but he was worried and dismayed at Kiril's unfortunate and untimely frame of mind. This was a new and unexpected obstacle, and it was dangerous. He realised that instantly, and decided not to let Kiril out of his sight that night lest he should return to his brooding solitude. He stuck to him like a leech, and to divert their minds, they went to a cinema, took good seats, and gave themselves up to the soothing effect of an American film, in which Harry Peel, long one of Kiril's favourite stars, played the leading part. In his later wanderings, Kiril frequently recalled Peel's sharp, penetrating eyes. A concealed orchestra played a dreamy accompaniment while Harry Peel leapt across chasms to the sounds of sobbing violins and staccato piano chords. But, at the time, Kiril hardly noticed Harry Peel or his exploits, and the music to which he listened was the sobbing of his own unhappy, broken, and despairing soul.

As Sverbeev was capable of forgetting everything, then he certainly had the right to live. But, as he, Kiril, was not made that way, would it not be best, as things had turned out, that he should simply wait until the end of the picture, and then go away from the cinema, not to return to the hostel or to Sverbeev's room, but never again to return to anything? There flashed into his mind the song sung impudently and without a touch of sadness by a little begging urchin at the tram halt on the Arbat:

> 'No one will visit
> My unknown grave,
> When the nightingale's song
> Is heard in the spring. . .'

281

But, if Sverbeev was right; if one should stick at nothing, because there was still civil war, if one were justified in flinging a man from the train without so much as a thought of his fate, whether death from the fall or death from exposure, if the only thing that mattered was to achieve one's own ends? Why, then, one could live a splendid, carefree life. Then, having, in the newspaper packet, this sum of money, which was so enormous for him, he would grapple with this recalcitrant life and bend it to his will. He would not lose his money in one night this time, he had paid too big a price for it, but he would abandon himself to days of such pleasure as he had never dreamed of.

With the help of a pole, Harry Peel had leapt across his last chasm, and the globes suspended from the ceiling were lighting up as though filled with luminous milk. Kiril was torn from his reflections. He saw Sverbeev's long sensual nose beside him. Sverbeev had been dozing through the performance, perhaps he, too, had been absorbed in his own thoughts.

They left the cinema soon after nine, and, tired though Sverbeev was, he stayed with Kiril until he saw him into the hostel just before it closed at midnight. Kiril made his way to his room, stumbled past his sleeping room-mates, and, overwhelmed with fatigue and all that he had gone through, fell into the oblivion of unconsciousness.

Sverbeev had been full of apprehension and mysterious doubts all evening. For the thousandth time he had gone over the whole business. Had they left the slightest clue? Had they cleared away every trace? In the most carefully thought out plan, one was always apt to overlook some tiny detail which eventually proved to be the pivot on which everything turned.

His misgivings proved to have been well-founded. On

reaching the narrow street in which he lived, some instinctive and inexplicable presentiment warned him to be cautious. So, instead of going into the house, he walked past it stooping, with his face well muffled in his collar. He saw a man standing in the shadows on the opposite side of the road and staring up at the house. His window looked out on this street. Sverbeev went round the corner and stopped, his heart beating violently. Who was this man, and why was he staring up at the windows? Sverbeev waited round the corner for a quarter of an hour which seemed like a thousand years. Then he re-adjusted his collar, and, shuffling along very slowly, like an old man, returned to his own street. His heart was still thumping. He glanced sharply across the road out of the corner of his eye. There, in the shadows, was the solitary figure, motionless, mysterious, menacing, his eyes still fixed on the upper windows of the house. An unreasoning dread seized Sverbeev, and he could not force himself to go back to the horrible spot. He hurried away aimlessly, into the inhospitable night, not knowing where he would find a resting-place, conscious only, with his unerring instinct, that the man was not watching the house without a purpose.

He had been right when, in reviewing all the details of the case, he had suggested the possibility of some oversight. And Feskin was the knot that, when untied, would unravel all the clues, Feskin the shoemaker, to whom he had given a great deal of thought, but not quite enough.

CHAPTER XLI

AT the preliminary examination after Chelishev's murder, Feskin had been questioned, like all the other inmates of the house, and his evidence had been so well thought out that Sverbeev had come to the conclusion that he was not only thoroughly reliable, but a valuable ally. Feskin's statement was to the effect that he had been working later than usual on the night of the crime, because he had promised to resole the house-bailiff's* shoes by the next morning. He had not heard anything while he was working, and at about half-past twelve he had put away his tools and gone into the courtyard, as he always did last thing, to get a breath of fresh air. While he was standing in the yard he had noticed that there were still lights in Chelishev's flat. He had returned to his room and gone to bed, but, a little after two o'clock, he had been awakened by screams and noises on the back stairs. He jumped out of bed, and ran to the backdoor, thinking that the house must be on fire. The screams came from the pianist, who had returned from a party and had been the first to discover the crime. On hearing that Chelishev's flat had been broken into – at that time he had known nothing of the murder – he had hurriedly dressed and run for the militia, returning with Petrov, who had been on duty at the barracks, and another militiaman whose name he did not know. By that time the whole place had been roused, and the bailiff and other tenants were in Chelishev's flat. The militiaman and he, Feskin, had got

* Under the Soviet regime, all houses are regarded as State property and a bailiff is appointed for each of them, to manage it, allocate rooms, collect rents, etc.

284

the others out of the flat, and had lifted Chelishev's body to the sofa from the floor, where it had been lying in a pool of blood. Then an ambulance had been called, and both the body and Madam Chelishev, who was still unconscious, had been taken away to the emergency ward. Although he had seen worse sights at the war, he had been so upset by the whole thing that he had been dazed and half crazy for days after.

When he was questioned for the second time, Feskin had repeated the same story, but had added a detail which the examining magistrate considered to be of great importance. He asserted that three days before the event, he had run out to buy some cabbage, and had noticed a bearded man in an Astrakhan hat, standing on the opposite side of the road and watching Chelishev's windows. He had supposed at the time that the man was waiting for someone, but he had seen the same man walking up and down in front of the house next day. He had not seen him since, but he realised now that the man had not been there for nothing. Feskin gave a pretty full description of the man's high Astrakhan hat, his neatly trimmed red beard, and also of his grey leather boots – he was naturally inclined to notice what people had on their feet.

The authorities, of course, could not ignore this bit of evidence, and the search centred round an unknown man with a red beard, wearing an Astrakhan hat, who had been watching Chelishev's windows.

It was at this point that Sverbeev somewhat relaxed his usual caution. He ceased to burden his mind with Feskin, as he was convinced that he could be relied on and was clever enough to be trusted. He prematurely gave him three hundred roubles on account: the rest was to follow. And those three hundred roubles completely turned Feskin's head. If Sverbeev had waited a little, and given

him the money when he had had time to calm down somewhat, everything might have turned out differently. But it
came to Feskin at a time when he was still excited, and
it filled him with all sorts of aims and ambitions. Life
opened up before him, a life of wonderful possibilities, of
hope realised, and, that very day, dressed in brand-new
clothes, with his concertina hanging from his shoulders,
wearing a pair of shoes which he had made for a customer
but now decided to keep for himself, he sallied forth for a
quiet and decorous celebration of his great piece of luck.

He went first to a café at the corner of Little Bronni
Street, where there was always a good Tzigan choir or
minstrels. Sitting down at a table, he placed his concertina
beside him, and ordered a double beer. There were no
Tzigans that night, but instead, the celebrated minstrel
Seliverstov – for whom all the taverns in Moscow were
competing, because there were only two such voices in the
whole town, his and that of Deacon Holmogorov. The
café was filled with a swarm of admirers, patriarchal old
men, and youngsters who were having their first taste of the
joys of life.

A very loose-limbed young man sprang on to the platform,
his coat tails flying, and walked quickly up and down, rubbing his hands.

'Citizens,' he cried, his voice unctuous with loving sympathy for all his dear clients – 'Citizens, in a moment you
will have the best item on our programme, the minstrel
Seliverstov, the great singer of Russian folk-songs. . .'

He was interrupted by a storm of applause, which he
tried in vain to quell by raising his birdlike hand. Feskin
found it very jolly to be sitting in that tumult and was so
contented with his lot that he smiled in sheer happiness.
At last the applause died down, leaving the young man
master of the situation.

286

'I beg your pardon, citizens,' he began again, rubbing his hands, 'but before the minstrel appears to give you his folk-songs, I think that I ought to remind you that we change our programme every Wednesday. Next Wednesday the famous Roumanian cymbalist Prohasko will make his appearance – please make a note of it, my dear guests.'

'All right, we'll make a note of it. Give us the minstrel.'

At that moment the minstrel appeared, and the whole room was electrified by his arrival. A boy dressed in a long coat like those worn by choristers in the Russian church, reminding one of an icon with his gentle mien and his hair with its central parting, led the minstrel across the platform to a high oak chair placed in the middle. Seliverstov was wearing a blue coat of same cut as the boy's, and loose knickerbockers that flopped over his soft leather boots. His face was deeply pock-marked, and his blind eyes, raised to the ceiling, were quite white. As he stared upward, he seemed to be sensing the limitless outside space which rose above the smoke-laden tavern.

He touched the tenor keys with his long fingers, as he drew out his concertina to its full length. It gave out the sad note of a bird, and that was answered by full, bass tones, in a foretaste of the music to come. He knew how to stir the human heart, how to find his way to its innermost depths.

'A war song about a cossack's son,' said the bard, addressing the space overhead. The concertina at once began a lilting march; the cossacks were off with spurs and bells jingling. He let them ride on for a mile, and then began his song:

'All the plain is covered
With bushes and coppices.
Just in the foreground,
Rises an acacia tree,

287

And in the tree, a
Nightingale is singing,
While just beneath it
Lies a young soldier,
A young sergeant lies.'

Here came such deep notes, and the music so stirred the
soul of the audience that even the most callous could not
resist its appeal. They listened spellbound as the bard
sang on and on, his song rolling over their bowed heads,
and so great was the volume of his voice that, at times,
the empty glasses vibrated in harmonic response to it.

Feskin listened with his cheek resting on his fist, and the
minstrel's song filled him with such delicious sadness that
he ordered another double beer. He decided that he would
stay where he was till the minstrel had finished, and then
go on somewhere else, say to Sergo's in the same street, and
take his concertina with him, so that he, too, could sing sad
songs, and make his concertina sob.

The minstrel sang on and on, his voice filling the hall, and
he so worked up his audience that, at last, it, too, joined in
the song. Loud uncouth voices shouted in chorus, as though
the singer had roused some wild animal. He was singing
now about a cossack named Moros:

'Oh Moros, Moros, glorious cossack,
All the Ukraine bewails your loss;
Oh Moros, Moros, glorious cossack,
A prisoner now. . .'

Feskin's head swam; it was all so beautifully melancholy.
He emptied his tankard, and looking round, saw that the
audience had been just as much stirred by the wonderful
voice as he had. One last song, and the boy led the minstrel

away. Feskin rose, paid for his drink, and went out, intoxicated by the beer and the music. He began to play his own
beautiful concertina in the street, but a militiaman on duty
said, with offensive contempt, 'Playing is not allowed,
citizen.'

The concertina emitted two squeaky notes and became
silent. But this untimely interference, which had prevented
him from pouring out his soul as he wished, made Feskin
quite miserable; so he turned his steps to Sergo's restaurant,
where nobody would thwart him, and he could behave
exactly as he liked.

The place was empty, and there was nothing on the
counter but a dish of greenish calves' feet, a few baked
eggs, and a sausage that was dry with age. Sergo, with
Asiatic dignity and indifference, welcomed him with his
hand on his heart.

'The militiaman won't let me play in the street. I should
like to know who'd mind if I did? They won't let a man
express himself even if his heart's breaking. A nice state of
things, isn't it?' While he was talking, Feskin chose a table
at the back of the room, and sat down. He was hurt that he
had been forbidden to sing when his heart was overflowing,
and he felt that no one had a right to order him about now
that he had so much money. He had more in his pocket
than that militiaman could earn in three months by standing
on point duty in the frost, and he could spend it all in one
night if he wanted to, and no one could interfere if he did.
All these feelings made him long to show off, to make
everyone understand that he was a man to be respected.

'Well, Sergo, what have you got to offer a first-class client?'
he asked slowly, almost breathless with the pleasurable
excitement that he was trying not to show. 'I want to play
and sing, and you must give me the best of everything,
because the minstrel Seliverstov has stirred up my soul.'

With his customary dignity, and trying to hide his greedy hopes, Sergo answered with ingratiating flattery:

'If you want to enjoy yourself, you won't find a better place than Sergo's. I'll send for the Sasanders if you like; they'll sing Georgian songs for you, and if you give them wine they'll sing all night till you're sick of them. What wine would you like? Caucasian? And I've got some wheat vodka, as clear as crystal?'

'Yes; get your people; let them sing,' said Feskin, 'and give me the best wine you've got, and some *shashlik*, only do it all in double quick time, Sergo.'

'It will be ready in one minute,' answered the host, and he disappeared into the back regions, whence issued a sound of much whispering. The chef, in a dirty white cap, poked his head through the door, and Sergo returned and began to carve some fat pork.

Feeling bored, Feskin took up his concertina, and began to sing a sad little popular song:

'Dear girl, tell me, tell me, my dearest one –
You are my life, the joy of all my life –
Why does the blood come rushing to your face,
Why do the blushes redden your fair cheeks?'

In a tone of complete dejection, he went on:

'It comes in rushes, it burns up my cheeks;
Cruel it is to me and my true love. . . .'

He sat there singing while Sergo was doing everything he could to dissipate his gloom. Dark faces, with protruding eyes, glanced into the room from time to time, and the feast at last began. Musicians appeared from somewhere, and hurriedly took their places in a recess in one of the walls,

290

and their flutes and tambourines at once began to emit their piercing or bell-like tones. The choir began a guttural recitative as though they were running a race with their instruments. Feskin liked the singers and their song, but what gave him most pleasure was the thought that all this was being done for his sole amusement. At the end of the first song, he said to Sergo:

'Give them all some vodka and shashlik.'

At that moment, one of the musicians approached Feskin with a tambourine in his hand, and, touching his forehead with his other hand, said in honeyed tones:

'Be our Tamada,* master; we will sing for you, master.'

That completely upset Feskin's balance. After that, the festivities reached such a pitch that he, himself, could never remember what followed. Vodka and shashlik were handed round to everyone – the 'crystal' vodka was really good – the musicians played, they beat and rattled their tambourines, they roared out song after song in their penetrating tones.

Not only was the proprietor now sitting at Feskin's table, but other men, total strangers, but all extremely pleasant. They all held out their glasses to be filled, and they all gave him the incomprehensible, but obviously honorific, title of Tamada. Feskin had reached a state of complete bliss. He would let them see what sort of man he was when once he let himself go. He looked round the company with drunken eyes, and, slowly and softly, in the tones of one who is a frequent and appreciated client, said:

'Well, Sergo, let's have another three bottles. And what about some apples?'

But Sergo did not stir. He, also, spoke in a low voice: 'You've had a lot already, master, you must pay for that first.'

* Tamada=King of Revels.

291

It was at that point that Feskin made a slip. The blood rushed to his head, and the whole room swam before his eyes. Blindly, almost unconsciously, he drew from one of his top-boots the rag in which he had wrapped up his three hundred roubles. In a voice hoarse with offended dignity, almost hitting Sergo's nose as he thrust the rag into his face, he said:

'Do you see that? You don't trust Feskin, don't you? Once Feskin orders anything, it means that he can pay for it. Perhaps I've got enough money to buy you up, you Georgian devil.'

He was beside himself with fury, but the music began again, and the revel became noisier than ever. A blue-cheeked young man, a perfect stranger, came up to Feskin, and said hurriedly:

'Allow me to clink glasses with you, citizen.'

The storm blew over, having produced nothing worse than a few flashes from Feskin.

The rest was a sheer riot. Sergo, forgetting his dignity, danced the lesginka with a beerbottle on his head, the instruments shrieked and moaned, and the blue-cheeked young man with a small black moustache, who was now sitting beside Feskin, kept on saying:

'What a wonderful revel. Life to the living, and let the dead sleep in their graves, don't you agree?'

And Feskin joyfully replied: 'Right you are, brother,' while he sank more and more happily into a condition of such complete intoxication as he had not experienced for many a long day. All he remembered afterwards was that the blue-cheeked young man very carefully put him into a cab because, for some unknown reason, they were going on to the Petrovsk Gates to the 'Cellar.' Feskin could not recall whether they had ever gone to the 'Cellar,' and he could not say anything about it to the magistrate, before whom he was taken, after his room had been searched, at about nine o'clock next morning, at which hour he had by no means slept off the effects of the night's orgy.

It was the first time that Feskin had ever been in a motor car. As they went rapidly and skilfully through the morning traffic, he kept asking himself how it was that everything had been discovered so quickly.

While he was undergoing his examination, he noticed a young man who was very like the blue-cheeked fellow who had been at the tavern the night before. This one was clean shaven, but he might have been his twin brother, and Feskin kept looking anxiously at this mysterious and impassive creature throughout the proceedings. Feskin began by denying everything. But he had to account for the large sum of money which he had had, the remainder of which had been found on him, and he was completely shattered when he was told that the others concerned in Chelishev's murder had been arrested, and that he had been the last to be taken. Whether it was because he was not yet quite sober, or because he had been so upset by the resemblance of the young man to the stranger of the night before, Feskin swallowed the bait, and made a complete confession. He made a clean breast of the whole affair in all its details. But he did not reveal the most important thing of all – the names of his confederates – because he did not know them. He supposed that that did not matter, because, since they had been arrested, their names must be known. He laid all the blame on the students as having dragged him into the sanguinary affair entirely against his will.

His statement gave the authorities their first clue as to the status of the criminals. They were students, but there are thousands of students in Moscow. Which were they? It would be a difficult problem to solve, and they would probably have found themselves up against a blank wall, but for one circumstance. A pair of shoes which Feskin had been mending had been found in his room, bearing the initials 'T.S.' in indelible pencil on the soles. That provided a starting point. Lists of students in all the Moscow colleges were examined, and all the names beginning with those letters were extracted. That made a list of about a score, which were then thoroughly sifted. Several were at once eliminated: One had been in hospital for a month after an operation; another was in Archangel; a third was a member of the Communist Party, and therefore, of course, above suspicion. The rest served as material for investigation, and special attention was paid to two who were students at the Institute where Chelishev had lectured: Theodore Sverbeev and Thavel Straich.

Thus, the nut was cracked, and, the kernel reached proved that the terror had not been baseless with which Sverbeev had been stricken that night when he had gone home to find a man in the shadows outside the house silently watching his windows. The game was up, and just at the moment when they thought that they had won. Not only had they not won; but, as he saw clearly next morning, after he had heard of Feskin's arrest, by evening, if not sooner, they would all have succumbed to the same fate. He did not go back to his room, nor did he venture to show himself at the Institute, but he sent a note to Kiril by a messenger, telling him to meet him in the private room of a restaurant at the other end of Moscow. Kiril did not dare to refuse, and drove across Moscow to keep this new, futile appointment. What on earth could Sverbeev want with him now, after all that had happened? But, one look at Sverbeev's eyes, usually so lifeless and now burning so fiercely, made him realise that something dreadful had happened.

'It's all up,' said Sverbeev immediately, not giving him

time to collect himself. 'Feskin was arrested yesterday morning, and you and I will be arrested before evening. I sent for you out of pity. If you want to be ruined, stay here: if not, run.'

'Where to?' asked Kiril in a toneless, despairing voice. 'Where can we go if, as you say, it's all up?'

'Rot,' replied Sverbeev fiercely. 'I'm not going to give in. I didn't climb up that hill just to roll down it again. I want to live, not to be stuck up with my back to the wall to be shot. It's the wall, all right, or at best ten years hard labour, you can be certain of that. There's nothing to argue about. If you choose ruin, stay: if you choose safety, run. I've got a plan, I've thought it all out carefully. We leave Moscow to-night, and go to the Caucasus in the first place. We take different routes; we'll discuss the routes later. We've got to reach Batoum, I lived there once, and have got friends there. Then we get a Turkish boat, and make for Turkey. We've got enough money to manage for a bit: three thousand dollars ought to last eighteen months, and then we'll start afresh, begin a new life. It would be stupid to go to the wall for a trifle, Kiril.'

It was strange, but the more Sverbeev talked of impossible plans for escape from the hopeless situation, the more inextricably Kiril felt himself to be encircled by a suffocating tight ring of expiation, the more intense and passionate became his desire to live. To live, to live, only to live! An hour ago it had seemed to him that he could hear any verdict with desperate calm, so desirable had it seemed to break the thread of his useless existence. He had fingered the cold steel of his Browning with thankful hopefulness. But now, when the abyss actually yawned at his feet, he sprang back in horror from the cruel prospect. What? Was he to be plunged into the pit, before he had even tasted life; to give himself up just when the cup of sparkling wine was within reach; to face a shooting party with his back to a wall, to end life when life was just beginning? All his recent thoughts of suicide seemed now to have been mere mental aberration. Oh no; life was what he desired. What if that did mean flying from justice, Batoum, an unimaginable Turkey? What if it even meant the end to-morrow, arrest while on the way? To-day, he must escape; to-day he must live!

He listened to Sverbeev eagerly and greedily. In an hour they had worked out their plan. They would leave Moscow that evening by different trains for different destinations. They would go their separate ways, and eventually, say in ten days, meet in Batoum, where Sverbeev had reliable friends. It seemed an impossible plan, but Kiril accepted it in its entirety, for it offered the only chance of escape and safety, and he clutched at it as a drowning man clutches at any straw. He accepted it instinctively and instantly and with his whole being.

Bewildered, full of doubts, but consumed by a passionate will to live, Kiril spent his last troubled day in Moscow.

CHAPTER XLII

. . .I remember golden days
In the heart of my own dear land. . .

Tutchev.

MARCH had not melted the vast snowfield which stretched
for hundreds of miles beyond Moscow. Standing in the
corridor of his train, his face pressed to the window, Kiril
watched the snow-covered villages and towns go by; so
Russian, with their church cupolas, their streets winding
uphill, their provincial cabs at the station, driven there to
the sad sound of their jingling bells. In all those towns and
villages, human beings were living under the snow, like
hibernating bears. They were all absorbed in their own
affairs, but no one of them all could be as unhappy as he
was. There lay Russia, spread out in all her enormous
extent; yet there was not room for him in the whole of it;
he was lost, hopelessly lost, by reason of his follies and his
crime . . . Now that he was confronted by the fact that he
was exiled from all this, he felt an ardent passionate longing
to return to it. He had done what Sverbeev had told him;
because, with the feeling that he was a hunted animal, that
seemed to offer the only chance of safety. Safety, life at
any price, that was his one desire; no matter what that life
might have in store for him. What did it matter whether he
was in Constantinople or some other town, so long as he
could be free from the fear of arrest and need no longer
meet with a shudder the dawn of each new day.

Through fields, past towns, over rivers still icebound,
still waiting for the floods of spring, on and on. . . .

The train to Tiflis went on Tuesdays, but it had been

imperative to leave Moscow on Monday, so he and Sverbeev had gone to different stations, and started in different directions. Kiril had taken an early evening train. He had slit the seam of his coat, and put his money between the cloth and the lining. The wooden seats of the long-distance train were crowded with all sorts and conditions of men. Two brothers, tall, quiet, grey-eyed carpenters, were on their way back to Simbirsk. Some land-surveyors and fitters were going to work on the erection of an electric power-station. A doctor was bound for a hospital which had been established in connection with some mines. There were two jolly girls, who had promptly won the hearts of their fellow-passengers, going home after having spent their leave in Moscow, which they had never seen before.

They all had something to relate, each of them had some purpose, and all of them knew exactly where they were going, and why. Kiril alone, in his self-inflicted isolation, was without definite aim and was unable to foresee what fate held in store for him, except that it was heavy-laden with his inexpiated crime, and that all the hopes with which he had gone to Moscow, the unattainable city, had been shattered and in their stead was such a bitterness of vanity and sin that he was afraid even to glance into their evil depths.

He stayed alone in the corridor till midnight, listening to the song of the wheels, dozing and waking, until at last he fell into the blessed oblivion of deep slumber. Early the next morning, he left the train in a small station to get some boiling water. He had sprung from the carriage without an overcoat. It was cold, and the pure air held the scent of some pine timber which was stacked close by. He turned up the collar of his jacket as he ran, teapot in hand, to take his place in the queue of still sleepy passengers who were bent on the same errand. When he turned the copper tap, the boiling water poured out in a broad silky stream, and he hurried back to his compartment at the other end of the wooden platform, refreshed by his run.

Dawn was just breaking. Through the haze he could dimly see the little town on its hillside, the cross on its church and the spire of its fire-station; while the rest of the buildings were still veiled in clouds of mist. Drivers were stamping about beside their wide, low sledges with painted wooden backs, hoping in vain for passengers. The red-capped station-master was strutting about, huddled up in his fur coat, his small eyes still full of sleep. Kiril stood outside the door of his compartment, teapot in hand, breathing in the snowy stillness the early morning silence, shedding something of yesterday's nightmare. Spring had not reached here yet, it was still only the eve of it, one of its dreary Russian precursors; but one felt that it was in the air for all that, and close at hand. And spring brings so much of hope and promise with its first pale flowers as the emblem of the ever-recurrent renewal of life. Kiril was longing to begin life anew, a newborn life, freed from all the horrors of the past.

Gazing at the modest, quiet little station, with its hamlet on the hill waiting for spring, he looked for its name, and gave a start when he found it – Razlougia. Why was the name familiar? When had he been here before? Then, in a flash, he remembered, and realised by what route he was travelling. He had passed through this station on his way to Moscow. There had been an accident on the main line, and his train had had to make a detour. He had been looking out of the window, and the name had imprinted itself on his mind. He had been starting out then at the beginning of a new life. And now the same road was perhaps taking him into exile, his life ended. But if this was indeed the same place, he was near home, and he might break his journey for an hour or so just to say good-bye, to see friendly faces and familiar scenes, to visit the graves of those who had first inspired him with dreams of wonderful lands where everybody lived happily ever after. What joy, what pain, what sorrow! With throbbing heart, with shining, aching eyes, Kiril watched the snowplains through which the train was rolling, bringing him hour by hour nearer to the place he loved best in the world. Thus, not knowing how it had come about, he was returning on this, his last, journey to the town where he had been born and bred.

About nine o'clock next morning, he got out to break his journey for the day, intending to take the train for the south in the evening. At that early hour, though the light was dim in the station of his native town, everything seemed familiar. He noticed that the building had just had a new coat of whitewash, but there was the same artificial palm on the long table of the refreshment room, the same row of cabs stood in the station yard, and the only novelty was the yellow motor bus waiting for passengers. With what a wealth of experiences he was returning to his old home!

Along with several others, he got into the motor bus, which, hooting and jolting, took the steep road into the town, passing cabmen who were urging their steaming horses up the hill. On his right, between some houses, Kiril caught a glimpse of the still frozen river. How often as a child, his strong, tireless legs had carried him up that hill. How was he going to meet Yagodkin, what would their interview be like with its necessity for him to lie from beginning to end? It was a holiday, and the town seemed drowsy with provincial sleep. There were carts standing in the market-place without their horses, and beyond it was the stone archway where Makar had sold books. He left the bus in Revolution Square, which used to be called Cathedral Place. His heart was straining as he walked along a wide street overhung by trees in the gardens.

Yagodkin lived in a little grey timber cottage at the end of a garden behind a white house which used to belong to a merchant but was now full of pale-faced orphans. Kiril stood at his gate for some time, afraid to enter, and trying to overcome his emotion. When at last he went in, he found Yagodkin enjoying the holiday leisure of a newspaper spread out on the table in front of him, reading it with spectacles to help his weak eyes. The samovar was out, and already cold, and the old widow who looked after Yagodkin, was clearing out its ashes with a cock's feather.

'Yakov Ivanovitch,' said Kiril on the threshold, not daring to enter. Should he kneel down before the old man, make his confession and tell him of his repentance, hide his face in the horny old hands which bore the marks of forty years of toil? But Yagodkin looked at him over his spectacles with glad, shining eyes, and came joyfully towards him.

'Kiril, dear boy,' he cried, putting his arm round his shoulders, 'you have come?' Still holding him, he led him to the table, and made him sit down by him. 'My friend Kiril has come.' And he said it in such a tone that Kiril, already strained by the meeting, could hardly hold back his tears. 'Why so suddenly with no letter or word or warning?'

Mastering his emotion and bitter pain, Kiril managed to say: 'I'm only here for the day, I'm just breaking my journey on my way to practical work.'

Yagodkin, full of affectionate admiration, kept nodding his old head: 'So, you're getting on, my boy? You'll soon be coming back here to build the new railway line to Skvir that they say we're to have. And there's to be a bridge over the Lapan. Well, how have you managed? All right? You're used to it now, and are making a success of it?'

Kiril told him all about the life he had not led in Moscow, how he had worked, about the practice he was going to in the south, all that he had dreamed of as a boy and that had

301

not come true. Yagodkin went on nodding his white head as he listened to the wonderful story.

'So you're a man at last,' he said lovingly, 'you'll be ready to carry on our work. I always did believe in you, even when you were a little boy. I've worked at the factory for forty-two years, and that has developed a lot now. Two new shops are being started this spring, and they're building a village for the workmen. A big thing has come out of a little one. They're making me out to be a sort of hero of labour,' he added in confusion.

Kiril had a passing vision of Yagodkin's life with its long years of toil and wisdom. Here was hard work, honour, truth – all that he had dreamed of – but what had he brought back, what honour, what truth? He had burnt up everything that it had been possible for him to burn, and the wind had blown away the ashes. He was standing before Yagodkin a beggar, while Yagodkin was giving his blessing to the false dawn of his future: Sverbeev, Vera Nikolsky, Cooperov, Naoum Robertovitch, various poets in short fur coats, Dontsev in his dressing gown diverting not a few simple youths from work and study by his promises of that fame which was concocted at the Poets' Club or at Madam Dolivo's long table. All these whirled in a mad dance before his mind's eye, with himself in the centre of them, tossed like an autumn leaf into that void from which there is no return.

'Wait a bit, Kiril,' said Yagodkin suddenly, 'I'll tell you someone who'll be glad to see you, and that's Varinka. She often talks about you.'

'What Varinka?' said Kiril, who did not at first understand, and then turned crimson.

'Varinka, don't you remember? – Arina Ivanovna's niece. She's here. She came back to this town.'

And Yagodkin went on to tell him all about Varinka,

how she had returned and had set herself, with all the vigour and determination of youth, to create a new life for herself. He seemed to be leaving something unsaid, but it was obvious that he liked talking about her, and that he had begun with some definite object in view. It was as a dream that Kiril later remembered this last day spent on his native soil: The meeting with the friend who had blessed his earliest hopes and watched his first unfolding, seemed to serve only as a terrible reproach and reminder. How was it that Varinka was back in the town; how was it that he himself was there? Why had their paths crossed again after having apparently diverged with such completeness and finality?

When he met Varinka, she at once brought back to him long-forgotten memories of the serious, charming girl whose rare smile had so enchanted him.

'Do you recognise me, Kiril?' she asked with soft shyness. 'I didn't expect to see you here so soon.'

He dare not keep her hand in his, but he could not take his eyes off the vision she presented.

'It's really you, Varinka?' he said at last as he dropped her hand. 'So this is how we meet. I've thought about you very often, I've never forgotten you, and I think that I have always been looking for you in others.' He was thinking at the moment of Tania and her ominous and terrible fate, Tania, who had been so like Varinka in her quietness, Tania, with whom he had thought of linking his life.

He had met her in the old glazed gallery where the linen was usually hung to dry in winter, and they had gone down the creaking old stairs together.

'I came back here to make something of my life before it was too late,' she said in a matter of fact tone. 'I left Arina Ivanovna five years ago. I stayed at Kazan but got work and studied a little, on my own.' She laughed, but it was a sad little laugh. 'You have grown, Kiril, I should never have known you,' she said, looking at him with her dreamy grey eyes.

They left the yard, and walked along the familiar street, down the hill. The wind, fresh from the plains beyond the town, was singing in the naked garden trees as they passed, bringing with it the vivifying breath of snow.

'Tell me all about yourself,' Varinka began again. She was wearing a shabby coat with a cheap fur collar and cuffs which were badly worn but had been mended with a careful neatness that was characteristic of the girl's whole being. In the far away noisy capital such neatness had had no place.

'As for my life,' began Kiril, shuddering with horror as he thought of it, 'it's not been much of a success, Varinka – but it's not worth talking about.'

'I thought you were very pleased at being able to go to Moscow to study, Kiril. That means a lot, you know,' and she looked at him with enquiry in her eyes.

He did not reply. They went down to the wide, still icebound river, past the houses which ran down hill, to the quay with its warehouses and wharves. The snow was still white here.

'Are you staying long?' said Varinka, as though the question had no importance and was merely a passing remark.

'I? Only till to-night. I just broke my journey here between two trains. I'm on my way to practical work.'

That instantly brought to mind the awful meeting with Sverbeev which awaited him, their fantastic plans for escape, while perhaps in Moscow the authorities were already on their track, searching for them, sending telegrams to have them arrested on their way. He, a criminal, a murderer, was walking beside this innocent, trusting girl, whom he had found again only to lose her once more. On the path which he had been following for so short a time, he had lost all his best friends by the way, and there remained no one but Sverbeev who had entangled him, urged him on to terrible deeds; and was now trying to effect their escape.

They went as far as the steamer company's booking-office, and sat down on the wooden railing. Varinka unfastened her collar, and turned her cold face to the wind as she stared past Kiril at the greyish surface of the frozen river. Her lips were slightly parted, as they always used to be, when she was a little girl, and to have her beside him filled Kiril with such joy and sorrow that for some moments he was unable to speak. At last, he asked:

'How have you been getting on all these years, Varinka? Have you ever thought of me?'

Even while he was saying it, he felt horrified that one who had fallen so low should dare to ask such a question, but Varinka turned her clear, steady eyes to him, and answered radiantly:

'I've often thought of you, Kiril. I had a pretty hard time when I left Arina Ivanovna – I had to go because of Valerian. I couldn't do what he wanted; so life became impossible. How could I ?' she asked with disconcerting simplicity, 'how could I when I did not love him?'

Overwhelmed by pleased excitement, Kiril asked passionately, 'Was there someone else. . . . ? In all these years haven't you been in love with anyone?'

She looked at him a little sadly, a little surprised, and shook her head slowly.

'No, I have not loved anyone, Kiril,' she said, sighing.

He stretched out his hand, and laid it on her worn fur cuff: 'Do you remember, Varinka?' he said in a strained voice. 'It may have been all very silly and childish, but there it was.'

'I have not forgotten anything.' She spoke with sudden

305

firmness. 'It was perhaps because I had not forgotten anything that I came back. Of course, we were too young to understand anything then; but still, I have never forgotten.'

She did not take away her arm, and his hand stole down the fur cuff and took her hand, and her fingers faintly responded to the timid pressure of his, or so it seemed to him.

With a quick movement, he pressed closer to her, gazing with insatiable hunger into those eyes which were unlike all others. Many were the faces into which he had looked to find their like, and he had once found eyes that reminded him of them in poor, unhappy little Tania's. . . . After a moment she raised them, beautiful eyes, full of warmth and tenderness. For a long time they looked searchingly at each others', with mingled joy and sorrow, glad to have found one another again. Kiril felt as though a warm breeze had come into the frozen waste of guilty isolation into which he had been cast.

'No, that won't do,' she said suddenly, speaking with great simplicity, and stroking his fingers. 'We must find out what we really mean to each other. Perhaps what it used to be will never come back. And why do you say that your life has not been a success?'

'If only you knew what a mess I've got into. It may be that we are meeting like this on the very eve of my ruin just to make it easier for me to face it,' he said with bitter sincerity. 'But don't ask me about it, Varinka,' he added in a burst of fear. 'Don't let's talk about it. There is night, a terrible darkness, within me, while you are the day with its light and warmth, your soul is so simple and pure and transparent.'

She listened in silence, and asked no questions, but said at last:

'Cannot the day break for you, too, Kiril? I do not know

what your trouble is, but I don't believe that there is any trouble that has no way out.'

'There is a way out,' he answered hurriedly, 'to disappear, to die; that's the way out. But I haven't got the courage. I want to live, Varinka. It's cowardly, but I do, although I know that life can never be the same again. There are people who are like the foam at the meeting of two rivers, just scum. And men of that sort never create anything, they only destroy life, and they end by destroying themselves. Well, that's what I am, Varinka, foam, scum. There is no reason for anyone to pity me or to try to save me. Forget here and now everything I've told you, and don't say a word about it to Yagodkin; do you hear, Varinka?'

'I hear,' she answered meekly. 'I won't say anything. But perhaps you may someday need my help, and, if you do, remember that I never forget you, perhaps it was because of that that I came back here; but, above all, Kiril, do trust me and confide in me.'

She put her hand on his shoulder, and her eyes, full of tears, of warmth and love, appealed to him in pain. United, they looked into each others' eyes for what seemed hours, years – she took off his cap, and stroked the golden curls she knew so well, then put it back, and hid her face in her fur collar.

'It's too late, Varinka,' said Kiril, ruthlessly twisting his fingers without noticing the pain. 'If only it had been sooner, a little sooner. I don't know, I can't imagine, how my life is to shape itself in the future.'

'However it shapes itself,' said Varinka quickly, 'whatever happens, Kiril, remember that I shall be waiting for you, that I shall never be untrue to my feeling for you, indeed, that I could not be untrue after having had it for all these years, waiting for to-day. . . .'

307

He stood on the wintry quay in a whirl of emotion, not knowing what to say or do. Should he take this new found treasure in his arms and carry her away, or should he fly before she learned the bitter truth, while she still believed him to be all that he had been when they parted years ago? Memories of the years that were gone and of the part which he had played came drifting through his mind. That which would once have given him supreme happiness was holding out both hands to him now, and he did not dare to touch them. The chance to achieve his ideal came irreparably late; he had sought for it among the dregs of humanity, and so all hope was vain. He felt that his life was, indeed, froth, scum.

They said nothing more to each other, but climbed the hill silently, both absorbed in thought. In Kiril's heart a knell was tolling, a cold wind was blowing away all hope, while Varinka walked at his side with her eyes still shining in spite of everything, as though she could hear her own triumphant song of life. At the corner of the square, where the wind was blowing about the stray wisps of hay left from the market, they stopped.

'I want you to remember every word I've said to-day,' came the even tones of Varinka. 'Every word I have spoken is true, and I have not in the least exaggerated. . . .'

She held out her hand to say good-bye. He was probably taking leave of her for ever, taking leave of this girl who had re-awakened his soul by her nearness and her love.

Just beyond the square was a lane which led to the little garden where they used to sit. With her hand in his, he glanced toward the lane, and Varinka understood. Without a word, she crossed the square, and they soon reached the crooked grey house in which he had spent his childhood, where Arina Ivanovna had fed him with her left breast. The house was damp and falling into decay. They went up to the fence and looked at the leafless apple trees in the garden, where life had given them their first dreams.

A slight frost gave the windows a look of mother of pearl, those windows behind which the cooper's wife had moped and sung while her warbler, in his red waistcoat, spilt his seed on her hair. The apple trees were the same trees, and spring would soon deck them with beautiful new tender blossoms.

Kiril and Varinka stood in front of the tumbledown house for a long time. It seemed to be giving them its blessing for a new life, such a life as Kiril could never have or Varinka share with him. Oh, if he could but make restitution, and then start afresh a life of toil and love! But that was barred forever. With a last glance at the house of their childhood's hopes, they turned back to the square, meeting the sharp, cold wind coming from the snowclad plains. There, in the empty square, they said good-bye; he, forever; she, till their next meeting.

Yagodkin looked steadfastly at him for some time, and then asked:

'Didn't you come to an understanding, Kiril? I'm talking straight out. I can't beat about the bush . . . I've meant Varinka for you for a long time.'

'Yes, we did,' said Kiril simply and unaffectedly and without any false shame. 'It's all over now, and there's nothing to fear . . .'

'What should there be to fear? What has a man to fear when he's the master of his own life? I don't mean that, Kiril, only it's a pity that you're only here for such a short time, like a bird of passage that has dropped out of its flock and perched on a roof to rest for a bit . . .'

'Perhaps I have dropped out of the flock,' said Kiril suddenly, 'dropped dreadfully behind.'

The old man gazed at him with weak, startled eyes. 'Is

309

that what you mean?' he said in a casual tone. 'Well, a stork got left behind here one autumn, and it lived through the winter with a crow. It got through the winter all right.'

'I didn't mean anything,' said Kiril soothingly, putting his hand on the old man's knee.

They spent the rest of the evening together till it was time for him to catch the midnight express. Yagodkin told Kiril a great deal about his father and his own life and the factory. Forty-two years of toil, to which the yellow callouses on his hands bore witness. But Kiril had preferred idleness and ruin to toil, and he had found at last, in his native town, the love for which he had longed; found it only to have to renounce it.

At eleven o'clock, he and Yagodkin took the bus on the square where he had said farewell to Varinka for ever. The old man was looking very proud and solemn as the bus rushed down the hill, hooting and bumping on its way.

'The river will be moving soon,' he said as they passed the lights shining on the quay. 'There's a lot of strength in that river. If a man could wake up every spring, and make himself felt, if he could store up all his energy to use when the flood came! If you've got any trouble, if anything has gone wrong, you'd better tell me right out,' he added, bending his head toward Kiril with an air of mystery. 'If that's the case, you come back here. You can always get work in the factory, you could work under me to begin with; I'm still good for a bit, and I'd teach you.'

The bus jolted him up and down on the springs of the cushion while he was talking, and Kiril was wondering whether the joy of his welcome or the bitterness of his parting was the stronger of the impressions which he was carrying away with him.

It was cold in the station, with a strong wind threatening snow, and they soon felt frozen. The express rumbled in the distance, over the bridge, and then came into the station, triumphantly brilliant with its lights, and making the very earth tremble. It stopped for only a few minutes at this out-of-the-way station. The backs of the seats had already been raised, and the travellers were making ready for the night.

'Well, good-bye, Kiril,' said Yagodkin, putting his arm round the lad's neck. 'And, if there's anything in that flock story, you come back here to winter with me, with the old crow. And perhaps we can find a dove for you such as you won't find anywhere else. You understand, don't you?' And the old man slipped something into his hand.

'What's that?' asked Kiril, but Yagodkin was pushing him into the carriage and waving his hand. He went alongside the train smiling as it left the station. It soon left him behind, but he went on smiling. Once again, Kiril looked out at the town, with its lights dropping down to the riverside like a golden chain. It was late, and the people had gone to rest. Kiril stood in the vestibule watching the lights that he would never see again. He was leaving in the darkness over there the only creature he loved in all the world, and the only man who had offered to share his nest with him when everyone else rejected him. How passionately, with that painfully bitter and desperate longing he wanted to live? He suddenly became conscious of the paper that Yagodkin had thrust into his hand. He unfolded the fragment of newspaper and found inside it two worn five-rouble notes, all that the old craftsman had to give. It was more than Kiril could bear, and, for the first time in all those days, he wept, his sobs shaking him as he leaned against the end of the car.

The conductor came through, and, flashing his lantern in Kiril's eyes, said crossly:

'You're not allowed to stand there, citizen.'

CHAPTER XLIII

'WHICH would you like, my young friend, the upper berth or the lower? I don't mind whether I'm up or down.'

'No, I'm younger, I'll climb up.' Kiril was sharing his side of the compartment with the talkative old man. He had a grey beard, too thin to look dignified, and one of his eyes was white with cataract. He did not look very well-to-do, but was obviously a friendly, kindly soul.

'Do you want to go up at once?' he asked in a businesslike tone, and he looked pleased at Kiril's negative, being glad of the chance to while away a part of the night in talking to a newcomer.

'Well, if you're not going to bed at once, fellow-traveller, I'll get out at the next stop to fetch some boiling water, and we'll have tea. We're both going all the way to Tiflis, so we can talk to our hearts' content, and maybe we shall find something interesting to tell each other.'

He carried out his suggestion, got some boiling water at the next stopping place, and made tea. He carried his tea leaves tied up in a bit of rag. Then, to the accompaniment of the snores of their fellow-passengers, they settled down to talk through the night.

'I don't know who you are, young man, but, as an introduction, I'll tell you about myself. If you're from Moscow, we're fellow-townsmen. I expect you've heard of the Somov rope factory? Well, I was foreman of the machine-shop there for eighteen years, and before that I worked for twelve years at the Nevski cotton mill, and for ten years I worked at different places, wherever I was sent as instructor. If it hadn't been for my eyesight, I should still be doing the same thing, but now, in a sort of way, I'm a reservist – they only send for me on special occasions. My name is Serge Simonovitch Larkov. Of course, that doesn't mean anything to you, but anyone who has worked in the textile industry would know me as a master craftsman. There's not a man who can put new machinery together better than I can. Sometimes they send a new model all in pieces, and no one knows how to assemble them. Do they have to send to Germany for an engineer? No: they send for Larkov. I puzzle my head over it for a day or two, and then I always get it right.

'Since the revolution we've had an incredible number of new machines distributed all over Russia. You just think – what's your name young man? – You just think, Kiril Alexeevitch; the factories in Riga were evacuated, that's one; then Moscow, that's two; Lodz, three; and Petersburg, makes four. And all the machinery was lugged all over Russia. A loom might go to Kharkov, say, while all its parts were at Rostov, and as nobody knew anything about either, the whole thing lay idle in the two distant towns. Just you think: there they were, sending to Germany for spools, sending them good money for nothing, while our own gold mines were running to waste. Such things are death to me; I'd rather not hear about them, because it's my job to set machines going. When every spool is in its proper place and working it makes me glad, because then I can see that the whole machine is in order.

'I've worked for two years at some places erecting machinery. I'd find out where such and such parts were, and I'd travel over the whole of Russia spying and begging – it all needed a bit of cunning. And the papers I'd get about it! You could fill a truck with the official papers! One department refuses, another department says that it's just on the point of looking into it, though the stuff has been rusting for three years for the lack of any attention. It was something dreadful, but you stick to it, and perhaps in another year you've got another factory going. I dare say you don't understand, but order and everything working properly is what I like more than anything!

'If it wasn't for my eyesight I might go abroad for a bit, to see what they're doing there. They tell me that they've got about twenty new models. I'll tell you – only mind, this is a secret – why I'm going to Tiflis. There was a rumour a little time back that there were forty cases of machine parts in Tiflis and that no one knew what machines they were for. There was a time when somebody maliciously scattered parts all over the country, as widely as possible, so that they should never be re-assembled. There was plenty of treason afoot, there's no doubt about that. Yes: so there are forty cases at Tiflis, and when I heard about them my heart went pit-a-patter. Because, you see, and this is the main point, there is a factory at Rostov, a first rate textile factory that used to turn out the finest goods. Well, when the Whites were surrendering the town, in all the confusion that followed, someone took all the parts from the looms, and sent them off no one knows where. I've been worrying over that business for three years. Where are those parts? They're nowhere to be found, and the factory is standing idle. To get them from abroad costs money, and it's not every sort of part that will fit. There's the factory, and I can't sleep for thinking about it. I've hunted for those parts everywhere: Novorossisk, Vladikavkaz, wherever I heard that any parts had been found. I'd find something, but never the right thing; and the factory remains idle, and I'm eating my heart out. And then I heard this about Tiflis: forty cases of parts, and nobody knows for what machines. It's quite true, even a specialist can't tell unless he knows his machine. You've got to know it just as you know your wife or your own child. So, I'm off, and I'm all

314

agog – suppose I find my Rostov parts in Tiflis? I shall go dotty with joy, I can tell you. . . .'

Larkov looked slyly at Kiril with his one eye. 'Ah, I wish I could throw off thirty-five years. I should like to live and see what machinery man is going to invent next. I look at you, and I'm envious of your youth, sinful old man that I am.'

'You needn't be envious of me,' said Kiril. 'If I had an aim in life like you, Larkov, I might appreciate life at its true value. But I have not got one, and without that youth is worse than old age.'

'No, no Kiril Alexeevitch, what you say sounds very feeble, and I won't believe that you are weak, that you haven't any force of character. Of course, one does have times of doubt, especially in one's youth. But that is only the husk, and you've got to pull that off, and then live with all your strength, not with all your weakness. Perhaps I look at life from an old man's point of view, but the longer I live, the more I want to live. It's so interesting. It used to be ever so much duller, but people didn't complain about it as they do now. They're a bit bored; they're tired, and so they're bored. But I see it like this, there's no time to be bored. You've got to live with might and main, with your whole being.

'Do you know why I'm saying all this? Why, because I can feel that you haven't lived yet; you've only run your first lap, so to say, and you're running away from life. No, no, a man may commit a robbery, even a murder, and still not go under – still not lose his warp. When you're weaving you have to set up the warp, and once you've got that, you can work at your pattern thread by thread. The warp is something inside yourself, and you've got it, or you wouldn't be sitting in judgment on yourself. And so long as you've got it. you're alive and can go on living, adding thread by thread as you weave.'

315

The tea had been cold for a long time, but they talked on and on into the night, while outside the sparks from the engine turned the darkness into a piece of golden embroidery. Kiril listened to the mechanic with fervent gratitude, for he had something wise to say about all sorts of human affairs. The world is full of remarkable men, and Larkov was himself not unlike one of his own looms, the rapid shuttle darting to and fro and in and out of the fixed warp, and the more rapid the movement, the more rapid the growth of the pattern for which it supplies the thread. . . .

They were together for all the three and a half days that the journey lasted, and they became intimate. This old man with his ragged beard, his one white and one childlike blue eye, his sinewy peasant neck and his cotton shirt, knew a great deal that was interesting. It seemed as though Kiril had met him, and come into touch with his humane wisdom, in order that, at the last moment, he might the more simply and easily accept his fate.

Larkov became very excited as they neared Tiflis. Were his long-deferred hopes to be realised? Would he find the parts lacking for the Rostov machines in those forty mysterious cases? If so, he would once again experience all the triumph of a victory.

Spring had made great strides as they travelled southward, and when they reached Tiflis, it was in full swing. They were met by the dark southern evening; crowds strolling in the streets; cherry trees in bloom, and the scent of roses. Kiril left the station with Larkov. The wonderful old man had become a friend, almost a father.

'A fine town,' Larkov stood on the station steps, holding his basket in his hand, and looking at the bustle of the unfamiliar place. He was obviously pleased as he watched the guttural crowd with the air of an experienced traveller, and he was particularly delighted when they got into a magnficent, roomy, well-sprung landau, and were driven across the town at a great speed by a coachman in crimson sleeves. Tiflis lay before them with its well-lit cafés and taverns, a golden chain of lamps, as though suspended in the air and with no relationship to the earth, an unbroken line up to the dark sky, pointed the way up the now invisible funicular railway to the summit of David's Mountain. They saw a town full of scintillating lights, of chattering crowds, the scent of flowers in the coolness of the evening amid well-watered lawns. Kiril watched the novel scene with excitement. Asses brayed as they passed with full baskets slung across their backs; windows were open, as though in summer, and snatches of music rose from some basement from time to time.

'Something like a town,' said Larkov contentedly, sitting very straight and not daring to lean back on the soft cushions. 'And you say that you despair of life? – Look how these people live; we have never seen the like of it. No: I'd like to live another hundred years; I should still be glad to be alive and to have things left to wonder about!'

The carriage rolled on and on, jingling the bells of the harness, till at last they reached their hotel. They engaged a double room, for they were loath to be separated on the last night they would have together. They went out after a wash, and Larkov was in high spirits. What if his hopes were at last to be fulfilled? – But that would be to-morrow, and to-night it was good enough to see something more of the town, and, if the occasion arose, to let the town see what sort of men they were themselves.

'First and foremost we've got to eat and drink. I should say that we are entitled to a drink after the journey. What do you think? We call our places taverns, the Caucasians call theirs dukhans, they're very good to their guests, they're a kindly people.'

317

And without more ado, he led Kiril into the first dukhan they came to. It had a very ornate sign, with the lettering all made up of fishes which crossed and recrossed each other. It was kept, as they learnt later, by the most hospitable inn-keeper in Tiflis, a man named Avetic. It was hot inside, where Avetic was standing behind a counter laden with dishes. He greeted them with a low bow.

'What would it be best to order first?' asked Larkov, 'some wine and a bit of fish? Look here,' he said, turning to the waiter who was dusting their table with a napkin, 'you do the best you can for us, and give us what you think is nicest.'

When the wine and the *hors-d'œuvre* came, Larkov filled his glass to the brim and raised it: 'Well, shall we drink to our friendship, and that you may find the warp of your life?' His old face broke into a charming radiant smile: 'No, this will be the best toast: may you find the warp, and may I find what I hope for in the forty cases.'

They drank the fragrant wine and tackled the food. A dish of delicate blue-fish was first served, Avetic himself having given the order that the new guests should be served with this incomparable dainty which is to be found only in the river Kura. Kiril sipped his wine, sitting opposite to the friend he had found in the desert, the friend to whom he had turned from his isolation as a criminal and a murderer, an apostate from life, and everything here was so peaceful that it did not seem possible that his past was burdened with a load of such dark memories of irreparable misdeeds that he would never again be able to lead the simple life of those all round him, or to clink glasses with this friend who had taken him to his heart on his last journey.

Avetic kept a watchful eye on them to see that they got enough to eat and drink. A dark girl, who was ugly but seemed at that moment to be quite beautiful, came in from the

318

street, offering for sale the large roses which were in full
bloom here, while snow still lingered in Moscow. Thus it
was that they spent their last evening together. While
they drank the golden wine, life seemed to be calling them
urgently and hopefully. Larkov became more and more
affectionate under its influence.

'Drop the life you're leading, boy – come along with me.
I'll teach you my trade, and you'll learn things that nobody
else knows nowadays. I've had forty years of experience,
and I'll show you how to work, we'll go on erecting machines
so that factories can be started. There's plenty of work for
us to do.'

And though what Larkov, cheered by the wine, proposed
so easily, was quite impossible, Kiril longed with all his
being to take up the proffered life, and he felt so wretched,
and so broken by the consciousness of his doom, that it
seemed as though the best thing that he could do would be
to return to the hotel and shoot himself or strangle himself
with a towel. But a thirst – no, not a thirst, a passion, a
burning, flaming passion for life was consuming him, and
it was that passion that impelled him to hasten to his meeting
with Sverbeev, who should by now be awaiting him in
Batoum; to renounce Varinka, his new-found love so unexpectedly encountered; to deceive Yagodkin, so simple,
so affectionate; and now, to leave Larkov, his latest friend.
When a battle is lost and the defeated army is compelled
to retreat, it has to relinquish all that it most values, loves
best, and regards as most necessary. Even if Sverbeev's
plans were crazy, even if at the best they meant only exile,
the loss of everything and everyone, the betrayal of friendship
and of love, even fresh crimes – even so, let him but live,
if only as an animal, to feel with his hands, to feel his heart
beat, be alive!

There was still a loophole of escape until the telegrams,

probably sent broadcast throughout the whole country, reached the local authorities and detectives were set to watch all railway stations. He must hurry on, from train to train, on to Batoum, his only refuge, where Sverbeev was already making preparations for their safety. He was wretched at the thought that it was impossible for him to continue his journey that night.

They left the inn, respectfully bowed out by Avetic who had given them the fleeting glamour of the golden wine. The southern night was aromatic with the scent of flowers borne on the mountain breeze. The Mountain of David was dark now, and the silence was broken only by the everlasting thunder of the meeting of the two rivers, the roar of rushing waters which had been heard here for untold centuries. Pushkin had heard it sorrowing here in exile; but he, Kiril, had no excuse for his sorrow, and there were no memories that he wished to evoke as he listened to it on this his one night in the southern city. For he had made his choice, and his choice was apostasy.

They drank some mineral water at a street kiosk on their way back to the hotel, and Larkov was soon peacefully snoring. But Kiril could not sleep. He hoped that Larkov would find what he wanted in his forty cases, but he was hopeless for himself, because there was nothing for which he could hope. He lacked that ultimate courage which is needed for the taking of one's own life, and he had, therefore, to rely on Sverbeev — Sverbeev was his only, his fatal, chance.

Happy was Larkov, for he had known how to train the tree of his own life.

He slept at last, lulled by the night breeze blowing through the open window, beneath which he could hear the faint sounds of the town's night life, the echo of passing footsteps. And with the cool night air came peaceful dreams.

CHAPTER XLIV

SVERBEEV reached Batoum from Odessa, feeling old and ill-tempered, after four days of violent seasickness. His bed went on heaving throughout the first night after his landing, but, early next morning, mastering his weakness and nausea, he set about carrying out his plan of operations. His first move was to take an early morning train to go in search of Ferat, a Turk with whom he had once been a lodger. Hiding from the Whites, Sverbeev had found refuge in Ferat's house among the hills, just below the nearly impracticable bridle-path along which smugglers led their asses laden with sacks of forbidden wares from Turkey. The whole coast was full of mysterious deals: dirty little steamers from Smyrna arrived with cargoes of lemons, and left by night with barrels among which a man in need of a change of climate could easily get away. Ferat knew a good deal of what went on on the coast, and though he was very busy with his tea plantation and his tangerine orchard, he pulled a good many strings in his little Turkish house with its red roof and its wide balcony, on which his two wives spent their unexciting evenings. Sverbeev had pinned all his hopes on Ferat. Even if they were unable to get out of the country at once, he might give them a hiding place until the hue and cry died down.

Sverbeev caught the first train, and travelling by the route which was familiar to him, gazed with eyes full of misery at the hated sea, still surging in great grey waves. Incessant rains had drenched Batoum and scoured the mountain paths, and the leaden sea was still beating monotonously on the shore. If it had been a question of hiding only himself, it would have been easy enough, but Sverbeev was very anxious about Kiril, because he was so weak that he might ruin everything. Fear, not pity, was the cause of his anxiety to save Kiril. His train at last reached Green Cape, and disappeared into the tunnel. Everything was soaking wet and slimy, and rain was still falling, beating down the stinking smoke from the engine. The wet, shimmering leaves of the trees in the Botanical Gardens glittered like tinsel.

Sverbeev began to drag himself up the hill. He had no stick, and kept on slipping on the greasy path. When he caught at bushes to save himself from falling, thorns tore his hands. Cursing the mountain, and cursing himself for having entangled himself with anyone so insignificant as Bessonov, he toiled on. The path seemed interminable. It curved roond private gardens, it skirted the very edge of a precipice, and the same thorny bushes bordered its entire length. Ferat's house was set on the mountain side like a bird's nest. The warm, damp air was enervating, and perspiration poured down Sverbeev's face as heavily as the rain fell from the clouds. At last he caught sight of the Turk's white house behind the impenetrable prickly hedge which surrounded it. A small Turkish boy, squatting over a hole so arranged that man might manure his fruit trees, forgot his natural needs at sight of Sverbeev, and ran away with his knickers still unbuttoned. A woman on the balcony promptly drew her veil over her face, leaving nothing but her eyes uncovered.

Ferat was pruning an apple tree in his garden. He wore black trousers, gathered in at the ankles, and looked very handsome with his crescent-shaped black beard. His slow movements gave him an air of dignity which was not at all in keeping with his dark, contraband dealings. But the whole scene was familiar to Sverbeev. There was caution in the friendliness with which the Turk welcomed him, for

322

he did not know what paths Sverbeev might have trodden since their last meeting.

Then and there, in the rain, under the apple tree, Sverbeev laid his plans before him, telling him frankly that he and a friend were in danger of being shot for something they had done. Ferat heard him out, and then asked him if he had got any money. He went on to say that the times were hard, that a very strict watch was being kept on all the roads, and that all boats were searched before they could leave the port. But, for all that, Memed Helvashi, who was famous for the daring of his exploits, had just brought a cargo of lemons from Smyrna, and would leave Batoum in a day or two, and it was possible that he might take the risk of smuggling out two passengers who were in danger of death from the Bolsheviks.

Setting aside all his other business, Ferat returned with Sverbeev to the town at midday. The accursed sea was very rough, and there seemed to be no prospect of better weather in the immediate future, so the boat might be detained in harbour for several days, or even weeks. Sverbeev's heart raged as he looked at the sea from the railway carriage. The palms were flinging their pointed arms about in clumsy fury, the cypresses swayed and bowed this way and that with wild movements, and the odious sea maintained its ceaseless rushing to and fro.

Walking along the Batoum quays from the Customs House to the Turkish bazaar, you have the harbour on one hand, and, on the other, an interminable row of Turkish coffee-houses. You will see in the unruffled harbour a white steamer which plies on the Black Sea, and perhaps a dozen feluccas, their masts spiring toward heaven, which would not venture out to sea in a spring storm. Bulky, slow-moving Turks sit in the dark coffee-houses, looking out at the sea or clattering their dominoes on the marble tops of the tables. All sorts of odds and ends of jetsam, such as the bits of leather which the Batoum shoemakers cast into the sea in such quantities, are thrown up by the incessant waves. The coffee-houses offer welcome shelter from the rain as well as the pleasure to be derived from the stimulation and warmth of the black beverage which they provide.

Entering one of these agreeable resorts, Sverbeev and Ferat sat down well at the back of the room. The proprietor, continuing to puff at his short pipe and without changing his position, glanced at them from the corner of his dark almond-shaped eye. An alert boy, not unlike a girl, brought them two cups of coffee. When the little stir this made had subsided, and when the dominoes were rattling once more, the boss rose and walked past them as though bent on some errand of his own. Ferat, clutching his beard with one hand, had time to whisper a word as the boss went by. Winking at Sverbeev a minute later, he rose, and Sverbeev followed him through a door concealed by a curtain behind the counter. They found themselves in a room containing three unoccupied tables.

The same boy brought them fresh coffee, as they sat down in silence. No one else entered the room, and Sverbeev began to feel impatient, and none too sure of Ferat, who, however, sat on calmly, taking little sips of coffee, with his eyes lowered and a look of mystery. At last a side door opened, admitting a man in oilskins. He took off his oilskin sou'wester, and Sverbeev saw that he was a Turk with sharp, penetrating eyes, a clean-shaven blue chin, and a large hooked nose like a beak. He lifted his hand to his forehead and his mouth, and Sverbeev and Ferat responded with a like salute. Sverbeev was introduced to Memed Helvashi.

Many were the cups of coffee consumed by the three men in that little room, coffee that made their hearts beat with violence.

324

Ferat had been right: Helvashi was nervous. The watch lately had been very strict, and it would be impossible to embark passengers in the harbour, because the boat might be searched at the last moment. Helvashi was going from Batoum to Smyrna, where he had people of his own, who would not betray them, but there would be the difficulty of getting through the customs there.

How many dollars could the effendi pay?

Sverbeev said two hundred.

Helvashi sighed with great dignity, and said five hundred.

At that, Sverbeev sprang from his seat in alarm and disgust.

Five hundred was very cheap for two, it ought to be a thousand for two.

More coffee was brought, and the haggling went on. Helvashi smoked his pipe, and would not hear of Sverbeev's offers.

But they came to terms at last, agreeing on four hundred. Sverbeev took a cup of sweet coffee at a gulp, and wiped his mouth with his fingers. It was out of the question for them to board the felucca in the port, and Ferat would have to row them out to sea to be picked up. But they could not get away at all while the storm continued, and there was no prospect of their being able to do so for the next three days. After that, Helvashi and Ferat began a discussion about some bolts of cloth and fifteen dozen boxes of Coty face-powder.

They wanted a deposit at once as earnest money. Sverbeev got up, turned his back to them, and took out fifty dollars.

'Too little,' said Helvashi calmly.

Sverbeev lost his temper. 'What do you mean by "too little," when the whole thing may fall through?'

'In that case, you'll get your deposit back; Helvashi's word is safer than money.'

325

Sverbeev reluctantly produced another fifty.

They agreed to keep in touch through Ferat. Helvashi put on his oilskins, once more mysteriously put his hand to his lips and his brow, and went out by the side door, while the dominoes went on rattling in the main room. It was arranged that Sverbeev should move to Ferat's house that same day. He expected to hear from Kiril; there ought to be a telegram from him at the *poste restante* to-morrow. He returned with Ferat to the house in which he had hidden some years ago in wretchedness, and disgusted with life. But, now that he was here once more, there was no cause for wretchedness and no reason to be disgusted with life, but only to treasure it and preserve it from ruin. He would know how to enjoy it. He would reserve all his energies for the fullest possible enjoyment of the time for which his money lasted. His enterprising character would be appreciated in other countries, and there would be room for the full play of his strong will, his power to mould life, not according to chance circumstances but in accord with circumstances which he would himself create.

Meanwhile the pouring rain never stopped, and it was dull and damp in the Turk's house, where the women hid their faces from the stranger, and the feeble flicker of an oil wick made unavailing efforts to dispel the gloom. After eating some tasteless concoction of peas and rice with Ferat, Sverbeev went out on to the wide balcony. He felt dismal and lonely in this foreign house perched on the mountain. The steady downpour went on and on, and in the blackness of the night the cries of a child awakened the echoes of the hills, penetrating as the cry of a man at the point of death. Sverbeev was horrified by the sound for a moment, and then he recognised it as the familiar howl of a hungry jackal. Somewhere down below, in the abyss, the invisible, menacing sea was raging under the lashes of the storm. For the

326

first time he became obsessed by dread presentiments, and a realisation of the actions which had characterised his life. His loneliness was so acute that he was even glad that Kiril was coming. If he telegraphed from Tiflis to-morrow, Helvashi would take them both away in a few days to a new and attractive life of safety. The rain streaming from the roof was like an invisible snake—there were so many snakes in these parts – Again the cry of a child, how beastly those miserable jackals were!

Shuddering, Sverbeev returned to the house. He would not admit it, even to himself, but he was frightened of the night, the darkness, the rain, and the sound of the distant sea. He wrapped his coat round his head, and tried to go to sleep, but the gusts of wind and rain beat against the house with such force, the mountain storm raged with such fury, that in spite of all his efforts, he could not get to sleep before daybreak.

Next day, rid of the terrors of the night, he went to Batoum, where he was relieved to find Kiril's telegram. The rain was less heavy, the clouds were breaking; and between their ragged edges – ragged as a beggar's shirt – there were glimpses of a pale blue sky, weak and watery as the eyes of an old man, but promising an end of the storm, and the opening of the way to safety.

CHAPTER XLV

KIRIL left Tiflis, not as though he were on his way to a new life of safety, but as though he were leaving his life behind him. It was as though in that town he had taken leave of all those who stood on the other side of that abyss by which he was now separated from life. It was true that he had put his trust in Sverbeev, and that Sverbeev had promised safety; but what did that safety mean? Did it hold any possibility of real life? Was not that what he had left behind him? What were the hopes with which he had started his ill-starred career? To become a poet? Hundreds, as good as he, who had been torn from their studies, their work, their peasant existence, had to sleep on the boulevards every night. To be a cinema actor? But had not Cooperov, who had given him his first chance, told him that he had not got a farthing's worth of talent? And he could hardly make a success out of wearing dusty old calico costumes and hovering round brilliant screen stars at three roubles a day! He had wanted money, leisure, comfort. But what did anyone sprung from his class know of such things? Had not Yagodkin, his father, and the wonderful and romantic Larkov built themselves up on a foundation of solid work? Had they not toiled for thirty, forty, years, and had they not pointed out to him that that was the only way? And what were the false and rotten notions which he had allowed to seduce him from his first, virginal ideals? Instead of Varinka, whose image he had striven to recapture in Tania Agourov, he had found the cynical sensualism and half masculine indifference of Vera Nikolsky. How puerile, how stupid! And what had Sverbeev to offer him far away beyond Batoum? Nothing but flight; to become a fugitive,

328

like some hunted animal, and, to make that flight possible, the proceeds of robbery, money, to obtain which – and not in the least to avenge Tania – he had murdered Chelishev.

He ground his teeth and moaned as he pressed his forehead against the window of his empty compartment. The evening train was panting slowly up the steep incline, making its way with difficulty.

Yes; with every physical instinct, with every atom of will power, with every breath, he wanted life! But he would not find it with Sverbeev; he would find it here, where there were people of his own race, his own blood, with his own outlook. Truth was here; not there, whither he was being dragged to complete his ruin. But, if truth was here, and life – the life which he had begun with such stupidity, shame and criminality – here, on this side of the abyss, was it not better to go back and to confess, rather than to escape? To say 'Yes, I am an apostate, I have sinned, I have followed after false gods, I have committed crime, but I am not utterly degraded, not completely lost; I want to live, because I am young, but I want to live a different life. I will accept my punishment, the hardest, the most severe, so that, when I have served the term set for my atonement, I may return once more?'

With some such words as those on his lips, he could go back, like the prodigal son, from his wanderings, and Varinka – longing with youthful ardour to build up her future; Yagodkin, with his experience of toil and hardship; Lebedkin, with the truth which he had found; and Larkov, who had so generously offered to teach him his skilled craftsmanship; all of them would understand, and would forgive him his fearful crime, and would take him back into their midst. The path of atonement made an irresistible appeal to him: it offered the only way out.

And surely Sverbeev could not be so base and criminal

but that he, too, would realise all this. Perhaps he, too, would return and confess and make atonement. . . . The fatherland, which they had meant to leave was so vast, there was such scope in it for filial devotion and labour, and its future held such promise that all would be forgiven and forgotten! A pure heart, waiting for that, could keep alive the flickering flame of hope. He had started wrong, but he would return to the strait path. He would say all this to Sverbeev, and surely Sverbeev could not fail to understand and acquiesce. Perhaps at that very minute Larkov was experiencing his greatest joy, because he had found in the forty cases the machine parts for which he had been searching. Yes: to be with him, with those others, that – or nothing: destruction, obliteration, death . . .

Absorbed by these thoughts and emotions, and determined in his repentance, Kiril spent a sleepless night on his way to Batoum. The storm which had raged against the coast for a week, was dying down, and in the hazy morning sunshine, which here and there broke through the grey clouds, he had his first sight of the sea. It was still flinging masses of water on to the shore, huge breakers were still rolling up from the depths of its blue immensity, but it was gradually calming, ridding itself of its fury. Standing at the window, he could not tear himself away from the glorious sight which seemed so much in keeping with all that he had been through during the night. His bitter suffering assuaged, he too was calmer now. He did not want to go to lands beyond the sea: his own land, the land in which he had been born, the land which he loved and in which he had gone astray and sinned, was calling him now with the voice of a mother.

When he arrived at Batoum, a few hours later, his face was so clear, so radiant, that Sverbeev was sincerely glad to see the comrade who had come to share his loneliness.

He carried him off towards Ferat's house in the very next train, for he had no wish to show himself in the town more than he could help. Once in the hills, they could discuss their plans further.

It was warm, and now that the rain had ceased, the houses on the hillside did not look unattractive with their white walls and red roofs, and the shade of wild apple and plum trees. Tangerines grew all down one slope, and, on the opposite side bamboos reared their feathery spires. Kiril gazed in astonishment at this unfamiliar world. They climbed the hill to Ferat's house, and looked down from the heights at the bright shimmer of the waves falling on the beach below. The storm was over, and the sea was calm. A sailboat was already leaving the harbour for the open sea, making perhaps for the Bosphorus, or perhaps for the Aegean.

'Things are going first rate so far,' said Sverbeev as he toiled up the steep path. 'If that Turkish devil does not let us down or play traitor, we shall be far away from here in a few days. If he does, we shall have to hide here for a few months till the chase cools down, and then get new passports so that we can go back somewhere, say to Baku or to Rostov. Meanwhile, we should be putting on a bit of weight. And then, we'll see – The most important thing is to have money, and we've got that, and if we're sensible we can have a jolly good time.'

After listening to Sverbeev's perturbing remarks, Kiril said quietly:

'I've come for something quite different, Sverbeev. I don't see it that way at all – Hear me out, and try to understand what I've got to say, I beg you.' He paused, and looked sadly and pityingly at his companion, who was just as much enmeshed as he was. 'This is what I think, Theodore'– And brooking no interruption, he poured out all that he had gone through during the night, the conclusions he had drawn, and the decision which he had reached, and the certainty that he had that Sverbeev would understand, and cast in his lot with him.

Sverbeev listened, his face distorted with rage, deadly pale, as always in his moments of great excitement. So, that was what his dangerous accomplice, so stupidly drawn into his plans, was up to? That was why his look at the station had been one of such brazen impudence? He had made up his mind to play Judas, had he? He had not understood a word about the motives behind Kiril's complicated, somewhat hazy, ideas, but he was filled with fury and hatred that, at the last moment, when all his plans were on the verge of accomplishment, the ground should be dragged from under his feet.

'When did you invent all that?' he said sourly, stopping to take breath. 'Very nice and clever, but what right have you to reach decisions of that sort without consulting me? You want to play the saintly simpleton at my expense? Not much, no, no, my boy – It's no use for you to try to tempt me with talk of prison or a trial in the criminal court; you can't wake my conscience up that way. I've got a conscience all right, but it tells me not to be a rotter or a mere dud, but a man, and to live like a man, with attractive women and clean beds, not to have to sleep in a doss-house at so much a night and bring your own bit of matting to lie on. Your conscience is worrying you, is it? Indeed! You expect that to convert me, do you? Well, where was your conscience when you killed Chelishev like a dog? I never put you up to that; that was your own bright idea. . . .'

'I know,' answered Kiril firmly. 'I will take all the blame for that – that was entirely my fault, but the rest, we were both mixed up in all that, Theodore. I am simply asking you to go back to pay the full price for what we did, so that

332

we can begin life afresh. If only you knew how much I have suffered, how bitterly I repent, how terrified I am by the thought of our ruin –'

Sverbeev walked on, his eyes lowered, listening to Kiril with contemptuous anger. New ideas were springing up in his mind, his jaws working, his cheeks drawn in, and his lips contracted, so that he looked terrifying.

'It may be very noble to lie down and rot,' he said at last. 'Do so, by all means if you want to, but don't ask me to. But perhaps,' and he suddenly bent towards Kiril as though he wanted to jab him with his long nose, 'perhaps you would like to take all the blame on yourself? Perhaps your heroism is so great that you would like to shield your companion, to save him? Your heroism would acquire still further merit by doing that.'

'I only asked you to come with me,' said Kiril simply. 'If you don't want to, I'll go back alone.'

'Do you mean that you'll go back and say "I killed Chelishev"?'

'Yes,' said Kiril without hesitation. 'What else can I do? I can't see any other way out. To run away? But that doesn't mean safety, that would mean my ruin.'

The mountain path and its thorny shrubs wound upward along the edges of precipitous chasms dropping down to tropical green depths. It was a hard climb along the rough, stony track; Sverbeev was walking just behind Kiril. What were the thoughts passing behind that lowering, perspiring brow? Was he to let this silly dreamer, this golden-haired lad, thrust him down from the heights to which he had climbed with so much difficulty and risk? Dark forces were working in his bowed head. The scenery became more and more wild as they went upward, on and on. The little white houses of the Turks and the villas of the former landowners now lay below and behind them. Every now

333

and then they had to pause to take breath, their blood throbbing, and the world below becoming less distinct.

'Is it far?' asked Kiril, nearing the limit of his endurance.

'Just round the next turn,' replied Sverbeev.

Pushing on, they entered the deep shade of a copse.

'Wait a minute, Kiril,' said Sverbeev in a strange voice. 'You don't suppose I brought you up here to admire the view, do you?' His colourless eyes, now filled with a new determination, were fixed on Kiril's. 'I ask you for the last time, will you leave the country with me or not? You'd better think before you give your answer; there's a lot depending on it.' His voice had fallen almost to a whisper.

Kiril took a deep breath of the cool mountain air, as he gazed for a minute at the world around him.

'I'm going back, I'm going back, Sverbeev,' he repeated exultantly, while he looked with a rapt stare at Sverbeev's hand, in which a small black object glinted with ominous menace. 'Kill me with that Browning, or let me go back; it must be one or the other; there is no other choice for me.'

Sverbeev, with hatred, adjusted the safety catch with his thumb, with hatred he glared at the tired, perspiring, but radiant face of his erstwhile confederate. It wouldn't take more than a second to rid himself of this detestable shadow which had been dogging his footsteps. Then his face, ashen in the green shade, was distorted by a sudden convulsion.

'You fool! You coward!' he hissed with bitter loathing. 'You're too vile for me to soil my hands over, or I'd kill you without the slightest compunction; and not a soul would know, not a soul! I'd drag your body into that bush, and you could lie there to manure the earth and feed the jackals. But you're not worth the trouble. Go where you like; go to the devil, but give me the money; go, but don't you dare

334

to give yourself up for three days, I must have time to clear
out, you understand?'

'There's the money,' said Kiril, still gazing at Sverbeev
with eyes full of elation, while he hurriedly got out the
packet and handed it to him, 'take it, and release me from
my awful burden.'

'Go to hell then, you fool, you worm!' Sverbeev answered,
pocketing the money. 'And while you're rotting in prison,
think of me. I shall be having a jollier time than you've
ever dreamed of.'

He strode up to Kiril, and stood over him, his face still
white with passion.

'Well, our roads have parted for good now,' said Kiril
in sadness. 'Time will show which of us has established his
life on solid foundations. But I know that you can't build on
a foundation of lies and crime.'

'Go to your ruin! Go and rot in prison, or, still better, go
and stand with your back to a wall, preacher, and be shot!
That is what I wish for you with all my heart!' cried Sverbeev, dashing up the mountain path without a word of
farewell or a backward glance. For a few moments, Kiril
could hear the sounds of his heavy breathing and the scutter
of the stones which he displaced as he climbed. He stood
there for a little, then wiped his streaming face on his cuff,
turned back and began to scramble down the path up which
he had so recently struggled. Emerging from the copse, he
stood once more in the open.

Far below, lay the blue panorama of the sea. Slopes
covered with wild bushes, orchards or crops, and dotted
with white dwellings, ran down to the shore, and the waters,
in their exquisite blue, seemed to Kiril to be offering him a
welcome that was almost human. He was suffused with a
feeling of serene joy at the thought that he was returning
to his own world. There he would learn the values of life,

335

of human blood, of toil, and of love, and it would be through his awful ordeal that he would acquire his knowledge. In spite of his sorrow and remorse, his elation still persisted as he looked at the loveliness of the earth with the sea caressing its coast. A light mountain breeze cooled and dried his burning face.

There, in the distance, he could see a white sail, the symbol of man, who sails to every point of the compass, who tries every course, until at last he reaches the infinitude of space which waits to enfold him, that space in whose immensity lies pardon for all things, for all wayfarers – even for the apostate.